GRAHAM KUAN SINCLAIR: the most despised man on Earth. Convicted of murdering millions of people and despoiling the oceans. Sinclair is sentenced to the most remote prison ever devised—the planet Mars.

There's only one catch: Sinclair is innocent.

If he's ever going to clear his name, Sinclair must find the real criminals. But first he must learn to survive the red planet's dangers.

RED GENESIS

The Next Wave
BOOK 1

RED
GENESIS

S.C. SYKES

BANTAM BOOKS
New York • Toronto
London • Sydney • Auckland

RED GENESIS

A Bantam Spectra Book/August 1991

ISBN 0-553-28874-1

Published simultaneously in the United States and Canada

Bantam Books are published by Bantam Books, a division of Bantam Doubleday
Dell Publishing Group, Inc. Its trademark, consisting of the words "Bantam
Books" and the portrayal of a rooster, is Registered in U.S. Patent and Trademark
Office and in other countries. Marca Registrada. Bantam Books, 666 Fifth Avenue,
New York, New York 10103.

Printed in the United States of America

OPM   0 9 8 7 6 5 4 3 2 1

For
my mother

Many thanks to Gordon, David, and the North
Penn Writers Support Group, Martin and Tracy,
Sally, Billy, Pat and Sharon, Mrs. Tam, and
David M. Harris

We had him to dine in
our mess once a week,
and the caution was
given that on that day
nothing was to be said
about home. But if they
had told us not to say
anything about the
planet Mars or the
Book of Deuteronomy,
I should not have asked
why; there were a great
many things which
seemed to me to have
as little reason.

—EDWARD EVERETT HALE,
   The Man Without a Country

INTRODUCTION
BY ISAAC ASIMOV

Mars differs from the other bright planets in being distinctly reddish in color. The ancient Sumerians who, about 3000 B.C., were the first to study the heavens systematically, associated this with blood and, therefore, with their god of war, Nergal. The Greeks accepted the association and called the planet Ares; the Romans called it Mars—and so do we.

People might have associated the ruddy color with rust, but at the time Mars was named, iron was known only in meteoric remnants and these did not rust. By the time people learned about rust, the association of Mars with war and blood was fixed for thousands of years.

In early times, there were speculations that the planets might be worlds, but this remained only speculation until the invention of the telescope in 1608. Astronomers viewing the heavens through the telescope magnified the planets into small orbs and it was clear they were worlds as the Moon was.

The first person to get a reasonable idea of the scale of the solar system was an Italian-French astronomer, Giovanni Domenico Cassini (ka-SEE-nee, 1625–1712). In 1670, he worked out rather roughly the distance of Mars and from that the distance of the other planets.

It turned out that the nearest planet to ourselves was

Venus, which, at times, can approach to within twenty-five million miles of Earth. Second closest was Mars, which, at times, can approach to within thirty-four million miles of Earth.

This meant that Mars and Venus were the sister-planets of Earth. Of the other planets, Mercury was far too close to the Sun to be habitable, while Jupiter and Saturn were far too distant from the Sun.

Mars, being half again as far from the Sun as we are, would be colder, but perhaps not too cold. Venus, being only two-thirds as far from the Sun as we are, would be warmer, but perhaps not too warm. Venus might even be cooler than expected because it has a permanent cloud layer that reflects most of the sunlight.

Once the distances of the planets were known, and the diameters were measured under known telescopic magnification, the size of the planets could be worked out. Whereas Earth has a diameter of 12,740 kilometers (7,920 miles), Venus has a diameter of 12,100 kilometers (7,520 miles). Venus is virtually a sister-planet of Earth, with just about the same size.

Mars, however, is distinctly smaller than Earth. Its diameter is 6,790 kilometers (4,220 miles), only a little over half that of Earth. Still, Mars is distinctly larger than our Moon, or than Mercury. The surface area of Mars is equal to the area of all of Earth's continents put together, so it's a sizable world.

Venus, for all that it is closer to Earth and almost the size of Earth, can't be studied. It is just a featureless white body because of its clouds. We can't see the surface, we can't tell if it's rotating.

Mars, on the other hand, has no cloud layer to speak of and markings on its solid surface can be seen. The first person to report a marking on Mars was a Dutch astronomer, Christian Huygens (HOI-genz, 1629–1695). In 1659, he noted a triangular dark marking he called "Syrtis Major" (SER-tis), which is Latin for "large bog." By following Syrtis Major as it traveled around the planet, he found that Mars rotated on its axis in just about 24½ hours, almost the rate at which Earth turns.

Of course, Mars is farther from the Sun and sweeps about it in a longer orbit, so instead of turning on its axis

365 times during one revolution about the Sun as Earth does, it turns on its axis 669 times in one revolution about the Sun.

When Earth turns on its axis, that axis is not bolt upright compared with Earth's motion around the Sun. The axis is tipped about 23.45 degrees. It is this tipping which points the northern hemisphere toward the Sun at some times in Earth's orbit and from the Sun at other times. It is this which gives Earth its seasons.

The German-British astronomer William Herschel (HER-shul, 1738–1822) studied the way in which the markings on Mars moved around the Martian globe as it rotated and found that Mars's axis was also tipped, and just a little more than Earth's was: just over twenty-five degrees. That means that Mars has seasons just as Earth does, but each season is twice as long as Earth's is and is colder, of course, since Mars is farther from the Sun.

Once Herschel knew how Mars's axis was tipped, he knew where the Martian North Pole and South Pole were. In 1784, he announced that Mars had ice caps about its poles just as Earth had.

All this seemed to be making Mars a true sister-planet of Earth: a little sister, a chilly sister, but a sister. People got more and more interested in Mars.

With Mars so much like Earth in a number of ways, astronomers were more interested than ever in mapping its surface. It was, however, a hard job to do so. The markings were just barely at the edge of vision and no two astronomers seemed to see the same markings.

A German astronomer, Johann Hieronymus Schroeter (SHROI-ter, 1745–1816), tried to make a map in 1800 and, on the whole, failed. Another German astronomer, Wilhelm Beer (BAYR, 1797–1850), had made an excellent map of the Moon, and in 1830, he began to try to map Mars. He was the first to see light and dark areas covering the entire globe of Mars but, on the whole, it was a very poor map. Others kept trying and didn't do much better.

Mars could best be seen when it was exactly on the same side of the Sun as Earth was. It was then at "conjunction." However, Mars's orbit is lopsided and at conjunction, if it is at the far part of its orbit, it may be sixty million miles from Earth. If it is at the near part of its orbit it may be only thirty-four million miles from Earth. Every thirty years or so, Mars comes quite close to Earth at conjunction and, of course, that is when astronomers are particularly interested in studying it. What's more, every time it makes a close approach, telescopes are better than the time before.

In 1877, Mars made a close approach to Earth and telescopes turned to it. It was in 1877, that the American astronomer Asaph Hall (1829–1907) discovered two tiny satellites circling Mars. He called them "Phobos" (FOH-bos) and Deimos (DY-mos).

The star of the 1877 opposition, however, was an Italian astronomer, Giovanni Virginio Schiaparelli (skyah-pah-REL-lee, 1835–1910). Schiaparelli had an excellent telescope and he made painstaking observations. He was the first to draw a map of Mars that other astronomers all agreed on.

Schiaparelli, in observing Mars, had noticed—as had a few other astronomers before him—that there were rather thin, dark lines present on Mars. To Schiaparelli, it seemed that they connected larger dark areas, in the way that straits or channels connected two seas. Schiaparelli therefore called them "channels," and he used the Italian word "canali" which means "channels."

Perhaps because people had awaited the 1877 opposition with such expectations, and perhaps because the discovery of the satellites of Mars had been so exciting, Schiaparelli's map and his "canali" were greeted with great interest and enthusiasm.

Nobody besides Schiaparelli had seen the "canali" in the course of the 1877 opposition, but afterward astronomers started looking for them in particular and some reported seeing them. What's more, the word "canali" was translated into the English word "canals."

This was crucial, for whereas "channels" are natural waterways, "canals" are man-made. Once the British and the Americans began thinking of the markings as "canals," they began, automatically, to think of them as being artificial and therefore as having been built by intelligent beings.

At once there came to be enormous new interest in Mars. Mars had only one-tenth the mass of Earth and its surface gravity was only two-fifths that of Earth. Perhaps its gravity was not quite enough to hold on to water permanently. For that reason, Mars, over the ages, was drying out. The picture arose of intelligent Martians setting up a system of canals interlacing the planet, in order to bring water down from the polar ice caps and irrigate the desert areas in the warmer regions of the planet so that they could grow food.

This caught the imagination of other astronomers. The American astronomer William Henry Pickering (1858–1938) reported round dark spots where canals crossed each other and called them "oases." The French astronomer Nicolas Camille Flammarion (flah-mah-ree-OHN, 1842–1925) published a large book in 1892 called *The Planet Mars* and argued in favor of a canal-building Martian civilization.

By far the most influential supporter of the notion of Martian canals and of an advanced civilization on that planet was an American astronomer, Percival Lowell (1855–1916). He was a man of independent wealth so he established a private observatory in Arizona, where the mile-high dry desert air and the remoteness from city lights made it particularly easy to study Mars. The Lowell Observatory was opened in 1894.

For fifteen years, Lowell avidly studied Mars, taking thousands of photographs of it. He saw more canals than anyone else ever did and was convinced that there was an advanced civilization on Mars. Nor was he bothered by the fact that other astronomers couldn't see the canals as well as he could. Lowell simply said he had better eyes, a better telescope and a better observatory.

In 1894, he published his first book on the subject, which he called simply *Mars*. It was well written and it was clear enough for the general public, so that people began to take it for granted that there was life on Mars. Lowell wrote two more books on the subject—*Mars and its Canals* in 1906 and *Mars as the Abode of Life* in 1908.

If anything was needed to arouse public interest further, it was the work of a British science fiction writer, Herbert George Wells (1866–1946). In 1897 he published a novel called *War of the Worlds* in serial form in a magazine, and the next year it appeared in book form.

It was the first popular book of interplanetary warfare ever written. The Martians were pictured as advanced beings who felt no consideration for Earthmen.

As a result of this book, the picture of Martians was firmly fixed in the public mind. The Martians existed and they were advanced and they were evil. For over fifty years, science fiction writers continued to write stories of Martian invasions. Mars became *the* science fictional world. Even if the Martians were viewed as decadent and harmless, it was Mars that would someday be settled by human beings.

Not everyone accepted the Martian canals, however. Asaph Hall, who had discovered the Martian satellites, never saw a canal. Another American astronomer, Edward Emerson Barnard (1857–1923), who had extraordinarily keen eyes, never saw one, and thought they were optical illusions. A British astronomer, Edward Walter Maunder (1851–1928), even put it to the test. In 1913 he set up circles within which he put smudgy irregular spots and then placed school children at distances from which they could just barely see what was inside the circles. He asked them to draw what they saw, and they drew straight lines such as those Lowell had drawn of the canals.

Then, too, astronomers were beginning to learn more about Mars, and the chances of intelligent life on it seemed to dwindle. In 1926 two American astronomers, William Weber Coblentz (1873–1962) and Carl Otto Lampland (1873–1951), measured the wavelengths of light from Mars. From this they could calculate its temperature. Mars turned out to be colder than had been thought; during the Martian night, the temperature dropped to levels as cold as Antarctica on Earth.

What's more, the temperature dropped so quickly at night that the Martian atmosphere was probably very thin.

In 1947, the Dutch-American astronomer Gerard Peter Kuiper (KOY-per, 1905–1973) detected carbon dioxide in the Martian atmosphere, but he did not detect any oxygen or water vapor. It began to look as though the Martian atmosphere was not only very thin, but was unbreathable.

None of this affected the general public, however. They continued to accept the canals, and to believe there was life on Mars. Certainly this view continued as far as science fiction writers were concerned. Edgar Rice Burroughs (1875–1950) from 1917 onward wrote a series of popular stories about an Earthman-adventurer on Mars, picturing the planet as full of life and as quite Earthlike. Ray Bradbury (b. 1920) wrote stories about Mars in the 1940s, which were put together in *The Martian Chronicles* in 1950. These also pictured an Earthlike Mars.

What finally put an end to the myth of Martian life was the coming of the space age. On November 28, 1964 a rocket-probe called *Mariner 4* was launched and shot Mars-ward. On July 14, 1965 it passed within 10,000 kilometers (6,000 miles) of Mars and sent back twenty photographs. Those photographs showed craters like those on the Moon. They showed no canals. The Martian atmosphere turned out to be even thinner than had been thought. It was only $1/100$ as dense as Earth's and it consisted almost entirely of carbon dioxide.

Later Mars probes, which were more advanced and took more and better photographs, also showed no canals.

Finally, on May 30, 1971 *Mariner 9* was launched and on November 13, 1971 it went into orbit about Mars. It ended up taking photographs of the entire planetary surface. It showed the presence of large, extinct volcanoes, a large canyon stretching out for thousands of miles, and what looked like dried river beds—but there were no canals. Lowell had been fooled by optical illusions exactly as Barnard and Maunder had insisted.

And yet, of all the worlds in the solar system, Mars remains the most Earthlike. In fact, it is the *only* world that resembles the Earth at all closely. The worlds beyond Mars are too large (like Jupiter), too small (like the asteroids), too cold (like the various satellites) to offer us inviting objects for colonization, especially in view of the science fiction training we have all had.

Mercury is far too hot, and Venus is the biggest disappointment of all. Beginning in the middle 1950s, its properties were studied. It turned out to be hot—very hot —hot enough to melt tin and lead everywhere on its surface. It had a thick, poisonous atmosphere and it was bone-dry. It is unlikely human beings will ever be able even to land on its surface, let alone colonize it.

Mars, however, does have a thin atmosphere; it does have some limited supply of water; it is cold but not unbearably cold. Human beings could easily land on its surface, as they have already landed on the Moon's surface, and they might be able to colonize the planet.

Settlements on Mars will be much like settlements on the Moon; they will have to be underground or under domes. There will have to be a trapped environment within the settlements, a breathable atmosphere, a water supply, perhaps farms. It will be impossible to leave the settlements without a spacesuit, and the difficulty of doing so may make most of the settlers prefer never to leave the settlements, so that they will be isolated from other settlements except for communication by radio and television.

Mars will have one disadvantage as compared to the Moon. Mars is many months away from Earth, whereas the Moon is only three days away.

In other respects, however, Mars has the advantage. One thing that the settlements on either world cannot modify is the surface gravity. On the Moon, the surface gravity is only 1/6 that of Earth, but on Mars it is 2/5 and is closer to what the human body is adapted.

Then, too, on the Moon, the days and nights are each two weeks long and during the two-week day, the Sun beating down on an airless world raises the surface temperature in places to the boiling point of water. It is very likely that Moon settlers will never come out of their settlements during the lunar day.

On Mars, however, the days and nights are just about as long as they are on Earth, and the sunlight is weaker than it is on the Moon. The thin Martian atmosphere may also offer some protection.

Finally, Mars has an indigenous water supply (not much, but enough for the settlers), whereas the Moon will have to import all its water.

Yet can human beings adjust themselves to a form of life so different from that on Earth? Can they bear to live in settlements of limited size instead of having an entire planetary surface open to them? Can they be indoors at all times? Prisoners? Isolated?

My own feeling is that we ought not to underrate the human capacity for adjustment. My father, in the year 1923, traveled from a small town in western Russia to the slums of Brooklyn, and never returned. It was a sudden and very drastic change, from the rustic to the urban, from the educated (in Russian) to the illiterate (in English), from a world he knew to a world that was utterly strange.

He adjusted.

I live in Manhattan, a most artificial region of the Earth, not very different from a settlement on Mars. I am far removed from nature and I like it that way. I do not like to leave Manhattan, and I rarely do. I live on the very border of Central Park and I sometimes walk through it to please my wife, but I view it with suspicion myself. I am at home only with concrete and asphalt beneath my feet. I don't want the open sky; I want the warm enclosure of tall buildings.

In short, I, too, am adjusted to the life I lead even though it is not the life that uncounted ancestors of mine have led.

It is possible, of course, that individual human beings will not be able to adjust to a settlement on Mars. After all, many of the settlers who came from England to the American coast in the 17th century, undoubtedly could not adjust.

Most will, however, and for those born on Mars no other life would be comfortable. I imagine that Martian settlers visiting Earth would feel the heavy pull of gravity and would find the openness and the unlimited vistas frightening. They would hardly be able to wait to get back to Mars—to the comfort of home.

Perhaps the most unsettling problem on Mars will involve the matter of population growth. Mars is a more fragile world than Earth is, being smaller and having less in the way of resources. It would be far easier to overload and, very likely, the Martian settlements would have to ration babies just as they ration water. This, in itself, would produce a society quite different from that on Earth.

And there may be other changes that the active imaginations of science fiction writers will deal with, as in *Red Genesis*, which you are about to read.

RED
GENESIS

CHAPTER 1

The fish surfaced first, belly up and white in the moonlight. They popped up in tens and twenties and in small schools, then more rose, some still flashing silver bodies into the air, as if escape from the sea might save them. Marlin, tuna, mackerel, cod, and eel rolled on the waves and drifted with the current, mouths gaping, gills wide and still.

From the depths a luminous green shimmer began to ooze upward. It rose slowly, almost gracefully, like some gelatinous dinghy-sized amoeba. The syrupy bubble burst upon the surface, shifting into a gaseous state. The vapor floated over the water in a phosphorescent green fog, blanketing the dead fish, curling in wisps on the night breeze.

Two miles off the coast of Virginia Beach the party aboard the yacht *Tolan's Folly* was in full swing. Music blared and the sound of laughter and clinking glasses wafted over the water.

The pale green cloud drifted toward the boat. Lights from the shore flashed and glittered like a tight cluster of stars in the darkness. As *Tolan's Folly* was softly enveloped by the fog, laughter stopped. Somewhere below deck a glass broke.

The cloud drifted on, farther out to sea.

.   .   .

Graham Kuan Sinclair watched the *wayang* from his balcony while he finished dressing. The Chinese street opera was performed mostly for the tourists now, but there had been a time, when he was very small, that his grandmother had led him down to Singapore's Old Chinatown district and told him the stories behind the broad gestures and fiercely painted faces. He had been frightened then, of the loud clanging cymbals and gongs and drums and the leaping actors who swung silver swords high in the air. In a soft Mandarin lilt she had explained the battles between Good and Evil and how Good always won. He had believed everything she told him, so much so that his parents had packed him off to a Swiss boarding school the following year.

He had not intended to stay over in Singapore more than two days, this trip, just long enough to finish business with Chiang Heng Lee and attend the Hungry Ghosts Festival, where he would burn paper money and offer prayers to the spirit of his grandmother. It wasn't that he believed in the ancient custom, but somehow the ritual eased some vague ache that had clung to him since her death three years ago. He had felt no such ache at the death of his parents when he was fourteen. They were passing strangers who allowed him brief visits to their various and sprawling homes in Southampton, or Buenos Aires, or Nice. Most of his holidays had been spent with the old woman, and that had been the way he had preferred it.

The *wayang* ended with Evil defeated once again and the red-and-gold-draped hero brandishing his sword in triumph. Graham tossed money down into the street to the players and withdrew from the balcony. He was having trouble with the pearl cuff links. Exasperated, he held out his wrist for Ti's assistance. The young valet was irritated and not properly trained for his position, so he allowed his irritation to show. "Why do we stay in this place?" he sniffed, yanking at Graham's silk cuff. "It is beneath you, this place. It shames you."

"You mean it shames *you*," Graham said, holding out the other pearl cuff link. The boy had attached himself to

Graham three summers ago while he was on Sentosa Island looking over some land development possibilities. The youth had been hawking hand-knotted sandals and was overwhelmed by this American who so effortlessly spoke the Hokkien dialect.

If pressed, Graham would have to admit to a mild pleasure in the reactions of those who mistook him for a Yankee American tourist. He spoke Mandarin Chinese, Tamil, Malay, and Cantonese, plus a smattering of dialects of the outlying provinces of Central China. He did rather enjoy sitting at meetings in Singapore's Golden Shoe financial district, listening attentively as Chinese corporate directors argued among themselves, shutting him out as if he were deaf. Then, in the heat of their debate Graham would casually offer a suggestion in fluent Mandarin, or Cantonese, or whatever dialect was dominant at the moment. The room invariably froze and everyone instantly reverted to business English, Eton- and Oxford-tinted.

Ti held out the formal black evening coat for Graham. If the boy had been trained officially as a valet, he would have held the coat properly so that Graham would not have had to dip slightly to ease into the garment. "So, you would prefer we stay in the Orchard Road district?"

"It would not bring such shame." Ti nodded, whisking Graham's shoulders with a soft-bristled brush. "A man must know his place. You do not belong here. There is no respect for one who lives in Chinatown. It is full of the old ways. You are top-notch dog. People will think you are poor. This is not so. You have billion, maybe fifty billion credits, I bet you."

Graham adjusted the white silk collar and tied the sash around his waist. It was far more than fifty billion, he thought, but frugality was not the point. How could he explain the allure of this small, carefully preserved section of old Singapore? The wood-and-tile buildings had been spared, almost too late, from the rapid urban renewal that had all but erased the pre-twenty-first-century culture and oriental architecture. In fact, it had been he who had fought for its preservation, likening the structures to those of old New Orleans, which had recognized its French-Creole heritage before it was completely razed.

Ti, Graham mused, was much like his mother, trying to eradicate all traces of his ethnic roots. His mother had suppressed the Chinese mixture of her blood, preferring to accentuate the French-English blood of her father. Perhaps it was for that very reason he had embraced his grandmother's world, to spite her, to further alienate the woman who had birthed him but who had never loved him.

"Well, next time we come, I'll put you up at the Raffles, and I'll stay here. How would you like that?"

The youth seemed to mull over the offer for a moment. "No. I belong to you, even if it brings dishonor to stay in this place."

"You bear your disgrace well."

"Why you pretend to be poor?"

Graham smiled as he headed for the reception hall. To own one square meter in Old Chinatown was a coveted status symbol. He owned two whole blocks. It was something Ti would never understand. There was a serenity in the simple rooms and inner courtyard with its small fountain that he could not duplicate elsewhere. There were dark lacquered tables, an elaborately carved armchair, which was to be offered to an honored guest, and a few pieces of bronze from the T'ang dynasty placed here and there on low chests. In the south room, where he slept, a golden-hued painting from the Sung dynasty hung over a carved-dragon bed. Most of his prized Ming porcelain was in New York, but he kept a few pieces of cloisonné for personal pleasure when he visited Singapore.

He was about to ring for his driver when the wall phone flashed a blue light, indicating a scrambled overseas call. It was inconvenient timing and Graham considered ignoring it. He would be late for the banquet if the call became involved. That would be awkward, especially since he was the guest of honor. He pushed the receiver button and Peebles appeared on-screen, clearly upset.

"Make it fast, Marcus, I'm on my way out to court Chiang Lee and his people. The merger's not going as smoothly as we anticipated. It's a rather delicate . . ."

"Tolan's dead."

It took a moment for Graham to absorb what Peebles was saying.

"And Brock. And Senator Crane."

Graham's first thought was that the corporate assassinations had started up again. "How?"

"We don't know yet. Their boat was found drifting off the Outer Banks early this morning. There were, ah . . . some women aboard. Dead. All . . . dead." Peebles wiped his high forehead as if polishing an apple.

"Does it look like a corporate maneuver?"

"No. It doesn't look like . . . anything. I mean, no foul play. They're just very . . . dead. Warner's headed down to check it out."

"Good. You have my itinerary. Keep me posted."

Peebles nodded. "G.K.? You don't think it's starting up again, do you?"

Graham checked the time. "It has never stopped, Marcus. We simply get more clever in the dispatching of whatever . . . whoever impedes the corporate goals. You know that. I know that. Everybody knows that."

Peebles looked like a man whose mission was to maintain the command post while everyone else was leaping out of windows, Graham decided. He seemed to desperately want someone to say that it must be an isolated accident. The deaths were a fluke, a random tragedy. Instead, Graham ended the transmission with a warning. "Be careful, Marcus. What you know could kill you."

Peebles mustered a faintly cynical smile. "And what you don't know could kill you twice as fast."

Ti bowed and presented Graham's street shoes in the outer hall, removing the man's dark slippers, which were worn only within the confines of his home. It was a custom that had always appealed to Graham, and one which he had imported to his New York headquarters, and wherever his business concerns demanded days of his time. His insistence on the removal of shoes within his office and boardroom had been met with some resistance by the older members of the Organization, but in the last several years the custom had gained social approval among the most chic trend-setters of New York's social set. He knew that within the next year or so the custom would gain acceptance throughout Western culture.

That the West embraced social change less readily than the East never ceased to amuse Graham. When the Peo-

ple's Republic of China had begun to implement its new
open-door policies in the late twentieth century, no one
had been prepared for the swiftness with which power
structures shifted, least of all the West.

China's experimental Special Economic Zones had
been phenomenally successful, blending socialist and cap-
italist ideals into an economic system that sang to foreign
investors. Graham's maternal grandfather had been one
of those early investors and his arranged marriage to the
daughter of a high-ranking SEZ official had probably been
more a business merger than due to any passionate urging
from the loins. Graham suspected that his grandfather
had ultimately planned offspring who could be molded
into multinational executive material. His mother, however, the only progeny of the union, had stubbornly refused to become the bridge between East and West that
her father had so desired. On the day of her marriage to
James Edward Sinclair she swore she would never again
speak a word of Chinese, and as far as Graham knew, she
never did. It was only with his birth in 2021, the year of
the ox, that the old man could at last foster the traits he
knew would ultimately enable his grandson to move into
positions of power few dreamed of.

Graham sat in the back of the limousine, an antique
luxury he indulged in only while in Singapore. Classic
automobiles had been a passing fancy when he was in his
early twenties, and he still kept a few, although internal
combustion travel was now outlawed in the West. He had
been a member of the Auto Racing Association, the only
American organization allowed to engage in limited exhi-
bition races for charity purposes. The sport had been exhilarating and dangerous and he had given it up most
reluctantly. The Organization was too fearful for his
safety and finally forbade the pastime. Still, there had
been a few occasions, after a night of celebrating a business coup, that he had roared off down empty moonlit
highways flagrantly ignoring the antiinternal combustion
laws. There was so little exhaust he couldn't see any harm
in the act. True, before the A.I.C. laws the world had almost choked on such air pollutants, but that was long
before he was born. After Greenpeace and the Sierra Club
and the European Greens and the more militant ecologi-

cal groups united under the political auspices of the Gaia Movement, things changed.

"Cha pah bway?" Madam Xiang bowed, greeting her guest of honor with the traditional inquiry as to whether he had partaken of nourishment.

Graham replied in the customary affirmative although it was clearly not the case. He was pleased to see that she remembered him. On his last visit, a year ago, the aging matriarch was having mild memory lapses. She had known his grandmother as a small child, and he regarded her with an affection he accorded few. She chose to dress in the ancient tradition of those of her station and that, too, charmed Graham. The evening would go well. He sensed it. The merger would be completed before dawn. Madam Xiang would see to it.

Chuck Bently's Irish setter growled again and stood facing the surf, his back bristling into a stiff ridge. "What's he yapping at?" Paul Jacobs grumbled, opening another beer for his fishing partner.

"Waves," Bently said, tossing a log on the camp fire. He whistled for the dog, which was still down beyond the dunes. He could hear Rusty snarling in the darkness.

Jacobs spat into the fire. "Damn city dogs. Can't take the great outdoors."

Joe Cobbs, the youngest of the three, and in his last year of law school, chuckled. "You should have brought your wife's poodle along, Jacobs. We could use it for bait. Fou Fou—Fi Fi—what's it called?"

"Fart Fart." Bently yawned. "God, this has to be the worst fishing we've had in five years. We've been coming down here to Nags Head how long now? Six, seven years? It's never been so bad. Not a bite, not even a teaser. I don't understand it. Tomorrow we should take the boat out beyond . . ."

"Chuck, will you go shut your damn dog up?" said Jacobs. "If a coastal patrol catches us out here with an open camp fire because of your stupid mutt, I'm not paying the fine, I can tell you that." The Department of Environmental Protection enforced the stringent coastal protection laws with stiff penalties—two thousand credits for a first offense. A second breach of trust would result in a three-year forfeiture of environmental privileges, or permanent banishment from any and all national park sites if the infraction was of a serious nature.

The setter continued to bark, racing back and forth along the beach. Bently took a flashlight and went to bring the animal back and put him in the tent for the night.

"Hey, Rusty, what's the matter?" he said, trying to smooth down the dog's hackles. It was then that he noticed the pale glowing cloud drifting toward the shore. It shimmered green in the darkness and it was rolling in fast like a neon fog.

Bently called to his two friends. They came reluctantly, stumbling more from too much beer than from the soft sandy beach.

"What the hell is that?" Jacobs frowned.

"Some kind of phosphorescent fish?" Cobbs offered.

Jacobs swatted at him with his fishing cap. "You fleabrain. It's on *top* of the water. In the *air*. It's some . . . kind of fog, it looks like."

"That glows? Green?" Bently said.

"Maybe some kind of will-o'-the-wisp." Cobbs shrugged.

Bently watched Rusty in the light of the lantern Jacobs had brought. The dog was trembling, whining now.

The night breeze was blowing in off the Atlantic and carrying the green cloud with it. Bently sniffed the air. "Smell that . . . what do you smell?"

Cobbs breathed deeply. "Oh, jeez . . . it smells like . . ."

"Dead fish," Jacobs murmured.

"Yeah. Dead . . . fish," Cobbs agreed.

And then they saw the first sluggish silver wave roll in, bearing dead and dying fish—thousands of fish, flowing with the tide and the sea foam, pushed up onto the wet sand.

Bently slowly began to move away from the water, tugging on his dog's collar. "Guys . . . let's . . ."

"Yeah," Cobbs said, retreating slowly.

They got as far as the camp fire before the glowing fog rolled in on them. Jacobs felt a moistness on his upper lip. Instinctively he wiped at it and saw the blood on his fingers as his knees buckled. Muscle spasms rippled up his body. In another breath the muscles of his diaphragm stopped functioning.

Cobbs wheeled to face his friend, his own nose beginning to bleed. His last conscious thought was an awareness that he had lost control of his bladder and bowels.

Bently saw his dog drop just as he lurched and fell facedown into the fire.

CHAPTER 2

Graham thrust a white paper yacht into the flames and watched it curl into ashes. Next came a brightly colored tissue house. It burst into flames, gone in an instant. The Hungry Ghosts Festival was becoming a tourist attraction, which irritated Graham, but he ignored the humming cameras and continued the ritual prayers for the dead. A large yellow sign on a wall opposite the open brick ovens warned in four languages: BEWARE OF PICKPOCKETS. Such warnings were still needed in this part of the world, he supposed, since yuan was still favored over the much more efficient subdermal banking chip used by the Universal Credit System. Graham tossed paper money into the fire, then took a step back and bowed to honor his grandmother's spirit.

Ti, waiting in the limo outside the temple, displayed his impatience by drumming his fingers on the dash. Soon they would be on the monorail, in their private compartment, speeding toward mainland China. One day in Shenzhen, an afternoon in Guangzhou, a wrap-up business meeting in Shantou, and then home to America, to his beloved Manhattan. There, he would again become indispensable to his master, able to please this American who was the center of his existence. Only he, Ti, knew how to prepare tea properly and what dishes pleased most and what music should be selected in accordance with the mood of his master. Only he knew exactly the temperature of the bath, the proper clothing to be laid out, the art of manicure, the mixture of oils for the skin, and the anticipation of his master's whims before they were spoken. It was only in Singapore that he felt his position threatened. It was here that he sensed a drawing away by Master Graham, a detachment and a strangeness that he did not understand. It was as if the city itself became a woman who whispered enchantments and lured his master from his high place, calling to him, making him forget his power and position. Ti always felt a great relief when they returned to the West and his master remembered who he was.

The driver turned to watch for the approach of the foreign businessman with the careful Chinese manner and spoke to the youth in Malay. "This man, your boss, is of two worlds, yes?"

The boy, indignant that so lowly a man would step beyond his designated station, rebuked him sharply. The driver turned back to face the street.

Graham watched the others crowding toward the funeral fires, burdened with the paper promises of material wealth in the afterworld. Something within him remained unsettled. Some ghost was still clinging, straining for his attention. He wondered if it was the shadow of Tolan or Brock. Certainly not Senator Crane. The men had moved occasionally within his somewhat extensive social circle but only Bill Tolan approached what Graham would acknowledge as mild friendship. No man moved any closer than that. It wasn't good business. A soured loyalty could produce a powerful enemy. Graham had seen the destruction it could cause. It was his father's best friend who had arranged the car bombing that took the lives of his parents.

He returned to the kiosk near the arched doorway, looking for a replica of a horse. Tolan had been a good adversary during polo and had talked of investing in breeding stock someday—Arabians, he said. There were no tissue horses. He reached for a white paper unicorn and handed the wizened vendor more yuan than necessary. The old man looked up at him and bobbed his head several times, smiling broadly.

Waiting on line was not something to which Graham was accustomed, but he waited patiently for the women in front of him to finish offering their gifts, then tossed the paper token into the flames.

He knew the Corporation had sent them, even before the two men politely introduced themselves at the rail station, presenting proper credentials. They positioned themselves outside his compartment like matched Dobermans, and Graham knew that he would not be rid of them until he was safely back in New York, if then. That he had escaped his guardians even for a day was a small act of cunning, and now that there was a Corporate Alert, he wouldn't be let out of their sight, not even in sleep. They would examine his food, test his wine, and guard against minute threats until the Alert was lifted or he was dead.

"You wish I should pull shade down?" Ti asked, already mindful of the beginning signs of nausea in his master. Graham nodded, glancing once more out the window at the rapidly shifting scenery, which was beginning to blur into horizontal streaks of green, darker and lighter, flickering beyond any recognizable patterns. He longed for the slower sky-rail trains of his youth, when he had traveled from Switzerland's icy gray and white mountains to the tropical jade-greens of Malaysia in a day. There was time to adjust to the change, to prepare for the lush humidity, time to gaze out windows and to wish things.

Ti pulled down the shade and drew the russet velvet curtain. Rapid-rail travel always made Master Graham uncomfortable, and tea was the only refreshment he would accept during such trips.

The boy put away garment bags and luggage and began to brew the specially blended tea as Graham stretched out on a lounge, closing his eyes. His six-foot-two frame seemed slightly cramped even though he had reserved the largest compartment available. The Trans-Atlantic Sky Rail system was far superior and wider than the antiquated Indo-China Monorail. The system had not been updated since the second generation of superconductors were put into service. Graham took a measured breath, fighting the encroaching motion sickness. He held bodily discomforts in contempt, tolerating any internal imbalance until his constitution took care of the problem. Sickness was never part of his agenda.

"Must I offer *them* tea, also?" Ti asked, extending a black-lacquered tray to Graham. The youth nodded toward the compartment door, referring to the bodyguards stationed in the corridor.

"No. They'll fend for themselves, I should think." Graham sat up, folded his legs into a lotus position, and reached for a sheaf of documents and papers in his briefcase. As he sipped the tea and read, he found a sense of excitement beginning to push aside any earlier physical discomfort. The next stage of the Lee-Qwang-Sinclair merger was clicking into place. The enormous strategies of the business game fascinated him, each component's interaction with the others carefully orchestrated, dependent on the completion of the whole, in order to become a fully functioning organism. He had been born for this, his grandfather had crowed, watching Graham's first corporate takeover at the age of twenty-two. After that he was the crown prince of the international business world. The old man had groomed him well. By the time he was twenty-six Graham was accustomed to the peculiar mixture of corporate-level deference, awe, and tension that emanated from those who surrounded him—men much older than he, who exuded a salty fear in their haste to please him. Only the subversive counsel of his grandmother had kept Graham from total disorientation in his perception of power. "Remember. Be at one with the dust of the earth," she had whispered. That in itself was the balance he had needed for his continued success in a world of impeccably dressed savagery.

Ti had to repeat his question before Graham surfaced from his paper strategies. "You think maybe there is going to be war?"

Graham shook his head. "This is merely company policy, until the Alert is over. It's happened before. You know this."

"Yes. People die before. Alert means war."

"Not necessarily."

"But often."

"Rarely."

The boy watched him from a knee squat on the carpeted floor. "If you die . . . I will die also."

Graham jotted notations in the corner of a document. "No one is going to die."

"But someone is already dead."

"An accident."

"You are not so sure." The youth's gaze was probing. There were times when Graham wondered why he tolerated the boy's insolence. A properly trained servant was invisible when not called to serve his master. And yet, it was the very directness of Ti's childlike manner that most fascinated him. He had been unable to shake the fourteen-year-old that day on Sentosa Island. The youth's persistent tour-guidance through the park and his gutter-wise manipulation of vendors bent on making unfair profit of the "Yankee tourist" amused Graham. Each morning the boy was waiting for him when he emerged from the Raffles Hotel, eager to show the American Big Boss places Graham already knew well from his childhood vacations and from the teen years he had spent living with his grandparents in their villa outside Singapore. He knew that he puzzled the boy with his extensive knowledge of the area and his command of so many languages and obscure dialects. But it was Ti's unflagging devotion and laughable aloofness that finally allowed the boy unprecedented closeness in Graham's world. Like a puppy that had chosen its master, the boy would not leave his side. Graham hired an English tutor for his young valet and within two years had produced a fanatical Anglophile who rejected with vehement scorn anything remotely oriental in nature. The tutor was summarily dismissed but irreparable damage had been done. Ti regarded his own ancient heritage with contempt. For that Graham would be eternally sorry. Like an improperly imprinted chick, which confused any moving object for its mother, Ti would never again recognize the surroundings from which he had been plucked as his own culture. He was always sullen and miserable on these trips to the Far East, and was never so pleased as when they again reached American soil.

Ti poured more hot tea into Graham's cup from the small solar pot. "Something is going to happen." The statement was more like a whispered confession, as if he were ashamed of a secret knowledge.

"What?"

"Something . . . very bad."

"No one is going to kill me, I assure you."

"No. This is much worse. Worse for you. Worse for me."

Graham laid aside his work. "What is going to happen, Ti? And how do you know this?"

The boy looked down at the floor. "I asked . . . a wise man. One who sees . . . a *sheng jen* . . ."

"When?"

"Yesterday. In Singapore. He say there is a great darkness coming. You cannot fight this darkness. It will eat you up."

"I didn't know you believed in *sheng jens*, the holy men."

"I do not. But sometimes . . . it is good to know, even what one does not believe."

Graham laughed. "Just in case. Yes." That would have been much like a move by his grandmother, another who took no chance, just in case. Perhaps that was why he honored the traditions of the Hungry Ghosts Festival, Graham thought. Just in case.

The small news article was buried in the back pages of the *New York Times*. Will Warner took a pair of scissors and cut it out. By itself the news meant little, but added to the other articles, a pattern was beginning to take shape, one that Warner desperately wanted to deny. On an enlarged wall map of the whole East Coast, from Maine to Key West, there was a scattering of red map pins, and clusters of blue and green map pins. The pins seemed busier along the Outer Banks, but there were a few isolated colors sprinkled out to sea, and a couple near Daytona Beach. Warner reached for three red pins, which represented

people. He stuck them into the map near Nags Head, on
the Outer Banks. Next was a green pin, representing a
massive fish-kill or unusual beaching of sea life. Then a
blue pin, for animal life. There had been a dog, a hunting
dog, found near the bodies. And all around, for a radius of
a half kilometer were dead rabbits, birds, raccoons, and
insects.

"I think you can call off the Alert," Warner said as
Marcus Peebles examined the collection of articles. "I
think it's something else, something much worse."

"What?" Peebles moved to the wall map and frowned.
"So some dead fish washed ashore."

"It's more than a few dead fish, Mr. Peebles. If it's anything like what I suspect it might be . . . things are going to get far worse before they get better. You should
alert Mr. Sinclair. Get him back here."

"G.K.—Mr. Sinclair will return on Friday," Peebles
said, moving back to his desk. He liked that, letting people know that his was a first-name relationship with the
head executive. "Mr. Sinclair is a very busy man. I'll not
disturb him with speculations. His time is too valuable . . ."

"Did you *read* the autopsy reports? On Tolan? And the
others?"

"Yes, I read them. Suffocation. Cause unknown. So?"

"And a fish-kill the next day."

"If I had to sail through a lot of rotting fish, I'm sure I
would die of suffocation, too. Terminal breath holding, I
believe."

"You don't see the pattern? It's like all the other reports."

"Pins. I see pins. I see no correlation between some fish
washed ashore and the deaths of two members of the
Organization—and assorted hangers-on. And I am not remotely interested in various and sundry obituaries of people with no corporate ties."

"What about this? The fishermen they found?" Warner
pushed the article across the table with a pencil eraser.
"And another massive fish-kill at the same spot, same
time."

Peebles leaned back in his chair, swiveled slightly

from side to side as if chewing over a reluctant decision, then sighed. "Check it out."

After Warner left, Peebles stared at the wall map. The pattern was there. No doubt about it. Like bloody little soldiers straggling onto the beachhead—things were coming home to roost.

CHAPTER 3

Graham watched Ti's expression as the boy pointed to their luggage and snapped orders at the skycaps gathering on the platform. The youth had begun to regain his imperial air and sense of superiority the closer they had gotten to the United States. Like a balloon with a fresh shot of helium, Ti seemed to radiate energy the moment he spotted New York's monolithic skyline. Graham, still surfacing from a deep meditative state, was relieved that he did not have to speak, or to make any demands of those around him. Trans-Atlantic Sky Rail, smooth though it was, still left him queasy for hours in spite of an altered state of consciousness. Once, speed had been coveted by the rich. Private air travel, the faster the better, belonged to those who could most afford it. Now, Graham mused, placing a hand on Ti's shoulder to steady his legs, only those who were among the most wealthy could afford slowness.

The two bodyguards, whom Ti had nicknamed Stick and Stone, followed behind their chauffeured Solar Beam limo as it descended below the bicycle- and trishaw-choked streets of Manhattan and headed for the Sinclair Towers.

Graham's personal living space covered the two top floors in the East Tower. There were gardens where fruits and vegetables were cultivated, plucked, and served within the hour, their life-aura and freshness still clinging to them. There was a waterfall and a stocked pool for trout and bass, and a sea aquarium for lobster and squid and shrimp.

Room after room in the Towers reflected Graham's exquisite taste in fine art and sculpture. His ability to recognize talented young artists, as well as his vast collection of Chinese jade and porcelain antiquities, made him a sought-after patron of the arts.

Peebles was waiting in the black-and-cream-marbled vestibule as servants scurried to relieve Ti of luggage from the elevator. "A successful endeavor, I see. I can tell. Good! You look well. The Orient agrees with you. Me, I never know what I'm eating over there. It all looks suspicious."

The man habitually perspired without reason, Graham noticed, moving on into the foyer. He removed his shoes and glanced back at Peebles who followed suit.

"If the Alert is over," Graham said, "isn't it time to dismiss the . . . hounds?" He nodded toward the two bodyguards who stood in the archway, trying to decide whether or not to remove their shoes.

"Oh, yes, of course." Peebles spoke briefly with them, and clapped them on their backs. They towered over the small man like two dark vultures who had not been recently fed. There seemed to be a reluctance on their part to accept dismissal until Peebles produced appropriate corporate identity.

Peebles returned to the large living room just in time to snatch the stack of mail Ti was sorting for Graham. "I'll take those, thank you. Where is he? Where did he go?"

"To the W.C. You wait here. I will take mail, thank you." Ti reached for the stack of letters, but Peebles moved away, sorting fast.

"That's quite all right, Ti. I'll take care of this. Just . . . business . . ."

The boy frowned. "Not business. Personal. You not mess with Mr. Sinclair's mail, please."

"I'm not messing. I'm simply sorting."

"I sort."

Peebles eyed the boy. "Very well. Here. Sort." He held out the stack of mail. "But if there's a letter bomb . . ."

"Bomb?"

"Oh, yes. Conceivably. Yes. Boom." Peebles accompanied the sound with small explosive hand gestures, and smiled.

Ti considered. "You sort."

"Very wise of you."

"I watch."

"By all means. Watch."

Graham, wearing a navy burnoose, leaned against a column on the balcony above, his arms folded. "May I watch, too?"

Peebles visibly fumbled. "Oh . . . I'm terribly sorry, G.K. I mean . . . it's just a precaution. You remember Clelland? During the Peterson merger . . . who would have thought . . ."

"We have scanners for that. What are you looking for, Marcus?"

Peebles stared down at the mail and sighed. "I didn't want to upset you. I was afraid . . . the autopsy report . . . I thought a copy might have been sent to you, here, by mistake. You don't want . . . I mean, it's not necessary that you go through . . . ah . . . The details are . . . just . . . unnecessary."

Graham moved down the staircase and took the letters from the man. In a voice little above a whisper he said, "Never attempt to censor my correspondence again. Ever. Is that clear?"

"Yes." Peebles flushed, perspiration beading across his smooth forehead. "I apologize. I simply wanted to spare you . . ."

"Yes, I know. The details."

As the man was about to leave, Graham added, "I want *all* the details on my desk Monday morning. Do you understand me?"

Peebles nodded and escaped, a walking jumble of misfiring circuits.

Graham turned to his young valet. "And, Ti, please, when someone asks my whereabouts you do not inform them as to the specifics. Simply say that I am indisposed. Say it."

"Master Graham is in the spoze."
"Indisposed."
"They will still know it is the W.C."
"That's not the point. Just—do it."
"Yes. I will do it. You are in de spoze."
Graham sighed. "Close enough."

Tamara Voss-Frieling cut through the gallery crowd with the agility and speed of a downhill racer the moment she spied Graham Sinclair entering the room. He was already surrounded by a self-appointed entourage, but she would take care of that with a few slicing glances. It was no secret that the Brokerage was assembling dossiers on a number of carefully selected marriage candidates from which Graham Sinclair might soon select a bonding-wife. Whatever the corporate merger sealed by the betrothal, it would be The Marriage of the Season. It was also no secret that Voss-Frieling Industries was a prime candidate.

Tamara extended her right hand to Graham, palm up, exposing a small crescent moon tattoo on the Mount of Venus. The fertility symbol adorned only those women genetically approved by the Barbican Society, and the mark was coveted for its relative rarity.

"Graham! Dearest! I'm so glad you were able to come after all," Tamara said as the man covered her hand with his own. It was an intimate gesture, and she was unprepared for such total envelopment in public. The usual custom was fingertip-to-fingertip contact—no more, unless the relationship was close to betrothal. Without disengaging from his touch, she drew him away from the others. "When did you return?"

"Yesterday."

"You must be simply drained, then. I'm always a disoriented mess for at least a week after I return from"—she discreetly slipped from his grasp to gesture, waving her hand like an escaped butterfly—"wherever. Oh! Then did you know . . . ?" Briefly her flutter paused on his chest. To touch clothing was acceptable, even preferable to skin contact unless one knew the other well. "Did they tell you? About Tolan? And the others?"

They were standing near a fountain where several art critics were arguing the merits of two of the city's most popular water sculptors. Graham studied the fountain for several moments and then made a notation in his program. "Yes. I was in Singapore when I heard." Without looking at her he said, "Do they know the cause?"

Tamara, momentarily somber, shook her head. "Everyone thought it was business-directed, at first. It *is* what one thinks of first, of course. It's a mystery. I understand there will be an inquiry. It's frightening. It makes one think of the Boniface thing from the thirties."

"Yes. My parents were two of the sacrifices from that venture."

"I lost an uncle." Tamara nodded. "It was an ugly, senseless little war. Now we have . . . skirmishes."

A servant paused with a tray of champagne and the woman removed two crystal glasses, handing one to Graham. "Enough of grim tidings. Tell me what you're after this evening. Have you seen the Myrmidon pieces? Grisly things, so barbaric. Quite controversial, but I suppose you knew that." She led him along the fountain displays, pausing in her chatter to see if he might fill the silence. He did not. Graham Sinclair's stoic manner was legend among her friends, but Tamara pirouetted gracefully around any potentially awkward moments, displaying a formidable knowledge of contemporary art.

"I find that I'm left in a bit of a quandary over the issues raised by the works," Tamara said as they approached a formally attired crowd gathered around a series of lifelike sculptures. Marble bas-reliefs depicted executions, historical war crimes, military maneuvers with disastrous consequences frozen at the moment the executive order was carried out.

Tamara shuddered delicately. "To function without scruples, to carry out orders like an automaton. It's a debasement of humanity."

"To execute orders without question?" Graham studied the sculptures. "In business it's a trait to be cultivated."

"As long as the head executives retain a sense of honor, yes. But tell me, Graham K. Sinclair, would *you* obey an order that went against your own principles?

Could you carry out a command, without question, when every ounce of conscience said it was wrong?"

"That's what resignations are for."

Tamara laughed. "Come. You must see Jasmine Wyncote's latest interactive piece. It's marvelous."

She led him over to a glass elevator, depositing the empty goblets on a marble balcony. "I heard a rumor that she was once your father's mistress. Is that true?"

"No, she wasn't." The fact was, Jasmine Wyncote had been his grandfather's mistress. The woman had occupied a spot in the periphery of his awareness for as long as he could remember. Like an affectionate great aunt, she had always been there.

On the third level they passed by a number of tableaux vivants re-creating famous masterpieces, with living models caught in freeze-frame poses, unblinking, for minutes at a time.

Jasmine Wyncote greeted Tamara, fingertips spread wide, and air-kissed the woman's cheeks. She was gaudily bangled and overly robed in colors only an artist could wear, Tamara decided, and why a woman in her sixties didn't bow to the simplest cosmetic restructuring, she could not fathom. Even if she was a naturalist who opposed antiaging agents and flaunted the silver in her red hair, to display prunelike skin so early was repugnant to Tamara.

"Graham! It's so good to see you," the older woman crooned, fingertipping the man's right hand lightly. Her own hand was heavily draped in finger jewels, meant to cover marks of sterility or sanctioned genetic alterations. Under any other conditions the woman would never mingle with those of higher station, but since she was an artist, social boundaries were muted. She was, after all, Jasmine Wyncote, one of the most famous interactive artists in the world.

"Show him," Tamara said, gesturing toward a darkened doorway.

Jasmine Wyncote pushed a button on a wall console and the darkened room began to glow. Graham stepped forward and stood in the doorway. Inside, hanging from a high ceiling, were hundreds of pale lavender and white tentacles. They shimmered with a soft, transparent quality, coiling slightly, like a slow-motion octopus or anemone wavering with sea currents. Near the top of the tentacles, which were of varying lengths and thicknesses, was a parachutelike silken dirigible of deep fuchsia and pink and purple, billowing on a gentle breeze.

"I call it *Portuguese Man-of-War*," Jasmine said. "Like the jellyfish. To interact with it you must wander among the tentacles. Each one gives off a mild electrical shock. More like . . . a vibration on the skin, most of them. Quite pleasant, actually. But somewhere in there are tentacles that could stun a man. And if you increase the power"— she smiled, pointing to a dial on the panel—"the interaction becomes . . ."

"Deadly." Graham nodded.

"For those with a taste for Russian roulette. Care to try it? Low voltage, of course."

"Just . . . walk in?"

"There are a number of ways one can approach it—to try to reach the far wall and back without getting stunned, or try for endurance, or"—she glanced at Tamara—"a love chase perhaps."

"I'll watch, thank you," Tamara said.

Jasmine's eyes glittered, betraying her own excitement as Graham took a step into the room. "It's best appreciated sans clothing, of course," the woman said, chortling.

Graham paused, then began to shed his clothes, handing them to Tamara. She watched him move slowly into the room and admired the beauty of his body. There was a grace in his movements that was not altogether Western, she thought. Possibly he was a practitioner of T'ai Chi Ch'uan. She had heard rumors that he had once lived for a year in a Buddhist monastery in Tibet, but there was much about this man that remained rumor. His striking features hinted of a Mongol bloodline, and indeed, she had heard that his mother had been an exquisite beauty of French-Chinese descent. His dark hair and eyes and high cheekbones added to his faintly exotic appeal.

By the time he touched the far wall, word had spread through the gallery and a hushed audience crowded the doorway. He was halfway back across the room when a tentacle's shock dropped him to his knees. As it brushed by him again he rolled away and rose to his feet, sweat sleeking his body like a fine oil.

His arrival back at the entrance was met with applause by the onlookers.

"I'll take it," he said as he dressed.

CHAPTER 4

He should have known, Graham thought later. There had been signs. All along there had been signs. But he had not heeded the inner instinct that had guided him so well for so long. It was best to keep one's enemies close, to hear their thoughts, his grandfather had once cautioned. Perhaps there had been too many enemies kept too close, and all the whispers had become senseless babble. By the time the message was clear it was too late.

The early warning was Warner's absence at the board meeting on Monday. Graham was mildly annoyed and made a note to have the man report to him as soon as the tracer located him.

Another warning was the report on the "Tolan Affair," as it was being referred to by almost everyone. The rambling research, several inches thick, spouted garbled statistics and data, structured to bury facts under sheaves of documentation ad infinitum. It was a classic business maneuver, and one which governments had long ago perfected. "If you want incriminating information hidden, document it to death," his grandfather had advised. "Only the dedicated will bother to wade through it." The old man had leaned close, his breath heavy with the smell of nicotine. "And the dedicated"—he winked—"disappear."

Graham pushed the reams of paper aside and looked

down the long table at Peebles. "In a word. Cause of death."

Eleven heads swiveled toward Peebles who fastidiously aligned his own copy of the report with the edge of the table. "Ah, well. I would rather that Warner explained, when he, ah, arrives."

Heads turned in unison back to Graham. "Try" was all Graham said.

"Well, it seems that, as I understand it, that is, speaking in layman's terms as it were, ah . . . Tolan and the others were—ah—victims of a natural . . . occurrence. A simple act-of-God turn of nature. You've heard, no doubt, of something called the, ah, red tide? It's a rapid-growing toxic algae that depletes the oxygen in the water and clogs the gills of fish so, ah . . . they suffocate, and well, it was something on that order. Just a freakish act of nature. You'll see, on page . . ." Peebles flipped frantically through pages of the report. "Yes. Here. There have been numerous reports of similar incidents which have occurred periodically all along the coastal waters—fish-kills, ah, other . . . incidents. It happens."

James Hartman, one of the elder board members, cleared his throat. "I don't recall ever hearing of any red tide that proved fatal to *humans*."

"Well, it's not *exactly* red tide, per se . . ." Peebles said, still thumbing through pages. "It's on the *order* of that type of natural occurrence. Research indicates that this is a relatively new *form* of, ah, whatever . . . algae, or whatever. It depletes the oxygen *above* the water, as well. Tolan's boat just had the misfortune to drift into a patch of it. Accidental death due to suffocation. Clear and simple."

It was too clear. And far too simple, Graham knew. Warner's absence from the table already told him that. And when the man still did not turn up after two weeks, he knew that whatever Warner had found out was still buried. Warner was a dedicated man.

There were other signs, of course—a rash of phone interference, message videos blanked out on his home screen, calls with no message, small clusters of executives who calmly drifted away as soon as he appeared, pauses in conversation at the Club as he walked by, painfully small talk over dinners.

aham for the events that
l send his destiny careening
r remotely fathomed.

ntic at dawn and billowed
green, rolling avalanche. It
very living thing in its path
, guided by the whim of air
atica, a sea-based metropolis
nately three and a half mil-
the space of a breath. They
ey turned to marvel in be-
e time it took for a smile to
ath so quickly that bodies
owers, slumped over morn-
s, newspapers still clutched
d cradling nursing infants,
hildren were in their beds
eps. It was a Pompeian City
n, without so much as a

stiffly until the ballooning
It had been such a joyous
rieling estate in Kentucky.
drifted like lazy butterflies
fields. Tamara had seen to
rom trivial matters and for-
ith the world at large. Just
ed, coaxing Graham to join
conditions will be perfect.
ys. It would mean so much
he had come along.
rty was not what Graham
ought it was an awkward

he dark-suited man held up
the charges against him as
artment of Environmental
authenticity. A third man

produced belt cuffs and roughly manacled Graham before he could react. The indignity of the moment was surpassed only by the stunned silence of the guests and the hostess.

He was whisked away to an Interrogation Center and locked in an isolation room, still unaware of the immensity of the crimes of which he was accused.

And then they showed him the surreal horrors on a videoscan. And the proof of his guilt. The oozing, corroded barrels had surfaced from deep chasms off the continental shelf. Thousands of containers, bobbing like rusty corks, snaked along the Gulf Stream, spreading contamination for thousands of miles. The industrial codes and cover names and bogus serial numbers were nonetheless traced back to the parent company, Sinclair Enterprises. It wasn't the chemicals in and of themselves, he was told later, but the lethal combination with far older dumping, of nerve gas and chemical warfare weapons and banned pesticides, toxic time bombs long forgotten from the last century. No one knew how many more Clouds would surface in the years to come, or where they would drift, or how one might mount a defense against them. Graham's signature was on document after document confiscated from the head office. His home was searched and still more documents and memos were discovered that laid the finger of blame on the chief executive of the Corporation.

During the trial, held in the World Court and watched by millions via satellite, Graham remained silent, focusing his gaze on Marcus Peebles, no longer a sweating, nervous little man, but one who stood absolved of all blame, a little man who simply carried out orders from above. It did not matter that Graham had never issued such orders, that these executive cost-cutting, profit-making decisions had been made without his knowledge. His guilt was decided long before the verdict. He was condemned for his life-style as much as for his artfully forged signature on telling memos.

Warner's body was found, compacted into a metal drum in a New Jersey salt marsh. It was such a tacky disposal, one meant to be found, Graham realized, for New Jersey Patrols were militant about environmental standards. Had someone wanted Warner to disappear permanently, he would never have surfaced. Cryptic notes were found in the man's pockets, as if he had been trying to reach Graham just before he was dispatched.

"Were you not a frequent guest of one Terrington A. Schuler, a man known for brutal hunting parties on his North Carolina estate?" the prosecuting attorney asked Graham when he was called to the stand.

"I never participated in the hunts," Graham replied.

"But you *condoned* these entertainments by your very presence, Mr. Sinclair. In effect, gave your *blessing* to these savage rituals against nature. And were you not aware of charges brought against Mr. Schuler six months ago? Mr. Schuler and six of his gamekeepers systematically slaughtered hawks, eagles, owls, dogs, and any other predators, *including* family pets, that threatened the stocked game on his private hunting preserve."

Graham was well aware of the incident, and had been appalled by the revelations. He, as well as the social circle of which Schuler had been a member, immediately severed all ties with the man, just as Graham was now cut off, a social pariah among his peers. His defense attorneys had informed him that he was possibly the most reviled man on the face of the earth. Even if he should be exonerated of all charges, his future would be precarious. He would be safe nowhere. Already several attempts had been made on his life, one attack by a guard whose sister and family were among the Cloud victims.

"I knew nothing of the dumping," Graham told the lawyers, then again under oath on the stand. "It has always been the policy of companies under the auspices of Sinclair Enterprises to render inert any toxic compounds created as waste products. Our companies have always complied with environmental guidelines and restrictions."

"Until now," the prosecuting attorney said with a nod. "Your cost-cutting endeavors lined your pockets handsomely and those who connived with you. The blood of millions is on your hands, Graham Sinclair. You, and you alone, are ultimately responsible for the deaths of three and a half million people, not to mention the untold damage to the ecological balance of the earth. And the horrors are not over. A Cloud surfaced near the Bahamas only last week. Shifting winds and a storm squall were all that saved those people. And who knows when these Death Clouds will rise again from a poisoned ocean?"

It did not take an hour for the jury to reach its verdict —guilty on all counts, including the murder of William Warner.

Graham was not surprised. The hostility toward him had been palpable, even from the attorneys hired to save him. And they had been the best. It was the sentence that stunned him. The death penalty had long ago been abolished, worldwide. Crime rates, too, had declined drastically over the last half century, what with behavioral modification drugs, genetic engineering techniques that had weeded out psychotic criminal tendencies, and computer monitoring of repeat offenders. Most prisons had been bulldozed to the ground, or converted into low-cost housing and community malls.

Blatant criminal acts were dealt with on an individual basis. Child abuse, which had become rampant by the end of the twentieth century, was eradicated by mandatory sterilization of the guilty and by intense nurturing education of all youth of child-bearing age. Corporate criminals usually received a sentence of community service. Environmental crimes were dealt with more stringently, the guilty parties assigned to clean up industrial accidents and carry out ecological duties until thoroughly rehabilitated in the eyes of Gaia officials.

Graham had expected punishment harsher but somewhat along the lines of that meted out to Schuler and the gamekeepers—a term of indeterminate length on Galapagos, tending to the wildlife until it became a consuming passion. Graham was prepared for a life sentence, to serve mankind and the environment until he died. And he was prepared to accept that decision. When all the appeals were done and finished and the last argument was heard in World Court, Graham would accept that which Fate had bestowed upon him. But he was not prepared for the punishment that was finally imposed.

"Graham Kuan Sinclair, rise and stand before the Court," the judge intoned.

Graham rose.

"You are to be banished from the nurturing environment that you have so despoiled. You are hereby sentenced to spend the rest of your days on the outposts of Mars, never to return, even in death, to planet Earth."

The gasps from the courtroom were audible. Graham could not feel his feet move as he was led away. The only face he remembered was that of Ti, as the boy's tears fell, spotting his crisp white tunic.

CHAPTER 5

Jonathan Baker watched his charge through the small observation window in the cell door. "You say he's been like that for the last six hours?"

"Hasn't moved a muscle," the attendant said, nodding. "Won't eat, won't talk. Won't open his eyes. I had to check three times to see if he was breathing. He just sits there like that, cross-legged, on the floor, like he's checked out and left the baggage behind."

"I suppose he has, after a fashion," Baker said, unlocking the door.

"He can't, you know, delete himself, can he? Doing that?"

"I don't believe so." Baker moved slowly into the chalk-colored room. It was sterile and stripped clean of any object that might serve as a weapon or an instrument of self-destruction. Graham Sinclair, folded into a lotus position on a blue pallet, looked to Baker like some white-draped yogi in an ashram. It seemed a sort of rudeness to disturb the man's concentration.

"Mr. Sinclair?" Baker waited, then called his name again. There was no response. The file on C7740-J was relatively skimpy, considering the fame of the prisoner. Rather, *infamy,* Baker reminded himself. He had to keep a proper focus, to keep a distance and a politeness. Personal rage had no place here, nor did empathy. He had finally resorted to the society pages that told him far more about Graham Sinclair than did the official dossier handed over to him by the Mars Commission along with the assignment.

"Mr. Sinclair?" Baker touched the man's shoulder and Graham opened his eyes.

"I'm very sorry to disturb you, Mr. Sinclair, but we're already behind schedule and there's very little time to prepare you for . . ."

Graham blinked. "Are you one of my attorneys? I don't remember your face."

"No. I'm Jon Baker, your T.E. We were introduced briefly last Tuesday. There was a great deal of confusion so it's understandable that you might not recall it. I was assigned to your case rather hastily, I'm afraid. There isn't much time to prepare you. I apologize."

"My case?" There seemed a hint of interest in the man's eyes now. "Then there *will* be another appeal, after all? I was told . . ."

"No, no, oh, I'm terribly sorry." Baker was not a man who was easily flustered, but Graham Sinclair was no ordinary assignment.

"I'm your Transition Escort."

The vague spark of interest and cautious hope in the man's eyes shifted to wary confusion. Clearly, he had no idea of Baker's purpose in his life.

"I'm here to help you . . . to make the transition . . . to your . . ." Baker swallowed. The thought of this man's future was oppressive, even to him. ". . . new home," he said, and watched the blankness rise in the man's face. No, he decided, it was not so much a blankness as it was a wall, a bland, impenetrable wall.

"I have no need of your services, thank you," Graham said. The tone was meant to convey dismissal.

"I'm afraid my services are not a choice, Mr. Sinclair. My job is to prepare you physically, psychologically, and . . . emotionally for an environment much . . . different from that of Earth. Your case is rather unusual. Unique, actually. We don't quite know what to do about you. You present us with something of a challenge."

"Why?"

Baker avoided the man's eyes and examined the blank walls. "Is there anyone you wish to see, before . . . your departure? Any particular requests?"

"Why am I such a *challenge*?"

Baker began to slowly pace the small, rectangular room, running his left hand along the smooth walls. "Does the size of this room bother you?"

"I'm not claustrophobic, no."

"Good. That will work in your favor. Your ability to meditate will also help immeasurably, I believe. Privacy will be a precious commodity at times. There aren't many places to escape and be alone on a cycler."

Graham watched the man move about the room. "A cycler. I assume that's some sort of *space* vehicle."

"Yes. I checked your dossier, Mr. Sinclair. You've never ventured beyond Earth's gravity, not even one Moon excursion. A man of your considerable wealth and background, and not one off-world jaunt. May I ask why?"

"It never appealed to me. Is it my virginal space status that presents such a challenge?"

"No."

"Then what?"

Baker met the man's eyes. "That you did not *volunteer* to emigrate to Mars. No one has ever gone *in*voluntarily." After an awkward silence, he continued, "There are, at present, five colonies on Mars. The first civilian settlement was established in 2038 . . ."

"Wasn't it wiped out by a disease?"

"Yes. Martian Fever. But you'll receive inoculations for that. The Jeremian colony was established seven years ago, in 2046. A year later the Sera colony and the Ventures colony were established. The Keyote colony is actually the oldest, after the SURF base—that's the Scientific Universal Research Facility—everyone just calls it SURF for the sake of brevity. It was established in 2028. Keyote is primarily a water-mining operation . . ."

"I know. One of my companies invested in the Mediterranean Reclamation project."

Baker nodded. "It was mentioned in your defense at the trial. You also have stock in the SURF colony."

"*Had* stock," Graham corrected, without seeming bitterness. "Is that where I am to be sent?"

"Initially."

"To be a guinea pig of sorts?"

Baker was uncomfortable and knew that his embarrassment showed. "Well, there will be some . . . scientific curiosity as to your adaptability. Considering the fact that you did not *choose* relocation."

"I am unique to Mars, then?"

"And the fact that you understand there can be no . . ." Baker needed a deeper breath than the room allowed.

". . . no coming home," Graham finished.

"Yes."

Graham unfolded himself from the blue pallet and stood up. He was taller than Baker by at least four inches. "I *will* come home, Mr. Baker. Someday. I will come home."

Marcus Peebles strolled through Graham's palatial rooms, issuing orders to Ti as to changes that he wanted, now that he was chief executive of Sinclair Enterprises and would be moving into the Towers himself. He browsed among Graham's expansive collection of custom-tailored clothing and shook his head. "They'll have to go, of course. Such a pity we aren't the same size."

"You will never be Master Graham's size, I think." Ti made a minuscule bow, his eyes on the notepad in his hands.

"That will be quite enough of your impertinence. That you still have a roof over your head is due in no small part to my own generosity and Mr. Sinclair's wishes." Peebles removed a silk shirt from a hanger and held it out before him between thumb and index finger. "Never forget. You can be discarded as simply as this." He dropped the garment to the marbled floor. "I want all of this out by tomorrow. Make a note. Just the clothing, shoes, et cetera. The cuff-link chest, the watches, those antique pieces especially, I'll keep. And the colognes. I always did like G.K.'s taste in cologne. Follow me."

The boy followed dutifully behind Peebles as the man rejected or embraced Graham Sinclair's many possessions. "The Ming collection can stay. I do like his selection of

Chinese porcelains, but I'll sell the jade. It's so much clutter as far as I'm concerned."

He breezed by several glass cases containing medieval illuminated manuscripts and first editions of rare books. "Also, get rid of these musty old books. I don't care how rare they are. I couldn't for the life of me understand his acquisition of Poe's *Tamerlane*. So there are only two copies in existence. It's fodder for the auction houses. And the art. My God, what am I to do with the art? Our tastes simply don't mesh at all in that area. Make a note to get in touch with an appraiser. I'll simply have to sell off what I can't stomach. Like this." Peebles frowned at a silver coil of sculpted abstraction. "I suppose it could be melted down. Hold on this."

Ti had stopped taking notes. "Master Marcus, sir. I wish to tender resignation."

Peebles turned and looked at the youth. "You'll be dismissed when I decide, not a moment sooner. I'll need your paltry services until I've adjusted to the—shall we say—idiosyncracies of the place. Then I'll be happy to ship you back to Taiwan or wherever he found you."

"Not Taiwan. Singapore. I stay in America. I am American citizen."

Peebles continued his room-by-room appraisal of the mansion. He paused at one point to examine a wall console. "Now what is this? Some sort of temperature control?"

"Part of art in next room. Please do not touch control. Very delicate."

Peebles pushed buttons. "I can touch anything I please. What does it do?"

"Master Graham say not to touch. Is very dangerous to change numbers."

The adjoining circular doorway opened up to reveal rich shades of violet and lavender and pinkish light. Long translucent tentacles swayed from the ceiling, coiling slowly, entangling, unwinding.

"Very . . . interesting, I must say. Is that it? Is that all it does?" Peebles moved a dial and the colors seemed to intensify slightly.

Ti folded his hands behind his back. "Is interaction art.

Must go inside room to appreciate. Master Graham go inside naked, only. Stay long time."

Peebles raised an eyebrow. "Oh, really?"

"Not for faint of heart. Master Graham only move this dial to five." Ti pointed to the console. "But he is very big man. Can do this. Maybe you should turn dial to one. Maybe two."

The man began to remove his clothing. Ti took his coat and began neatly folding things, performing his valet duties with meticulous dedication. Peebles turned the dial to nine, the highest number, and stepped into the room, his pale, potbellied frame silhouetted by fuchsia and alexandrite hues.

Ti watched, a thin smile hinting at the corners of his mouth. It didn't take long. Lights dimmed for a moment and somewhere in the thick of the tentacles, there was a muffled gurgling sound that stopped after a moment.

"Master Marcus?" the boy called. "This mean I not get letter of recommendation?"

There was no answer, but then he hadn't really expected one.

CHAPTER 6

Books, manuals, charts, and holo-discs were stacked neatly on a table that had been moved into the white room, along with two chairs. Graham continued his T'ai Chi exercises, aware that eyes watched him outside the dark observation slit in the door. His forced isolation had sharpened his inner senses, and he often knew who would be interrupting his concentration before the bolt clicked in the lock. Jon Baker was tediously punctual, however, so there was nothing intuitive in recognizing his arrival, Graham decided. He felt a vague sympathy for the man charged with his care until he was handed over to authorities on Mars. He could sense the escort's suffocating pity mingled with suppressed repugnance for his fate, like an oily film over his every gesture.

"Did I disturb you?" Baker asked from the cell doorway. "That looks very relaxing, very peaceful, what you do. It's supposed to symbolize the movements of insects or something, isn't it? I don't know anything about T'ai Chi, actually. Perhaps you could instruct me in the discipline during the journey."

Graham looked at him. "If you like. It's more than movement of the body, though."

Baker entered the room, carrying several books and holo-discs. "I've never pursued Eastern philosophy. It's much too esoteric for my head to grasp. I'm rather concrete in my thinking. Graphics I understand. The essence of Taoism escapes me. Like what you said the other day about accepting blame. You compared your attitude to the movement of water. 'There is strength in what it is not,' you said. I still don't understand what that means."

"The truth often seems paradoxical." Graham nodded.

"See, there you go again. I don't understand that either." He put the new books on the table and stacked the others in a pile.

"Then we're even," Graham said. "I don't understand half of what you bring me to read." He flipped through a book. "What are libration points?"

Baker seemed pleased to be asked something, at last. It was an indication that his pupil had begun to study. "They're also referred to as Lagrange points, after—"

"—after the French physicist and mathematician who first calculated their existence. I know that. I still don't know what they are."

Baker sketched a circular diagram on a sheet of paper. "Here's Earth in the center. The circle around it is the orbit of the Moon. There are five Earth–Moon Lagrange libration points where space stations can remain with an insignificant expenditure of energy or propellant." He drew a rhombus within the circle. "Libration points one through three are somewhat unstable in that any spaceport or space station placed along this line"—he bisected both the circle and the parallelogram in one brief stroke—"could begin to drift away and it would keep drifting. L1, L2, and L3 are all on the Earth–Moon line. Now, L4 and L5 are stable because they're on the orbit of the Moon around Earth. Any facility located at either of those libration points will return to that point if it should be displaced."

Graham leaned over the table. "So they're simply the points at which the gravity of the Earth is canceled by the gravity of the Moon."

"Exactly." Baker was obviously relieved at his studious interest. "There are corresponding libration points between the Earth and Sun, and the Sun and Jupiter. Jupiter has a group of asteroids associated with its L4 and L5 points."

"And the *Shepard* space station is located—"

"—at L5, here." Baker pointed. "But we'll be leaving from L1. It's been proven to be the best jumping-off point for the Mars run."

Graham sat down at the table. "From what I understand, there are about ten steps from here to . . . there. The first step is the *Shepard,* pausing only long enough to buy a few postcards. Then, step two, we move from the *Shepard* to the Libration Point Spaceport, the *Glenn,* perhaps for an overnight stay? Then, it's to some sort of transfer vehicle that will match orbits with a cycling spaceship. That's step four, the cycler. Six months, six more steps and 400 million some-odd kilometers later . . . home . . . sweet home."

Baker opened a holo-disc. "This will give you a brief introduction to life aboard a cycler. It's not as unpleasant as it sounds. It has artificial gravity that starts out at one g and the rotation will be decreased gradually until it's 0.34g—the surface gravity level of Mars. Time is adjusted in the same way. The Martian day, or sol, is 24 hours 39.5 minutes long. You adjust gradually to the sols along with the change in gravity. When you arrive you're fully acclimated and ready to function."

"And the return trip simply reverses the process."

Baker kept his eyes on the disc. "Yes . . . just the reverse."

Graham had not intended the remark to trigger an awkwardness between them. He was beginning to realize that the man's knowledge and guidance would be needed for a future rapidly being thrust upon him. Baker did not look like a space commuter, he thought, although he did look like a social volunteer, one of those who felt a need to give comfort to the less fortunate. It had never, even remotely, crossed Graham's mind that he, himself, would one day fall into just that category. "How many of these . . . runs have you made?" he asked, more to ease the strain than because he was curious.

"Four. This will be number five."

"That puts you in space for approximately a year at a stretch. How old are you?"

"Two years older than you. Thirty-four."

Graham was surprised. He was usually a better guesser

and he had estimated Baker to be several years younger than himself. With his dark blond hair and youthful physique he could still be lifeguarding on some summer beach, he thought, instead of taxiing convicts to other planets.

Baker picked up the stack of books and discs that Graham had finished perusing. "I lived there for two years, on Mars. In the Jeremian colony."

"I thought you had a missionary look about you. The holo-discs weren't all that helpful about the colonies. They were armchair travelogues. Water mining. Get rich quick and get out. Research facility. Do the experiment and go home. The Ventures colony—what's the turnover rate? Three years, maximum, and they come back to Earth. And then there is the Jeremian colony, bent on Christianizing Mars." Graham ticked off the groups on his fingers. "What did I leave out? Oh, yes. Them. The Contaminants. The . . . what do they call themselves? The Sarah colony."

Baker's demeanor altered slightly, as if he were prepared to defend himself against a verbal attack by taking the offensive. "Not 'Sarah.' *Sera*. It stands for Selective Environmental Reproductive Adaptation. They believe in the acceptance of whatever genetic mutations are bequeathed them, no matter what the environmental source."

"They refuse genetic engineering techniques that could help their offspring to have a normal future in society," Graham countered.

"They inherited the fruits of their parents and their grandparents and their *great*-grandparents, victims all. Victims of PCB spills and toxic dumping and poisoned water and poisoned air and pesticide-laced baby food and contaminated breast milk. All because of people like you!" Baker's face was ruddy with rage. "People like you! Faceless corporations with three-monkey innocence, out to make a profit no matter what the cost. After all, who gave a damn? Those corporate directors sat back and smiled at their company charts and counted their money. They would never have to look upon the children of their children and wonder at the distortions of nature. They would never have to answer to the genetic seeds they scattered, the inheritors of the Bhopals and Love Canals and Minamata Bays and all the others . . . the secret spills and unreported contaminations . . . the ones in the middle of the night, down back roads, and into the water supplies. I won't even go into the results of all the toxic dumping in the third-world countries. We both know the tragic harvest we reaped from that!"

A guard, a stun gun in his right hand, had opened Graham's cell door to see what the commotion was about.

"It's all right," Graham said to the man. "We're having a philosophical discussion."

Baker slumped back into a chair, momentarily drained.

"Does it feel better, having a face to blame for guilts half a century old?" Graham asked.

"I'm sorry. I wasn't expecting the anger after so many . . . years. I worked among the Contaminants—the Sera colonists. We built a church . . . and . . ."

"You bonded with one of them?"

Baker nodded. "The Jeremians expelled me from the commune. I lived with the Seras for a year, until Matina . . . died. They die early, you know, most of them, from things we've never heard of, from internal scramblings of misplaced hearts and tiny . . . broken things inside."

"Are you still a Jeremian?"

"No. I'm"—Baker spread his arms slightly—"nothing. And I belong nowhere. Not here, not Mars. I live in between. That's where I'm happy, I suppose." He tapped the fresh stack of books and discs. "Do your homework, Mr. Sinclair. We have only ten days before rendezvous with the next cycler."

He called for the guard to unlock the door. "Funny, how is it that you know more about me, now, than I know about you? I'm not being a very good teacher, I'm afraid."

Graham returned to his pallet on the floor and assumed a lotus position. "One who does not treasure a teacher is greatly deluded. You are a good teacher, Jonathan Baker."

"Jon."

"Graham."

• • •

The prison made Jasmine Wyncote nervous. That it was a prison elaborately disguised as a medical facility made her even more uncomfortable. She had tried to visit Graham since his arrest and had sent him notes of hope, but was not sure anything reached him. Now, on the eve of his departure from Earth, forever, she had received word that a brief visit would be allowed. A guard led her through security checks and Jon Baker met her in a conference room adjacent to Graham's cell.

"I'm glad you could come . . . to see him off," Baker said.

"See him off?" the woman snapped. "My God, man, this isn't some holiday cruise he's going on! We're not here to throw confetti and down champagne! You're sending him to hell. That's what you're doing."

Baker looked upset. "Please. He needs a sense of . . . family now. I asked him if there was anyone he might like to see, before . . . he left. You were the only one he mentioned. And the boy, his valet."

"Ti?"

"Yes. He's waiting in the next room. One visitor at a time. There was no one else. Just the boy . . . and you. He said you had sent notes of encouragement, even after the trial, and he wanted to thank you."

"He's an innocent man," Jasmine said. "He should never have received so cruel a punishment. I will fight to my last breath to bring him home. I want him to know that."

A door opened and Graham, flanked by two guards, was ushered into the room. He wore hospital-white pajamas and a pale blue robe. Even in rumpled, ill-fitting clothes he still possessed a princely aura, Jasmine thought. She had painted his official Corporation portrait when he was twenty-one, and had done a nude study when he was twenty-six. He was one of her earliest supporters when she had first begun to explore interactive art. She had just begun to work on a bust of him when the world closed in and brought him down like a stag among dogs.

Jasmine stood and held out her hand in the traditional

fingertip greeting, but Graham did not respond. Instead, he opened his arms, a most intimate gesture, and embraced her.

"Thank you," he whispered.

The warmth of his body made her want to hold the contact forever. Bodily touches had become so rare in a frightened world, she thought. *Cling to this instant. It will not come again.*

They sat and there was a brief awkwardness as Baker excused himself. "Ten minutes, Gray. And ten for the boy. It's all they will allow."

Graham wasted no time. "I have a favor to ask of you, Jasmine. You needn't say yes unless . . . it's about Ti. I set up a trust for him, but I don't know how long Marcus will allow him to stay at the Towers. If he's turned out . . ."

Jasmine sat back. "Then you don't know. They didn't tell you?"

"What?"

"Oh, my." She quickly told him about the inquiry and how Ti had been exonerated in the man's death. "Luckily the surveillance cameras were on at the time and caught it all. It was perfectly clear that the sludge, excuse me, Marcus Peebles, refused to heed the boy's warnings. Accidental Death Due to Arrogance, the report should have said. I was also called in for questioning. After all, it was my creation. They were going to dismantle it, but Tamara Voss-Frieling bought it. I hope she fries, too. Oh, I'm sorry. They just make me so . . ." Jasmine took a deep breath and erased the air. "The way they closed you out . . . so . . . completely . . ."

Graham smiled. "It's the custom. I would have done the same to another man. You risked a great deal in coming here today. It may hurt your standing in the art community."

"Then they weren't friends worth having." Jasmine shrugged. "You have never understood that, have you? The depth of friendship. Those in your circle have no concept of *real* friendship. Unless there's something to gain from the contact, unless the connection is socially or monetarily beneficial . . ." She shook her head. "Forgive me. What a waste of precious minutes. I'm sitting here expounding on the vacuousness of the rich when . . . but you were always a bit different. You always knew something was missing. You collected your art and you opened your home to those lavish parties—oh, they may not miss you, Graham Kuan Sinclair, but they will miss your parties! I watched you. None of it made you happy, Graham. Not for long. Where you're going . . . make it a good life. Promise me you'll seek out the things that matter."

Graham reached out to touch her hand. "Ti matters to me. Will you look after him? He's strong-willed and impudent and he will never become a Class-A valet or anything else, for that matter. But he needs . . . someone. Is there room for him, with you? As an assistant . . . anything, a fetcher, whatever might make him feel some sense of worth."

There was a soft rap on the door and Baker stepped in. "Time's up, Gray. Do you still want to see the boy?"

"Yes."

Jasmine touched his face gently, an impossible breach of protocol under normal circumstances. "I'll take care of him. Don't worry. I'm told you will never be . . . allowed further contact from anyone on Earth. And no messages may be transmitted by you from Mars. Is that correct?" She looked at Baker.

"Yes," Baker said, and looked away.

She leaned close to Graham and whispered, "Then watch for a sign—the sign of the ox. You'll know the message is for you."

Ti entered the room after Jasmine's departure, a tense frown masking what Graham knew to be complete terror. He bowed stiffly, then scowled at Baker. "They did not beat you?" he said to Graham.

"No. I'm treated very well."

Baker reminded them of the brief time limit and left the room.

"He is your new valet?" the boy asked. "He is no good. He shames you."

"I have only one valet. You are that one, Ti. But now I

must say good-bye to you, and you must offer your services to someone else."

"No. I will go with you."

Graham shook his head. "You can't go with me. You wouldn't like it there. You would miss your great American city."

"I would miss you more. Please! Let me come with you. I will make myself very small and be like a shadow no one will notice. I would eat very little and I can do many things. Tell them. Make them let me come with you. Please, Master Graham!"

"I believe Marcus Peebles is no longer with the Corporation," Graham said.

Ti retreated slightly. "He not appreciate art."

"So I understand. Where are you staying now?"

"Many places. Judge say to stay in children home, but I do not like. I am not child. I will go with you to Mars."

Graham again shook his head. *'Pu shih!* No, Ti. You can't go. But I have a friend. You've met her. She's the artist, Jasmine Wyncote. She wants you to come and work for her."

"I will not be valet to lady!"

"No. You would be . . . an assistant. You would help her with her art."

The youth thought for a moment. "I could learn art, too?"

"I'm sure she would teach you whatever you wish to learn."

"I will consider."

"No. I must know now that you will go to her. She's waiting outside. I want to know that someone is going to . . ." Graham swallowed. He hadn't expected this to be so difficult. ". . . look after you. I respect her and I trust her. I would not send you to anyone else. Tell me that you will go with her."

Baker knocked on the door as he opened it. "I'm sorry, Graham. Time is up."

The boy turned to leave, then suddenly flung his arms around Graham, weeping.

"Tell me," Graham whispered.

"I will go with her."

"Good."

"I will not forget you, Master Graham. Do not forget me. Here." Quickly he removed a small leather pouch on a string from around his neck. "Something of my ancestors inside. Small piece of jade. From Singapore. You keep. *Tsai chien.* Good-bye." He pressed the treasure into Graham's hand and was gone.

Baker cleared his throat. "You can't keep it, Graham. They won't allow it. Nothing of Earth. They were explicit. I'm sorry." He held out his hand to confiscate the gift.

"Not even this?"

"Nothing of Earth may be taken with you."

Graham held the small brown pouch, darkened from years of sweat and body oils. It was the only possession the boy coveted, his only link with his own meager heritage. Slowly he placed it into the man's palm. "Will you keep it for me? For when I come home?"

Baker looked at him. "I'll keep it for you."

CHAPTER 7

The one thing for which Baker had not prepared Graham when they boarded the aerospace plane at dawn was the presence of other passengers. He had been so insulated from the public since the trial that he was momentarily puzzled by their stares as he moved down the narrow aisle between rows of seats toward the reserved section. And then, hearing their whispers among themselves, he remembered that his was a notoriously recognizable face. He moved past twenty pairs of eyes, braced for any sudden assault from any direction. Baker, close behind him, murmured, "Just ignore them. It will give them something to tell their grandchildren about."

" 'I rode with Villa'?" Graham said.

"More like, 'I rode with the Cloud Man,' I suppose."

Graham settled into his seat and Baker helped him adjust the safety harness. "Is that what they're calling me? The 'Cloud Man'?"

"That's what they're calling you. Is this comfortable?" He tugged at the harness and tightened it slightly.

Graham closed his eyes. "I forgot to mention that I have a tendency toward motion sickness. Meditating helps."

"You won't have time. If you start feeling uncomfortable breathe into this." Baker pointed to a clear plastic inhaler attached to the side of the seat. "It'll take care of everything."

Graham was glad that the man had forced him to go through repeated holo-simulations of a typical Earth-to-orbit flight. He knew he had only five minutes left of his last contact with Earth when he heard the auxiliary power units start up. Three and one-half seconds before his severance with the planet of his birth, the main engines roared into life. As the aerospace plane lifted, the noises and vibrations were overwhelming. Graham felt vaguely like Jonah, experiencing whale indigestion from the inside. The acceleration, approaching three g's, pressed down on him like a serious carnival ride. He tried to lift his right arm, but the invisible giant pushing him deeper into the semihorizontal seat allowed room only for slight lung expansion. A sudden noise that sounded as if the craft were breaking up made him flash-sweat until he remembered it was only the SCRAMJET reaching Mach 20. Minutes later the main engines cut off and Graham experienced zero gravity for the first time. The sensation was both pleasant and mildly disorienting. Two short burns later and the ship was in LEO, low Earth orbit.

Baker unfastened his safety harness in the seat across the aisle. "See? Not so bad when you're prepared and know what to expect. Any motion sickness?"

Graham released his safety harness. "Not yet."

One of the other passengers, a woman in a red jumpsuit, pulled herself toward Graham's seat like an awkward mermaid. "You *are* Graham Sinclair, aren't you?" she said, grinning nervously. "The Cloud Man? Could you sign my autograph? I mean could I have your . . ."

Baker blocked her advance. "Sorry. This area is reserved, ma'am. Please return to your seat."

The woman appeared ready to argue, thought better of it, and pushed off to float back to the others. "He's so Class-A gorgeous," she said, giggling, to a second woman. "More handsome even than on TV."

One of the men leaned toward her. "You so much as acknowledge his existence again and you'll spend your vacation in a sling."

"Hush. He can hear you," said the woman.

Graham turned away to gaze out at the Earth hanging

large and resplendent against the blackness of space. The neon blue aura around it seemed to affirm the Gaia theory. Earth was a living organism. No photograph, no hologram, had prepared him for her indigo and white-marbled beauty. He was becoming aware of a creeping coldness beginning somewhere in the center of his chest and radiating outward. He had to force himself to take slow breaths, to remain calm. He tried to identify the peculiar feeling. It was unlike anything he had ever experienced before. He breathed deeply. It was like being buried alive. That was the closest he could come to pinpointing the sensation. He had to speak, to smother the growing distortion within.

"Is it true that the only man-made structure on Earth that can be seen with the naked eye from the surface of the Moon is the Great Wall of China?"

"It's true," Baker said.

Graham smiled slightly. "My grandmother would be pleased to hear that." The coldness, however, continued to spread.

Only four of the other passengers followed Baker and his charge from the *Shepard* space station to the L1 *Glenn* spaceport. The others were headed for the Armstrong lunar settlement to visit relatives or to vacation or work. Of the four men who joined them, two were also headed for Mars.

"Everyone else on this Mars run arrived weeks ago," Baker explained, flashing credentials to an ID monitor.

Graham ducked to get through the exit hatch and followed his escort along a snakelike tunnel ribbed with a flexible material he could not identify.

Four guards and the commander of the *Glenn* were waiting for them as they emerged into the spaceport's terminal.

Baker introduced Graham to Commander Weems, who did not offer so much as a perfunctory fingertip greeting. "I will tolerate no mishaps while this man is under my jurisdiction. I want a twenty-four-hour guard on him. He is not to leave his quarters until the transfer to the *Olympus Mons.* Is that clear?"

The guards led Graham to a small room with two bunk beds, a wall-molded desk unit, and a personal hygiene compartment. Baker stood in the doorway, watching him explore his temporary quarters. "Be glad of the artificial gravity." He chuckled. "Toilet facilities in zero g are no fun, believe me. I'm sorry he was curt with you, Graham, but you're too important a person to be assassinated under his nose. It wouldn't look good."

"Are you staying in here, also?"

"No. But I'll be nearby. The door will have to be locked, you understand. It's only for your own safety. Do you want anything? You didn't touch your meal while we were aboard the *Shepard*."

Graham removed the soft-soled shoes he had been given to wear upon his arrival at the space station. There had also been a brief but thorough physical inspection and a complete change of clothing to insure that he was not smuggling aboard any mementos of his life on Earth. He unzipped the gray jumpsuit and assumed a lotus position on the floor. "I would just like to be alone, if you don't mind."

Baker nodded. "I'll come back at fourteen hundred hours. If you need anything before then, just call one of the guards outside the door."

His eyes were closed but he heard the door shut and a heavy bolt hum into place. As hard as he tried to let go and remove himself, the subtle vibrations and sounds of massive machinery reminded him of the reality of the nightmare. It was happening. Like some cartoonish conveyor belt, powers beyond his control were dragging him to another world. Nausea surged upward, and deep breaths did little to help. His first impulse was to call for Ti, who would have come with a porcelain bowl and waited, dampened linen cloth in hand. Graham lurched toward the toilet and divested himself of the remnants of his last Earth-cultivated meal.

The transfer vehicle that would rendezvous with the cycler, *Olympus Mons*, was cramped and uncomfortable, Graham discovered. It was also without gravity. The novelty of zero g had worn off quickly, and he was looking for-

ward to a sense of weight and balance again. The concept
of up and down took on new meaning, and he was
vaguely bothered by the fact that no one could seem to
agree on exactly where they were located. Passengers
floated in any direction they pleased, much at home and
quite comfortable in what Graham perceived as an up-
side-down position.

"We should dock with the *Mons* in about an hour,"
Baker said, checking his watch. "How are you holding
up?"

"I'm all right. I would, however, appreciate it if you
wouldn't stand on the ceiling."

Baker chuckled and did a slow-motion somersault.
"You should unharness and enjoy the moment, Sinclair.
You're an old, old man sometimes. Did anyone ever tell
you that?"

Someone had, in fact, told Graham that, once. It had
been his grandmother, who had accused him of aborting
his youth for "the games of old men."

"You can be old the rest of your life," she had chided,
and splashed fountain water at him from where she stood
among the goldfish in the pond, drenched and laughing.
Her hair had still been mostly ebony, and hung in a
heavy braid down her back. He could have nearly encir-
cled her waist with his hands, had he been a man. But he
was nine and embarrassed by her inappropriate behavior
before the house servants.

"Come into the water, Kuan. There are no dragons to
bite you. Just golden little fish to nibble at your toes. It
feels so cool." Her wet silk shift outlined her small breasts.
Those, he could have cupped in his hands with room to
spare. Small apricots, his grandfather had called them.

"Where did you go?" Baker said, watching him from
what Graham considered an upright position.

"Nowhere." He wished now that he had gone into the
water.

CHAPTER 8

The *Olympus Mons* deserved its name, Graham realized, as the gigantic spaceship slowly came into view against the black velvet void and stars. It was impossible to grasp its enormity since there was nothing against which to compare it. He was reminded of a childhood excursion to the Pyramids with several boarding-school chums and an Egyptologist engaged by his father to keep him busy during his Christmas holiday. His parents were vacationing on the Greek island of Mykonos, and did not relish the thought of a ten-year-old chattering about the place. The Nile trip included a camel ride up to the Great Pyramid of Cheops. He had been relatively unimpressed at first, as they had approached the ancient wonder—so many stacked bricks, he had thought, squinting in the white heat of the Sahara sands. He swayed and clung to the camel's back, and the thumbnail-sized bricks seemed to grow larger. It was only when he finally saw the human figures sitting in the shade of the stone blocks that he began to comprehend the immensity and power of the structure.

The *Olympus Mons* looked nothing like a spaceship in the classical sense of the word. It consisted of a number of modules clustered together and linked to tethers that extended like the fine cross-hairs of a theodolite. Graham understood little of the multiple functions of the tethers other than that their lengths could be varied, and thus the artificial gravity of the ship could be altered. Solar arrays spanned a portion of the ship in a design that seemed a wedded combination of box kites and windmills. It was hardly a beautiful piece of engineering design, but, he decided, it did have an almost crystalline fragility about it that intrigued the mind. It was as if a spider had begun an organized and methodical web, running the main foundation lines, then became distracted and wandered away.

Once the transfer vehicle had docked with the cycler, everyone was forced to synchronize directions. Feet were on the floor, and "up" and "down" returned. Graham's stomach had definitely rediscovered "up." He felt heavy, as if coming out of a pool after a long swim.

"Are you going to be okay?" Baker asked as they moved into the linking corridor.

Graham simply nodded.

A welcoming committee made up of two members of the security patrol; Dr. Maggie McKay, the head of the ship's medical staff; and the ship's captain greeted the twelve new passengers.

Graham saw the subtle changes of expression as he was introduced. It seemed as if an air of reserve, a vapor-thick distancing, transpired the moment his name was spoken.

The group was led down narrow corridors and through air locks and chambers not unlike those of an ocean liner, just as the holo-discs had described, Graham noted.

Their guide, after the captain had departed, was Dr. McKay. She was not an unpretty woman, Graham thought, although devoid of feminine touches. Clinical and crisp would have been as terse a summation as he could have delivered if pressed. Perhaps in her mid-thirties, of average height, with short-cropped brown hair and features unenhanced by cosmetic decoration, Dr. McKay had, nevertheless, a smile that broke all boundaries of professional formality.

As the group toured the facilities, the two security guards positioned themselves behind Graham. Baker, who spoke to the doctor in a way that indicated a long-standing friendship, seemed to elicit an inordinate number of smiles from the woman.

"If any of you should become a bit confused by your surroundings at first," the doctor explained, "you'll find a number of location maps that will guide you back to familiar quarters. You may frequent any area not restricted to ship personnel only. Those areas are so marked, in red."

Graham turned to Baker. "Am I to be allowed the same freedom as the others?"

"Yes, Mr. Sinclair," said McKay, "with the exception of two security officers who will remain with you at all times. For your own protection, of course. There are people aboard this ship who are not pleased by your presence, I'm afraid. We want no incidents." She glanced at Baker. "You were assigned the top Transition Escort in the business. Jon . . . Mr. Baker has a wealth of experience, and you would do well to learn all you possibly can from him. It's a bit like having your own private wagon master to see you over the Rockies or through Death Valley and Indian country, to get you to the gold fields of California. Usually, a T.E. has ten or more clients per trip. You are a very privileged man, Mr. Sinclair. But then, I suppose you're quite used to privilege." She paused, as if waiting for a retort, and seemed somewhat surprised by Graham's silence.

Baker offered the return volley instead. "Keep in mind, Maggie, the man never asked to go West."

Her gaze faltered for a moment. "True."

They moved down long corridors while McKay pointed out features of the habitat. There was a recreational module that included a swimming pool, a running track, and a gym. A round-the-clock cafeteria-style commissary provided a relatively wide range of foods, including seafood, all harvested from a synthetic biosphere. "The CELSS, or Controlled Environment Life-Support System, offers just about any food whim your taste buds desire," the doctor said with a touch of pride.

"Beer?" joked one of the other men.

"Yes. And wine." McKay nodded. "As well as a number of medicinal plants, should medical supplies become critical."

"Beer's medicinal," said the man, laughing.

"It's made outta tofu, Denny," said the man next to him.

"You're kidding," Denny said. "Tell me he's kidding."

"How about something like chocolate? Or coffee?" asked another man.

Dr. McKay smiled. "We make something pretty close. You couldn't tell them from Earth-grown."

"Made out of tofu," someone else said, which provoked mild laughter.

"And the women, all made outta tofu," chimed in another, to louder chuckles and hoots.

Graham listened to the verbal one-upmanship. The sport had always slightly puzzled him. It seemed B Class, somehow, a quick verbiage rated by the loudness of the laughter, often cruel, and almost always sexual in nature. He had never understood it in school and he had never participated in the ritual during business dealings. On the few occasions an executive new to the Corporation launched into such prattle, either out on the golf course or during social engagements, he quickly realized his mistake. Graham's silence and inscrutable gaze caused an excruciating sense of humiliation in the perpetrator. The gaffe was never repeated thereafter. The custom belonged to a fraternity of which Graham had never been a member—male fellowship. He had understood only subordinates and superiors. In school the subordinates were laddered by age and academic progress, and he had moved to the top as quickly as possible, leaving behind most students of his own age, which further isolated him. He had no peer group to which he could belong and be accepted as an equal. He did, however, have followers. In business, subordinates and superiors were designated by the power allocated to them. Again, Graham moved to the top at an uncommonly young age. It was as though the position was the only one he understood. Again, however, the position allowed little room for unguarded friendships.

He watched Baker as they moved through sections of the vast cycler and realized that he had begun to look upon the man as much more than an obligatory host or something akin to a hired guide. Jon Baker was the closest thing he had to a friend. He was one of the few who did not look upon Graham with hostility, curiosity, or indifference. The concern for his comfort and well-being seemed genuine, and he was suddenly grateful for the gesture. That he did not know how to express his gratitude was of some concern to Graham. In the past, such a man in the Corporation would have been rewarded with a promotion. Elsewhere, he would have been handsomely tipped for his work, or gifted with some tangible extravagance. Since Graham's banking privileges had been abruptly frozen upon his arrest and his subdermal account chip removed from his right palm, he now survived on the beneficence of the State. There was nothing he could give this man. Except his cooperation.

"Down this corridor are our research facilities," Dr. McKay explained at a junction. "Only those with security clearance may pass beyond this point. Anyone who attempts to penetrate the area without proper credentials will find himself in a lot of difficulty."

"Sounds like the rules of my last marriage," quipped one of the men in the group.

"Now, if you'll please follow me, I'll show you to your living quarters, gentlemen," the woman said. "I'm sure you will want to settle in and unpack before dinner."

Graham found his room to be more spacious than that on the *Glenn*. It was equipped with a few more amenities, somewhat like lesser hotel accommodations in places he had visited on business, where a two-star establishment was the best the province had to offer. On the narrow bed was a Day-Glo orange duffel bag with his name on it.

"I took the liberty of ordering clothing and personal items you'll need," Baker said, watching Graham open the bag. "I believe everything will fit."

"Did it come out of your pockets or the State's?"

"It's part of the allocation for your transition."

Graham examined the toiletries. Nothing had an Earth-marked brand name that he recognized.

"Everything you see before you was manufactured either aboard this ship or on one of the space stations."

"What am I going to do, Jon? When I get there? Continue to live on whatever is doled out by the penal system?" He had never in his life been in such a position, the recipient of a governmental allowance. It was he, Graham Kuan Sinclair, who dropped coins in beggars' cups, and designated portions of business profits for a multitude of organizations dependent upon the charity of the wealthy.

"What am I going to do?"

"We have six months to explore your options. I doubt that your executive skills will be in great demand. What is needed most is manual labor. The Jeremians, Seras, and Ventures are agrarian colonies for the most part. Primary needs—food, clothing, shelter—take precedence over material comforts. They're a curious amalgam of survival basics and high tech. You'll see what I mean. Don't worry about living on charity. There will be plenty for you to do."

"Do they use a local currency or the Universal Credit System?"

"The miners at Keyote are paid through the U.C.S., and so are the people at the SURF base. But the other three colonies use a combination of credit and barter. The last time I was there I saw that some barter was being carried on at Keyote—food crops, mainly. Seems one of their CELSS modules was destroyed during a dust storm and they lost about half of their soybean crop. The Ventures got the use of a couple of the company stone fusers in return for a share of their crop."

Graham folded his new clothing away in wall storage units. He didn't know what a stone fuser was, but he had a feeling his ignorance would be short-lived once he reached Mars. Manual labor. He had never done manual labor in his life. He had seldom prepared his own bath. He had never cooked, or dug so much as an herb garden. He had once built things out of wooden blocks, but he had been three years old at the time. The nanny had disassembled all the constructions and put them away in a large carved-dragon chest at the end of play. He was ill-prepared to face a pioneer life, he thought. It was not the life his grandfather had foreseen for him, certainly.

"Want to come up on the observation deck to watch . . ." Baker flushed suddenly. "Forgive me. Maybe you'd rather not."

"Watch what?"

"Earth."

Graham placed a hairbrush and shaving equipment on a metal shelf in the hygiene compartment, aligning the articles neatly, as if their positions were critical to his well-being.

"It's always been a custom . . . to watch for a while. I understand, if you'd rather not." Baker turned to leave.

"No. I want to see it. I'll go with you."

The two guards stationed outside the door followed them up a spiral flight of stairs. The deck was a large circular observatory covered over by a clear dome. Ceramic panels partially shielded the area from direct rays of the sun. A number of passengers were already there.

"Take a good look, ladies and gentlemen," said a crew member. "No telling when you'll see her again. The most prized marble in the game, I can tell you that."

Graham was jarred by how small Earth had become, compared to his glimpses from the spaceport windows. The Moon partially eclipsed it now. He felt no real sensation of movement, only a constant low vibration and the relentless hum of machines circulating air and performing invisible tasks he could not begin to fathom. He assumed the ship's noises would fade into the unconscious, somewhat like one's lack of awareness of one's own heartbeat. Each time he blinked he knew that Earth was shrinking, although he couldn't see the change. It was like staring at the hour hand on an old timepiece. It was moving all the time, but the only way to tell was by comparing where the hand was at that moment with where it had been ten minutes before.

"It *is* a beautiful sight, isn't it?" a woman next to him murmured.

"Yes. It is," Graham said.

"I won't be back this way again for three years," she said with a smile. "How about you?"

Graham did not shift his gaze from the sphere. "I don't know . . . when I'll be coming home."

The woman turned to look at him for the first time. "Oh! Oh, dear, it's you! I didn't realize . . ." Flustered, she looked about as if searching for a familiar face, then bolted for the staircase.

Graham's eyes remained fixed on the dwindling world.

· · ·

He was in the ship's library with Baker, viewing updated information on Martian conditions when Dr. McKay found them. "You had an appointment with me, Mr. Sinclair, at fourteen hundred hours. Weren't you informed?"

Baker sat back in his chair and slapped his forehead. "Blame me. I meant to tell him."

"He can't put it off, Jon. He has to start the series next week. His physical was scheduled to begin today. Tell him to report to the infirmary A.S.A.P."

"I *am* in the room," Graham said. "You might address me directly."

"So you are, Mr. Sinclair."

"I was recently given my annual physical by my personal physician. If you need my medical history, I believe Mr. Baker has it in his files somewhere. I won't waste your time, or mine, in the retrieval of redundant information."

Dr. McKay placed both hands on the table and leaned toward him. "Are you averse to being examined by a woman, Mr. Sinclair?"

"Only in the medical sense."

Baker laughed. "A joke! You made a joke. An old one, true, but there's hope for you yet!"

Graham frowned. He had meant it in all sincerity.

It was the most thorough physical examination he had ever undergone in his life. He was punched, probed, scanned, scoped, pricked, snipped, gouged, tubed, tapped, starved, filled, flushed, and stuck. Stuck a number of times. And then stuck some more. All in a matter of three very long days. Days on the *Olympus Mons* were artificial, as were the nights. Lights dimmed and ceramic panels fanned out like a dulled peacock's tail to simulate an Earth night. Graham found sleep difficult to come by in the open infirmary. He was unused to sharing sleeping quarters with others but suspected that a request for privacy would be met with something akin to incredulity by those around him.

"Can't you get to sleep, Mr. Sinclair?" Dr. McKay asked, passing by his bed.

"I usually function on approximately four hours of actual sleep, if I have the opportunity to meditate. Unfortunately, that hasn't been the case."

"How come?"

"I'm constantly interrupted by the various and sundry ministrations of your medical staff."

McKay moved over to his bed. "Would you like me to order a sedative for you?"

"No. Thank you."

"You don't take any medications whatsoever according to your medical history. Not so much as an aspirin. Is it your religious custom?"

"No."

"Then why?"

Graham watched her tap in notes about him on a compu-chart. "Most of what we administer to our bodies simply gets in the way of its work. With a little patience the body can correct a lot of malfunctions."

"Then you have a holistic approach to health?"

"I don't know. It simply works."

"Apparently. You're one of the healthiest people ever to come through here. I must compliment your stoic cooperation through all of this, Mr. Sinclair. I know it hasn't been pleasant. But it is necessary. The brain-picking hasn't even begun, yet."

"That, too?"

"Oh, yes."

Graham clasped his hands and rested them on his chest. "It doesn't really matter, though, does it?"

"How do you mean?"

"It doesn't really matter—the condition of my mind, or my body. Whatever you find won't change anything. If I'm found to be mentally, physically, or emotionally incapable of thriving in a Martian environment, it still won't matter. All of this . . . data you're gathering is merely for scientific documentation of a unique specimen. No one else has been put through such . . . rigorous investigation. I've watched. I know what you're doing."

"Do you mind?"

Graham closed his eyes. "I'm grateful you haven't carried your enthusiasm to the point of vivisection."

He could feel her still watching him, even though he had, in effect, dismissed her.

"Good night, Graham Sinclair." There was a softened tone in her voice that he had not heard before. Most of her remarks to him during the three-day ordeal had been of an almost combative nature when they weren't outright clinical instructions. If she wasn't telling him to bend, cough, hold on, hold still, push, or breathe deeply, she was sniping at his class status or privileged background. She seemed to be trying to goad him into some form of verbal retaliation. His continued silence only stepped up her barbed jabs. The prejudices of which she was guilty were not new to Graham. He had endured since childhood far more caustic remarks from those who were made uncomfortable by the presence of extreme wealth. The unprovoked attacks had puzzled him when he was young and had caused more than a few bloody noses and skinned knuckles. Only as he had matured had he discovered the proper response. Silence. Now, however, there was an undercurrent in this woman's tone against which he knew no defense. And it threatened to awaken a long-dormant dragon of rage that he had thought tightly chained. And the message in her voice that stirred the dragon was pity.

CHAPTER 9

Graham was sitting on the observation deck at what would have corresponded to dusk on Earth when Baker appeared. "I can count on finding you here if I can't find you in the library or the pool."

"It's still the brightest jewel in the sky," Graham said.

"If you don't count the sun." Baker pulled a lounge chair over and sat.

"What does it look like from Mars?"

"The sun?"

"Earth."

"You can see it easily, in the early morning hours or early evening, if the weather's good. It looks . . . blue-white on a clear night."

They sat in silence for several minutes. Usually it was Baker who spoke first, as if the lack of conversation was his fault. But this time Graham initiated the topic. "Why did you leave?"

"Why did I choose to emigrate to Mars? Oh . . . partly because . . . it was there. I felt there was little need for my help where I was. Things seemed to be operating pretty smoothly at home so I felt called to go where I might be of more use."

"From what I understand of the Jeremians they're

pretty certain Earth is facing imminent cataclysm. Do you feel that way?"

"I did. When I was much younger."

"What changed your mind?"

Baker laughed. "Living on the brink of personal annihilation on a day-to-day basis makes the uncertainty of the cosmic deadline look pretty damned reassuring. A bit of serendipity, if you will—'Hey, it's tomorrow and I'm still here!'"

"That sounds more like a bit of Eastern philosophy."

"The 'Be-Here-Now' variety?"

"The garden variety." Graham nodded.

"When are you going to teach me T'ai Chi?"

"I don't know that I can."

"Why? It doesn't look all that hard. You just move in slow motion, right? I can do that."

"You're too . . . Western-minded."

Baker stood up and imitated what he supposed was a T'ai Chi stance. "You just said I was talking Eastern. I'm ready."

Graham smiled slightly. "About as far east as Coney Island from New Jersey, I think. Jon, it's all right. I know what you're trying to do. I'm not . . . I'm all right."

Baker stuck his hands in his pockets. "Maybe you shouldn't spend so much time up here . . . watching. It can't help."

"If the powers that cast me out succeed in keeping me on Mars, I'll never be closer to Earth than I am at this very moment. Don't deny me that."

Baker sat back down. "Do you mind the company? I hate to see you alone up here."

"I'm never exactly alone," Graham reminded him, glancing at his two bodyguards who stood discreetly near the far wall.

Two other passengers, a man and a woman, reached the top of the steps, spotted Graham, and retreated to a corner, whispering. He was not unused to such avoidances, except that the circumstances of the situation had altered. Once, he had been a man of such power that Corporation underlings scattered at the rare sight of him in their midst. If he paused for a cup of coffee in the office refreshment center, people scurried away on urgent missions elsewhere. Finally Peebles had suggested that it was in poor taste to mingle with office personnel, that it would be best to avoid common meeting areas. If he wanted anything, someone could be sent to fetch it. It had been a grave error, he knew now, to allow such insulation. Now he was avoided not because of any power he wielded, but because of the stigma that would cling to him forever. He wondered if he would be so isolated once he reached Mars. Would there be no colony willing to accept him? Or would he be forced upon them, passed around like an unwelcome guest for short stays? A dignified exit would be preferable, Graham thought, but some small core deep within kept persuading him to stay, to see what future would unfold.

"Are you hungry? I'm hungry," Baker said, seemingly uncomfortable with his silence.

On their way to the commissary Graham broached the subject of what he assumed were the more sought-after job skills on Mars. "It seems that everyone aboard this ship has been given some kind of job assignment and will have another job assignment waiting when we reach our destination. I'm the only one without training or without a marketable skill that would be of any use to anyone. I'm tired of Martian history lessons, Jon. Teach me a skill I can use."

Baker reached for a slice of hydroponically grown tomato as they moved down the line. "All in good time. After the brain-picking sessions."

"What if I refuse to be brain-picked?"

"Why would you refuse? It's only for your own—"

"—good. I know. Let's say I have an aversion to mental probing."

"Wait until you see the size of the tomatoes on Mars. All the food, actually. It sounds like a tall tale, but they're just tremendous." Baker made vague circular shapes with his hands, cupping imaginary tomatoes the size of basketballs. "The taste isn't quite the same, but it's good. Let them pick a little, Graham. They're not going to ask you for your sperm count."

"They already know my sperm count."

"Oh. Yeah, I guess they do."

They moved to a long table where several other men

sat with trays. Baker seemed oblivious to the fact that they got up and moved elsewhere, but the blatant rebuff was not lost on Graham; nor did he miss the small silent drama that passed before Baker had so much as unfolded his napkin. One of the men, in an orange jumpsuit, picked up a table knife in a manner that conveyed use as a weapon, not a meat-cutting implement. Graham braced himself for possible attack, but the man released the knife, dropping it on his tray. The two ever-present guards behind Graham had not missed the gesture, either, taking a step forward.

"Would you pass the salt, please?" Baker asked.

Graham passed the salt.

"How can we assign you to any work detail if we don't have an aptitude test or psychological profile upon which to base our decision?" Dr. Bartlett argued.

Graham sat before the psychiatric panel and flipped through the myriad questions he refused to answer. Dr. McKay, as a member of the panel, seemed almost amused by his stubbornness.

"Let me try a job. If it doesn't work out, I'll try another," Graham suggested. "Whether I have an Oedipus complex or delusions of grandeur or a fetish for small feet has little bearing on my professional qualifications."

"It would save all of us a great deal of time, Mr. Sinclair," said Bartlett, "if you would simply comply with the request." The man reminded Graham of Marcus Peebles, grown older and more grating in his rigidity. He had a fleeting impulse to hurl the phone book-sized aptitude test at the man. But the gesture would have been aimed at a dead man and it would only complicate the situation. Someone on the panel would be certain to label the action as infantile hostility and add it to his psychological profile.

"*Do* you have a fetish for small feet, Mr. Sinclair?" McKay asked, smiling.

"That's hardly relevant, Dr. McKay," Bartlett snapped.

Dr. Ushakov, the third member of the panel, said nothing. She was a matronly woman who, thought Graham, should have been draped in aristocratic finery and attend-

ing operas instead of being clothed in a white medical
jumpsuit and whirling through space.

"Why won't you cooperate, Mr. Sinclair? It's for your
benefit, you know." Bartlett sighed, drumming his fingers
on the table.

"It's for *your* benefit, Dr. Bartlett," Graham corrected. "I
will not contribute further to your petty scramble for literary immortality in the annals of medical science."

McKay studiously examined a file in front of her.

Bartlett exhaled audibly and pushed his chair back
from the table.

Silence ensued.

Finally Ushakov closed a report. "If that's all, then?
Should you reconsider, Mr. Sinclair . . ."

"Thank you, I won't."

"If you *should,* please let us know. This meeting is adjourned."

Dr. McKay held an impressively large cartridge syringe
while Graham shed the upper half of his jumpsuit. "There
will be seven in the series," she explained, positioning his
right arm.

"Will there be any side effects?" he asked, eyeing the
unsavory-looking greenish serum.

"You mean like excessive hair growth and fangs?"
When he didn't respond, she shrugged. "Side effects can
range from a slight headache and double vision, to
death."

"I would call that a rather severe side effect." Graham
nodded as the pressure syringe made a small pheeping
sound.

Severe fever seemed to be the side effect most prevalent, followed by a semicomatose state of a week's duration. Graham vaguely recalled faces and voices, some of
which logically had no place in reality, like his grandmother's face. But he had felt so comforted by her presence that he resented rising to consciousness.

"Welcome back." Maggie McKay smiled, punching
rapidly on the compu-chart in her hands. "You speak fluent Chinese when you're delirious. Did you know that?"

Graham attempted a response but discovered that he

was temporarily voiceless. His mouth was sore and tasted medicinal. There were lines and monitors and beeping medical devices attached to his body that left him feeling invaded, pinned to the bed like a not-quite dead insect under scrutiny.

"Who is Lihwa? I assume it's a lady. You called to her rather frequently."

Graham closed his eyes. Since he had refused the psychological interrogation they had attempted to inflict upon him, he was not about to let them inside his head now.

"It was his grandmother," he heard Baker say.

Graham opened his eyes.

"His *grandmother*?" McKay arched her eyebrows, as if she had found a soft spot she hadn't expected.

"How do you feel, Sinclair?" the man asked, resting his arms on the metal bed rails.

Graham managed a hoarse whisper. "Death might have been a more pleasant . . . option. Why didn't . . . you warn me?"

Baker chuckled. "I was afraid you might be disappointed if the joy juice didn't hold up to expectations. Congratulations. You've survived a mild case of Martian Fever. You should be immune to just about anything in the known universe now. You have an early member of the Seras to thank for that distinction."

Graham frowned. "A Contaminant?"

Baker nodded. "When the Fever first struck in 2038 it wiped out almost the entire population of Mars. There's always been a debate as to whether it was brought to the planet by colonists, and it mutated from something benign, or maybe it was something SURF was working on that escaped. Only seven people survived—two women and five men. One of them was a Contaminant who carried an antibody that was spread through intimate contact. The researchers finally isolated the enzyme and developed the serum that allowed us to return to Mars and start over. End of Mars history lesson. Get some rest." As he was about to leave, Baker turned to McKay. "Oh, Maggie, if he starts walking around in slow motion it's just a T'ai Chi exercise, not a relapse."

The only exercise Graham could muster for several

more days was deep breathing. The first day he swung his legs over the side of the bed, one of the bodyguards caught him before he fell to the floor. Physical weakness was an intolerable condition to him. He had no patience with illness.

"You'll have some mild recurrences of fever and some chills and sweating for a while," McKay told him. "It's to be expected. Just report to the infirmary when you feel it coming on and you'll be given something for the discomfort." She held out two yellow capsules in her right hand and Graham noticed the small tattoo on her palm.

"You wear the quarter moon," he said, not taking the proffered medication.

The woman closed her hand. "That was a long time ago, when I was young and foolish and such things seemed important."

"You're genetically clean. I would think you would want to contribute to the betterment of the human race."

McKay smiled. "Now who's brain-picking whom, Mr. Sinclair? How do you know I haven't?"

Graham bowed slightly. "I apologize."

"Apology accepted." She paused, as if considering something. "You're scheduled to begin a work detail when you've fully regained your strength. Since you refused to fill out the profile, would you like to start here?"

"In what capacity?"

"Menial chores. Custodial work. Would that be too far beneath you, Mr. Sinclair? Then, perhaps you could begin basic nursing duties, as an aide. Just to see if it interests you enough to pursue further. Paramedical assistants are highly valued in the colonies."

Graham's tolerance of other people's illnesses was only slightly greater than that for himself. He didn't think a medical career was where his future lay. "I'll consider it," he said.

"He's not suited for physical labor," Baker argued when Maggie told him of her suggestion the next day. They were in her office, going over Graham's progress report, which would be sent back to Earth.

"Do you think he's going to get there and whip up a

corporation to run? The man has no marketable skills. He has no knowledge of what it takes to run his own life. You said so yourself. He's been waited on his whole life. I'm surprised he knows how to dress himself. Do you see how he acts with the bodyguards?"

"How does he act?"

"Like they're invisible. Like he's so accustomed to their presence he hardly knows they're there. Could *you* do that? *I* couldn't ignore them. They'd drive me nuts."

Baker sighed. "Maggie, the guy has had bodyguards around him most of his life. Since he was a baby. To ward off kidnappers, and later to protect him from corporate assassination. It's part of his world."

"A little floor scrubbing might be just what he needs." McKay smiled.

Baker slammed a chart down. "Examine your motives. He's a proud man. Don't humble him through humiliation."

"He killed three and a half million people, Jon. You seem to forget that."

"He wasn't responsible."

"Like Hitler wasn't responsible?"

Baker looked at her, angry. "That doesn't even deserve a reply."

"You're right. Three and a half million is a paltry number compared to . . ."

"Read the transcript from the trial. Before you accuse him further. Do that much for me, Maggie. You misjudge this man."

The woman flipped through the thick document on her desk. "I'll read it. But he still starts scrubbing floors come Monday. The Committee already gave approval."

Graham ran the floor sterilizer while Maggie watched from her office. He had not appeared to be embarrassed by the lowly tasks he was asked to perform and for some reason it irritated her. He had not balked at anything thus far, and Chuck Anderson, the male nurse in charge of his training, had begun giving him minor medical duties to perform. A few of the patients had refused any contact with the Cloud Man, but others seemed less particular. He was not reacting at all as she had supposed a man of his station would, under the circumstances. Maggie glanced at the trial transcript she had steadfastly refused to read, much to Baker's chagrin. Over coffee she began to scan the first few pages, disinterested, sure of her impressions of Graham Sinclair. Her own father had been a man much like him, a corporate executive whose priorities did not include a child.

As she read, however, the words began to take on the aspects of a mystery novel. She continued to read after her shift was over, and read far into the night, until she had completed the transcript. The man who had been tried and convicted was not the man she was beginning to understand. Baker had been right. She had to talk to him. It was 0200 hours, but knowing Baker, he would still be up. She slipped into clothing and headed down the corridor toward his quarters. She had already passed Graham's room when she realized the two guards assigned to watch his door were absent.

"Mr. Sinclair?" She tapped on the door and opened it when there was no response. The room was empty. Turning on a light, she looked around, momentarily jarred by its starkness. The bed had not been slept in. Nowhere was there any evidence of personality, nor even of habitation. No personal photos on the shelves, no favorite books, keepsakes, idiosyncratic clutter that invariably accumulated wherever a human being took up residence for more than a day. In the hygiene compartment there was an immaculate hairbrush, a razor, and a teeth-cleaning implement. That was all. Nothing in the cabinet. Not even a Band-Aid. Prying unabashedly, Maggie opened storage compartments. There were the regulation navy-blue jumpsuits of off-duty personnel and the whites, assigned to the medical staff. Engineering wore orange, CELSS attendants wore green, science and research technicians, yellow, and the mechanics and robotics department wore gray. Security personnel wore black. Maggie counted six pairs of underwear and socks and six white T-shirts, also regulation. Nothing else. No personal items, no lucky hat, favorite shirt, perfumed scarf given as a parting gift from a lover. The emptiness of Graham Sinclair's world made her feel scooped out, hollowed. Maggie closed the storage compartments, shamed by the abrasiveness of her earlier attitude toward the man.

"Did you find what you were looking for?" Graham said, standing in the doorway. A guard moved in front of him, looking for an attacker, stun gun raised.

"I was on my way to see Baker." Maggie felt the heat rise in her face.

"This isn't his room."

"I'm well aware of that, Mr. Sinclair. I saw that your 'chaperones' weren't on their post and I was concerned."

"Do you usually do room inspections at two A.M.?" he chided, seeming to enjoy her embarrassment.

"Yes. And everything seems to be in order." She pushed past him and moved down the corridor.

"Baker's quarters are to the left." Graham pointed, watching her.

Maggie made an abrupt U-turn. "Yes. I knew that. Good night, Mr. Sinclair."

"Good night, Dr. McKay."

CHAPTER 10

Orange juice on the *Olympus Mons*, even fresh-squeezed, did not taste quite the same as at home, Graham decided, leaving the glass half finished. The vaguely off-kilter differences in flavors would be the least of the things he would miss, he knew, but somehow a facsimile of the real thing only seemed to taunt him.

"An apology gift," Maggie McKay said, plunking a lumpy white-tissued package in front of him. She slid into the seat across from him and set her breakfast tray down.

"For a late-night room inspection? What were you looking for?"

"You. Some . . . tangible evidence of your existence, I suppose."

"And did you find any?"

Maggie watched him continue his breakfast. "No."

"My corporeal state isn't sufficient evidence?"

Maggie nudged the gift toward him. "The apology is for more than nosiness. It's for . . . severe . . . misjudgment. I read the trial transcript. You were, how do they say, royally shafted, I believe."

Graham looked at her. "I'm guilty."

"So they say."

"No. I *am* guilty. Ignorance was no excuse. I was ultimately responsible. I accept the blame."

Maggie poured cream into her coffee and watched it swirl and blend. "Is that why it was so easy for you to . . . oh, scrub floors and clean up messes? A form of religious penance? Why did you take my crap? You never once came back at me. Why?"

"It's not my custom."

"Are you going to accept my peace offering or not?"

Graham opened the tissue. Inside was a small cactus in a clay pot.

"From Arizona," she said. "That's my home, where I came from. This little guy has been to the Moon, looped around Mars four times, and now . . . it's yours."

Graham turned the sharp-spined plant around to observe it from all directions. "That's very . . . kind of you, Dr. McKay . . ."

"Maggie."

He gently pushed the gift back toward her. "I can't accept it."

"Of course you can. I'm due R and R on the return trip. I can always get another."

"No. I'm not *allowed* to accept it, Maggie. I'm allowed nothing that originates from Earth. I couldn't even keep the clay pot. It's made from . . ." He didn't finish.

The woman stared at him. *"Nothing?* Not even a . . . family picture, a few keepsakes?"

Graham shook his head.

"It isn't fair. What they're doing to you. They've made you a scapegoat for the whole damned planet! At least it explains the sterility of your room."

A sudden series of sharp blaring sounds caused them both to jump. People began to run in all directions, emptying the commissary.

"What is it?" Graham asked, following Maggie.

"Solar flare. It may just be a drill, but never take the chance. We have to get to our station. The alarm indicates a malfunction in the C Sector."

"How do you know?"

Maggie pointed to a wall diagram of the *Mons* in the corridor. Flashing lights circled a portion of the ship far from their own area. "Solar shields open up automatically if there's a flare, but the alarm sounds if something goes wrong. Anyone in that sector has to evacuate the area immediately."

Baker arrived at the infirmary moments after Graham and Maggie and the two bodyguards. "It's just a drill," he reported. "The all-clear will sound in a minute. I meant to warn you about it, Graham. You were up and out too early."

A moment later a long, uninterrupted wailing siren sounded the all-clear.

Graham handed Maggie the small cactus. "You forgot this."

She looked at Baker. "Can't he keep it? It couldn't hurt . . ."

Baker shook his head. "Maggie, you're in violation of World Law just by offering it to him. I'm sorry. Gray, I'll meet you in the library at fifteen hundred hours for your lessons."

In the weeks that followed, Graham learned every medical technique and procedure permitted to a paramedic, and advanced so rapidly that Maggie gave approval for the equivalence of advanced nursing study. "If you want to pursue a medical field once you reach Mars, you'll have to apply for an apprenticeship under Dr. Vladimir Krolov. There are no schools thus far, for any training in any field. People either come already prepared in their field of knowledge or they get on-the-job training. You fall into the latter category." She watched Graham examine cultures under a microscope and correctly identify each one.

"Why aren't there any schools?" he asked. "What about the children?"

"There *are* no children. Didn't Jon explain that?"

"No. Not yet."

Maggie leaned against the counter. "There's just too much to cover in the time you've been given. Any potential colonist to Mars must study and train for at least two years before he is given permission to emigrate. Part of his training is to live in a biosphere on Earth for a minimum of ten months. That tends to separate the Space Larks from the true pioneers. Many people can't take it.

You already know that the turnover rate of the Martian population is rather high. The environment isn't for the fragile-minded. Do you want to know the most common complaint of the returnees? They couldn't take the pink sky. Constant, dusty pink sky. They craved a blue sky. Researchers are doing color studies to try to understand the impact of color deprivation on the colonists. They've found that those who work in the mines need green after a while or they become listless and quarrelsome. So you'll see a number of them working in the CELSS crop areas periodically.

"The colonies are rather carefully balanced in an ecological sense and that balance must be maintained. There can be no births until there is room for food expansion. And there can be no expansion until there is a sense of permanence within the colonies themselves. It's only been seven years since the new settlements dug in."

Graham handed her the slides as he identified them. "I thought the first outpost on Mars was established in 2015."

Maggie nodded. "It was. But an outpost is not the same as a settlement. Nor is a base the same as a civilian settlement. The first full Mars base was established in 2028. The longest anyone stayed was two years. After the first civilian settlement was all but wiped out, it was difficult getting volunteers to return, even with the vaccine."

"I can understand how the inoculations could curtail one's enthusiasm," Graham said. "In fact, I meant to ask you—is brain damage another little side effect you forgot to mention?"

Maggie laughed. "My God, no. Why would you think that?"

"I'm doing peculiar things lately."

The woman seemed to be trying to suppress outright mirth. "Such as?"

"Stumbling on steps. Dropping things."

"Clumsiness has never been one of your traits, hum?"

"Hardly."

"Graham, could you move this desk for me? I don't like where it is. Oh, never mind, I'll move it myself." With little effort, she managed to adjust the heavy desk against another wall. "There. I've been meaning to do that for a while."

"Gravity. It's lessening," said Graham, clearly relieved.

"Exactly. You'll adjust. Don't worry. Where was I? Oh, yes. The colonists who have elected to settle on Mars did so because Earth no longer offered whatever it was they sought. They're an unorthodox bunch, Graham. Be prepared for that. They have their own rules, their own value systems, their own . . . prejudices. They're proud of their world and they look upon new immigrants with a great deal of suspicion. You have to prove your use to them. You have to offer something they don't have, that they want and need.

"The Jeremians are the most austere. They're trying to get back to basics, and reject much of the technology available to them. They use no robotics, but their farming techniques seem to surpass the CELSS of the other colonies. No one is sure why. They do everything by hand, even to the weaving of cloth. You feel as if you've stepped through a time warp and are in 1800s America. Except for the domed enclosures."

"And the pink sky?" Graham said.

"And the pink sky." She handed him a final set of slides. "If you correctly identify these you'll qualify for your lab technician merit badge."

"My what?"

"Scout badge. You know . . . Eagle scout stuff. Ah, I'll bet your kind never go in for scouting, do they? You went to boarding schools or prep schools or military academies."

Graham ignored the small slice of sarcasm and identified the cultures. She had been much better over the past months, the elitist jabs tapering off to teasing nudges. He supposed this was another small discrimination that separated him from those of other stations.

"What about the Ventures? What do you know about them?" he asked as she replaced the slides in a compartment.

"They're a wild bunch. Few women, that I recall. And the few who are attracted to the colony aren't remotely interested in domesticity. The Ventures go out in the rovers a lot to explore. I don't know what they're looking for. They probably don't know what they're looking for either. They don't handle farming well. Frankly, I don't know how their CELSS modules have survived. Nothing gets tended, particularly. Things grow wild and tangled, but they *have* developed some architectural structures with the stone fusers that hold up very well in the seasonal changes. The other colonies have begun to adapt the style for their own needs. Their modules remind me of, well, you know how, when you were a kid, and you built sand castles at the shore . . . to get those candle-drip kind of layered looks to the spires, you had to drop really wet sand in little dribbles . . ." Maggie stopped, hand poised in the air. "Don't tell me you weren't allowed to play in sand when you were a kid . . ."

Graham decided against pointing out that Nice, on the French Riviera, had a stone beach. It also seemed best not to mention that his nanny had occasionally taken him by train a bit farther down the Mediterranean coast to Cannes where there was indeed an imported sand beach. And lovely bare-breasted women. He had never bothered building sand castles.

"Well, these structures look like layered, melted stones. Which is what they are. Ventures are a bit on the rough-hewn side, you might say, but fantastic individualists. Eccentric as hell, and somehow . . . they seem to have preserved the best part of childhood within them."

The second shift arrived and Maggie walked with Graham up to the observation deck. "Why haven't you asked about the Seras?" she said, sitting back in a lounge chair while he stood, searching for the blue-white light. "It's the only other permanent settlement. I don't consider the Keyote miners or the SURF researchers settlers."

"I have no interest in the Contaminants."

"Don't call them that, Graham. Not to their faces. It's a painful insult."

"They contribute genetic impurities to the human race. I have little sympathy for their selfishness, when there are alternatives available to them."

"Voluntary sterilization isn't a pleasant choice," Maggie reminded him. "Genetic manipulation is just as drastic. I don't know that I could subject myself to those choices if I walked in their shoes."

Human imperfection of a gross nature was, Graham thought, his area of greatest intolerance. Especially when there was help available to the afflicted to prevent further malformations in any progeny. The prejudicial flaw within himself was a stone of enormous size, and though he had tried throughout his life to wash it away, it had not budged. Nor had the flow of a lifetime's river worn it down.

"The Seras probably have the closest thing to what we would recognize as traditional Western values. At least as close as anything you're likely to find on Mars. They have a great reverence for the arts. There seems to be an inordinate amount of creativity among them. I'm not sure why. Possibly because of their shorter life spans. Brief candles burning brightly." Maggie folded her legs up. "How do you get your legs in a lotus position? I try, but it hurts."

"You should sit on the floor if you want to try it." He turned to watch her.

Maggie held her hand out. "Help me up, Sinclair. I'm a tired old woman."

He looked at her hand, hesitating.

"Oh, for heaven's sake. I have touched you over practically every centimeter of your body. If I was going to give you anything you'd have gotten it by now." He pulled her to her feet. "Jon says you're teaching him T'ai Chi. Is he a good student?"

"No."

"Why?"

"He moves his body but not his mind." She didn't laugh, as he had supposed she would. "Also, I don't think I'm a very good teacher for him. I don't know how to teach what has taken most of my life to learn. He only asks to know the physical, but the spiritual can't be separate from the body. He doesn't want to know about that."

"Are you a master of the art? Of T'ai Chi Ch'uan?"

Graham shook his head. "I don't know that I ever will be. To be able to execute every movement by remaining absolutely still . . . then you can truly be called a master. And there is one step beyond that, called the Taoist Wand."

"What does that entail?"

"It's . . . complete control of energies by the mind. I

could . . . stand here . . . and"—he pointed outward, toward the blue-white brilliance that was Earth—"be there."

Mars grew larger each day until it was a dull orange ball in the ebony emptiness of space. Somehow, it reminded Graham of a chick embryo in the early stages of development. He could almost make out veins and a dark smudge of an eye and where the heart was beating. He was growing accustomed to the lighter gravity now, and felt less clumsy. Steps were no longer miscalculated. The weight of objects was not so drastically misjudged.

Baker pointed to a Martian map on a wall in the library. "We'll be landing here, in the Lunae Planum, in the Northwestern Quadrant, about fifteen degrees north of the equator. You'll get a good aerial view of the two biggest tourist attractions of the planet—Olympus Mons and the Valles Marineris. If the Olympus Mons were a volcano on Earth, it would extend from San Francisco to Los Angeles. It's twenty-seven kilometers high, the tallest mountain in the entire solar system. Makes Mt. Everest look like a pimple. And the Valles Marineris makes the Grand Canyon look like a little scratch in the Earth. Over 4,500 kilometers long, 192 kilometers wide in places, and six or seven kilometers deep in the central sections. Now *that's* a canyon."

"What about the Face?" Graham asked.

"We don't discuss the Face. It's only shadows, a freak design of nature. That's all."

"It *looks* like a face. A 1.6-kilometer face."

"It's not a face. What have you been reading?"

"It's mentioned in several books."

"Old books. With incorrect data. Stick to the holo-discs for the most up-to-date information. Forget the Face."

Baker pointed out the locations of the five colonies. "The Keyote Mining Operation is in the Acidalia Planitia, northeast of the SURF base. We'll be staying at the research facility for a while . . ."

"We? You're staying?"

"Until you're . . . acclimated. I'll catch the *Romanenko* cycler on its swing-by. That gives you six more months to

teach me T'ai Chi. Maggie thinks you may have a marketable skill there that no one considered. There are bound
to be colonists interested in learning the movements. It's
something to consider."

That Jonathan Baker would be remaining on the surface of the planet to guide him, even a little longer, eased
a growing tension that Graham had been unable to shake
for the past month. The *Olympus Mons* had become his
home, after a fashion, and the aspect of being uprooted, to
face again possibly hostile strangers, was not something
he had relished. And he would have missed Baker. The
realization surprised him. He had never "missed" anyone
in his life. He had, however, known the ache of loss with
the death of his grandmother, and the pain was similar
when he now thought of Ti. The boy had gotten closer
than he ever intended. He had appeared suddenly, within
days of the old woman's death, ragged and scrawny, and
hungry in a way that no food would assuage. Graham
saw it as a sign he couldn't ignore. Somehow there was a
link between his grandmother and the youth, as if some
small part of her soul burned in his eyes. Now he had lost
them both.

"Gray, concentrate. How are you going to get your
bearings if you drift away while I'm talking to you?"

"I'm glad you're staying . . . longer. I didn't know
you were."

Baker laughed. "Did you think I was just going to push
you out with a parachute on a flyby? What kind of Transition Escort would I be? The World Court was hard on you,
Graham, but they're not without mercy. T.E. service *had*
to be created, even for those who *wanted* to come to Mars.
Guides through the wilderness . . . though the wilderness be stars . . . Now, pay attention here . . . I'm
guiding. Have the decency to follow."

The colonies had not strayed far from the original outpost. The Jeremian commune was located to the west of
the Lunae Planum at the foot of Tharsis Tholus. The Seras
were farther west, between Pavonis Mons and Ascraeus
Mons. Although the Ventures had established their colony southwest of the original base, at Hebes Chasma, they
had begun to explore areas along the Valles Marineris and
were beginning to build a series of CELSS modules. In

ever-expanding forays outward, like artificial oasis points along a trade route in the Sahara Desert, the rock-fused mounds provided underground shelter and enough food, water, and breathable atmosphere to support three or four people for days at a time.

The marking of time was another lesson Graham had to learn. Unlike Baker, who sported a watch that kept Earth time as well as that of Mars, he would need to keep track of Martian sols only. The Martian calendar, like the Julian dating used by astronomers, measured sols consecutively, rather than in months, Baker explained. There were 687 sols in a Martian year.

"A long time between birthdays," Graham said. "When you're a hundred I'll be about half your age."

"And probably look it, too," Maggie said, entering the library. "Less gravity, less sag. I've always wondered about that. Would either of you gentlemen care to join a lady for dinner?"

Graham wasn't sure, but thought he detected the faintest application of makeup on the good doctor. Something about her had been softly enhanced. For the last several days, in fact, he had become increasingly aware of Maggie McKay in a way that was decidedly not clinical. Whether she had actually altered subtly in some mysterious way women could, and which had always fascinated him, Graham couldn't tell. There was, however, something in the way he perceived her that had shifted. There was a soft scent about her that was not perfume and not antiseptic, but it made him acutely aware of her closeness.

On the way to the commissary Maggie handed Graham a sealed document. "It's a letter of recommendation to Dr. Krolov at the research facility—if you should choose to continue your medical studies. My personal advice, on the other hand, is to explore all options open to you, Sinclair. Look around, test the waters. You have a whole new world and a whole new life waiting for you down there." She paused as they were about to enter the commissary. "You may well be better equipped to handle it all than anyone can imagine. I think you're going to do fine, just fine." She gave his arm a comforting pat.

•   •   •

"There they are." Baker pointed as they stood on the observation deck. "Phobos and Deimos. Fear and Terror, the
charioteers of Mars, god of war." Phobos, the larger of the
two moons, was twenty-seven kilometers across and
highly pocked with craters.

"See that big indentation on Phobos?" Baker said. "Like
somebody took a big bite out of it? That's Stickney. The
crater is over nine kilometers, rim to rim."

There was an enthusiasm in the man's voice, thought
Graham, like that of a homesick traveler spotting much-
loved landmarks.

Deimos, only fourteen kilometers across, was
smoother, like a water-worn gray pebble.

"Will we land on Phobos?"

"No. We'll use the transfer vehicle that brought us up
to the *Mons.* It'll take us to the *Ninotchka,* where there will
be a brief wait, and then a lander takes us on in."

"Step ten," Graham murmured.

"Weather conditions seem to be cooperating," Baker
continued. "If there were a severe dust storm we would
be stuck on the space station for God knows how long."

"Is it winter or summer or what down there?" Graham
was still unsure of the Martian way of dividing seasons.

"Summer is 178 sols long, winter, 154 sols." He glanced
at his watch. "I suppose you could say it's early spring
now."

Graham's peripheral vision caught the movement first.
Before his bodyguards could begin to react, a heavyset
man hurled himself through the air, aimed at Graham's
midsection. Graham stepped aside and swiveled to meet
his attacker, who rolled to his feet and lunged again.
There was time to notice the knife in his right hand, and
to identify the face. It took only two quick moves to put
the man in a heap against the wall. By then Graham's
guards were alert and rushing over with stun guns out.

Baker was frozen, his arm still poised to look at his
watch. "Oh, my. I hope you didn't kill him, Gray. He's
from the engineering department."

They followed the bodyguards as they carried the unconscious man on a stretcher to the infirmary. "I suppose

there will have to be an inquiry into this." Baker sighed. "It'll use up precious time we don't have to spare. Why now? He had all this time to try to kill you."

Maggie met them in the commissary later. "You just have to fill out an accident report," she said to Graham, "if you stick to your silly story. He *tripped*? The man *tripped* and broke his collarbone and right wrist? What was the knife for? To clean his nails? And of course nobody saw anything until it was all over. 'Bozo' and 'Bippo' over there"—she jerked a thumb in the direction of the two bodyguards—"just saw him tumble. Can't say quite how it happened. You don't have a credit, not a penny, Sinclair. How could you pay them off?" She looked at Baker. "You? You paid them to shut up?"

Baker shrugged. "They don't like inquiries any more than we do. Maggie, it's over, done, and forgotten as soon as we're out of here . . . if you'll just tend to your own business."

Graham signed the pink form and Maggie snatched it back. "Tripped. My ass."

Graham folded his few belongings into the garish orange duffel bag. He had not been able to sleep, nor had he been able to meditate for more than a few minutes. Tomorrow at 0600 hours they would disengage from the *Olympus Mons* in an elliptical trajectory, to link up with the orbiting space station *Ninotchka*. All night he had heard and felt shifts in the internal workings of the ship. The transfer vehicle was being refueled and made ready. At dinner he had eaten very little, remembering his queasy response to zero gravity. The *Ninotchka*, Baker had assured him, would have gravity equal to that of Mars. "It will feel no different from what you feel now, on the *Mons*."

A soft tap on the door made him turn around. "Room inspection," Maggie said, balancing a tray in one hand and grasping the long folds of a rose-colored caftan in the other.

Graham wasn't sure of the hour, but estimated that it was well after midnight. All watches, being Earth-made, were denied him.

Maggie bowed slowly. "A tea ceremony, honorable sir.

A parting gesture . . . only I think it's Japanese." She placed the tray on his desk and poured, the herbal aroma wafting from the steaming pot. "There's a ritual to it," she said, handing the plain white cup to him, "but I don't know how to do it. I had to improvise. There wasn't anything in the library files on the custom."

Graham slowly took the cup from her hands and sipped the strong hot liquid, keeping his eyes on hers. He watched the color rise in her face, aware that she was attempting to do something that was more foreign to her than a tea ceremony. He handed her the cup. "You're supposed to drink from it now."

She held the cup, her eyes dropping from his gaze. "I think I'm to turn it around, or something . . ."

He took the cup from her and set it on the tray. "Don't imitate a custom you don't understand," he said, his voice soft, close to her ear. "Do what you *do* understand, Maggie."

"Ah . . . I may still have to improvise, Mr. Sinclair." She began to unzip his navy jumpsuit.

"That's quite all right, Dr. McKay."

CHAPTER 11

The transfer vehicle was crowded to capacity, forcing everyone to stay harnessed in their seats, much to Graham's relief. Baker was deep in conversation with another T.E., Jim Simmons, who was bringing eight new emigrants to Mars.

"Six men and two women," he told Baker. "Maybe half will stay. The others, two or three years max and they'll run screaming for home."

"They'll succumb to the 'Pink Sky' syndrome?" Graham asked.

"Or the dust." Simmons nodded.

"Or the feeling of confinement," Baker added. "Or the just plain alienness. Everywhere you turn, everywhere you look, she reminds you of her difference. Mars makes no compromises. You either learn to love her, or you get the hell out."

"That narrows my options considerably, I would say."

Baker looked at him. "You'll make it. You have it in you . . . whatever it is that lets a man carry his world within him. I've watched you, Graham. You settle into your surroundings well. Maybe it's due to your religion or your philosophy or whatever it is that gives you that calm place inside you. I don't know. But you'll survive. I have no doubts about you."

A shuddering vibration caused a few stifled gasps from several passengers. Simmons turned in his seat to address his nervous charges. "That's just the aerobraking, folks. Nothing to get alarmed about. We're entering the upper regions of the Martian atmosphere. In a few minutes we'll be in LMO, that's low Mars orbit, then we'll dock with the *Ninotchka.*"

Graham gazed out his window. Mars was a burnt umber and rust color. In places, wispy cirrus clouds hazed over tiny portions of the planet's surface. It seemed odd that there were no continental patterns defined by azure and sapphire oceans. It did not look inviting, this world, with its pockmarked face and deep scars. Graham swallowed, trying to make his ears pop.

The majority of the passengers aboard the transfer vehicle were miners headed for the Keyote colony. If they could endure Martian life for two to three years they would return to Earth considerably wealthier men. Or women. Three of the miners were women, Graham noted, and another seemed somewhat neuter in appearance, so he wasn't sure.

A bearded man sitting behind Graham leaned forward and tapped him on the shoulder. "Hey, Sinclair. Is it true you killed some guy back on the *Mons*?"

Graham said nothing.

"Did you put another notch on your gun, Sinclair? What's that make it, now? Three million five hundred thousand and one?"

"That's enough, Jessup," Baker said. "Leave the man alone."

"How'd you do it, Cloud Man? Breathe heavy on him?"

Baker unharnessed himself from his seat and pushed over to Jessup. Hovering over the man like a balloon, Baker said quietly, "One more word and you'll be in quarantine when we reach the *'Notchka.*"

"I'm just talking to the man."

"You're quarantined." Baker reached out and snapped a small flashing yellow emblem onto Jessup's collar.

"Oh, shit!"

Two of Jessup's companions snickered. "He warned

you, stupid," said one. "Twenty sols in quarantine. You'll be left with the grunt jobs."

"Hey, Baker, come on. What'd I do?" Jessup complained as the man glided back to his seat across from Graham.

"A T.E. carries the full power of the law between planets," Baker explained, in answer to Graham's obvious puzzlement. "We have the power to arrest, judge, and sentence anyone. He can appeal the judgment aboard the space station, but the *Ninotchka* has a reputation for hard-line law and order, especially any case brought in by a Transition Escort. When Jessup gets to Keyote the best job assignments will have been snapped up."

"He wasn't bothering me," Graham said.

"He was bothering *me*. I know Jessup. He was just warming up. I'd swear the man has a genetic defect somebody missed."

The *Ninotchka* was a busy station from what Graham could tell, and there was an electric atmosphere he had not sensed elsewhere. He was surprised to hear lively music and laughter from the direction of the canteen. Compared to the almost stately dignity of the *Olympus Mons*, the military severity of the *Glenn*, and the interplanetary shopping-mall atmosphere of the *Shepard* space station, the *Ninotchka* was a curious pastiche of border town, carnival, and English pub. The air carried odors of human involvement: not unpleasant, Graham decided, when compared to the clinically pure air on the *Mons*.

The canteen was crowded with an energetic, transient population and Baker had a hard time finding a table for them after going through the food line.

"Most of the food here is home grown," he shouted above the accordion music accompanied by a boisterous sing-along in several languages. "I mean from Mars. Try it. See what you think."

Graham couldn't eat. He drank strong tea and thought briefly of the night before, which already seemed long ago. Baker looked mildly disappointed by his lack of appetite and Graham knew it was a socially rude thing to do. But he couldn't eat.

"I'm sorry. It's not the food . . ."

Baker looked at him intently. "Do you feel all right? It

could be a flare-up from the inoculations. Stress triggers it sometimes."

"I'm all right."

"You're sweating."

"It's warm."

Baker nodded. "The ventilation system here has never functioned properly. And the place is always over-crowded. The Phobos fuel workers come down here for R and R and there's always a load of people coming or go-ing, or waiting to come or go. And those who can't make up their minds whether to come or go. The *Ninotchka* is a lively purgatory. I think we should get you checked out, just in case a flare-up is in the works."

The infirmary, too, was crowded. Graham, in an ear-lier time, would have assumed it was his right to step to the head of any line. His table in the finest restaurants was always held in reserve, and velvet ropes were un-hooked to let him through crowds at the opera or the symphony or the sold-out Broadway musicals. He by-passed crowds wherever he went. Now, following Baker, who held up his T.E. credentials like a magic wand, he was embarrassed to step ahead of those who had been waiting in a long line that spilled out of the infirmary and down the corridor.

The medical staff looked overworked. A doctor con-firmed that Graham was, indeed, experiencing a flare-up, dumped a number of small yellow capsules into a plastic pill bottle, and ordered bed rest and fluids.

"We're due out on the lander tomorrow," Baker said.

"Then get him prone now or you'll have to carry him aboard tomorrow, and if you have to carry him aboard, they won't *let* him aboard. He does know the bottle is returnable, doesn't he? We're running low. Nobody's re-turning the damn things. What are they doing with them? They're hard to get, you know."

The sleeping quarters to which they were assigned were three-tiered berths in a compartment for eighteen people. Baker was apologetic. "I tried to get private rooms on the A-Deck, but they're booked solid. Put your gear in the cage at the end of the bed and lock it. Don't forget your shoes. Lock them up, too."

Several men were already sleeping in the bunks, some

with curtains closed for a modicum of privacy. Others, nude or clad in undershorts, snored, oblivious to the constant coming and going of passengers. The dimly lit room was stuffy and warm and smelled of body odor and unwashed feet. Behind some curtains a dull yellow light glowed, indicating that the occupant was awake, possibly reading or watching the TV hookups attached to the wall. In his youth, Graham had once visited an opium den with several school chums, and the room reminded him of the place. All that was lacking was a haze of pungent smoke. His fever was beginning to supply the distorted intoxication of that night, enhancing the memory to the point of reality. He peeled down to T-shirt and undershorts, his navy jumpsuit already soaked with perspiration. He was feeling shaky now, and thirsty.

"Where is the . . ."

"Hygiene compartment? Down the corridor to the right, about four doors. Do you need any help?"

Graham shook his head. "How long does this go on?"

Baker shrugged. "It varies with each individual. Two or three sols, then it subsides, usually."

"Usually?"

"Martian Fever is something like malaria. Once it's in you, you've got it for life, but the flare-ups taper off. It only makes an appearance if your resistance is low, like if you're working without rest for long periods—if you push it and get stressed out."

"I'll keep that in mind," Graham said, wobbling off to find a toilet.

He woke shaking, his teeth clenched, his bunk covers drenched with sweat and urine.

"Take it easy." Baker wiped his face with a towel. "You've peaked, I think. Here, drink this." He held out a blue cup and helped prop Graham up.

Graham gulped the brackish-looking liquid and gagged.

"Finish it. It stops the chills."

"What is it?"

"A little of this, a little of that. A home-grown concoction." Baker smiled.

"Home grown. Meaning from Mars."

"From Mars. With a dash of good *Ninotchka* vodka. To give it a zing."

Graham drained the cup. Something was working. Warmth seemed to be returning to his feet.

"Can you stand up long enough to switch bunks? You soaked the bed."

Baker helped him down and stripped him while Graham leaned against the bunks, so dizzy that he wasn't sure where the floor was. Gently, Baker wiped his body with warm, wet towels, dried him, and helped him roll into the lower berth.

"I'm taking your stuff down to the laundry. Think you'll be okay till I get back?"

Graham was already drifting off. He felt someone pull a blanket up around him and thought his grandmother said something, but he couldn't think of an answer.

The flight official, a woman in a crisp red and blue uniform, eyed Graham suspiciously as he weaved down through the air-lock tunnel, Baker close behind. "Hangover," he mouthed, and flashed T.E. credentials as they passed.

The woman checked them against her list and nodded. "I know a flare-up when I see it, sir. As long as he's on his own two feet he can pass through."

"He'll be fine."

"Yes, sir."

Once in his seat, Graham let out a long breath. "Are they going to take me away?"

Baker fastened his seat harness. "You made it. Just don't pass out. You can throw up, but don't pass out."

Graham concentrated on trying not to do either.

This was it. The final step of a very long voyage. The New World he was coming to did not have a Lady with a Torch to welcome him. There was, possibly, an ancient stone Face somewhere below, officially denied but eerily human, carved by nature or by an intelligence long dissolved into dust. This would be his home, his future, his destiny. Until he could change it, anyway.

The lander swooped in over the Arcadia Planitia and

the Amazonis Planitia, descending in an ever-tightening spiral. Graham could see Olympus Mons rising from the barren red plain like an angry carbuncle. Nowhere was there a single sign of life. Not a road, not a house, nothing. And certainly no Great Wall. A deep, jagged canyon came into view—Valles Marineris. It looked as if someone had spilled cream into it. Baker explained that it was an early morning fog that would burn off by noon.

The plane banked and turned in a slow counterclockwise direction. "The Keyote Mining Operation is off to the northeast," Baker said, pointing. "They may still have the night lights on. Yeah . . . there, about two o'clock."

Graham thought he spotted a brief white sparkle but wasn't sure. Moments later, however, he did see a number of shielded domes set in a geometric pattern below. And a number of landing strips. Rectangular CELSS covering several acres were linked to the circular domes by long covered passages. They vaguely reminded Graham of a molecular diagram, something jotted on a chalkboard in a science class and left unfinished.

The moment the wheels touched the ground passengers let out whistles, whoops, and applause.

"Welcome to Mars, Graham Sinclair," said Baker.

CHAPTER 12

Graham's memories of his first few Martian sols were hazy. He wasn't sure, later, if it was because of the lingering fever or the shock of the reality. He was on Mars. They isolated him for what would have passed as a week on Earth and he spent most of the time sleeping. The infirmary was almost empty except for a miner with a broken leg and another new arrival, a woman with an emergency appendectomy. She would be going on to the Ventures colony, she told him during one of her shuffling constitutionals down the length of the room, out into the corridor, and back.

"Where are you headed?" she asked Graham as he lay in bed, trying to down his first solid Martian breakfast. There were eggs, toast, coffee, and soy bacon that tasted very close to the real thing. "I don't know yet," he said.

"You didn't put in for a particular colony?"

Graham pushed his tray away. "I thought I'd browse a bit first."

"You can't just go around and pick a place. Who said you could do that? Are you going to eat that toast?"

"No."

"I'm starving."

Graham pushed his tray toward her. "Help yourself."

She reached for the food, then hesitated. "You haven't got anything catching, have you?"

Graham shook his head. "A flare-up of Martian Fever, they tell me."

"Oh, that. God, I thought I was gonna die when I saw the first dose coming. It was nothing. I was a little barfy for a few days. That's all. And got the sweats. Nothing else."

He watched her dig into the food, settling in on the edge of his bed. Such familiarity at home would have been unthinkable, Graham mused, then reminded himself that he must stop thinking in terms of "home." This was home for the present. For better or worse.

"Tucker, Paris," the woman said, wiping her right hand on her robe and extending it.

Graham didn't respond at first. Obviously she didn't recognize him, he thought. She had to have been on the *Mons*, but it was a big ship with a lot of people. Maybe there were a few who didn't know. He touched her fingertips with his. "How do you do, Tucker Paris."

"Oh, you're one of them. What's an A-Class doing on Mars? I didn't think your kind had the pioneer spirit. Your idea of roughing it is plastic champagne glasses on a safari. Air-conditioned howdahs on the elephants . . . that sort of thing."

"I'm . . . broadening my horizons, Miss Paris."

"No. Tucker. I mean it's Paris Tucker, not Tucker Paris."

She was probably in her early twenties, Graham decided, and commonly educated. She was tall and coltish, with an ungraceful way of moving, possibly due to the recent appendectomy, but there was also an energy about her that appealed to him. With shoulder-length chestnut hair that seemed to do what it pleased, and hazel eyes, she had a no-nonsense bluntness that amused him. "It's a nice name, either way."

"My mother always wanted to go to Paris, but she never made it, so she thought maybe I'd be the one to go, in her place, like. And you know something? I never got to Paris, either. I should have gone, you know? Before Mars."

"That *is* overshooting your mark, a bit." Graham nodded.

"Just a tad, yeah. But the way I look at it, if I get bored here, I can always go to Paris. No matter what, someday I can tell my grandkids, 'Hey, I once lived on Mars.' But maybe by then they'll be living on a planet we haven't even discovered yet. Things go fast."

A male nursing attendant came to take Graham's cleaned breakfast tray. "Good. You're getting your appetite back. Miss Tucker, keep ambulating. No rest stops. Up!"

Paris made a face and got up. "You know, I remember you from the *Mons*," she said to Graham. "I thought you were a doctor. I mean you wore the whites and worked in the infirmary and all. One of the T.E.s was always hanging out with you."

The attendant snorted. "You don't know who this is? He's Graham Sinclair."

Paris looked momentarily bewildered. "*The* Graham Sinclair?"

"The one and only." The attendant nodded and whisked the tray away.

The woman stared at Graham. "*You're* the Cloud Man? Why didn't you say so?"

"It would have cut short a pleasant conversation."

"Yeah. I guess so." She moved away from the bed as if something contagious might be clinging to her. He was sorry to see her go. Baker, waiting for him to recover enough to get around, had gone off to the Keyote mines for four sols and wouldn't be back until tomorrow. Boredom was the last thing Graham had expected to encounter on Mars.

"Did you really kill two men aboard the *Mons*?"

"No."

"People talked about you being on the ship. I just never . . . I didn't know it was you they were talking about. You don't look like . . . the way I pictured you." She turned, flustered, and made an awkward escape.

For the next two sols Graham watched her during her walks. She avoided eye contact with him when he began his own shaky ambulations down the hallway. Baker had been by to visit, loading him down with more books to read and holo-discs to study as if he were a student cramming to catch up to his peers in time for graduation. He was in the solarium reading when Paris sat down at the table, joining him.

"What are you studying?"

He looked up, vaguely surprised. "You're speaking to me?"

"Why not?"

"Most people don't, once they know."

Paris pushed a lock of hair behind her ear. "I noticed. That T.E. talks to you, though—Baker."

"It's his job. So why are you deigning to converse with me again, knowing about me as you do?"

"Deigning?" She rolled her eyes. "A-Class talk, if ever I heard it. *Deigning.* I changed my mind about you, that's all."

"Why?"

The woman turned his book around to read the title. "This is premed stuff. You training to be a doctor, Sinclair?"

"It passes the time. What changed your mind?"

She got up and began to pace the room, a small domed hub that connected several spokelike corridors. The corridors, Graham had discovered, led to other CELSS modules and various sections of the medical branch of the research facility. Much of the rest of the SURF community was off limits to unauthorized personnel.

"I thought about it," she said, "and what it comes down to is this: We all are guilty. Every one of us. With every single thing we buy we contribute to the toxic by-products of the companies that make the things we demand in our daily lives. From shampoo to cute little plastic toy ducks to the paper we write the grocery list on to the apples we eat, brought to us by courtesy of the pesticides and chemical fertilizers used to grow our food."

"We don't use pesticides and chemical fertilizers anymore."

"We don't?"

"They were phased out years ago."

"Well, we did. That's what I mean, though. We still contributed to the process, to the waste . . . all those barrels of poison. How was anybody to know they would mix with nerve gas and chemical warfare stuff dumped in the Atlantic before we were born? You aren't the sole blame for that awful tragedy. I have to accept my share of the guilt, too." She held out her hand.

Graham started to touch her fingertips, then grasped her hand in the old custom. "You realize, of course, that socialization with me might well cause you to be ostracized by the planet at large."

"I'll take my chances."

She told him a little about her background and how she had yearned to travel to the raw edges of life. Climbing Everest had not quenched her thirst, nor had gold prospecting in the Australian outback. She had been raised on a wildlife preserve in Kenya where her parents were doing studies on the return of the black rhino to the open. "I climbed Mt. Kilimanjaro before I was twelve. Do you climb, Sinclair?"

"No." He could not explain to her that the risks he took were on paper, but just as challenging to him. Corporative peaks were charts and mergers and takeovers that only the players could truly appreciate. "So, do you plan to climb Olympus Mons?" he asked, wishing she would sit back down. Her restless movement was adding to the queasy feeling in his stomach that persisted despite all the little yellow capsules and other various medications inflicted upon him by the medical staff.

"Maybe. Someday. If I stay. It's been done already, though. But they cheated. Some jerk geologist flew a hover-lander to the top to scoop up some soil samples. Big deal. I'd like to explore along the bottom of the Valles Marineris. Maybe train to become a T.E. I could be the first woman Transition Escort. That would be nice. Your guy, what's his name—Baker—I hear he's the best there is. I suppose even an A-Class outcast rates only the best in escorts. He's taking me out to the Ventures colony when they let me out of here. The T.E. who brought us from Earth couldn't wait around for me to die, which he thought I was gonna do. So he went on ahead with the others." She settled on the edge of the table.

"Why did you choose the Ventures?" Graham asked.

"It was more like they chose me. I mean, I qualified in the aptitudes. I had a skill they needed . . ."

"What?"

"Cartography. They like to explore. They needed a

mapmaker to plot all the CELSS pods they've been building. The Jeremians would have taken me, but I'm not crazy about Bible thumping. Mining's not my passion, although I've spelunked a couple of times. And forget the Contaminants. They don't want you unless you're one of them. Reverse prejudice, I'd call it." She spun around on top of the table like a child making do with available toys, then crossed her legs, facing Graham. She flipped his medical text shut.

"So, what are you gonna do here, Sinclair? Become a doctor? That's some career change."

"Like I said, I'm browsing around."

"Meaning they can't find a colony that will accept you?"

That no colony would take him had fleetingly occurred to Graham. He fully expected a cold or indifferent welcome wherever he went, but he hadn't seriously contemplated complete rejection. He wondered if Baker's quick trip to the Keyote colony was for the purpose of ascertaining the climate should he be sent there at a later date. Dr. Krolov, among others at the SURF base, had introduced himself to Graham, exuding a clinical formality that placed him on guard. It might have been his fevered state, he thought, but he had the distinct impression of being perceived as a specimen for study. Krolov, heavy-set, with bushy graying hair and wild, wiry eyebrows, informed him that Dr. McKay's letter of recommendation was most impressive. Graham could begin work under his tutelage as soon as he was able. That he had no special interest in medicine didn't seem proper to bring up. So he had thanked the man and gone back to sleep.

"Somebody *has* to take you in, don't they?" Paris asked. "I mean, it's not like you have a lot of choices. You can't turn around and say, 'Screw it, I'm going home.' Is it really forever? You can never go back? To Earth?"

Graham nodded. The subject was becoming uncomfortable. She was like a child trying to understand blindness, asking the blind man just how dark was it? Could he imagine blue? She could not comprehend the wounds she inflicted with her bluntness. But then, she could go home. She could always go home.

Paris was silent for a moment, obviously trying to

grasp the concept of banishment with no chance of return. "Wow. Forever. Stuck here forever. Now that would
be scary. I can go anywhere as long as I know there's a
way back. Cripes. Even a murderer gets a shot at parole.
You sure they aren't going to say, hey, it's okay, after a
few years?"

"Paris, do you mind if we change the subject?" Even a
child had to be told when enough was enough.

"Yeah. Sure. I mean, I understand." She scooted to the
edge of the table and got up. "Graham? You could come
stay with me, if you want. All it takes is one member to
say okay, to be accepted by the Ventures. I could teach
you about surveying."

Graham studied her face. He had been wrong. This
woman knew what it was to not belong anywhere.

"I'll definitely consider your invitation. Thank you,
Paris. For offering me refuge."

He felt awkward enough in the white cooling garment
that fit him like a snug pair of long johns, but he felt
downright silly as Baker helped him climb into the Mars
Extravehicular Mobility Unit. It was a hard suit, true
spaceman gear. And he would have to wear it anytime he
was out on the open surface of the planet. Graham had
been carefully measured, and the suit was custom-fit.

"On Earth this little number would weigh about
twenty-two kilograms, but here it only weighs nine,"
Baker said. "The LCG—that's the liquid cooling garment
you keep calling long johns—controls the temperature inside the suit by circulating warm or cool water. The upper
torso of the MEMU goes on first, then you slide into the
lower torso." He watched as Graham maneuvered awkwardly into the lower torso.

"Good. Are your feet comfortable in the boots? Okay,
now, feel for the upper torso ring with your right hand.
Higher. That's it. Now attach the lower torso ring to it. It's
connected when you hear it snap. You got it."

"What if you have to . . ." Paris made a face.

"You go before you get into it."

"You didn't tell me that."

"Logic should have told you that."

"Well, it didn't."

Baker *tsk*ed. "Pain makes for indelible lessons in life."

Paris, like a poorly coordinated robot, moved across the room. "I can't make the muumuu snap together."

"MEMU." Baker guided her verbally but did not fasten the rings for her. "You have to keep doing it until you get the feel of it. Let's try it again."

He made them climb in and out of the suits for the next hour, finally timing them. He wasn't satisfied until the movements were completed within one minute—speed suiting, he called it. "Now the gloves and the helmet," he said, presenting the final accessaries like diplomas. "The helmet has a sunshade that's sensitive to ultraviolet light. It's the same material used for the CELSS domes. Go ahead, put them on."

The novices moved clumsily about the room, bending, turning, testing the restrictions of the suits.

"How do you feel?" Baker asked.

"Like a lobster," Paris mumbled.

Baker smiled. "That's enough for today. Tomorrow we go for a walk."

"Outside?" Paris was elated.

"Outside," Baker said, nodding.

Graham removed his helmet. His one fervent desire was to shed everything and enjoy immediate and total nudity.

Graham was browsing among the books and discs in the SURF library when Baker found him. "I'm taking Paris Tucker out to the Ventures colony tomorrow. I wondered if you'd like to come along. Do a little sight-seeing."

"You mean check out the colony and see what I think."

"That, too."

"Paris tells me you have to be approved by a member of the group before you're welcome to join them."

Baker shrugged. "It's not like it's a closed fraternity. Besides, I understand the girl has already extended an invitation to you. See, you're not universally loathed, after all."

"How long will this take?"

"About three sols round trip if we stay overnight. It's a

little over eight hundred kilometers, but I thought you might like to take a look at the Valles Marineris up close, and I want to show both of you one of the homemade CELSS pods the Ventures are building all over the place. It's good to know where they are, in case . . ."

Graham shelved a book. "In case of what?"

"Just . . . in case. If you should find yourself between safety zones and a rover breaks down . . . or if you lose your orientation in a dust storm . . . things like that."

"Do these little emergencies happen often?"

Baker smiled. "Very seldom."

"I suppose wearing a MEMU is de rigueur for this excursion."

"We have to take them along, but the rover is something of a CELSS on wheels. You'll only need to climb into the hard suits when we transfer to a pod or get out and walk around."

The Martian landscape did nothing to take Graham's breath away, he decided, after a full hour of barren volcanic plains, a sparse scattering of craters, and endless chunks of rust-tinted rocks. The rocks had been cleared on either side of the meandering path of the big-wheeled rover, but there seemed to be no actual road in places. Powdery fine dust had obliterated the tracks of earlier vehicles and drifted in small rivulets across the road. Baker had declared it a lovely day. Graham thought the air looked parched and hazy and there was nothing remotely lovely about it. The dawn was a dusty vermilion, which faded to a cloudless pastel salmon and stayed that way. The terrain looked hot. It wasn't, he knew, but the hues gave every indication that they traversed a baked waterless desert. The actual temperature was a pleasant 62 degrees, according to the instruments inside the rover. When they had departed from the SURF base at daybreak the temperature was well below freezing.

"The Tharsis Bulge is there, off to the west." Baker pointed. "It's the highest region on the entire planet. Since Mars has no sea level, an atmospheric pressure level of 6.1 millibars was designated as a kind of artificial sea level. Below that datum water can't liquefy, but pressure above that point could allow liquid water to exist during the summer sols. Plans are under way to transport water-ice from Keyote to the Fesenkov Crater north of the Jeremian colony. Once filled and covered it could become an artificial lake and reservoir."

Paris gazed out the fishbowllike windows. "Tharsis averages about what, six or seven kilometers above datum?"

"Good girl. You did your homework." Baker nodded.

"I just wondered why two colonies chose that area. Now I understand. Looking to a green future, I guess."

"If it starts anywhere it'll start there," Baker said.

The rover was heavily laden with supplies for the colony, including a machine Graham considered very weaponlike in appearance. It reminded him of a combined rocket launcher and laser cannon. The contraption, carefully hauled aboard the vehicle by a crew at the SURF headquarters, was identified by a metal plate on its side as a V-175 Igneous Bore. A stone fuser. The Ventures, Baker explained, had suggested various modifications on the mining tool, and the new model had just arrived from Earth. If it worked to their satisfaction, more would be ordered for the expansion of each colony.

They bumped along, with Baker pointing out various sights like a bus tour guide. "Anybody hungry?" he asked at last.

"Me!" Paris said, raising her right hand.

"Be on the lookout for a solar wand up ahead. It's where one of the pods is located. I thought we'd stop there to have lunch, so you can see how they're set up and you can stretch your legs."

A solar wand, Graham discovered, was a tall vertical rod sticking out of a dirt mound with an array of solar panels attached. It supplied the homemade CELSS with heat and power and sustained the vegetation inside.

There was no way of maneuvering in the MEMU suits other than awkwardly. They exited through the rover's air-lock hatch one at a time and followed Baker toward the pod. To Graham's mild surprise the mound that arched above ground was not a pile of Martian dirt but a thick layer of glasslike irregular plates forming a pattern that vaguely reminded him of a tortoise shell.

"By altering settings on the stone fuser," Baker explained through the MEMU transceiver, "they're able to make a somewhat transparent glass dome for sunlight. It's quite effective in shielding occupants from too much ultraviolet light. Follow me."

The entrance, akin to an igloo tunnel, forced them to crawl a short distance before they could stand up. Steps made of fused stone led downward. Only small circles of sunlight from singular glass panels set into the tunnel arch provided enough light to see.

There was an outer chamber, a cramped middle chamber, and finally they were inside. Baker removed his helmet. "It's okay. You can breathe the air."

The module was like an illustration out of a childhood book of fairy tales, Graham thought, turning slowly around. Above them arched the tortoise-shell dome, like a concave free-form rose window in a Gothic cathedral. Slabs of colored glass rainbowed over them in shades of amber, lemon-yellow, honey, and wine. Green vines clambered up walls and hung in lush tendrils like weeping willows. Water trickled from a stone crevice, creating a miniature waterfall down into a small pond. Baker removed a glove, cupped water into his hand, and drank. "There's no water anywhere as pure as that of Mars." He sighed, wiping his mouth. Clearly, he was enjoying their speechless awe.

"Are they *all* like this?" Paris said finally, climbing out of her MEMU.

"Some are larger, some smaller. I've seen one that has become a multichambered burrow." Baker shed his own hard suit and deposited it on a carved stone bench. "In that module to the left you'll find edible mushrooms, carrots, potatoes, peanuts, squash, onions . . . I forget what else. You can whip up a damn good vegetarian stew in an emergency." He turned around, looking for something. "They usually leave a couple of pots around . . . there, above you, Gray, on that ledge."

Graham reached for one of the much dented and abused pots and watched as Baker filled it with water.

"Aren't you going to get out of your MEMU? I know how much you like the thing." Baker plucked several leaves from a nearby bush.

"What are you doing?" Graham asked, climbing out of the suit.

"Making tea. Of a sort. I think you'll like it." He clamped a solar coil to the rim of the pot and set it on a long stone slab that passed as a table. "Should be ready in a few minutes. Sandwiches are in that case I brought in."

"Is there, like, a little girls' room around here?" Paris asked.

"There's an Ecolet in the hygiene compartment to your right. Your contribution to the compost will be greatly appreciated."

Paris wrinkled her nose. "Crude, Baker. Very crude."

"Well, what did you think happened to waste aboard the *Mons*? Did you think it got flushed out into space?"

"I preferred not to wonder about it, frankly. If you really want to know, I thought it was compressed into neat little packages and sent back home."

Baker chuckled. "Go back to your training manual and read Section Five again. Without the use of water or chemicals, without any form of septic tank or sewer system, the Ecolet causes all biodegradable waste to decompose into a powderlike compost. One Earth year's worth of contributions by five people would fill a pot no bigger than that." He pointed to the half-gallon pot that was beginning to steam. "It's a fine fertilizer. The best."

Paris moved off toward the smaller chamber. "I don't think I want any tea, thanks just the same."

Baker set about preparing the picnic lunch. "There should be a canister of seasonings, sugar and the like," he said, rooting through thick foliage. "That's the only trouble with these pods; the plants grow wild if nobody comes around to tend them once in a while."

"Is this what you're looking for?" Graham asked, lifting vines off of a long metal box.

"No, that's medical supplies. Wait, somebody may have stored the can in there. Take a look. It's aluminum, about so big." He gestured, making a cookie jar-sized shape with his hands.

Inside the metal chest were all kinds of emergency supplies. Graham recognized some of the packaged implements from his recent medical training and realized that one could perform surgery, if necessary, from what was available. He found a silvery canister nestled in among blankets at one end of the box. "Is this it?"

"Yeah. Pitch it over."

Inside were sugar, salt, spices, oils, and vacuum-packed coffee and soy flour.

"Are all these pods this well equipped?"

"Most. The larger ones, out beyond the Ventures colony, contain sleeping compartments separate from the central dome. If we camped here overnight we'd have to sleep right here—not that it would be uncomfortable. I hear they're planning to build a way station out on the Solis Planum that could house ten to twenty people for the duration of a half-year dust storm."

Graham watched him set out food and pour hot tea into insulated metal cups. "Half an Earth year or Martian year?"

"Earth year. The storms are greater in the southern hemisphere, not that we don't get them this far north. We do. We get our share. Sugar? No, you don't take sugar. Hey, Tucker, did you fall in back there? You want sugar or straight?"

The woman emerged, still velking up her cooling garment. "Lots of sugar. Dump it in." As she passed Graham she said, "It's okay as long as you don't look down inside. There's even a stone sink in there with a heating coil for hot water. Amazing. This is not a bad place. Not bad at all. I'd fix a sleeping loft up there, though, near the dome. And blast out a hot tub next to the pond, maybe. Very . . . cozy."

The tea was strong and vaguely mint-flavored. As they ate in silence the only sound was the trickling water. The environment appealed to Graham in a way he hadn't expected. It was natural and cavelike, the antithesis of the geometrically precise structures of the SURF modules that had been constructed of Earth-made materials. The only wood thus far on Mars grew as small fruit-bearing trees and was not to be used for any other purpose. He supposed that cultured forests were on the drawing board, many years down the line. It was difficult for him not to envision a business enterprise that would corner the market on lumber. It would be a rare and precious commodity for those demanding an aesthetic alternative to metal or plastic. Momentarily he saw fortunes amassing, then remembered where he was. One did not accumulate a fortune in barter, and what would he do with any credits that accrued? Buy his way back home? It was hard letting go of old habits.

Baker began packing up. "There's a custom that's developed around here that you should know about, both of you. Anytime somebody uses a pod, and takes something from it, he leaves something in its place. I put powdered milk packets into the canister. It's a nice custom. I don't know how it got started. It's just something people around here do."

Graham put the aluminum canister back into the supply chest. With customs like these cropping up he doubted that wood hoarding would go over very well. "Different value systems," Maggie McKay had said. They had different value systems. He was beginning to understand what she meant.

CHAPTER 13

Sunset on the arid plain was rather spectacular, employing all the warm shades of the visible light spectrum from scarlet to deep plum. A smattering of cirrus clouds on the horizon offered some texture to the otherwise smooth canvas, and Graham began to look for the blue diamond glitter of his beloved Earth. Deimos appeared in the early evening sky as an intense light not much brighter than the surrounding stars. Phobos, which rose later, almost full and butter-yellow, was about one third the size of Earth's moon.

"I see it!" Paris said suddenly, pointing off into the darkness. "The colony! There it is!"

From a distance the community looked like a warm light glowing beneath a settling parachute. As they got closer, however, Graham could see that it was more like a number of parachute silks clustered together that gave the appearance of one large dome. He began to feel a touch of anxiety as to how he would be greeted by these people. Paris would be welcomed. They were expecting her. And they would be expecting Baker, or someone like him, as escort for the new member of the commune. But what about himself? How would they deal with him, once they heard his name?

They did not need to don the MEMU suits to transfer

from the rover to the Ventures colony. Instead, the vehicle entered a double set of air locks similar to those of the SURF base, but on a smaller scale. Several men, jumpsuit- or denim-clad, came to meet them and unload supplies. They seemed especially interested in the new stone fuser, lifting it from the top of the rover as if it were a woman about to give birth.

"We were expecting you earlier," Simmons said as they climbed out of the rover. Graham noted that the T.E. was now cultivating a beard, which promised to be quite red in contrast to his dark hair.

"We was about ready to set out to look for you," a second, much shorter, man said.

Baker smiled. "Worried about the new fuser, huh, Vogel?"

The other men laughed.

"Damn right," Vogel said, nodding.

Paris, scratching a spot on her stomach, explained that Baker had shown them a sample of Ventures handiwork on a CELSS pod. "Terrific workmanship. How many are there, so far?"

"Nine," Simmons said.

"Seven," countered Vogel. "One croaked last winter. Pod 8, the one near Ophir Chasma. We think it was pierced by a fragment from a shower sometime after the Winter Solstice. Killed everything. Haas and Waverly are working on it to bring it back, but we can't risk going out to work on the one at Gangis till Pod 8 is in working order again. And we don't count a pod till it's completed, Simmons. So we got seven, not nine. I keep telling you that." Patting the stone fuser, he said, "This baby should speed things up, though."

A statuesque woman with straight white-blond hair pulled back in a loose ponytail entered the chamber. She wore jeans and a sweatshirt and soft cloth boots. She sized Graham up and grinned. "Thank God! A man of decent height. All they send us is shrimpy little vermin like you, Vogel." She turned to Paris. "Please tell me he's not yours. You're Tucker, right? I'm Waverly. Flora Waverly."

Paris looked at Graham, uncertain. "He's . . . with me, if he wants to be."

Vogel gestured with a thumb. "This here, my little persimmon, is the freakin' Cloud Man. Graham K. Sinclair himself. Killed—what was it—besides the three or four million back home—four guys on the *Mons*? Not to mention putting three guys in the hospital on the *'Notchka,* I hear. So don't go looking at the man, Waverly. He'll break your sweet chops. And if he don't, I will."

Vogel reminded Graham of a hairy troll. He was barrel-chested and stubby-fingered, a perpetual scowl furrowing his forehead. One long unbroken eyebrow accentuated the unpleasantness of his face. He wore a faded blue jumpsuit, much frayed at the cuffs, and shower sandals. Black chest hair curled beneath his Adam's apple. Vogel, Graham decided, was the result of two people who had rejected genetic counseling somewhere in the remote past.

"So get outta the LCGs and meet us in the Lodge, half an hour," Vogel said. "Waverly, show 'em where the hygiene unit is." As he turned to leave he looked at Baker, but pointed to Graham. "I take it you're both staying for the night? Him . . . he staying for good, or what?"

Baker picked up a duffel bag and pitched it to Graham. "He just came along for the ride. But he could stay if he decided to."

"How come? I don't hear nobody asking him."

"I did." Paris smiled, hefting a green duffel bag to her shoulder. "You got a problem with that?"

Vogel seemed to be trying to force his eyebrows down over the bridge of his nose. "No problem, lady. Just watch it he don't kill nobody else before dinner, okay?"

Paris nodded, solemn. "I'll do my best. You do have chains? We left ours behind."

"Very funny lady, this one," Vogel muttered to no one in particular. "Just what we need. A comedy queen."

Graham followed Paris and Waverly down a long laser-blasted corridor. Baker brought up the rear. They came out into an underground grotto complete with a splashing waterfall and pond surrounded by tropical plants. For a moment he was reminded of Singapore and the home of his grandmother, with its walled garden and exotic flowering plants.

"This was a little pet project of mine," Waverly said. "I do plumbing. I figured if the water's got to circulate anyway we might as well enjoy it. And why should fish farming be so dull? There are catfish in that pond. Excellent eating. You can't see it now because it's dark, but there's a skylight up there made of fused glass. At dawn the whole place just lights up."

She led them down another corridor and pointed out sleeping cubicles where they would be staying. "There's not a lot of privacy around here but we're working on it," she said to Paris. "The hygiene area is communal at the moment but Vogel has promised to carve out another compartment with this new fuser. If he doesn't I'm going to stop up the plumbing until he does. There are only seventeen of us"—Waverly shrugged—"eighteen now, with you. We have to stick together if we want to make any changes. Welcome aboard, Tucker."

"How many men are here?" Graham asked.

Waverly made a quick mental count. "In the actual commune, right now tonight, or in the colony at large?"

"At large."

"Forty-seven. If you really want to count Vogel as a whole number." She laughed, flashing perfect teeth. She was very Nordic in her bone structure and her eyes were of such pale blueness that they seemed to be without irises. When Waverly looked at him, Graham felt almost unclothed by her directness.

"Forty-seven?" Baker said. "I thought there were forty-eight, counting the new arrivals."

"Hughes died last year. You didn't know? Got disoriented during a bad dust storm, got out of a rover and wandered around in the thick of it. We found him about two kilometers from a pod. He just couldn't locate it. The beacon had snapped off in the storm. That's why we're putting up several at each pod now. So it won't happen again." She spread her hands in a "that's life" gesture. "Well, I'll let you guys get cleaned up and changed. I hate those LCGs. They itch."

"I thought it was just me," Paris said, scratching her shoulder.

"The Jerrys, excuse me, the Jeremians, weave an under garment you can put on beneath the LCG. It's terrific. I'll loan you one if you like. I think we're about the same height. Baker, you can show them how to get to the Lodge, can't you?"

Baker nodded. "Through the grotto and to the left."

"You got it." Waverly smiled again, this time directly at Graham.

The Lodge was a large, rounded communal meeting hall, dining room, and entertainment center. Long metal tables with attached benches reminded Graham of one of his childhood prep school dining halls. Only there the tables had been of heavy oak, worn smooth from countless hyperactive bodies and obsessively whittled upon by discreetly gouging penknives when the headmasters were elsewhere occupied.

Dinner, served chow-line style, consisted of a variety of overcooked vegetables and roast chicken. There was also wine, served in large glazed clay pitchers.

Waverly settled in across from Graham. "So, what do you do, Mr. Sinclair, aside from killing people on impulse?"

Graham looked at her, trying to decipher her intent. She was smiling in a way that intimated that she was joking.

Paris reached over to break off a chunk of bread from a round, slightly burned loaf. "He's a surveyor. I mean he will be, if he wants to stay here. I mean he *could* be, if he wanted . . . to stay."

Waverly speared a potato. "What we could use is a cook. I understand one of the new guys is something of a chef. I hope so. We rotate duties around here. Every two cycles. That's twenty sols. So far nobody's much of a cook. The chicken you're eating tonight comes from the Jeremian commune. We don't get it very often. The only chickens we keep are for eggs. The Jerrys are farming fanatics. So we leave the chickens, rabbits, goats, and such to them. In return we help blast a foundation for a new module or help during harvest time. We can get cloth from them, too, or one of the women will make your clothes if you work it out in some form of barter. Real nesters, those women. The hardest part is letting them pray for you all the time. I can't imagine Baker

living with them for as long as he did. Where is he, by the
way?" She looked around, licking her fingers clean of
chicken in a sensual manner that intrigued Graham. He
had never seen a woman eat so lustily and still retain
such highly sexual mannerisms. She ran her tongue
slowly over her lips, seeming to savor the flavors. A
trickle of wine escaped the corner of her mouth as she
drank from a pottery goblet, and she drew the back of her
hand slowly across her cheek as if caressing it. She did not
look at him but he knew that she was keenly aware that
he watched her.

"I think he's off talking to Simmons," Paris said, dis-
turbing the subtly erotic display. "They're probably comparing notes and laying bets on who'll crack and go home
first."

Waverly looked at Graham. "Guess they can't bet on
you, though, can they? Vogel says you can't go back
home. Ever. Is that true?"

"He'd rather not talk about it if you don't mind," Paris
snapped, tossing a chicken bone onto her plate.

"What are you, his interpreter? The man has a voice. If
he doesn't want to talk about it, let *him* tell me, all right,
sweetie?"

"I'd rather not talk about it," Graham said.

"See?" said Paris.

Waverly dipped a strawberry into her wine and sucked
at the ruby sweetness. "I totally understand," she said.

Several of the other women came by to greet Paris and
introduce themselves. They were for the most part
comely, Graham decided, healthy-looking in a way that
suggested severe physical workouts. They were quite unlike the women of his former circle, who maintained porcelain skin and skeletal bodies, all the better to parade the
fashion of the moment. He doubted that any of these
women had ever undergone any form of cosmetic pruning or plumping. They had faces of carved individuality,
not the molded masks that had begun to bore him by the
age of twenty. He tried to imagine Tamara Voss-Frieling
among these women and could not. That she refused to
travel without her personal hairdresser and manicurist
was perhaps too critical a judgment of her pioneer potential, he thought. She was, after all, a product of the society

to which she belonged. If he examined his own survival skills compared to the least of these settlers, he was sorely lacking and just as out of place, he realized. There was much to learn, and there was a lifetime ahead of him to fill.

After dinner Waverly guided Paris and Graham on a haphazard tour of the colony. Most of the modules were completely underground with narrow arched tunnels connecting them. There was an amorphous cavelike quality to the rambling structures, not unlike the pod they had visited earlier in the day but on a much larger scale. Several hubs where sunlight was needed rose partially to the Martian surface like translucent bubbles. Here vegetation thrived in wild abandon, clambering up walls, curling around every protuberance, dangling from ceilings. Grapes seemed to be a favorite agricultural crop, and the size of the fruit was unlike anything Graham had ever seen on Earth. One deep purple grape was comparable in size to an Earth-grown plum. Plums were the size of grapefruit.

"Wine we can make." Waverly shrugged. "Cheese, however, takes more patience than we seem to possess. For one thing, goats require more care, so we gave ours to the Jerrys. Now they send us cheese and we send them grapes. For jelly only, of course."

"What about the Seras?" Paris asked. "Do they barter with you?"

"Not much. They keep to themselves. The plates you ate off of tonight, and any pottery you see, came from them. They're experimenting with glass, too. They got a glassblower over there, a couple of years ago, but he died before he could pass on all the secrets of the trade. That was a shame. His work is highly prized, what little of it there is. You won't find much glass in any of the colonies, just the big slabs we make with the stone fusers. It's pretty primitive. We'd like to get down to something thin and strong. Maybe the new V-175 can manage it. We'll see."

There was no information center or library in any of the modules they passed through, Graham noted, although books and holo-discs had been among the supplies brought out to the commune. He did not picture Vogel as a remotely scholarly man, so he assumed that few of the people drawn to the Ventures were of a literary bent. They weren't without a sense of the aesthetic, however, as shown by their rambling architecture and the jungle-like freedom of the plant life in the colony.

It was only later, long after everyone had scattered to private cubicles, that Paris crept to Graham's quarters to express her doubts. She pulled aside the rough-woven curtain that passed as a door, to find him in T-shirt and shorts, sitting lotus fashion on a mat. She joined him, crossing her legs awkwardly in her green jumpsuit, and waited until he opened his eyes.

"You done?" she asked.

"I suppose I am. What's wrong?"

She looked around at the vaulted ceiling and smooth reddish walls, bare of any ornamentation. A shelf, empty, was chiseled into a far wall. A tall metal cabinet with numerous compartments was set into another wall. The narrow captain's bunk provided more storage space beneath. Otherwise, the room was stark and as impersonal as a monk's cell.

"You need a window. *I* need a window. I'm beginning to think I made a big mistake, here, Sinclair."

"In what way?"

"Every way you want to name. I don't like it. I want to go home. Only . . ." She fought to hold back tears, but they spilled over anyway. ". . . I have no place to go. I've got no home to go back to. What am I going to do? I don't want to stay here. I *hate* it here!"

Graham watched as she scrubbed away the tears, reddening her face further. "What is it that you hate?"

"*Everything.* They . . . they've got no damned *windows.*" She started to laugh. "Oh, cripes, I need a snot rag here."

He held out a clean T-shirt. "Sorry. It's all I have."

She looked at him and the combined tears and laughter spilled over again. "I never do this, I swear. I never cry. Never. I'm just not the type. It'll all be over in a minute, I promise." She blew her nose into the T-shirt. "I'll wash it. God, I'm sorry."

He waited until she seemed in control, then got up. "This room, I'm told, belonged to Hughes. When he died they divided up all his worldly goods because he left no will and there was no one on Earth to whom they could send his things. Nothing of him remains. Except the pods. He built the first one. It was his idea, the pods, the way they're built. He left something to pass on. He made his mark here, for those who will come later. Paris, something brought you here. You *chose* to come. You have something to contribute. Don't give up and turn around now."

"They don't need me. I don't belong here. It's like a private club. I'm on the outside looking in. And jeez, I don't even *want* in."

"When I was first sent away to school I was seven years old. I didn't want to go. I was accustomed to a tropical Eden, to an . . . opulence, if you will, and people, adults, at my beck and call. It was what I was used to. From that safe and very sheltered *and* unrealistic cocoon I was thrust into a cold, brittle world. Both figuratively and literally."

Graham sat on the bed and drew his feet up. "Boys know cruelties to smaller boys that you can't imagine. I hated it. I tried to run away. But there was no place for me to run to. I had no idea where my parents were wintering at the moment. My only memorable sanctuary was the home of my grandmother, near Singapore. My grandfather lived in New York. My father's parents were long dead. I had to stay, and I survived, and the strangeness faded. Eventually, I learned to love the school. I dreaded holidays with my parents and was eager to get back to an academic environment. I was very sorry when I grew older and had to move on to other schools."

Paris shoved a tear-dampened clump of hair away from her face. "You're saying I should stick it out. Big whoop."

"If you don't, what will you tell your grandchildren? That you were a pioneer failure? Paris Tucker, Space Lark?"

"Don't call me that." She tossed the T-shirt at him and he dodged it. "I guess I just panicked a little. I wish you would stay here, Gray. I really do. I'd feel a helluva lot better if there was at least one face I knew around here."

"You know plenty of faces—far more than I do."

"But you . . . you're a friend. They're just . . . people."

Graham reached over to a light above the bed and dimmed it to a soft glow, casting the room into shadows. "Thank you. Considering that friendships in my life are at a record low, I especially value the distinction you made, Paris."

She stood to go. "I'll give the place six months, until the next cycler. Then we'll see. Good night, Sinclair. Oh, pitch me the shirt. I'll wash it out."

"Would you . . . do something for me?"

"Sure. What?"

Graham rubbed his face. It felt slightly sandpapery. He hoped that his request would not be misconstrued. "Would you stay with me tonight? Just . . . share my bed . . . for the night. No demands, just . . . stay here."

Paris put her hands to her chest in mock dismay. In a deeply honey-dipped drawl she said, "Why, Mistah Seeunclaih, such fowahdness in ah gentleman!"

"I need your . . . protection. I fully expect a visit from a lady before the night is over. If the space is . . . occupied . . ."

"Waverly?"

"Baker tells me she's bonded to Vogel. Has been for well over four years. I don't want a door shut to me here because of . . ."

Paris grinned. "You're in a pickle there, okay. No matter what you do you're going to piss somebody off."

Graham nodded. He lay back and touched the empty space beside him. "For a friend?"

Paris moved to the edge of the bed. "Well, for a friend. Okay. I'd hate to see a stone fuser in action tonight if Vogel came gunning for you." She reached up and turned off the light.

He felt her slide between the covers.

"You do this often?" she asked in the darkness.

"Do what?"

"Use women to fend off other women?"

"Asking Baker would have been a bit too drastic."

Paris giggled. "Yeah. I guess so. This is kind of fun. Like a slumber party. We could tell ghost stories. 'Out of the mist rose the horrid xenomoth, fangs dripping . . .'"

"Xenomoth?"

"Yeah. A strange, foreign, constantly changing monster . . ."

"I think you mean xeno*morph.*"

"It's a fangy moth, okay? It's my story. You're no fun, Sinclair. I think I should get out of the jumpsuit, don't you? For the sake of authenticity you might also get under the covers, you know?"

Graham slipped between the covers. He could feel her warmth as she maneuvered out of her clothing in the dark. He heard it drop to the floor.

They lay still for several moments. "Just friends," Paris said. "You're gonna owe me for this, Sinclair."

"All right. I'll tell you a ghost story."

"Naked is not for telling ghost stories."

"Go to sleep, Tucker."

After another silence Paris said, "Don't you think you ought to sort of put one arm around me, like? So when she peeks in . . ."

Graham was asleep.

"Now you're *really* gonna owe me, Sinclair."

CHAPTER 14

He woke to find the room bathed in filtered sunlight and Paris propped up on an elbow, watching him. "Surprise," she said. "They have windows, after all. All that stone in the ceiling is glass. I couldn't tell last night. It just looked like fused rocks. You talk in a foreign language in your sleep. Did you know that?"

"I've been told."

"I'll bet. What is it? It sounded like Chinese or something."

"Possibly. I speak a number of languages. What time is it?"

Paris glanced at a heavy watch on her left wrist. "About six-thirty. What happened to your watch? You never wear one."

Graham climbed over her and got up. "They're all Earth-made. Can't have one."

She watched him from the bed, covers pulled up to her chin, as he rummaged in his duffel bag for his hygiene kit. "They won't even let you keep a lousy watch?"

"No."

"How do you tell time?"

"Other people tell me the time." He pulled fresh clothing from the bag.

She sat up, modestly draping herself with the sheet.

"You were right. About last night. The princess came prowling, about two."

"How did you know?"

"She tripped over my jumpsuit on the floor. Said something about cubicles all looking alike, and left. Then later, Vogel . . ."

"Vogel?"

"Yeah."

"Are you sure it was Vogel?"

"What other four-foot-nine hairy beast do you know around here? He poked his head in, looking for Waverly. Then Simmons came by looking for Waverly. I tell you, the traffic through here was incredible. How could you sleep through all that? Then Baker dropped by about an hour ago. Seemed rather pleased to see me here with you. Said to meet him in the Lodge, whenever."

Graham paused, towel in hand. "The showers are communal, I understand."

Paris scrambled from the bed. "Thought you'd never ask."

Baker was drinking strong black coffee when Graham appeared, Paris at his side, her breakfast tray heaped high. "So?" he said. "What are your plans? Staying or what?"

Graham slid into a seat across from the man. "It's not what you're thinking."

"He was fantastic." Paris smiled, her mouth full of toast.

Graham glanced at her, then turned back to Baker. "I'll explain later."

"The man is *amazing*!" Paris continued.

"Thank you, Paris. That's enough," Graham murmured between sips of coffee.

"*Extraordinary*," she whispered.

Baker smiled.

Vogel, in what passed as unusually high spirits, came by and slapped Graham on the back. "So, Cloud Man, you staying or what? We can all use the skills of a good corporate executive around here." His laugh had a malicious curl to it that made Graham want to step on him.

"I'll be heading back to the SURF base with Baker," he

said. "But I'd like to come out again once in a while. I'd like to see how a stone fuser operates. Maybe you could show me how to build a pod."

"Sure thing, Cloud Man. Anytime. We'll take good care of your little lady here." He clapped Paris on both shoulders, his stumpy fingers squeezing in a conspiratorial manner. Paris rolled her eyes heavenward.

Waverly, in anything but good spirits, plunked herself down beside Baker. She wore a dark blue jumpsuit unzipped far enough to create tension if she elected to bend over. Her blond hair was piled on her head in a wispy manner, silken strands escaping, falling to her shoulders. "Vogel tells me you're taking Sinclair out to the Marineris before you head back," she said to Baker.

"I thought we might take a look since we're in the neighborhood." Baker nodded.

"Mind if I catch a ride as far as the Ophir Chasma? It'll save Haas the drive in from Pod 8 to pick up the new fuser."

"Fine."

Graham marveled at her no-nonsense approach to eating breakfast. It was nothing like the performance of the night before. Paris reached over to stroke his cheek. "I'm going to miss you, shugums. Promise me you'll send me comp-letters every day. He's getting his medic certification," she said to Waverly. "Did he mention it?"

Waverly cut across an egg with fierce precision. "We've hardly had a chance to talk."

"And that's the way we like it," Vogel snorted. "Hey, Tucker, maybe you oughtta go along, start surveying stuff. Start out at Pod 8, why don't you?"

Waverly glared at him. "It can't sustain three people yet. I told you that."

"So one of ya sleep in the rover. What the hell."

"Terrific idea," Paris said. "I'll get my gear together." As she rose from the bench she draped her arms around Graham's shoulders. "It'll give us a few more hours together, darling."

The ride out to the canyon's edge was somewhat subdued. Baker talked about a bridge that was planned for a section of the Marineris. "Right now, in order to cross, you have to travel west, down through the Noctis

Labyrinthus. What this bridge is, what it does, is spiral gradually down to the valley floor, then a road will cut across to another spiral that goes up to the top of the cliffs. It'll be one nice shortcut to the Solis Planum."

The two women sat in seats behind the men, and on opposite sides of the rover. Paris made a stab at cracking the frost emanating from Waverly by praising the comfort of the "Jerry long johns" that the woman had loaned her.

"You guys should get a pair," she said. "In fact, they should be government-issue along with the LCGs and the MEMUs. Make a note of it, Baker. Tell them."

"I've made a note."

Graham pointed off to the right. "What is that?"

"A dust devil," said Baker. "I've been keeping an eye on it. You don't want to tangle with a Martian dust devil. It's like trying to discuss the weather with a tornado." The dark reddish whirlwind, approximately twenty kilometers to the southeast, undulated like a giant elephant's trunk, sucking up anything in its path. Graham estimated that it was at least one to two kilometers in height.

"A couple of years ago," Waverly said, "that's Martian years I'm talking about—three miners from Keyote tried to outrun a dust devil in a rover. The thing picked up the rover like a toy in a vacuum cleaner. They didn't find enough of anything to bury. I hope to heaven this isn't a sign of a storm coming. There was nothing on the tracking when we left."

"A storm?" Paris asked.

Waverly seemed to be thawing. "Dust storm. You'll see what I mean . . . if you stick around long enough. Usually, one is all it takes."

"For what?"

The woman caught a wisp of hair and tucked it behind an ear. "To separate the Space Larks from the Grits."

"Grits are the ones who stick it out," Baker offered.

"I figured," Paris mumbled.

Without turning around, Graham reached a hand behind him. Paris touched his fingertips, sat back, and smiled. Waverly, catching the small gesture, turned her gaze to the windows.

·   ·   ·

Haas, moving slowly in his MEMU, emerged from the damaged pod. By the overall dimensions of the hard suit, Graham decided Haas must be bear-sized. Through the face plate he could see that the man was dark-bearded, with startling blue eyes. He seemed ecstatic over the new stone fuser as supplies were unloaded from the rover.

"This honey can slice, dice, puddle, and pour," he crooned.

Waverly made brief introductions. "Tucker is joining us, maybe. Only time will tell."

"The cartographer. Yeah," Haas said, circling Paris. "She got a body? Can't tell for shit in a MEMU."

"I suppose," Waverly said. "But it's been claimed, Haas. Stop slobbering or you'll fog your face plate." To Paris she said, "They're all animals, but you get used to it. You forget what a true gentleman is. Unless you're reminded."

Haas had no reaction to hearing Graham's name until Waverly tacked on the "Cloud Man" appendage. "You don't look like a killer," he said.

Graham pulled a crate of food rations out of the storage compartment of the rover. "It's hard to tell in a MEMU."

Haas paused, then laughed. "Yeah. Hey, I like him. He can stay."

"Why don't you demonstrate how the fuser works for these good people?" Waverly suggested. "You need to test it anyway, to see how the modifications work out."

Haas, like an overgrown kid with a new toy, was quite willing to perform for his guests. He led them out to a roughly dug trench approximately three meters square and one meter deep. "This is for making the glass slabs. We had to haul the right kind of sand in from several locations. That's why you get the variation in color and clarity. Kind of potluck glass. You don't know what you got till it's cooled. This batch should be about ready for cutting. The fuser I've been using has only four settings, none of which were made for the stuff we use them for. Hell, they're just hole borers, essentially. But if you set it on tight focus, the laser cuts a narrow path, good for slicing." To illustrate, he strapped the new fuser around his hips, adjusted the shoulder harness, and aimed at a nearby outcropping of rock. In a smooth movement he cut off a piece. It tumbled into the dust, smoking.

"In short bursts it blows rocks up. The beam acts like bullets, maybe more like grenade bullets. That's the second setting." In a swift move, the still-smoking rock exploded into granules.

"The third setting makes puddles out of rocks, depending on how it's focused—you diffuse it a bit." He moved several mechanisms on the fuser and aimed again at the outcropping of rock. In less than a minute the stone began to droop like a brown crayon left in the summer sun. In a few more seconds it began to drip, a glowing, molten mass, pooling on the ground, running in brief rivulets until it hardened, cooling rapidly into a muddy solid.

"Oh, man, this is fan-effin-tastic," Haas said. "Waverly, did you see that? Oh, this is great!"

Waverly smiled. "Usually to get that result we have to wait a good three to five minutes. It gets tiring. Your arms start to ache. You can see why pod building is slow work. The V-175 is a lot more powerful."

"I'll bet this beauty could make clear glass if we handle it right," Haas said. "That's the fourth setting, for sand, for the slabs." He swung around and cut through the hardened material in the trench. "Like slicing through hot brownies," he announced. Reaching down into the shallow pit with a pair of metal pincers, he pulled out a brick-sized chunk of molasses-colored glass. It was flawed and imperfect, with bubbles and small lumps, but sunlight glowed through it. Graham was reminded of a translucent amber soap his mother used when he was a child. It was expensive and she carried a supply of it wherever she traveled. He could remember the clean smell of it on her skin, better than any perfume.

Haas, like an eager host who seldom received visitors, beckoned everyone down into Pod 8 to see what progress had been made to restore the environment to full operating status. "You can climb out of the suits. The air is thin yet, but it's breathable. If you're not into aerobics."

The central hub was untidy, like a house under construction. Metal scaffolding had been erected clear to the turtle-patterned dome. Dust and gravel were everywhere, on every surface. Haas climbed out of his hard suit like a cicada shedding its outer body and brushed off the stone-slab table. "If I'd known we were having company . . ."

He laughed, shoving empty food cans onto the floor. "I hope you brought some microwave meals, man. I hate cooking. I've had veggie stew up to here."

He was the grizzly size that Graham had suspected, but younger than he had first estimated, in spite of the beginning of salt-and-pepper streaks in his beard.

Waverly guided them on a short inspection of the pod, pointing out the fresh plant growth in both Latin and common terms. "With the new fuser, I'm thinking of enlarging the area somewhat. This pod will have heavier traffic as more and more"—she glanced at Graham— *"tourists* come out to see the Valles Marineris. It's a shame you both can't stay the night," she said to Baker. "But the environment is still fragile, as you can see. We're pushing it to the limit with three of us staying, as it is. It's the dawn that's most breathtaking in the canyons. The mists boil and swirl like an ocean of white foam. Everything burns off before noon."

They left Haas to tidy up while they walked out to the edge of the closest chasm. "This is Ophir," Baker said, pointing. "Beyond it is Candor Chasma, and beyond that is Melas Chasma. They run parallel, something like giant claw marks. Melas runs into Coprates Chasma, which forks to the east into Capri and Eos."

"Pod 9 is planned for the Gangis Chasma," Waverly added. "It's a little north of Capri."

Graham gazed at the vast canyon below him, the floor almost lost in shadows. The canyons beyond Ophir were hazy but offered purplish shaded walls in contrast to the rust-red and muted orange of the plains. After the monotonous sameness of the Martian terrain he had seen thus far, the rugged beauty of the Marineris was a jarring reminder of the world he longed for everywhere he turned.

Paris was silent for a long moment. "There should be birds" was all she said.

Haas had brewed tea by the time they returned to the hub. He handed Paris a cup. "Not bad. A little on the lean side, but not bad."

"Me, or the tea?"

"You. You bonded to the Cloud Man, here?"

Paris looked over at Graham. "We're . . . considering it."

"Too bad. Let me know if you change your mind."

It was later as Graham was climbing into his MEMU that Paris bent close and slipped something into his LCG at the crotch. "To remember me," she whispered, helping him into the upper torso. Aloud she said, "You will come back, darling? As soon as your medical training is complete?"

"Ah . . . yes, I will."

"You'll call? And write?" Leaning close, she muttered, her lips barely moving, "I mean that, Sinclair."

"I will."

"You will?"

"Yes."

In the rover Baker waited for Graham to climb out of his MEMU. "Okay, Gray, what did she give you?"

"Nothing. What do you mean?"

"That bulge is not a hard-on. Come on. Hand it over."

Graham reached down, unvelked the LCG, and removed the watch Paris had given him. "She didn't know she was doing anything wrong, Jon. Don't turn her in."

"But you knew it was wrong to accept it."

A brief flash of anger erupted in Graham. "I didn't know what it was!"

"The watch keeps Earth time as well as Martian sols. You know you can't have it. You have no use for Earth time. You've got to accept that, Graham. Until you do, you'll never . . ." Baker closed his hand over the watch face. "So, what do you want me to do with it?"

"Return it to her, through the courier, when we get back to SURF. But let me . . . explain to her first."

Baker placed the watch in a compartment. "One more thing. Graham, never lie to me. I'm here to help you. Don't break that trust."

The anger, like the molten results of the stone fuser, hardened in Graham. But it did not cool.

CHAPTER 15

The Martian sols slipped by as Graham returned to his medical studies under the supervision of Dr. Krolov. There was a tiresome sameness to the days and a relative social isolation that made him retreat into his own thoughts. Periodically, the 220 other inhabitants of the research facility would gather in a circular video theater to watch news developments and entertainments sent from Earth. The first of these social gatherings of which he was aware proved an awkward embarrassment to Graham and the rest of the population, in general. He had been one of the last to enter the room, at some loss as to the purpose of the meeting. He had attended lectures there at Krolov's invitation, but some meetings, for security reasons, he was told, were closed to him. Heads turned as he entered and murmurs rippled through the room. He did not realize at first that his presence was the cause of the stir.

It was Krolov who went to him finally and gently escorted Graham from the theater. Obviously uncomfortable, the older man explained that the information concerned Earth. "I am deeply sorry, Graham. No one thought to inform you. Jonathan Baker always sees to it that you are occupied elsewhere during these occasions. I had forgotten that he was taking a lander out to visit one of the colonies. You were supposed to go, also. Why didn't you go?"

"He was going out to the Contaminants. I . . . told him I needed to finish some work."

"In the lab?"

Graham nodded. "I finished early. I didn't know about . . ." He gestured to the closed door. "I just saw everyone going in. You needn't find things to occupy my time in the future, Dr. Krolov. Just tell me. Please extend my apologies to the others."

Krolov patted him on the shoulder as if comforting a small boy. Graham fought an impulse to recoil from the touch. The gesture, so filled with pity, nauseated him.

Krolov returned to the theater, leaving him to sit alone on a bench in the corridor. He slowed his breathing, straining to hear, even faintly, news of Home. Several times there was applause. Once, he heard laughter. Some small part of him wanted to continue sitting there until they emerged from the room, glutted on that for which he starved. Perhaps he could catch brief bits of chatter concerning the topic forbidden him, like an aroma curling out of the darkness. A half phrase, a word here and there, snatched like a beggar after coins and strung together in secret suppositions later in his room. And, too, his solitary presence greeting them as they exited would force them to see him, to acknowledge his existence. And if they felt some vague shame in their collective conspiracy, so much the better. He wondered if someone, even now, watched the screen and thought of him, of his absence among them.

"I was afraid I'd find you here." Baker ambled down the hallway, his hair still damp from a shower.

"You don't have to make up things to keep me busy during . . . these gatherings, Jon. You can still go in, I should think. You haven't missed much. All this time you've missed the news, because of me."

"I see tapes, later. Come on, I'm overdue for a T'ai Chi lesson."

Graham shook his head. "Please. Another night. Let me work this out."

"You can't just sit here."

"Yes. I can sit here."

Baker sighed and sat down. "Then I guess I can, too."

They sat in silence for several minutes before Baker cleared his throat. "We don't have a lot of time left, you know. The next cycler is due in about six weeks. Graham, if you're not settled into life here, then I've failed to do my job. I've failed you. I can't leave you floundering like this."

"You've done what you could. The rest is up to me. You seem to forget the circumstances."

"I've *never* forgotten the circumstances! Do you think I *enjoy* any of this? Do you think I like cutting every shred of Earth from your life?" Baker was on his feet. "I *hate* it. I hate every minute of your pain! Because I'm part of it. I feel the pain, too!"

Graham watched in silence as Baker stalked away. Gradually he slowed his breathing, and waited.

He didn't see Baker for the next three sols. Usually, the man would join him at breakfast with a crammed agenda for what free time Graham had. Krolov was a stern taskmaster, pushing his pupil to more advanced levels of training, and Baker snatched whatever time was left.

He was meditating in his quarters when he sensed that he was being watched.

"I believe this is yours," Baker said, dangling a small leather pouch on a string in front of him.

Graham opened his eyes. It was Ti's small treasure. He reached up to take it, puzzled.

"I quit," Baker said with a shrug. "If they find it on you, they'll take it away. Just don't tell them where you got it."

"What do you mean, you quit?"

"Resigned. I'm no longer your Transition Escort. I'm no longer anybody's Escort. I just quit. It feels terrific."

Graham held the pouch in his hands, a rush of mental images tumbling forth. He could see the boy clearly, as on the day they parted. One image triggered another, and that sparked yet another. He reached inside the worn leather bag and brought out the piece of jade. It was the green of a mossy pool where water trickled over stones. It was the green of tropical plants in shadows, away from the too-hot sun. It was a color from his home.

"What I've just done puts me outside the law, you know," Baker said, watching him caress the stone between his fingers.

"I know."

Baker turned to go.

"Wait. Why did you do it? Quit?"

"I didn't like what I was anymore. It seemed the right thing to do."

Graham stood, carefully placing the piece of jade back into the pouch. "Jade represents many things, among them friendship and loyalty. Are you leaving when the cycler comes?"

Baker shook his head. "No. I'm staying."

"What will you do?"

"I don't know yet. Maybe be a courier for the SURF headquarters. Maybe I'll build my own pod out in a canyon and grow a beard and do T'ai Chi. I don't know."

Graham held out his hand.

Baker shook it. "I could use a beer. How about you?"

"That would be . . . nice."

They started arriving several sols before the scheduled departure for the *Ninotchka* space station and the eventual link-up with the cycler *Romanenko,* headed for Earth. The returnees, the ones who had decided they had taken enough of an environment too alien to embrace, came like wounded animals to the SURF base. Graham worked beside Krolov and the rest of the medical staff, examining the arrivals for signs of any unidentifiable virus or disorder. It was their eyes that he remembered most. It was as if they had lost the ability to focus on distant objects, or on anything tangible at all. They gazed inwardly, rejecting the world they could no longer endure. A few wept for hours at a time. Some blinked rapidly, pacing the corridors, behaving like long-caged animals pushed to the point of savagery.

"Nature sifts and separates what we cannot," Krolov said, taking a chart from Graham. "Survival of the fittest. It is still a basic law. Some recognize that this is not the soil that will nourish their roots. Those are the wise ones. Others recognize the signs too late." They passed by the bed of a woman from the Sera commune. She was frail, her body wasted to little more than bones. Her skin, like a waxy blue-tinged paper, seemed too delicate to touch.

"She will not survive lift-off for the *Ninotchka*. She waited too long." The doctor tapped in notes on her chart.

Graham watched through a window as another rover pulled up to the air lock, red dust billowing behind it. Although he could not tell who the people inside were, he expected to see Paris at any time. He had come to enjoy her brief calls over the telecom. Now that Baker was a courier between the various settlements, he was often away for several sols at a time and Graham had no one to talk to. Krolov was slowly warming, in that he occasionally challenged Graham to a chess game. But there was little communication on a more personal level. Paris would talk to him, filling him in on the progress of the pod building. She had begun a tentative relationship with Haas. "Everyone thinks I'm jilting you," she said, laughing. "It seems to please Waverly. Better wear a chastity belt if you come to visit."

Krolov nudged Graham with a chart. "Please pay attention, Mr. Sinclair. Exams are coming up. If you pass, you will receive your medic certification. And then, if you like . . . you might specialize? You have been a very quick student for one who is not inclined to medicine. Whatever you decide, your services will be much in demand."

"You think that I would be accepted by the colonists?"

Krolov looked at him. "That, I am not so certain of. It is not your past that is the barrier, you see. Many come here to leave a past behind that is, shall we say, less than pristine. It is not your past, Mr. Sinclair, that frightens them. It is your future. You remind them simply by your presence that you can never leave here. And the idea of that finality is a terrifying thing to them. That's why they avoid you. You remind us that we are all aliens here and that some of us will die here. No one likes to consider that possibility."

After they had moved through the infirmary, checking charts and adding new input and observations, the two men headed for the commissary. The rowdiest bunch, which had just arrived, was made up of Keyote miners heading home. They paced the corridors and clustered in noisy circles in the commissary, laughter exploding. Most of them had put in two Earth years on the Red Planet, and would never set foot on her soil again. Graham sat in a corner of the room, watching them as they ate, feeling the electricity of their excitement. There were a few, Baker had told him, who came to love the environment and had stayed, once their job contract was completed. Haas was one of the former miners who had chosen to stay on, joining the Ventures colony. Graham wondered if Paris liked the man enough to stay. She had given no indication of her decision in the last several comp-calls, only that they had all been working hard on Pod 9.

"There he is, my prince, all in white," Paris said, coming to his table with a food tray. "They told me I'd find you in here." She was jumpsuited, her hair in a tumble of wildness.

Krolov rose in the old tradition and Paris motioned for him to sit. "Is he a good student, Dr. Krolov?"

The old man smiled. "One of the finest. If only he had the heart for it, as well as the mind."

"Heart? Sinclair, you're not giving it heart?" Paris sat down and hit Graham on the arm. "Still withholding heart. Shame on you! He has that problem in other areas, too, Doctor."

"This is your lady?" Krolov said to Graham.

Paris beamed and nodded. "In a manner of speaking. We've met, Dr. Krolov. Tucker, Paris. Appendectomy. 6.10.2054.159."

"Ah, yes. Yes, I remember you."

Graham knew that Krolov not only remembered her, but kept extensive files on every member of every colony. To the researchers of the SURF base, all colonists were, in effect, laboratory animals in a grand experiment. No move went unnoticed or unrecorded. He was sure that if he were allowed access to her files or, for that matter, to his own, he would find references to the night she had spent in his room at the Ventures colony. The scientists were quick to note any pairings or "cross-colonization" efforts made by any member of any group. They seemed very pleased with the barter trade-offs between the Ventures and the Jeremians. The Sera colony, on the other hand, seemed like the problem child, shy, withdrawn, and unable or unwilling to mingle with others. That they had begun tentative craft making in pottery and glassblowing was looked upon with the excitement of a parent for its least demonstrative child.

"It is their *needs*," Krolov had once said to Graham, "that will ultimately decide the fate of humanity on Mars. If we are ever to make life on this planet work, it will be because of that magical something inside the human psyche that drives it to create what it most needs for survival. We are amazing organisms, are we not? That we are here at all, against all the laws of probability, that we *survive* here, in the face of impossible odds, speaks well of us as a species. We make mistakes. But we learn, and we improve. We adapt and create from *nothing* a world moving toward Eden." Graham wondered how he was perceived in their grand design. His only true need, he thought, was to go home. He had no desire to contribute to any Eden-in-the-making. What they were to conclude from that he didn't know. He was the one rat that did not run the maze.

"Are you happy to see me, dearest love-of-my-life?" Paris smiled, kissing the air in Graham's direction.

"That depends."

"On what?"

"On why you're here."

Paris looked momentarily puzzled. "I'm here with Haas to drop Simmons off and pick up the new settlers. You thought I was going to leave? Hey, I'm a Grit. Well, half a Grit. Okay, get technical, a quarter Grit. But I'm staying, Sinclair. Happy now?" She turned to Krolov. "This man never smiles. Have you noticed? Sinclair, it wouldn't break your face to indicate faint joy over my decision, you know. If it hadn't been for you I'd be gone. In more ways than one. You're the reason I'm here."

Graham glanced at Krolov. He was sure that somehow a notation would be made in their files based on that simple statement.

"If you'll excuse us," he said to the man, "I would like to show Miss Tucker where she'll be quartered while she's here." He took Paris by the arm, ushering her toward the exit.

"My food . . ."

"It will wait."

In the corridor he said, "Paris, in the future never discuss me or any private matter in front of others."

"Why?"

"That I ask you should be reason enough."

Paris shrugged. "What did I do? Did I embarrass you? I'm sorry. I have a hard time with pompous formalities. You can be awfully tight-assed sometimes, Sinclair. You really can."

She looked angry, but started blinking, as if fighting tears. Graham hoped that she wouldn't lose control in front of him. He felt awkward during emotional scenes and usually dealt with them by walking away. Paris Tucker, however, was not a woman who would react quietly to such a move. Of that he was certain.

"Have you been assigned quarters?" he asked.

"Not yet. Things get crowded around here when a cycler comes, I'm told. They're setting up extra cots wherever there's room."

"Get your gear. You can stay with me."

"Same bunk?"

"There are two beds. Haas can sleep on the floor, or bring a cot in. There's not much room, but . . ."

"He's already made arrangements to bunk with some of the miners from Keyote. He knows most of them, the ones leaving. It's like a reunion with these guys."

He went with her down to the air lock, where her duffel bag was stored in the changing room, and signed her in, listing his compartment number.

"So, are you glad I'm staying or what?" she said, following him down through various corridors and surface hubs.

"That's difficult to answer." He arrived at his room, pushed an ID card into the wall slot, and the door slid open. "If I say I'm happy that you've chosen to stay, it's a bit like being happy to have companionship in purgatory. I don't know how to answer you, Paris."

"You have a point. Hey, go ahead and be happy, okay?

I'm happy. I just had that weak moment, you know?
First-day-of-school jitters."

She stepped into the room. "Still looks clinical. Like a
private hospital room. Or maybe a dorm room. You need
a football pennant up on the wall, or a few posters . . .
some pictures of—" She stopped and turned to look at
him. "Oh, Graham, I'm sorry. I wasn't thinking. I didn't
mean—damn! Tucker, chew your foot off, why don't
you."

Graham placed her duffel bag on the bed nearer the
door. "There's a private hygiene compartment—no communal showers, I'm afraid."

"The highlight of my day. Pooh. You know, since Haas
has been panting after my body, Waverly's been really
nice to me. She's not such a bitch after all. And you know
something else? I think she really loves Vogel. She beds
down with Simmons every chance she gets, but she *loves*
that little gnome. Strange lady."

Graham handed her the key card. "I'm still on duty. I
have to get back. There's a film in the auditorium tonight,
if you get bored. I could meet you in the commissary
afterward, if you like."

"I'll wait and go with you. We could pretend it's like a
date. Real old-fashioned, like."

Graham shook his head. "I'm not allowed, Paris."

"Not even a crummy movie? Jeez! Is *any*body fighting
for you back there? Isn't anybody speaking for you?"

"I don't know. I don't think so."

"If I . . . go home someday, Graham, I will. I won't
let them forget you."

Graham turned to go. "You know how to find your
way back to the main hub?"

"I think so. Blue floor stripe to yellow floor stripe, turn
right. When you hit the red stripe take a left. Up one
level, then to the right. One thing I've got is a terrific
sense of direction."

"See you about twenty-three hundred hours?"

Paris nodded. "Commissary."

She wasn't in the commissary. Graham watched the room
fill with what would have been called the "after-theater"

crowd in another place. Simmons, who had shaved his
beard, folded his lanky frame into a chair at Graham's
table. "So where's Baker tonight, Cloud Man?"

"The name is Sinclair."

Simmons blew on his coffee. "You sure as hell did a
number on the guy. I guess you know that. Best damned
T.E. there ever was, and you just screwed his head around
backward. I don't know what you did, but you broke
him. Nobody else would touch you. Nobody wanted to
take you on. Did you know that, Cloud Man? But Baker,
he thought he could do it—get you to make the transition.
You destroyed a good man. I won't forget that."

Graham could smell the alcohol on his breath from
across the table. "Have you seen Paris Tucker?"

Simmons slurped the too-hot coffee. "She was hanging
around outside the auditorium. Said she was waiting for
you. Maybe she's with Baker. Maybe they're . . ." He
made some crude hand gestures that seemed to slur as
much as his speech.

The room was getting almost as rowdy as the *Ninotchka*, except that there was no music. Graham scanned
the faces, thinking that he might have missed her in the
crowd.

"Is it true they ban you from even watching a crappy
little news roundup from Earth?" Simmons was adding a
clear liquid to the coffee. "Well, somebody's gotta be held
accountable, don't you know? And you're the man. King
of the hill back there, weren't you? You know what you
are here, Sinclair? You're"—he drew his right index finger
and thumb together—"nothing. Big as a freaking zero."

Graham rose, not quickly, but in a manner that would
not indicate hostility to the inebriated man. Simmons still
braced himself for attack, attempting to rise from his
chair, but it tipped back, causing him to fall over. Heads
turned in his direction, but Graham had already left the
room.

"Did you *see* what the guy did to Simmons?" said one
of the miners to another. "Knocked him over without
touching him. I swear!"

Somewhere, a bottle broke. A metal chair flew across
the room. In moments the air was filled with fists and

bodies and roars of approval as the miners entertained themselves in their own way.

Graham checked in the emptied auditorium but there was no sign of Paris. Nor was she in the library. He went by the infirmary but no one had seen her. Something, a very soft trickle of concern, pushed its way into his mind as he headed back toward his own quarters. He pressed on the automatic door release and it slid open. The room was dark, but from the dim light in the corridor he could see that there was a figure in his bed.

"Paris?" The door slid shut, leaving the room in total blackness.

"Don't . . . turn on the light." Her voice sounded muffled, but not from sleep.

Graham touched a wall unit that brought up a soft light.

"Don't!" Paris pulled the covers over her head.

At first he thought she had been crying and simply didn't want him to see her. He reached down to pick up her jumpsuit. He had never picked up after another person and was about to comment on the fact when he saw the spattered wet stains on the light blue collar. It was not tears, but blood.

"Paris . . ." He reached out to pull back the covers.

"Don't! Leave me alone."

Graham yanked back the covers as Paris curled up into a tight fetal position, covering her face with one arm. There were bloody smears on her upper arms and raw, angry scratches along her back. He could already see the beginning bruises across her thighs and the bluish marks where fingers had wrapped around her ankles and wrists. He sat down on the edge of the bed and tried to push her hair away from her face.

"Paris, who did this?"

She would not look at him, but curled into an even tighter ball. "Doesn't matter."

Slowly he drew her arm away from her face. It was puffy and tear-streaked. One eye was swollen almost shut. A cut on her lip still oozed blood. "It matters," he said.

She refused to go to the infirmary and begged him not to report what had happened. "I forgot . . ." she said as he washed her cuts and the smears of dried blood from

her body, "that there are still lower life forms in the universe. I was waiting for you. I didn't go to the film. I
figured . . . ow, I think a tooth is loose. I figured if you
couldn't see a damned movie, I didn't want to see it either. I went down to the far end of one of the CELSS, to
see what they have growing. SURF has things we don't
have. Did you know that? Do I look just awful, Sinclair?"

Graham gently washed her face. "I wish you'd let me
take you to the infirmary. You could use some stitches.
Your lip is still bleeding."

Paris ran her tongue over the split on her upper lip.
"It'll stop. It feels funny, like about out to here. I guess I'll
look worse tomorrow, huh? Anyway, there was nobody
around. Or so I thought. Then these two clowns . . . I
think, hell, I know they were miners . . . I've lived butt
to butt with men for almost a full quarter of a Mars
year . . . about a hundred and seventy sols so far. And
not one, not *one* has ever bothered me. Miners are scum,
here for what they can take, and then they split. Haas is
the only human out of the bunch and he's not real high
on the evolutionary ladder. Oh, Graham, don't look at
me. I'm so ugly. I feel so ugly all over!"

He could not elicit any description of the two men, but
let her talk out the wired tension until she finally fell into
a fitful sleep. He covered her with a second blanket and
sat across from her on the other bed, watching, for the
rest of the night.

CHAPTER 16

She would not leave his room the next day, nor would she describe her assailants to Baker when he came to ask her about the incident. "We'll get them with or without your help, Paris. No lander and no rover goes anywhere until they come forward and confess—"

"Don't hold your breath," she mumbled.

"—or until the computer scan matches the blood type and genetic print we picked up from the clothes Graham gave us."

"Damn you, Sinclair. Keep out of this!" She heaved a shoe at Graham across the room.

Baker sighed and sat on the second bed. "You have to at least sign the form, Paris, or we can't move on them once we know who they are."

"Fine. I don't care. Let 'em go. I thought you lost all your law clout when you resigned, Baker."

Graham placed her shoes together near the bed. "Couriers have legal authority above colony law, Paris. That's why I asked him to talk to you. But even Baker can't help you if you don't sign the complaint."

Paris pulled the covers back over her head. "Just go away. I want everybody to just . . . go away, okay?"

Baker got up. "I'm leaving the form here on the desk. Think about it. We'll know who they are before this day is over, Paris. The next move will be up to you." He gestured for Graham to follow him out into the corridor.

"I'm sending Dr. Siegler down to talk to her. Maybe she can convince her to act on this."

"Why Siegler?" Graham didn't know the woman well, but was under the impression that she was more involved with files and charts than people. In her late twenties, with a severe knot of copper hair at her neck, she seemed to speak in terms of statistics if she spoke at all.

"She has a background in trauma counseling. Besides, women deal with each other better in things like this. Maybe Paris will talk to her."

Graham had only a general idea of the structure of Martian planetary law and how it applied to him person-ally. He remembered references to the legal hierarchy when Baker tutored him on Martian colonial life while aboard the *Olympus Mons*. Each colony set up its own rules and punishments within guidelines approved by Earth law, as he understood it. The SURF base acted as final legal recourse for disputes that a colony couldn't settle. The research facility had the right to eject anyone from the planet and return them to Earth. They also had the ultimate right to decide what deterrents and monitoring devices to use, should there be any serious transgression of the law. Graham wondered if Paris had refused to co-operate because she knew the standard deterrent for sex-ual violence was a form of chemical castration.

"If they threatened her," Baker said, "then that might mean these were men who aren't leaving Mars yet. They may be here for R and R, or to pick up the next load of miners coming in on the *Romanenko*."

By evening Paris had signed the complaint, one miner had been identified and the second implicated in the as-sault.

Haas, when informed of the incident, was so enraged that he was placed in temporary seclusion until the two miners were safely off-planet. Their trial would take place aboard the *Ninotchka*, Graham was told, and sentencing carried out once they reached the cycler.

Paris would have to remain at the SURF base in order to be available for questioning via satellite, Baker ex-plained the next day.

"Will they be able to see me?" she asked. "On the screen?"

"Yes. And you can see them. It's the law, Paris. The accused has the right to be faced by his accuser. It shouldn't take long. The second one has already admitted his participation in the act."

Paris moved around the office that served all legal functions for the facility. Graham watched her from the doorway.

Dr. Siegler sat to one side of Baker's cluttered desk. "They won't be allowed to return here, if that concerns you."

Paris ran her hands through her hair, combing it with her fingers. The swelling of her left eye was almost gone, but her face still looked bruised. "How long would this . . . sentence last?"

Baker looked at Siegler. "Ten years for the second man," he said. "The other one had a prior conviction on Earth."

"That means for good, then? For the rest of his life?"

Siegler nodded. "Can you handle that?"

Paris shoved her hands into her pockets. "At first, I was just very embarrassed. Very confused, like maybe I had somehow brought it on myself, you know? Now, I'm angry. Now, a lifetime doesn't seem long enough. Yeah. I can live with that."

She turned to Graham. "Sometimes the law doesn't seem fair. Other times, it works. I just want to make sure I'm not the cause of an innocent person's pain."

Baker sat back in his chair. "In this particular case, Paris, you were the innocent person. The guilty ones will pay."

It was later, as Paris lay in her bed in the darkness of Graham's room, that she told him how her parents had died. "My father was accused of raping a village woman when I was fourteen. He was innocent. Later she recanted. But the damage had been done. The shame and the stigma destroyed him. He . . . shot my mother, then killed himself, while I was away at school. I always thought that if they could have just waited, let time put distance between them and that awful disgrace . . . But he couldn't let go of it. He couldn't wait. It was an ugly, cowardly thing to do. I suppose, if I had been home at the time, he would have killed me, too. Sometimes I still have this cockeyed impression that he didn't love me enough to . . . include me. I was left behind. This was a man who had taught me that life offers us endless options. He just picked a really lousy one. Am I boring you, Sinclair? Say something, or are you asleep?"

"I'm awake. It explains some things about you that I didn't understand."

"Like why I'm such a mess? The way I look at it, everyone's life becomes a Greek tragedy eventually. So you might as well enjoy the comedy parts while you can."

She was silent for a while, then he heard her get up and move across the room. "Graham? Tonight, I'm the one who needs the favor. Can I crawl in with you? No strings, no demands?"

He opened the covers and she slipped into his bed. She snuggled against him like a child and he instinctively put an arm around her. He could feel the healing scratches along her back and for a moment an acid fury raced through him. He had to withdraw mentally from the emotion in order to regain control. The suddenness of the rage surprised him. Overt anger was something he had long held in check. To let it loose in business was to destroy delicately constructed bridges between parties. Anger in business conveyed weakness and vulnerability. To unleash anger socially was a sign of poor breeding, immaturity, and emotional instability. It simply wasn't done. Graham stroked her back, gently. "I'm sorry this happened to you, Paris. I wish I had been there."

"Good thing you weren't," she murmured. "You would have added more notches to your myth. Rumor would make it ten men dead, seven permanently crippled."

"Starting tomorrow I'm teaching you T'ai Chi."

"T'ai Chi? Isn't that the exercise thing you do? Where you make like bugs and birds and stuff?"

"In a way. It's a form of self-defense, among other things."

"I was thinking along the lines of a gun, actually."

"This will be good to know, even if you never need to use it."

"Maybe two guns." Paris yawned. "One on each hip.

And bullets, bandoleer style, across the boobs. What do you think?"

"Let's try the martial arts first."

Paris put her arm around him. "Okay. Grasshoppers, then guns."

Graham watched her carefully for signs of delayed trauma, but Paris seemed determined to continue as if nothing had happened. She emerged dry-eyed from counseling sessions with Dr. Siegler, and reported for buddy training with new arrivals, helping them become acclimated to their new environment.

Each morning she went through T'ai Chi exercises with Graham in the SURF gym before he went to work. She was a good student. He hadn't expected her to embrace the philosophy, but she seemed eager to understand. Her movements, which had always seemed to border on awkward to Graham, became fluid and graceful. Several members of the SURF community who exercised in the gym stopped what they were doing to watch them, then asked to learn the movements as well. Before Graham realized it, he was teaching a T'ai Chi class every morning before he reported for duty in the infirmary.

The final lander arrived with the last of the new colonists and miners, and Paris finished her video testimony before the *Ninotchka* tribunal.

"I'll miss being your roomie," she said to Graham as they shared lunch in the commissary before her departure.

"What about Haas?"

"It's okay. I told him you're an ascetic."

"I'm not."

"Well, damn."

Graham smiled slightly.

Paris sat back and threw up her hands. *"Now* he smiles. All this time I thought you were practically going into the priesthood here, and you weren't abstaining at all. Just not interested, huh?" She threw an ice cube at him. "No sacrifice, no self-denial, just not interested. Thanks a lot. Does a helluva lot for my sense of womanhood."

"Paris, I admire you greatly . . ."

"But no heat in the loins . . ."

". . . and I respect you, your courage, your intelligence . . . I value your friendship. You know that."

Paris made a face. "I think I liked you better when I thought you were abstaining—denying your carnal lust for me."

He walked with her down to the changing room where the new Ventures colonists were easing into their MEMUs. Haas and Cabot, the T.E., were admonishing those who were slow. "Nobody's going to be around to help you in an emergency, Larson. Get with it, man," Haas said.

Paris turned back to Graham before heading off to climb into her LCG. "The Summer Solstice . . . the Jerrys make a big deal of it with some kind of festival. A bunch of us are going over on sol 343. Would you come?"

"If I can."

Paris rolled her eyes. "Jeez, it's *Martian,* not an Earth custom. Nobody's showing home movies for chrissake. Who would say no?"

"I'll come if I can."

She touched his face. "It'll make it easier for me if you just say yes."

"I'll check with Baker. I'll let you know."

After the last of the rovers had left, the new colonists had dispersed to various destinations, and the returnees to Earth had departed, the SURF base seemed emptied of life. "It always feels this way after the campers are gone," Baker said as he and Graham swam laps in the pool. "The external chaos settles, then the paperwork chaos starts. New files opened, old files closed, updates, logging new data. All the craziness goes on in the labs now."

"New guinea pigs for the cages," Graham said, pulling himself up onto the edge of the pool. "Jon, tell me something. Is Siegler in charge of my file?"

"Why do you want to know?"

"I'd like to take a look at it."

"You can't. It's classified. All colonist files are classified. What makes you think Siegler is in charge of yours?" Baker treaded water, then climbed out of the pool.

"Just a guess. I think she monitors Paris Tucker, as well. How do they divide the colonists up? Siegler gets the Ventures; Winston, the Jeremians; and so on?"

"No, not exactly. I'm not supposed to be talking about this, you know. You're not even supposed to be aware that files are kept, but since you're involved with the medical aspects of the process, we can't keep that information from you."

"Do you have a file?"

"Yes. Everyone does."

"Everyone's part of the grand experiment, then. Even the SURF researchers themselves."

"Yes, to a degree."

Graham brushed water droplets from his face. "Do you have access to your own file?"

"No."

"Just . . . how closely are we monitored?"

"Closely."

"Big Brother close?"

Baker didn't answer, which, Graham realized, was an answer, and one that did not surprise him.

"They don't interfere. They just . . . observe and record. Don't get paranoid about it, Graham."

"You still have to report on me, don't you? You didn't quit at all. You're still a T.E., still *escorting.*" He moved over to a bench and began to towel off.

Baker followed him over. "I'm not a T.E. anymore. I don't have to restrict your movements and I don't censor you."

"But you still report everything I do. Or is it all on-screen somewhere? Little devices tucked away in corners, in my room, behind mirrors . . ." Graham stopped and stared at Baker. The man's silence confirmed his growing suspicions.

"In my room? In my quarters?"

"Not in every room."

"But in *my* room. Infrared? Then they know that I have the pouch with the jade."

Baker nodded. "They know. But as long as you keep it out of sight they can't do anything about it. I got shit for giving it back to you, if that means anything."

"Where else do they watch? Where is there any privacy left us?"

"Surveillance equipment was installed in the main hub of every colony. And in the pods after they're built. The Ventures don't know. That's it. They don't watch everything, Graham. Just gathering places and the CELSS areas here, to observe social interaction."

"Like the social interaction that was inflicted on Paris? Did they watch that?" Graham could feel self-control slipping away like cut twine.

Baker did not look at him. "They . . . can't interfere. It's one of the prime directives in contemporary anthropology."

Without warning Graham slammed a fist into Baker's jaw, sending the man sprawling across the wet concrete. "Put that in your file."

In his room Graham searched for the bugging devices. He knew what to look for and the places most often chosen for such equipment from years of corporate surveillance tactics. As he located each one he ripped it out and dropped it in the toilet in the hygiene compartment. The final assault was on the mirror over the combination desk and bureau. He didn't bother to unbolt the mirror from the wall. Instead, he heaved a chair through the glass, shattering the elaborate camera equipment behind it.

"It won't do any good," said Dr. Siegler, watching from the doorway. "They'll just replace it all."

Graham ignored her and continued to yank the wires and equipment out of the dark space behind the splintered glass.

"Mr. Sinclair, if you can't calm yourself within the next thirty seconds I guarantee you'll find yourself in seclusion. You broke Baker's jaw. We have a right to restrain you . . ."

Graham upended a bed, then moved to the hygiene compartment where he broke the second mirror with a fist. "Do what you do so well, Dr. Siegler. Observe. Take notes. I'm not finished here."

"Oh, yes you are, Mr. Sinclair."

Graham had seen a stun gun in action but he had

never felt one. It was much more painful than he had imagined it might be. The security team rushed him once he was down, and Siegler finished him off with a potent sedative that was unceremoniously jabbed into his backside.

CHAPTER 17

He woke on the floor of a seclusion room, which was well padded, clear to the ceiling. Someone had put a fresh white jumpsuit on him and bandaged both of his hands and his right arm. He did not remember being cut by glass but vaguely recalled blood on his clothes. Or had it been on Paris's clothes . . . things were not clear. He sat up. His body ached. His left leg still tingled where the stun gun dart had struck him. Tentatively he touched his face with the tips of his fingers that were free of bandages. The stubble told him he had been unconscious for a number of hours, possibly all night. An overhead light was bright enough to read by, and he could see the outline of a door, also heavily padded, but no sign of any window.

He got to his feet, searching for the camera he was certain watched him. "I know you can see me," he said. "And hear me. I need to urinate."

No voice responded. After a moment there was a soft whir and a wall unit opened to reveal a urinal jug. As soon as he had relieved himself the unit closed and padding slid over the metal plate. Graham pictured specimen bottles being rushed off to various laboratories. Somewhere, Dr. Siegler was busily charting the results. He had an urge to laugh but supposed it was a lingering side effect of the sedative, or of something else that had been administered while he was unconscious. He sat down and tried to meditate, but the sense that he was being watched kept interfering.

He asked for water, and another slot opened in the wall to present a plastic cup with an attached top and spout akin to a baby's first drinking cup. Graham suspected that the liquid contained another sedative, for after he had drunk the water a sudden drowsiness came over him.

The next time he woke, the overhead light had been dimmed. The left sleeve of his jumpsuit was pushed up and a small bandage over a vein told him that they had taken a blood sample. Or perhaps he had been given an IV. He couldn't tell. Something about the situation reminded him of "The Pit and the Pendulum." He wondered who now owned his copy of Poe's *Tamerlane*, and what had been the highest bid. The longest anyone had been kept in seclusion in the SURF medical division was three sols, as far as he knew. He estimated that he had been there for at least two sols, although he was not remotely hungry. He wondered what would happen if he asked for food.

"May I have something to eat?"

A whir and a click behind him made him turn around. It was a liquid diet. "I was hoping for something a bit more substantial," he said. The wall unit closed. Nothing more was offered.

Graham sat back down on the padded floor and began unwinding the bandages on his hands and arm to inspect the damage. He counted twenty-seven very neat stitches and wondered if Krolov had done the work. He had watched the man perform several surgical procedures and had been impressed with his precision.

A wall unit opened, unbidden, to produce another filled drinking cup. "No, thank you," Graham said, not moving from where he sat on the floor, gauze bandages in a heap. "I don't care to be drugged into oblivion again. I would like to be released now, however." He waited for sounds of locks unlocking but there was only silence. He wondered what would happen if he started braiding the long gauze strips into a noose. It didn't take them long to open the door.

Dr. Siegler, her hands deep in the pockets of her white lab coat, looked irritated as a medic entered the room holding a pressure syringe. "You have another twenty-four hours in seclusion, Mr. Sinclair. Now either you co-operate and let Maxwell rebandage your cuts, or we can do it without your interference."

Graham sat still while the man wound fresh bandages around his hands and right arm.

"Why did you do that?" Siegler said, watching him.

"Do what?"

"Make the noose. There is no way to hang yourself in here, Mr. Sinclair."

"I simply wanted you to open the door. And you did."

Siegler, he decided, was one of those rare women who actually did look most striking when enraged. It pleased him to be able to enhance her looks so acutely. He would have to see how often he could manage it in the future.

"Not so tight, Maxwell," he cautioned. "It must be late if you're on duty. Who's filling in for me?"

"DeMarco."

"Did Krolov do the needlework?"

"Yeah."

"I thought so. He's very good."

"I assisted," the man said, not without some pride.

"Did you? Sorry I couldn't watch."

Graham glanced up at Siegler and thought that if she got much angrier she would fall over in a ravishing froth. He supposed that she had expected him to protest further time in seclusion. That he was not reacting in some pre-dicted manner seemed to be pushing her beyond what might be called livid, he thought.

"How is Baker's jaw?" he asked her.

"Wired!"

"Good."

Maxwell finished his work, gathered up his tray of medical supplies, and departed.

"Dr. Siegler?" Graham said as the woman was about to close the door.

"Yes, Mr. Sinclair?" Her eyebrows were arched, expec-tant, waiting for him to plead some kind of forgiveness in order to gain freedom.

"Would you please cancel my barber appointment for tomorrow?"

She slammed the door in a manner that indicated complete loss of clinical professionalism. Graham stretched out on the floor and went to sleep.

It was Krolov who released him finally, opening the door himself. Graham had the impression that the man had overridden someone else in order to free him, perhaps a whole committee of sorts. There was a subtle anger in his voice as he helped Graham to his feet. "There was some concern. You refused to eat, even when offered a general diet."

"I didn't care for the menu."

"I see."

"Also, the thought of being watched while sitting on a chamber pot didn't appeal to me."

Krolov chuckled. "Yes. I sympathize. Seclusion is a drastic measure. But you must admit, you were not yourself."

They moved out into a corridor that was empty. "I disagree, Dr. Krolov. I was very much 'myself.' You simply haven't had the occasion to observe that aspect of my behavior. I seldom have need of it. I assume it has now been well documented."

The older man nodded. "To an infinitesimal degree. Come. I would like to examine your hands. I must say I was most concerned about them, but the lacerations for the most part were superficial. If you feel up to it you may return to your duties this afternoon."

His room looked as if it had never been ransacked. Another mirror was over the bureau-desk, and all the surveillance equipment, he was sure, was back in fine working order. He removed a drawer and felt behind it where the leather pouch was taped. Everything was in place. He had a momentary adolescent urge to drop his clothes and moon the mirror. The thought jarred him slightly. He felt as if the veneer of his maturity and reserve was eroding, much as the Martian landscape was sandblasted by endless harsh winds. All of his cultivated remoteness was wearing down to painfully raw flesh. The feeling was dangerous and new to him. And somehow it was intoxicating.

Baker was in the infirmary, sucking a liquid meal through a straw when Graham appeared. "Feeling better?" the man asked through clenched teeth. "What the hell happened to all that Zen cool?"

"Taoist."

"Whatever."

"I never claimed to have reached perfection."

"Now you tell me.".

Graham looked at his chart, punching in a request for close-up views of the X rays. It had been a serious fracture. He knew that had he chosen to land the blow a few inches in any other direction he could have easily killed the man.

Baker held out his right hand. "Still friends?"

Graham put the chart away in the slot at the end of the bed where it would continue to monitor the vital signs of the patient as long as he was lying down.

"No."

"Graham, you're angry with a system. It doesn't have a face. Don't confuse it with our friendship. You can't break a system."

"Then you'll have to do." He moved on to the next patient, a miner suffering from a laser burn to the left shoulder.

That Baker was no longer someone he could trust or respect saddened him far more than he had expected. He had insulated himself from close relationships early in his life and separations had seldom touched him deeply. But those that had left wounds that had never truly healed. On Earth his isolation had been cultivated by his own design and he had relished it. Now, however, circumstances inflicted isolation upon him in a way that he was growing to loathe. He doubted that Baker could comprehend the depth of despair this severance of friendship caused him.

Baker made numerous attempts to engage him in conversation over the next several sols. Graham was courteous but coldly reserved. In business the tactic could push an executive to the point of nervous prostration. Graham had used such maneuvers at times to drive a man to resign from a company in which he was entrenched like an embedded hook. He made sure that the executive was included in every meeting, then was exquisitely ignored, passed over, or made socially invisible. It was a calculated cruelty, taught him by his grandfather, who found confrontational firings distasteful. Graham had used it only as a last-resort weapon, although the tactic was one of long tradition in corporations. That he used it on Baker, though in a far milder form, made his anger clear, even to himself. Baker, however, did not give up.

Several SURF staff members had asked Graham to continue the T'ai Chi training in the early morning hours, and Baker began to show up, jaw still wired, to receive instruction.

"What did you do to Siegler?" he asked as Graham adjusted his stance for the Snake Creeps Down movement.

"Nothing. Why?"

"She's royally pissed at you. Has been ever since you were put in seclusion."

"You're not concentrating. Breathe."

"I'm breathing."

"Deep. From here." Graham made a move to touch Baker's abdomen and the man instinctively drew back as if to ward off an attack.

"I don't think you're truly relaxed," Graham said to him, moving on to another student. "Remember, proper breathing is essential. *Chi* means breath-energy. It's your life-energy. You're filling the Tan Tien with this energy. Taoists call this 'Before the Gate of Heaven Breathing.' Carol, close your mouth. Breathe through the nostrils."

He watched as they moved slowly, some executing the movements with skill, others with little or no understanding of the underlying purpose of each motion. He was too aware of Baker's nearness, and finally called a halt to the day's instruction.

"I'm not sure I can continue to do this if you insist on participating," he told Baker after the others had left the gym.

"What am I doing wrong?"

"You exist."

Baker considered for a moment. "There's not much I can do about that."

"I've asked to be transferred to the Keyote mining colony."

"I know."

"If I'm free to come and go as I please, why are they keeping me here?"

"You wouldn't like the colony, Graham. It's not what you're looking for."

"You know what I'm looking for, and it's not on this planet. If I am to live in exile, then at least grant me the freedom to choose my place in hell!"

"You haven't completed your medical training."

"I have no desire to advance beyond certification as a medic. Keyote can make use of me at that level, I'm told."

"Why Keyote? Any of the other colonies would be preferable. You've never been to the Jeremian or Sera colonies. At least take a look at them. The Jerrys are celebrating the Summer Solstice on sol 343. Would you come with me? I know that Paris Tucker invited you."

Graham could feel a heat rising again into anger. "Of course you would know that."

"She *told* me, Graham. She wanted to know if you were allowed to attend. I said yes. That's all."

"You can rerun the tape of the encounter in the changing room if you like. I don't recall the exact sol, but I'm sure it's on record. It is a gathering place, after all. You realize someone is recording us now, all of this, watching." Graham looked upward. "Good morning, Dr. Siegler!"

Baker picked up the jacket of his sweatsuit from the mat. "You do this a lot? Talk to the cameras?"

"Every chance I get."

"Just to remind them that you know they know you know . . ." Baker rolled his hand to indicate endless loops. "No wonder Siegler hisses your name. Well, are you going to the festival or not?"

"I'm going."

"Good. So's Siegler. This should be a real fun trip."

CHAPTER 18

They left before dawn, the rover heavily loaded with boxes of supplies that would be divided up among the three colonies participating in the celebration. "It will save us a trip," Baker explained, wedging more supplies into every available space. The SURF base, like the Ventures colony, had an underground loading dock, but on a far grander scale. Rovers and landers passed through air locks, then moved down a tunnel and emerged in a hangar-sized area. Here, loading and unloading could be done and repairs could be made without the inconvenience of the cumbersome MEMU hard suits.

"It's about a twelve- to fourteen-hour drive without any detours, folks," Baker said as he set dials and tested instruments on the panel of the rover. "I've left just enough room for one person to sack out at a time."

It would be a five-sol trip, Graham was told, with three sols for the festival. "It's important to be there for the dawn service, to watch the sun come up," Baker explained as they waited for the outer air lock to open.

Siegler, sitting in the copilot seat, was scribbling notes. "It's a young tradition," she said, "in terms of planetary customs, but it's become a major symbolic gesture for those who observe the occasion."

"And this one is doubly important because . . ."

Baker caught himself when the woman shot him a look that clearly warned him into silence.

"Because," said Siegler, "it's the fifth one."

"And it happens to fall on December twenty-fifth, Earth time," Graham said from the seat behind Baker.

Siegler turned to look at him, making eye contact for the first time. "How did you know that, Mr. Sinclair? You aren't permitted a timepiece."

"I can calculate, Dr. Siegler." He had made a small Earth calendar aboard the *Olympus Mons* and hidden it inside a study manual, along with the circular Martian calendar Baker had given him. For some reason it was comforting to him to be able to know the seasons on Earth and how time passed at home as the Martian sols crept by with a deadly sameness. Graham wasn't certain that there would be any real exterior change of season on the planet as his first Martian year dragged by. He had been told there would be evidence of some snow in the winter, but that was all. The temperature inside the CELSS modules never varied more than a few degrees.

"Since you calculate so well, Mr. Sinclair," the woman said, "were you aware of the significance of your attack upon Mr. Baker? As to the date, I mean?"

"Yes."

Siegler's strawberry-blond eyebrows went up. "Really?"

"It was a year ago, to the day, that I was expelled from Earth."

The air lock clanged open and they moved off into the darkness. Baker cleared his throat. "I hope you don't plan to celebrate that anniversary in quite the same way every year."

"In seclusion?"

"Breaking my jaw."

"We took that into account, Mr. Sinclair," said Siegler, "that you might have been subconsciously aware of the anniversary and were under extreme stress at the time. We didn't realize that you were actively aware of the date."

"I didn't wake up that morning and decide to break Baker's jaw after breakfast. It was an impulsive reaction to something I considered an abomination."

"You were about a breath away from killing this man. Do you know that?"

Graham gazed at the woman. "If I had intended to kill Jon Baker, I would have. And you know that. Don't you, Dr. Siegler."

Baker sighed. "It's going to be a long trip."

Siegler seemed to be having some trouble controlling her flared nostrils. Her chest, Graham noticed, was becoming taut in an amazingly erotic manner. She reminded him of a tightly clenched bud swelling and unfurling into a rose of wrath.

"You might be interested to know, Mr. Sinclair, that you were under consideration for a mood stabilizer implant. If you lose control again as severely as your last little episode, the procedure is a certainty in your future. Be reminded of that before you display your oriental little . . . *talent,* again."

It had been an exhilarating game right up until she said checkmate. She had won, and they all knew it. Graham had seen—indeed—had dealt with M.S.I. recipients. They were frightening to the point that he avoided business contact with them as much as possible. Relentlessly pleasant, they moved in a way that made him think of poorly constructed cyborgs. He remembered how his grandfather had ranted against the medical devices when they first became the wonder drug of the day. "Give me schizos and suicidals and manic-d's any day over those damned smiley faces!"

They drove in silence through the Martian night, small wisps of ground fog swirling in the rover's headlight beams. It could have been any desert at night. Graham craved to see a jackrabbit race across the road, or a lizard scurrying off into the dark. But nothing alive was out there, watching. Not so much as a one-celled spark of life.

A voice over the radio transceiver broke the tension. *"Rover K-12, Rover K-12, this is SURF Base One calling. Do you copy?"*

Baker adjusted the headphone and answered the call.

"Rover K-12, you have a dee-dee on your tail, traveling approximately eighty kph in a southwesterly direction. It should appear on your screen in about four minutes."

Graham watched the green radar screen as a small blip

appeared. The dust devil, if it continued on its current path, would intersect with the rover within twenty minutes.

"We're hours away from the nearest pod," Siegler said. "Can we dodge it?"

"Well, we're certainly going to try," Baker said, nodding. "They're a tad whimsical, however. It may decide to dodge in the same direction."

The blip, like a heat-seeking missile, seemed to be looking for them in the darkness. That he could not see the ruddy-colored funnel shape undulating on the horizon did not comfort Graham.

"Is everybody buckled down?" Baker asked. "Hang on, we may catch the ring on the merry-go-round."

The green blip seemed to be racing parallel to them now and inching closer with every sweep.

"Oh, God," Siegler murmured. "I think I see it."

Baker veered to the right, bounced off the road, and headed out across open terrain, weaving between boulders and rocks big enough to damage the rover's undercarriage.

A fist-sized rock smashed against the window next to Graham. It was followed by pellet-sized stones that bounced against the rover like granite-hard hail.

"Everybody! Hard suits, now!" Baker shouted above the roaring wind.

Graham could feel the vehicle slide sideways, as if it had spun out of control on an icy road. He now appreciated Baker's obsessive drill in speed suiting. Supplies that were not securely tied down flew across the interior of the rover and spilled out over the floor. Another rock smashed against a window, leaving a spidery white crack in the outer glass. Rocks bounced off of the metal hull of the vehicle making so much noise that it was useless to shout. One of the headlights blinked out. In seconds the wind had passed, carrying its destruction down through dry ravines and broken craters and channels.

"We just caught the edge of the lady's skirts," Baker said, finally. "Just a slight breeze, if you will. Is everybody okay?"

Siegler had to be coaxed out of her MEMU. Once they

were back on the road she climbed over into the bunk space, turning the copilot seat over to Graham.

Sipping coffee through a straw, Baker said, "They don't come much closer than that and leave anyone around to talk about it. Is she asleep?"

Graham looked back. "If she sleeps with her mouth open, then yes, she's asleep."

"She does. Sleep with her mouth open."

Graham didn't have to ask how he knew that.

"About what Siegler said earlier, about them giving you an M.S.I.—she wasn't kidding, Gray."

"I've never considered the good doctor to be a kidder."

"Just . . . be careful. Don't give them any reasons. They think an implant would help you adjust better."

"Smiley faces in hell," Graham murmured.

"What?"

"Don't let them do that to me, Jon. If there is anything left of what was once a friendship, you won't let that happen to me."

"I don't have a lot of power with them. The only reason they listen to me now is because they think there's still a bond . . . that I have some influence over you. But if you . . . exhibit any more extremes, they'll do it. They will."

Graham watched the road which was illuminated by the one remaining headlight. "If . . . they do . . . promise me something. Kill me. Because I won't be able to. I would do it for you, if you asked me."

"I know."

"Promise me."

Baker looked over at him, his face lit by the greenish light from the radar screen. "Let's hope it doesn't come to that."

For a brief moment Graham thought he saw a jackrabbit caught in the beam from the headlight, but it was only fog.

CHAPTER 19

The Jeremian colony had a far different external appearance than the Ventures' eccentric architecture. Although its center dome was identical to the Lodge hub of the Ventures colony, and the initial spokes out to smaller hubs were of the same government-constructed materials, there were far more above-ground circular structures. The size of football fields and covered with geodesic domes, these were the farmlands of the Jeremians.

"There are 150 members at present," Siegler said to no one in particular as they approached the commune. "We aren't certain how the factions will split, but the division looks imminent. A number of the Ventures have begun work on an ambitiously large pod near Jovis Tholus in exchange for food, clothing, and other barter items. If the separation from the parent colony succeeds, it will be the first Mars-spawned colony."

"What's causing the split?" asked Graham. There had been no hint of disharmony in the cheery little travelogue introductions to the colonies he had viewed before leaving Earth.

"Philosophical and religious differences," said Baker. "I've always found it paradoxical that the very thing that draws us together also scatters us."

"How many factions are there?"

"Hard to say. At least three."

Siegler glanced over at Baker. "You will be civil to Jacob?"

"I will be civil to Jacob."

"You won't disrupt the proceedings?"

"My opinions will remain private."

Graham watched the two from his seat behind Baker. He wondered how long the relationship had been going on. There were moments that made him think they had been bonded for an eternity.

"Jacob is the leader?" he asked.

"Yes," Siegler said.

"For now," Baker added.

"How do they decide a leader? I know Vogel heads the Ventures, but how was he chosen?"

"Force of personality." Baker shrugged.

"The most obnoxious person wins?"

Both Siegler and Baker laughed, but it was private humor between them. Graham had never seen Siegler so much as smile before. She leaned toward Baker, placing a hand briefly on his right thigh. "He may be right," she whispered, but Graham still heard her.

Baker looked back at Graham. "Jacob is not what one would call congenial."

"He was the one responsible for your banishment from the commune?"

Baker's jovial mood dissolved, as did Siegler's.

"Yes. But there were other reasons, too."

Siegler could be eloquent with eye communication, Graham noticed. Her look now warned him to back off. "Mr. Baker's past is not your concern, Mr. Sinclair."

"It's all right, Risa. I told him a little about it."

"So," Graham said, "the SURF base is run by committee vote, the Jeremians and Ventures by charismatic personality, and the Keyote mining operation, from what I gather, is akin to a benign dictatorship."

"Not so benign," Baker said.

"And the Contaminants—the Seras—what about them?"

"A true democracy," said Siegler, going back to her computer notes.

"And every move, every decision they make, you document."

"Graham, don't start," Baker warned.

"I would just like clarification on one point, Dr. Siegler."

The woman turned in her seat. "And what is that, Mr. Sinclair?"

"If they had killed Paris Tucker, would you have simply watched? Made a small adjustment in your statistics and closed her file?"

"Yes, Mr. Sinclair." Siegler retreated to her most clinical pose. "That's exactly what we would have done. You needn't be so arrogantly moralistic about it. The human race has documented its own behavior since cuneiform tablets. At one time we watched our wars like daily installments of a soap opera. People died on the evening news while we watched from the dinner table. And if we happened to miss the little dramas, they were replayed endlessly, until we were comfortably glutted on gore. We are doing nothing that hasn't been done for centuries. We are simply trying to understand the human animal. We will not interfere with the course of its development."

"Thank you, Dr. Siegler. That's all I wanted to know."

The Jeremians had an air-lock system similar to that of the SURF base in that it could accommodate landers as well as several rovers at a time. Graham could see Paris waving even before he emerged from the vehicle.

"We were getting a little worried," she said. "What happened to the rover?"

"We skimmed a dust devil," said Baker as he directed the unloading of supplies.

Paris frowned. "Why are you talking funny?"

"A small accident."

"I broke his jaw," said Graham.

"Oh, jeez. Doing T'ai Chi? I mean it was just an accident, right? Oh, Baker, you poor baby. Can you chew?"

"Not yet."

"We've got this absolutely fabulous spread for tomorrow and he can't eat. My worst nightmare. He's a walking illustration of my worst— Dr. Siegler! Didn't know you were coming!" Paris grabbed Graham's arm and muttered, "My other worst nightmare. Why didn't you tell me she was coming?"

Graham looked back at the doctor. "Does it matter?"

"Only if one enjoys probing questions about one's pre-natal life. Come on, guess where you're staying while you're here?"

"With you?"

Paris released his arm. "Well, you don't have to, Sinclair. I'm not forcing you. But you might like to know that *your* worst nightmare is here, too."

"Waverly?"

"And Vogel."

"I would be delighted to share your quarters, Miss Tucker."

"That's what I thought."

A gray-haired woman in a long brown robe of coarse-woven material descended steps to the floor of the receiving room. She was followed by two other women, much younger, but similarly dressed.

"Jacob wishes to extend greetings to our guests," the woman announced. "Rachel and Hannah will show you to your rooms. I'm sure you wish to rest and freshen yourselves before the evening meal at six."

Baker, Graham noticed, seemed uncomfortable as he approached the woman and made introductions. "Graham, I would like you to meet my mother, Elisabeth Hobbs Baker."

Graham glanced at him as the woman extended her hand, palm up in the fingertip greeting to which he had once been accustomed.

"Yes"—Baker nodded—"Jacob is my father."

"Jonathan, why are you speaking with clenched teeth?" his mother asked. "Surely the occasion isn't that distasteful to you."

"Jaws are wired," he said.

"Oh, my. What happened?"

"Ran into an opinion."

The woman looked puzzled. Paris, however, gave Graham a look that clearly said explanations would be expected shortly.

Siegler greeted the woman in a cheek-to-cheek air kiss. "It's good to see you, Elisabeth. You look well."

Baker declined to follow the group, choosing to stay
and supervise the unloading of the rover.

"You'll have to see him eventually," the older woman
said to her son. "You can't avoid him entirely."

"I can try."

"Jon, don't be rude," Siegler warned.

Paris, with a questioning look, turned to Graham and
moved two fingers together. He simply nodded.

The room to which they were assigned reminded Graham of a combination of tropical bungalow and convent.
A plaster crucifix hung on one wall above a bamboo
double bed. All of the furniture, in fact, was made of
bamboo and woven rattan. He assumed that it was one of
the crops in the enormous CELSS modules he had seen on
their approach to the commune.

"I told them we were bond-pledged," Paris said, patting
the down-filled comforter on the bed. "So you'd better be
sweet to me, Sinclair. You'd better treat me like we're
betrothed, or they'll cut off something, and I'm not talking social invitations, here. These people take bonding
very seriously. Like for life, none of this renegotiable contract every-five-years business. I mean forever unto death.
Did you know Baker's parents headed the group?"

Graham moved about the room, looking for surveillance devices. "No. He neglected to mention it."

"Surprised the hell out of me. And what's this lovey
stuff from Siegler? When did that happen?"

"Quite some time ago, I suspect."

"Prunelips and Baker. Now that's an ungodly coupling,
if ever I saw one. Second only to Vogel and Helga the
Hun." Paris tried to bounce on the bed but there was no
bounce. "Our first double bed. Things are looking up.
What are you doing?"

"Examining the construction of the furniture. Very
nice workmanship." Graham stooped to feel beneath the
bedside table. His fingers felt the circular disc. He pried it
loose and slipped it into his sleeve.

"They're aiming eventually to duplicate every kind of
agricultural environment found on Earth, so I'm told. Cullen, rather *Brother* Cullen, one of the Jerrys here, told me
about an ecological disaster they had a couple of years
ago. The SURF researchers gave them some new stuff to

try on the soil. It killed every worm in the ground. I never knew how important worms were. The CELSS had to be closed off—smelled like dead fish, Cullen said. Now, nothing will grow in the pod. They're trying to bring it back, though."

She watched Graham slide beneath the bed. "Looking for dust balls?"

"Not exactly."

"It's a sturdy bed, Graham. It won't collapse or anything."

He found the second listening device against the wall and placed the first one facedown on top of it. It was a simple method of scrambling that would send any listener through the roof and yet afforded the person under surveillance some privacy.

"You about through under there, Sinclair?"

He rolled out from under the bed and sat up.

Paris, lying stomach down on the bed, narrowed her eyes. "Something's different about you. What's changed?"

"Nothing."

"No. Something's not the same. Graham, look at me. What's going on between you and Baker? What's with this broken jaw thing?"

"It was just an accident."

"No accident. You had a fight, didn't you? What about?"

Graham got up. "I would like to shower and change. I assume the hygiene compartment is shared."

"Two doors down. What was the fight about?"

"Paris, you may play at bonding mate in social situations, but I would prefer some breathing space in private, if you don't mind." He had not meant to sound irritated, but Paris was clearly stung.

She got up from the bed and grabbed her belongings, stuffing things into a duffel bag. "Hey, fine with me. Take all the breathing space you want. Fill the old Tan Tien till it comes out your kazoo, buddy!"

He caught her arm and she surprised him with a well-executed T'ai Chi movement that demonstrated her growing skill in the art. He countered with a maneuver that he had not yet taught her.

"You going to break my jaw, too?" she snapped, slugging him with the duffel bag.

"Paris, stop it." He yanked the bag out of her hand and flung it across the room. In one swift move he pinned her to the floor and whispered, "There are listeners."

"What?"

He put a finger to his lips. "Listening devices," he whispered in her ear.

"Now I know what's changed," Paris said aloud. "You've gone nuts."

He dragged her to the bed, lifted the bottom of the coverlet, and pointed to the two metal discs against the wall.

"Oh, wow. Why?"

"I think that's all in here," Graham said, helping her up. "They may not be in every room, but I tend to be somebody's pet project. Siegler's, to be exact. Or some 'committee' of which she's a part."

"It's okay to talk?" Paris whispered, tucking her feet under her on the bed.

"I've neutralized the two I found. Just use some discretion."

"Why are they bugging you?"

"It's not just me. This entire planet is one grand anthropological experiment. They don't want to miss a second of its development in any direction."

"How long have you known about this?"

"A little while."

"Like about since Baker got his jaws wired?"

"About then, yes."

Paris nodded to herself. "Your room back at the SURF base . . ."

"That included video."

"Oh, boy. Just your room?"

Graham shook his head. "Surveillance is everywhere, there. They observe everything."

"Then . . ." She looked up at him.

"Yes, they saw it."

Paris reached for a pillow and hugged it against her as if to smother a sudden rage. After a moment she took a deep breath and said, "You should have broken Siegler's jaw, too. Does everybody here know they're being watched?"

"I don't know. I doubt it. The equipment was installed in the central hub of every colony when they were constructed. And in the pods after the Ventures were finished and gone. Baker says that's all, but he may not know beyond that."

"I should break Siegler's jaw. We should do something."

Graham picked up her duffel bag. "I don't think there's much anyone can do except lodge a complaint about invasion of privacy. I have no rights so I can't protest anything they decide to do concerning me."

"What do you mean, you have no rights?"

"Mars is my prison, or have you forgotten that? I lost all rights and the privilege to determine my own future a year ago in a courtroom on Earth. They can do whatever they please with me, as Dr. Siegler recently reminded me."

Paris took her duffel bag and began to fold her clothing back into neat bundles. "You're right. I do keep forgetting you don't want to be here. That you didn't choose to come to Mars. I'm sorry. About the snit I was in. I . . . get a little possessive, but dammit, Graham, you keep sending these mixed signals, you know? I get confused."

"I don't mean to, Paris. I suppose it's because I've never met anyone quite like you before."

She looked down at her denim overalls. "Not your type, huh? Not the kind you'd take to the opera, or sailing on your yacht, or whatever you do with the kind of women you hang out with. All those A-Class types."

Graham watched her attempt to smooth down wild curls with her fingers. "First of all, I seldom had the time to 'hang out,' as you call it, and second, I've simply never had a woman friend. I don't know what to make of such a friendship. All I know is that I treasure it, and I don't want to lose it."

Paris stretched out on the bed and propped her head with an elbow as he placed his own belongings on a shelf in the corner. "Would you have ever maybe asked me out, sort of, if you'd met me back home?"

"I doubt that our paths would ever have crossed."

"That's true. I'd probably have been the waitress you'd have left an enormously obscene tip for, after a dinner at some hot-snot restaurant. Did you have a yacht?"

"Yes."

Paris got up on her knees in the center of the bed. "No kidding? How big?"

"I don't know. It belonged to my grandfather. I inherited it along with everything else."

"You never saw it? You never went sailing?"

"There never seemed to be time."

"You never took a vacation on your own boat? Didn't you ever have fun, Sinclair?"

He had to think for a moment for he knew that it was the business structure itself that seemed to give him the greatest pleasure. He wasn't sure what Paris would label fun, but he didn't think it was corporate dealings. "I occasionally played polo."

"*Polo?* Of course he would play polo," she groaned, falling back on the bed.

"And I rather enjoyed antique race cars."

"Antique race cars. Of course."

She was beginning to sound like Maggie McKay, he thought, making his background seem distorted and abnormal, somehow.

"You were *real* rich, weren't you?"

"Yes. Now, can we drop the subject?"

"Just *how* rich were . . ."

"Enough, Paris."

"Okay. I forgive you."

"For what?"

"Being A-Class. It wasn't your fault. Somebody raised you right, in spite of the money. You're all right, Graham Sinclair."

CHAPTER 20

Jacob Baker was an imposing figure. He looked to Graham like a man who could have easily added several more commandments after Moses had finished taking dictation from God, and no one would have argued with him. His face was framed by a flowing mane of white hair and a gray and white beard. At sixty-two, he was the oldest colonist on Mars, besting Dr. Krolov by five years. Graham discovered that Jon Baker was the youngest of five sons, and the one upon whom his father had depended to lead the Jeremians eventually. The older brothers, though they had entered the ministry, had all refused to follow the family to the new colony on Mars.

"So, Mr. Sinclair, you are the one responsible for breaking my son's jaw," the man said as the commune gathered in the large feast hall. "No doubt he deserved it."

"Jacob, please," said his wife.

" 'If I do not remember thee, let my tongue cleave to the roof of my mouth; if I prefer not Jerusalem above my chief joy.' " The old man glared at his son, who sat at the far end of the table, but within earshot.

Graham was seated to the man's right, and Vogel, somewhat slighted, was placed several seats down the long table. There was a hush, and heads bowed all around the room at other tables while Jacob turned grace into a fairly lengthy sermon on prodigal sons.

The meal was elaborate and well prepared, with a variety of meats Graham could not readily identify. He passed over them in favor of vegetarian fare. Paris lost her appetite only momentarily after discovering that she was feasting on guinea pig. "I thought it was rabbit or something," she mumbled.

"I noticed, Mr. Sinclair," said Jacob, "that you participated in our custom of bowing one's head during grace. I was under the impression that you were not a Christian. Was I mistaken?"

"I follow Taoist teachings, but I was exposed to Christian beliefs as well, in my youth. It has always been my custom to honor the customs of my host."

"I would never bow in your temple. I have no tolerance for pagan beliefs. 'I had rather be a doorkeeper in the house of my God, than to dwell in the tents of wickedness.' "

"Psalms 84:10," Graham said with a nod. " 'Because men do not understand, they have no knowledge of me.' "

Jacob frowned. "Are you quoting the Bible, Mr. Sinclair?"

"Lao Tzu."

" 'Should a wise man utter vain knowledge, and fill his belly with the east wind?' Job 15:2."

Graham sipped wine from a finely crafted goblet and decided that someone in the Ventures colony was getting more proficient in wine making. " 'Heaven's net casts wide,' Reverend Baker. 'Though its meshes are coarse, nothing slips through.' "

Jacob sat back in his chair, obviously relishing a worthy opponent. "Are you familiar with Proverbs 2:21 and 2:22, Mr. Sinclair?"

"Yes."

Baker, at the far end of the table, started to rise. "Father, the man is your guest!"

Siegler yanked his sleeve to pull him back into his seat. "You promised," she hissed.

Paris watched the confrontation, forgetting to chew.

" 'For the upright shall dwell in the land, and the perfect shall remain in it.' " The old man scowled. " 'But the wicked *shall be cut off from the earth,* and the transgressors *shall be rooted out of it.' "* Jacob waited while Graham tore bread from a round loaf.

" 'The Tao of heaven is impartial. It stays with good men all the time.' " With that, he offered the bread loaf to his host.

Jacob slapped the table so hard that Paris jumped. "I like him! Welcome, Mr. Sinclair!" He took the bread and tore off a generous chunk. The rest of the meal passed with the two men discussing the similarities in the teachings of various great religions. By the end of the evening it occurred to Graham that had this been a business transaction back on Earth, Jacob would be ready to sign any agreement that might have been proposed.

"How come you're so up on the Bible if you're a Taoist?" Paris asked once they had retired to their guest quarters.

"I was sent to a Jesuit school in Switzerland for two years when I was fourteen. My grandfather decided that since he couldn't eradicate my grandmother's influence on me, I should at least be armed with knowledge that would serve me in a Western society." That he had also been sent to the school to hide him from the assassins who had murdered his parents was something he didn't think Paris would understand. That he had gone from there to a Tibetan monastery for two more years was something his grandfather never understood.

"Well, you sure impressed the hell out of the old man. You were probably better than a rejuvie blood-wash for him. I don't think he has many people buck him publicly. Or privately, for that matter. I'd guess Baker was the last one to dare disagree with him, and he got pitched out bag and baggage, as I understand it."

Graham stripped down to T-shirt and shorts and settled into a lotus position on the floor while Paris watched from the bed. "I guess you can't do that and talk, too, huh?"

"They don't go hand in hand, no."

"Should I go for a walk till you're done?"

"You may join me if you'd like."

Paris slid out of bed and sat on the floor, facing him.

She had on a much-oversized white T-shirt. "It belongs to Haas," she said. "Are you jealous?"

"Why should I be jealous?"

"I was just hoping. That you might be. Just a little."

"Concentrate."

"I can't."

"Breathe."

"That I can do." After a moment she opened her eyes. "How long does this take?"

Graham sighed. "Forever, if you don't be quiet."

A minute of silence passed. Paris scratched her nose. "This is really boring, Sinclair."

He opened his eyes and looked at her in silent reproach.

"Okay, I'll be quiet," she said, closing her eyes as if about to leap into cold water.

Another minute passed before she asked, "But how *do* you know when you're done?"

Graham got up and climbed back into his clothes.

"I'm sorry. I'll be quiet. I will." Paris made a zipping motion across her lips. "Where are you going? Are you mad at me?" She jumped up, brushing her seat.

"For a walk, and no, I'm not mad at you."

"Can I come with you?"

"No."

"You're mad."

"I'm not mad. I don't get mad."

"You just break jaws during disagreements. I'm not criticizing! I wish I'd been there. You will come back?"

Graham opened the door and stepped out into the dimly lit corridor.

Paris watched the door close and plopped down on the bed to wait.

He was back in seconds.

"That was fast," she said.

"Waverly's on the move."

Paris smiled.

Graham carefully lifted Paris's left wrist to check the time. It was after two in the morning. Although he had not slept since two A.M. the day before he was restless and wide awake. He looked at the double timepiece and saw the Earth date. December 25, 2054. In two weeks he would be thirty-four. He had to think for a moment to account for his thirty-third year. It had gone too quickly, spun away too fast. Here, the year was only half over and he had spent only a little over a quarter of it on the surface of Mars itself. And yet, if one measured time by events instead of numbered sols, it seemed that a decade had passed since that last green day of freedom, drifting above treetops in a rainbow-colored balloon.

Slowly he rose from the bed, pulling the comforter up over Paris's shoulder as she slept. He slipped into his clothing and left the room. They had been given a tour of the various CELSS modules earlier in the day, and it was to the tropical rain forest that Graham was drawn. He felt an intense need to return to it, perhaps to meditate, or just to be reminded of the world he hungered for. The environment was sealed off from the rest of the adjoining modules to maintain the humid warmth, and he had to pass through two linking chambers before coming out into its lush beauty. Moonlight from Phobos bathed the cultivated jungle in a cold blueness. He could see the trickling waterfall splashing into the dark pool, but a vital ingredient was missing—the night sounds. There were toads and insects, but no birds, no monkeys. There was too much silence. The facsimile almost mocked him in its falseness.

A movement near the edge of the pool caught his eye. A woman stood, poised, her nakedness framed by plants like ivory against jade. Her body arced into the water and disappeared beneath the surface. Graham drew back into the shadows to watch as she burst to the surface and swam, rolling onto her back, her long hair flowing around her like dark seaweed. She emerged from the water, sleek and glistening, and wrung droplets from her tresses. He thought it best not to startle her under the circumstances and remained very still as she drew on a white robe and began to braid her hair there in the moonlight.

Suddenly she froze, seeming to home in on him in the darkness. "Who's there?"

He did not want to frighten her further and stepped

out so that she could see him. "I apologize. I didn't think anyone else would be here at this hour."

"Mr. Sinclair, is that you?"

"Yes. How did you know?"

She was across the pool from him and somewhat in shadow. He had no idea who she might be, although he had met a number of the Jeremians that evening.

"You're a bit taller than most," she said.

"I didn't mean to disturb you."

She moved gracefully through bushes and between vines, making her way around the pool to where he stood. "Please don't tell them you saw me. It's really not allowed, swimming here."

She was small-boned, her face a delicately carved cameo. Water droplets still glistened in her hair and on her pale skin. He had never seen her before. He would have remembered such exquisite beauty in any woman.

"The wrath of Jacob would be worse than the wrath of God if he knew I swam here. You won't tell?"

"No. I might have been tempted myself."

"You're up a bit early for the Solstice, aren't you?" Her smile reminded him of something but he couldn't remember what. It felt warm with approval and oddly reassuring. In the moonlight she looked no more than seventeen, but her voice had a soft richness that would place her in her mid-twenties, he decided.

"Up a bit late, I think, actually."

She blotted her face with a towel. "It will be two hours before the others start to rise . . . if you want to take a swim. I'll be a lookout, if you like."

"I'm afraid I didn't come prepared."

"Such modesty, Mr. Sinclair. It's only fair. You watched me."

"Unintentionally. But without regrets."

She laughed softly and put her hand to her mouth. It was then that he recognized the ghostly familiar allure in her. With the long thick braid down her back she looked as his grandmother, Lihwa, might have looked as a young girl. Her eyes, though dark, were not almond-shaped, nor were there the innate shyness and delicate mannerisms traditional with Chinese women of the old culture, but there was still something . . . haunting in her.

"Who are you?" he asked, suppressing an impulse to touch her, to confirm her reality.

"Anna Leah."

Graham felt the name reverberate inside. His grandmother would have chided him for his inability to accept cosmic similarities.

"I don't remember you from earlier, at dinner," he said, wondering if she sensed his inner turbulence.

"Because I wasn't there. We were rehearsing for the play. I understand you gave Jacob a good tussle. I'm sorry I missed it."

"Play?"

"For part of tomorrow's festivities. I have no lines," she said with a laugh. "But it's a leading role."

"What do you play?"

"That would be telling, Mr. Sinclair. This is your first Solstice on Mars, isn't it?"

"Yes."

She walked with him toward the linking chamber. The circular Plexiglas door was fogged over.

"Brace yourself," she said. "It's going to feel like stepping out of a sauna into an arctic spring."

He hadn't realized how damp his clothes had become in the humid CELSS, until the more temperate climate hit him.

"Do you know your way back?" she asked.

"Yes."

"You should try to get some sleep before dawn. You're in for a long day tomorrow." She hesitated, looking down at her bare feet. "We were instructed not to discuss certain . . . topics in your presence, Mr. Sinclair. Would I be overstepping bounds in wishing you a Merry Christmas?"

"What topics were you told to avoid?"

Anna Leah looked away, clearly embarrassed. "Things concerning Earth."

He had thought she was referring to religious topics. He was not prepared for mass censorship of those who came into contact with him.

"Jacob decided this?"

"No. It was understood from the beginning. We were told never to . . . I'm sorry. I shouldn't have said anything." She turned and fled down the corridor before he could respond.

Baker was not alone when Graham slammed his door open and turned on the light. Siegler sat up, then dove under the covers as Baker lurched naked from the bed.

"Christ! Graham, at least knock!"

"Don't let him hit you!" Siegler shouted from under the covers. "He's crazy, Jon!"

"Did you censor this whole planet?" Graham said, his anger quiet in a way that made Baker freeze.

"What?"

"Did you instruct everyone on this entire planet about what could and could not be discussed in my presence?"

"No."

"Then who did?"

"Who have you been talking to?"

"Who told these people never to mention things concerning Earth while in my presence?"

Baker sighed, pulling on a dark brown burnoose. "It was an edict from the court, Gray. No one expected it to be enforceable. They can keep current events on Earth from you, to a degree, and they can block all correspondence, but they can't actually stop people from saying things. Unless it's done in public. Then they could be punished, yes."

"What correspondence?"

"Mail. Addressed to you. Or to SURF officials. Tons of it."

Siegler stuck her head out from under the covers. "Shut up, Jon. You've said too much already."

"You shut up, Risa," Baker said. "It's not hate mail either, if that's what you're thinking. Most of it is from Universal Amnesty. It seems you're looked upon as something of a political prisoner now. You're becoming a cause célèbre back home. Nobody here wants you to know that, especially the Committee that was established specifically to look after your needs."

Siegler sat up in bed, her breasts at attention. "I'm going to have to report this, Jonathan Baker. You're interfering in Code One business. If you don't cease immediately—"

"He has a right to know!" Baker wheeled on her, his own anger spilling over. "Ow! Oh, shit." Blood began to dribble from his mouth.

Siegler gasped. "Oh, my God."

Graham reached for a towel on the back of a chair. "He pulled some wires loose in his jaw. He'll be all right."

Baker sat down on the edge of the bed and held the towel to his mouth while Siegler scrambled for a robe and ran to a water basin on a stand.

"All of this is your fault," she snapped at Graham, holding a straw in a glass while Baker rinsed his mouth, spitting blood into the basin. "Does it hurt?"

"Hell yes, it hurts," Baker muttered.

"Don't talk. Rinse."

"He had a right to know."

"He lost every right he ever had, for the rest of his life. You know this. Jon, you've got to separate yourself from him. You'll contaminate the entire project if you keep interfering."

"Project?" Graham said.

Both of them turned to look at him.

"Uh . . . your . . . adjustment," Baker said.

"To Mars," Siegler added.

Graham nodded. Baker did not lie well. It would take time, but he would find out. As he left he turned and said, "Oh, by the way, Merry Christmas."

CHAPTER 21

The dawn of the Summer Solstice was steeped in religious ceremony. Jacob, a true showman, Graham decided, mounted a long, pointed sermon on the subject of the division of seasons, ostensibly aimed at the factions within the commune, he assumed. Everyone assembled in a CELSS module called the Congregational Garden. It seemed an architectural blend of Greek amphitheater and terraced step garden. Concrete slab benches formed a semicircle up a steep incline that reached to the very top of the CELSS enclosure. All around the edges, on each tier, flowers bloomed in a heady abundance of sweet smells. A vine-covered rockery supported yet more flowers of every shade and hue. Bees were busily at work, and Graham noted several hives on platforms off to the edge of the garden. At the base of the semicircle were a stone-floor stage and a pulpit, also made of stone. Behind it was a cream-colored drape that extended to the edge of the stage, providing a neutral backdrop to the profusion of color. Jacob preached on as the sun rose in the pink and salmon sky.

Paris yawned. "I hope we can go back to bed when this is over," she whispered. "This dawn doesn't feel one bit different from any other dawn. They all start too early."

Graham sat beside her on one of the long concrete

benches, trying to search out one face in the crowd, one particular dark braid down a back.

It wasn't until another member of the congregation rose and began reading from Luke, chapter two, that he saw her.

" 'And it came to pass in those days, that there went out a decree from Caesar Augustus . . .' "

The drape was pulled back to reveal a living tableau of the Nativity scene and there, bent over a manger, was the face he sought.

What he had deemed lovely in moonlight was radiant at dawn.

"What are you smiling at?" Paris whispered.

"Paradoxes."

"He finally finds something funny and I don't know what it is."

"Intriguing, not funny."

Paris looked at him, then back to the stage. "You've gone gaga over the Virgin Mary. Wouldn't you know it. Sometimes I could really hate men."

"Do you know her?"

"Not personally. She was before my time."

"I mean the girl. Anna Leah."

Paris shrugged. "I've seen her around, but I don't know her. You want me to deliver your love note? I always got stuck passing the love notes in school. *I* never got a love note. I just delivered damn messages."

A choir burst into song and everyone stood up. Graham rose but did not participate in the singing. It was, he thought, the first music he had heard since his arrival on Mars, and he found it deeply moving.

After the service he tried to make his way down to the stage, but Jacob grabbed him and launched into a monologue concerning age-old theological issues. By the time Graham turned around the actors were gone, manger and all.

He could not find her at the Solstice feast that evening, although a number of the actors who had appeared in the Nativity tableau performed scenes from Shakespeare's *Twelfth Night*.

Graham waited until Siegler got up to return to a laden buffet table and Paris was off talking to one of the actors before he asked about her. Leaning over to Baker, who sipped a mushy liquid concoction through a straw, he said, "Is everyone here? All the Jeremians?"

"No. One group doesn't approve of all this. They're off fasting in their rooms. To them this is a hedonistic debauchery. Sodom and Gomorrah on Mars."

"I take it they're one of the splitting factions."

"Oh, yes."

"How's the jaw?"

"Tender. Kind of you to inquire."

"Is Anna Leah one of those who disapproves of this?"
Baker looked at him. "Who?"

"The Madonna, from this morning. She said her name was Anna Leah, but I don't see her here."

"Anna Leah Moineau." Baker smiled. "You do have fine taste, Graham. That's a rare tropical flower if ever there was one. She's . . . no . . . she's not one of the factions."

"Have you known her long?"

"Since she was sixteen. Six Earth years . . . no, seven, now. So when did you two, uh, meet?"

"Last night in the rain forest CELSS. Just briefly."

Baker nodded. "Ah. Now I understand about what had you ticked off. She must have mentioned Earth and got panicky about it. Graham, most of these people avoid Earth topics around you not because of the edict, but because they don't want to cause you discomfort. Anna Leah is a very . . . well, she senses things. She knows inside people. It's like a gift. And whatever she may have said to you must have upset you. And she realized it. And I'll lay odds she took off like a proverbial rabbit."

"Something like that, yes."

"Anna Leah's not fond of large gatherings such as this. She told me once that it was like a thousand whispers just beneath the surface of speech. She picks up what's being said and what's being thought and sometimes layers beneath that, where there are no words and no images, just core emotions. When people stare at her and keep saying, 'How did you know that?' then she knows she's been responding verbally to information that hasn't been *offered* verbally. It spooks people."

Graham declined more wine when a server came

around, placing his hand over the glass goblet. "And she's an actress? That's what she does?"

"No. She was just asked to participate in the Nativity scene. What she does, is that." Baker pointed to the goblet.

"She makes wine?"

"No . . . she made the goblet from which you drink your wine."

Graham frowned. "I thought the Seras were the glass-makers."

"They are."

Graham took his hand away from the glass. "She's . . . not a Jeremian?"

"No. She's one of your dreaded Contaminants. So are the actors who entertained you this evening."

Graham fought to maintain a neutral calm. Clearly, it did not work, for Siegler commented on his expression when she returned to her seat.

"Mr. Sinclair, you look as if you've swallowed something inedible. Did meat pass your lips by accident?"

"Risa," Baker began, shaking his head.

"What did I say?"

Graham excused himself and left the room.

Paris saw him leave and started to follow, but Baker caught her arm. "He's okay. Just leave him alone for a little while, Paris."

"What happened?"

"He found out that Anna Leah is from the Sera colony."

"I could have told him that."

"Graham does not react well to—"

"Yeah, to Contaminants. I know. A-Class prejudices are hard to overcome. They like their vestal virgins to arrive with a warranty."

He was sitting on the floor in a lotus position when Paris opened the door. She hesitated and started to withdraw, but he called to her. "It's all right. You didn't disturb me."

"You're finished?"

"Yes." He got up and moved to the bed, peeling down

to T-shirt and briefs. "It feels late. Are the festivities over?"

Paris waited until he was beneath the covers before turning off the light and undressing in the dark. "It's about two. Things were breaking up, yeah. Hey, Sinclair, I've got good news and I've got bad news. Only maybe you might think it's bad news and more bad news."

He could hear her moving about the room in the dark. He didn't think he wanted to hear any more bad news. Although he had gone longer than forty-eight hours without sleep before, he didn't relish the idea of embarking on a third day with no rest beyond brief meditation.

"Aren't you going to ask me the good news, at least?"

"What is the good news?"

"Thought you'd never ask. You're going to be staying here somewhat longer than you expected. So am I."

"How long?"

"I don't know. The most definite time Baker could give me was 'indefinitely.' That's the good news. I knew you'd be excited."

"I assume the bad news is the source of the delay."

"You got that right."

He waited, but she did not elaborate. "So, tell me the bad news, Paris."

"I don't know if you can handle it, you're so ecstatic over the good news."

"I'm pleased to be stranded anywhere with you, Paris. Did a rover break down?"

"No."

"An epidemic? We're all in quarantine?"

"No."

"Paris . . ."

"A dust storm. A dust storm's moving up from the south. They're tracking it and it should hit sometime within the next two sols." She moved closer to him. "You really mean you don't mind being stuck here with me for maybe quite a while? Like months, Baker said. It could last for weeks or months. It'll be our first Martian dust storm. And we're sharing it together. It's a little like being snowed in, don't you think?"

Graham hardly considered months of blinding red dust romantic, but did not say that to Paris.

"The Grits seem pretty calm about the whole thing," she continued. "I watched it on the radar. It looks like a green amoeba oozing up. It's really big. Fills the whole lower part of the screen."

"Sounds like a xenomoth."

Paris smacked him on the chest. "I'm talking facts here. Jeez, Graham, what is that? You've got a lump on your chest!"

He grabbed her wrist but she was squirming into a sitting position, groping for the light.

"Don't," he said, but she turned on the light next to the bed and reached toward him.

"What have you got under there?" As she started to reach toward his T-shirt he sighed and removed the small leather pouch from beneath the shirt, lifting it over his head.

"What is it, besides Earth-made and totally verboten?"

"It was given to me by . . . a friend when I left Earth . . ."

"A woman?"

"No. A boy. He was my valet."

"Your *valet*? You're kidding me. You had an honest-to-God valet? Like, 'Here, let me polish your shoes, sir'? 'Let me grovel at your feet, Master'?" She opened the leather pouch and dropped the smooth piece of jade into her left hand. Her expression altered from mocking incredulity to quiet somberness. "It's beautiful. It's so . . . green." She touched it to her cheek. "And cool." She looked at him and tears began to spill over.

"Paris, what's wrong?"

"Nothing. I'm just so glad they let you keep this."

And so he told her about Ti and how the pouch had been taken from him and then returned. "If it's discovered on me, they can still take it away."

"What became of him? Of the boy?"

"I don't know."

Paris returned the jade to its place of safekeeping and draped the string of the pouch around his neck. "Well, we'll just have to find out, that's all."

"No. You'd be breaking the law."

She turned off the light. "I'll think of something. Don't worry."

Long after he thought she was asleep, Paris whispered, "She *is* beautiful, Gray. I do approve. I just wanted you to know that."

It looked like a mountain growing even as he watched, an angry reddish-brown tidal wave building on the horizon. Graham stood in the Congregational Garden with Paris, who was not taking the approaching storm well at all.

"I feel like we should be heading for a shelter or something," she said. "Only we already *are* in a shelter. It looks ugly."

Waverly descended steps just above them, binoculars in one hand. "This is what separates the Space Larks from the Grits, sweetie. If you still think Mars is heaven after she's belched in your face for maybe five months or so, then you have the right to be called a Grit." She handed the binoculars to Graham. "Of course, in your case, Cloud Man, you'll always be a Lark, won't you? A very special Lark in a cage. That's a shame."

Graham grabbed Paris by the arm before she could swing at the woman.

Waverly backed away slightly, smiling. "Truths are truths, honey. He'll never earn the title of Grit. Because it's a *choice* you make. He understands. You think he'd ever set foot on this planet *voluntarily*? Or *stay,* of his own volition? Sweetheart, the man would be out of here on the next cycler if he had the choice. Am I right, Sinclair?"

"Why do you stay, Flora?" he asked, handing the binoculars to Paris.

"The challenge excites me. And the men. They're a breed apart, the men who come here. There's nothing like them left on Earth."

"In Vogel's case, that's a real blessing," Paris mumbled, watching the storm on the horizon.

Waverly stroked her neck and ran her hand slowly along her throat and down between her breasts as if wiping away sweat. "You can do better, Sinclair," she said, nodding toward Paris. "Let me know."

Paris shoved the binoculars back into Waverly's hands. "I think he's already let you know. You just don't listen."

Before Graham could step between them the two women lunged at each other, tumbling down into chrysanthemums and violets, rolling over geraniums, day lilies, and phlox.

"Don't you think you should do something?" Baker said, descending from the top of the tiered rows of seats.

Graham reached down and pulled Paris off of Waverly, ducking a wild-fisted backhand blow to the head.

Baker grabbed Waverly, whose face was hidden beneath a tumble of blond hair. Generous tufts of it were still in Paris's hands as she swore and kicked the air.

"This often happens just before a storm," Baker grunted, pinning Waverly's arms in a tight clinch behind her back. "It sets nerves on edge. Waverly, cut it out!"

"She started it!" the woman screeched.

Baker yanked her arm, making her flinch. "Listen to me. Vogel's not back yet. You know what that means. If they get caught by the storm . . ."

Graham saw the anger drain out of the woman. Her composure was immediate as Baker released her. "Where are they?" she asked.

"They were somewhere between Ceraunius Tholus and Ascraeus Mons when we lost radio contact. That's what I was coming to tell you."

Paris, dabbing at a scratch on her cheek, said, "What does it mean, no radio contact?"

"The rover has broken down and we don't know their exact location," Baker said. "Everyone was heading in from the construction site before the dust storm. All the rovers are back except the one carrying Vogel and the crew with him. We're sending a search party out. It's the timing that will be tricky."

"Do you need help?" Graham asked.

"You want to ride shotgun for me? The storm usually spins out a lot of dust devils ahead of it. I'll need somebody to track them."

"I'll go," Paris said.

"The hell you will." Waverly tossed her hair back and wadded it into a knot. "I'm going."

Baker sighed. "I'd like Graham with me this time. I've already chosen the third member. We leave in twenty minutes. You two please finish your fight in the gym, okay? You're going to face a pretty nasty storm from Brother Perry over the flowers, as it is."

"Who else is going with you?" asked Paris.

Baker kept his eyes on Graham as he answered. "Anna Leah."

Waverly nodded. "Good. She's better than radar, I swear. Well, go! Get out of here!"

Graham had not seen her since the morning of the Solstice, draped in virginal white and blue and posed like a statue in a cathedral. Now, in a cream-colored LCG, she moved like a ballerina in a warm-up suit, he thought. She would not meet his eyes as they boarded the rover in the docking hangar. He didn't know what to say to her, so he said nothing as they waited for Baker to finish a last-minute briefing with the other rover pilots.

"You've done this before?" he said finally, more to ease his own vague discomfort than to engage in small talk for social purposes.

"Yes."

"Do people get lost in these storms often?"

"No. Not often."

There was a long moment of silence before she finally looked at him. "It's more involved than a simoom."

"What?"

"A Martian dust storm . . . it's more severe than a simoom. And it lasts longer."

Graham had not been consciously aware that he was looking upon the approaching storm as if it were a dusty relative of the violent, sand-laden wind of African and Asian deserts. He wondered if this was an example of her peculiar ability, which he wasn't convinced really existed. Baker had a way of describing people that was, in Graham's opinion, less than clinically accurate. Still, he had a curious respect for the possibility of extrasensory perception. There were things in his life that he could explain in no other way.

Baker climbed aboard the rover and settled into the driver's seat. "I believe you two have met?"

"Yes." Anna Leah nodded. "Indirectly."

Five rovers fanned out across the plain, heading in a

westerly direction toward Jovis Tholus. Once they were off the road, maneuverability was more difficult in the loose red soil. Baker switched from wheels to tank treads, which slowed the vehicle considerably.

"We have two, maybe three hours, tops," Baker said. "Then we have to head back, whether they've been located or not. We can't risk more lives for the sake of the few."

Graham watched the radar blips. "You couldn't still search for them in the storm? On the radar?"

"The dust chokes any vehicle left out in the open for more than an hour. We could all be stranded. And you don't just sit tight and wait for the storm to blow over. Rovers don't have the capacity to sustain a livable environment that long."

Anna Leah sat forward, behind Baker. "Head off about eleven o'clock. Just a feeling."

The sky, which had been a relatively clear pink, was beginning to darken as if dusk were falling early. Graham spotted two fast-moving flashes on the screen. "They're directly behind us," he said. "They're too big and too fast to be rovers."

"Dust devils." Baker nodded.

Anna Leah watched the screen. "There's a ravine ahead about two kilometers. If you can reach that we'll be safer."

They veered off to the left of the path of the cyclonic winds that moved northward ahead of the storm.

"Move south along the ravine," Anna Leah said softly, closing her eyes. "One is hurt. The rover . . . is on its side."

Graham glanced back at her, then looked at Baker.

"She's never been wrong yet," Baker said.

Forty minutes later they picked up a faint signal. Baker relayed the message to the other rovers that began to close in on the area.

The dust storm was now so close that Graham could see electrical flashes dancing across the plain ahead of it. Seven dust devils swirled like a sensuous chorus line, dark umber funnels with an even darker roiling backdrop.

The sun was dulling into an orange ball in the west as

they spotted the overturned rover ahead in the ravine. Two other rescue vehicles arrived within minutes of Baker and helped to remove the men inside.

Graham knew who the injured man was, even as he was lifted from the damaged rover. By the giant-sized MEMU, he knew it was Haas.

"We was dodging three dee-dees," Vogel said as Haas was carried aboard Baker's vehicle. "There was no place to go but over the edge, into the ravine, and hope we landed right side up. We didn't. The walls of the damn ravine blocked our signal. I was about ready to take a hike when you guys showed up. Cloud Man, even you look good to me right now."

Six of the rescued men divided up to ride in the other rovers while Graham and Anna Leah eased Haas out of his hard suit. He was conscious, but the small trickle of blood from his nose and mouth indicated to Graham that there were serious internal injuries he could do little about. He administered first aid to the man and began antishock infusions and oxygen while Anna Leah assisted, handing him what he needed before he asked for it.

"He gonna be okay?" Vogel asked, looking back at them while acting as Baker's copilot.

"For now." Graham moved forward and leaned close to Baker. "We have to get him to the SURF hospital. There's internal hemorrhaging I can't stop. They could send a lander . . ."

Baker shook his head. "It might get to us in time but it would never make it back before the storm hit. Nothing can fly in that." He nodded toward the angry-looking cloud that loomed above them now, spanning the entire horizon to the south.

"Then radio ahead. Tell them to send Krolov."

He moved back to Haas, who seemed relatively comfortable except when the rover was jolted by rough terrain.

"Hey, Sinclair, why can't I have some water, man? I'm so dry I could suck rocks."

"Hold off till we reach the colony, then you can have a drink."

"Any wine left from the festival?"

Anna Leah smiled and wiped a trickle of blood from his nose. "We saved you some."

"Vogel said it was the best yet. Didn't bring us any, though."

"Don't talk, Haas. Save your energy." Graham watched the man's vital signs drop slightly.

"Am I busted up bad?"

"You'll be all right."

Haas tried to turn his head and flinched. "I'm afraid to ask her. She'll tell me. Sometimes you need lies, you know what I mean? If you hang on to lies long enough they might—" He closed his eyes as a jolt made him groan. "Are we about there?"

"Soon. About ten more kilometers." Graham added a drug to the IV cartridge. Anna Leah watched him, then looked away.

The dust storm hit before they reached the colony. The sun dimmed to a rusty flat circle hanging above Olympus Mons like the dot over an i, the way an adolescent schoolgirl might make it.

Anna Leah switched on interior lights as darkness enveloped them. Haas seemed to be sleeping. Graham checked his vital signs and increased the oxygen output.

The headlights of the rover illuminated only the gritty dust directly in front of them. Vogel let out a whoop as a horizontal beam of light pierced the blinding thickness. "The air lock! I see it. Straight ahead. Oh, baby, papa's coming. Keep smiling!"

The rover's engine was already beginning to sputter as they rolled down into the inner chamber after the outer air lock closed. It seemed to Graham to take an eternity for the air exchange light to indicate that it was safe to open the second sealed door. Once inside, the rover was met by a SURF team ready to rush Haas to the commune's hastily improvised trauma center.

Paris watched them converge on the man and then tried to follow, but Graham caught her hand and shook his head. "Let them do their work, Paris. They know what they're doing."

CHAPTER 22

It wasn't enough. Not even Krolov's consummate skill could repair the damage inside the man. Paris curled up in the huge T-shirt Haas had given her and wouldn't speak, choosing to remain in her room during the funeral service.

Graham sat alone in the Congregational Garden after everyone had left, watching bees go about their business despite the midday blackness outside the domed enclosure. The colony maintained an artificial day–night cycle, switching from solar power to auxiliary wind power. Even through the thick, insulated walls he could hear the howling wind and the white noise caused by the incessant pelting of sand and small stones against the sheltered environment. If he could see beyond the density of the atmosphere outside, Graham mused, and if trees could live in the openness of this savage display of Martian weather, they would be leaning almost horizontally. Occasionally a particularly large rock would bash against a window and cause a reaction from anyone in the vicinity.

"Thinking of taking up beekeeping?" Baker said, coming down the steps to sit on the tier of seats just above Graham.

"Jon, what happens when someone dies?"

"Are you asking me a theological question?"

"No. What happens here? On Mars."

"To the body?"

"Yes. And afterward."

Baker shrugged. "It's cremated. Just like on Earth. And the ashes placed in a mausoleum, or scattered, or given to the surviving family. Haas had no family, so there's no sense in shipping his ashes home. In fact he made a request to have his ashes recycled. Here. He would have stayed. He really did love the place. Not so many do after a few years. But Haas understood Mars. He was at home here."

"What happens after that?"

"I don't know. He goes to heaven. How should I know?"

"No, I mean, is there an inquiry? Does the SURF Council convene and review the circumstances of a death, to see how it might be prevented in the future?"

"It was an accident, Gray. Accidents happen. Are you feeling guilt because you couldn't keep him from dying? You did everything right. Even Krolov said so. Haas would have died no matter what anyone did. He was just out there too long."

"It was a preventable death."

Baker got up and moved down the steps to the floor of the stage. "Mars is a rough environment, Graham. Deaths will happen in ways we can never foresee."

"How do people die here? Aside from the Seras who die from genetic self-destruction. Accidents? Suicide? Murder? What has been the most common cause of death here?"

Baker leaned against the smooth stone pulpit and ran his hands along its edges. "After Martian Fever, accidental death."

Graham stood up. "Due to carelessness?"

"No. To . . . cosmic poor timing, okay? Dust storms. Zigging when they should have zagged dodging a dust devil. Not reaching help fast enough, like with Haas. Graham, what's the point? Nobody's going to stop death."

"No, but you could certainly slow it down. The average life span on Earth is 102.5 years. What is it here? Thirty-seven? That doesn't look good in the travel brochures. See Mars. Die young."

"We would prefer not to flaunt that statistic. So what do you propose we do?"

Graham moved down the steps. "For one thing you're appallingly disorganized as a functioning whole. You've let recurring weather conditions grind the entire planet to a dead halt. Nobody can get anywhere. Krolov is stuck here until the storm lets up. According to those who know, that could mean weeks or months. So what happens if someone in one of the surrounding colonies needs more than a medic can provide? There's no airlift, no rescue, no help whatsoever. No one is going to stop a planet-wide dust storm. And it's a fact of the Martian environment. Why in the name of common sense you haven't built some form of underground monorail system to connect the colonies, I can't fathom. Life on Mars will not flourish in isolation. It's the very interconnectedness that causes it to thrive."

"Supply and demand?"

"Yes. Among other things."

Baker wandered over to the geodesic-patterned windows. "Only so much financing is allotted us, you understand. Mars is still a losing proposition on the books. The only exportable product we have is the purest water available in the known universe. We're a curiosity and an exotic adventure, but eventually everyone returns home. Whether permanent settlement of Mars survives or perishes may well depend on the generation living here now."

"Then you had better start making some changes."

"How? Where do we start?"

"Isn't there any unifying leadership here? Some kind of council created by the leaders of each colony? To set long-term goals?"

Baker shook his head. "It's pretty much every colony for itself. These people are still trying to meet some basic survival needs, Gray. They don't have time to play politics. That's ribbons and bows on a box that's not even wrapped yet. Right now there's a hodgepodge of charismatic leadership. Can you picture my father and Vogel sitting down and working out long-range plans together? Jacob would pound the man right into the ground with a Bible. The barter system they have going now took two

Martian years and a lot of bickering and setbacks. It's very fragile, and nobody wants to mess with it."

"Who is the leader of the Seras? Is he here?"

Baker smiled slightly. "You've met her."

Graham frowned. "Who?"

Baker just looked at him.

"Anna Leah?"

Baker nodded.

"Then, with Krolov and Siegler here, you have representation from every colony, except the Keyote group."

"Actually, I don't know whether Keyote really qualifies as a legitimate colony," said Baker. "They're more a mining camp than a colony. They have no commitment to Mars other than how fast they can earn a fortune and get out."

"But anything that would make life here more tolerable should interest them. They're just as shut in as we are right now. If there's a serious accident there's no way they can reach the SURF base. An underground monorail system would benefit them as well as the other colonies."

Baker began to pace the stage. "Who should organize this meeting?"

"Why not you?"

"No, I can't. I'm no good at this sort of thing. Besides, sitting in the same room with my father is beyond his endurance and mine. Just my presence would doom the thing to failure. You do it! It's your idea. You've got the background for organizational planning. You understand the beast."

"Jon, you may forget my station on this planet. I don't. I have no rights and no voice in any decisions made here. Vogel would be the first to remind you of that fact. I doubt that he would consent to attend any meeting of which I was a part. He certainly would never agree to any idea I might suggest."

Baker bent to smell a cluster of violets. "I'm sure you've dealt with business adversaries much brighter than Vogel. How do you move a little mountain?"

"Make him think it was his idea."

"How do we do that?"

"Make Waverly think it was her idea."

Baker laughed. "Done."

CHAPTER 23

Vogel paced back and forth near Waverly's chair as Siegler, Krolov, and Anna Leah entered the conference room.
Jacob had already claimed the head of the table.

"What's he doing here?" Vogel said as Graham entered
the room behind Baker. "He's got nothing to do with colony business. He don't belong at this meeting."

"I invited him," said Baker, sitting down beside Siegler.
"He's acting as a Keyote representative."

"He don't represent Keyote. He's never even been up to
the mines, am I right?"

"Graham is being transferred to the Keyote mining colony as a medic. He can relay whatever transpires here to
the company reps—Tillman and the others."

Vogel made it clear that he was not happy about the
proxy representative, but he also could not cover his obvious nervousness about the gathering, in general. His
scowl was challenged by Jacob's own, which carried far
more power, Graham decided.

"Get on with this, Vogel," Jacob grumbled. "I have better things to do than listen to your petty sputtering."

"You want the Cloud Man here? Okay by me. Just
don't nobody say I gave him the invite. I want that clear.
Florie, write that down."

Waverly tapped a note into the clipboard-sized computer in front of her.

"She's gonna take down everything, stuff we talk about. That okay with everybody? I don't want none of this stuff, you know, like lost. I mean, it could be historical, right?"

Siegler rolled her eyes. "I assume she will correct your grammar for the sake of posterity?"

Vogel sneered. "I'll show you posterity, Prunelips." He turned his back on the group and started to wiggle his hips.

Krolov smothered a laugh with an attack of throat clearing.

Jacob pounded the table. "Either conduct yourselves in an appropriate *adult* manner or I adjourn this meeting!"

"You didn't *call* this meeting, old man!" Vogel shouted. "*I* called this meeting. Who says SURF has gotta have two reps anyway? Prunelips over there can take her la-de-da college degrees and her fat fanny outta here."

Baker stood up. "The SURF colony is the largest group, next to Keyote. Dr. Krolov would be representing the medical department and Dr. Siegler, the scientific department."

"Jeez, I should be happy you don't have a rep from the janitorial department," said Vogel. "Or is that why you're here, Baker? Just who invited you? You don't belong *no*-where."

"*I* invited him," Waverly said. "He's like an arbiter . . . if we should need one. He's involved with *all* of the groups. And he's committed to the development of Mars. We all know that. He belongs at this meeting."

"All right!" Vogel threw up his hands.

"Shouldn't Brother Perry have been included?" Anna Leah asked. "He is the leader of the Jovis grop, as I understand it."

"There *is* no Jovis group, Miss Moineau," said Jacob. "As long as they remain under the roof of this colony they are Jeremians. 'They are of those that rebel against the light; they know not the ways thereof, nor abide in the paths thereof.' "

Vogel paused. "Uh . . . yeah. Took the words right

outta my mouth. Okay, let's get on with this. I sort of like got to thinking—"

"An event in itself," Siegler muttered.

Vogel glared at her but continued. "—like maybe we oughtta put our heads together, united like, and come up with some ideas about . . . uh . . ." He looked at Waverly like a schoolboy stuck on stage without a vague grasp of his role in the play.

"How to utilize the resources at hand . . ." Waverly prompted.

"Yeah . . ."

". . . in a more efficient manner . . ." She looked at him, understood that the careful rehearsal in bed the night before had been for nothing, and turned to the group. ". . . for the betterment of the future of Mars. Our greatest resource is ourselves, the diversity of our abilities, our talents, and our interests."

Vogel nodded, excited. "Yeah. Like we've been wasting a lot of time and energy, taking care of our own in a pretty crappy, uh . . ."

"Less organized," Waverly murmured.

"Less organized way. I mean, we're catching on, like you guys, all the Jerrys are terrific farmers and such. We're not so hot at that. But we understand architecture better than you, right? So we been doing the barter thing. And you Seras, with the artsy-craftsy stuff . . . I'm not knocking it, don't get me wrong. I mean you got talents we don't even understand. Leah here, she's got talent so spooky I don't wanna think about it."

Vogel moved around the table. He started to put his hands on Anna Leah's shoulders, then seemed to think better of it and moved on. Graham felt a sudden tightness in his midsection relax and was surprised to realize that he did not want Vogel to touch her. Ever.

"Now Dr. Krolov . . . I mean it's clear we gotta have the bone-healers, right? We could use more than we got. Then we got Siegler. God only knows what you people are doing here. It's one big mystery to me, I can tell you that."

"And no doubt it always will be." Siegler smiled.

Vogel leaned close. "Count on it." His scowling smile in return made her sit back.

"Anyways," he continued, "we gotta start functioning

better as a whole. We gotta start working together, like. And I got this idea . . . Florie and me . . . that we should make the head honchos back home fork over more dough so we can build us like an underground. You know, like a monorail system to connect up the colonies, so when the dust storms hit they don't knock us out of commission no more. I mean, look at us, stuck here like we been snowed in for the winter. If we had us a monorail we could get around a lot faster. Hell, they ain't even gonna pave the roads we got and it takes forever to get anywhere unless you got yourself a lander. If we'd had us a monorail, underground, Haas might not be dead now. Maybe he woulda made it, you know?" Briefly, there was a huskiness in the man's voice that impressed Graham. He was certain that the moment of emotion was real. It was in that instant that he accorded Vogel, for the first time, a shred of respect and admiration.

Siegler sat forward. "Do you have any idea what such a system would cost?"

"Plenty," Vogel said. "And, baby, we're worth every friggin' penny. Think about it. They been carrying us for how long? How many umpty billion credits they been shoveling into a proposition so far in the red *they* don't wanna talk about it? Somebody back home has plans for us. It's real important to them that we make it, right? We're like the kid they spend all the dough on for tap-dancing lessons and piano lessons and orthodontist garbage and *elocution* lessons." He directed the last to Siegler. "And then pack 'em off to Harvard and Yale and teach 'em to eat little sandwiches with the crusts cut off"—now he smiled directly at Graham—"so the kid can be A-Class, all the way. Somewhere, it all pays off, don't it, Cloud Man? All that pampering and pruning. Somebody back home is sure we're gonna pay off when we're all grown up."

"So," Krolov said, "what do you propose we do, for the present? For the foreseeable future?"

Vogel's face went blank.

The silence in the room grew awkward.

"Excellent plan." Jacob nodded. "And in keeping with my expectations of you, may I add."

"How would you build this underground monorail system?" asked Graham.

"Dig a hole in the ground," Vogel snapped.

Graham nodded. "Something on the order of a stone fuser . . . only much larger?"

Vogel looked like someone had plugged him back in. "Yeah! We get 'em to build us one big mother of a fuser . . . that would do it like in no time. Instead of a hole borer it would be a tunnel borer. Yeah. Cost effective, too, right?"

Graham kept his eyes on Siegler as he spoke. "If the ultimate goal of the colonization of Mars is to make the planet self-sufficient . . . totally independent of Earth, then this unification is a major step in the right direction. I should think the request would be approved in budgetary meetings in the near future. The sooner Vogel's proposal is put in motion the better."

"I agree," said Anna Leah. "The longer we remain isolated, both as individuals and as colonies, the less our chance of survival. If Mars is to thrive we must reach for total independence from our mother planet. The child itself must sever the umbilical cord."

Graham turned to look at her and she flushed slightly.

" 'Let us break their bands asunder, and cast away their cords from us,' " said Jacob. "Psalms 2:3."

Waverly nodded. "We have to take care of our own. And that means all of us, together."

Siegler looked around at the faces now focused on her. "All right. Submit your proposal for this next stage of development to the SURF Council and they will relay it to the Mars Commission. And we'll see what happens."

Vogel looked like a man ready to pass out cigars. He slammed his hand down on the table. "Hot damn! Meeting adjourned!"

Baker watched from the bed as Siegler ritualistically creamed her face and neck and arms in a sensuously slow manner before the small mirror.

"I can't believe the meeting went so smoothly," she said. "It's actually happening. The seed is germinating. The only thing that galls me is that generations from now the historians will probably look upon that wart of a little man as the George Washington of Mars." She turned to Baker, smiling. "He'll sound like Jefferson and Lincoln and Gandhi and Mother Teresa and Segunda-Bal all rolled into one sweet-smelling rose."

Baker chuckled. "That's up to you people. How it goes down now will be how it's remembered."

She moved across the room and turned off the light. "Human manipulation is far older than genetic manipulation. So why do I feel so damned guilty? You can never tell him, Jon. Graham Sinclair must never know why he is here. The success of the project depends . . ."

"I know." He pulled her down into the bed. "I keep telling myself, better here than Antarctica for the rest of his life. But . . . Risa, I know what the heart of Judas feels like. I do."

"Shhhhh." She put a finger to his lips in the darkness. "He can never know. Never."

CHAPTER 24

Graham sat in the shadows of the tropical enclosure, oblivious to the sweat trickling down his body in the humid heat. No moonlight could penetrate the swirling dust that now blanketed much of the surface of the planet. Small lights, the size of fireflies, were positioned at points across the geodesic dome where the panels were conjoined. They seemed decorative, like artificial stars arranged in geometric patterns, but their purpose was far more serious. If a light changed to red and began to flash, it indicated a rupture in the CELSS environment. For now, however, on a night far darker than any on Earth, Graham allowed the lights to be stars. He breathed deeply, feeling the moist warmth like a memory.

He didn't know how long she had been standing there, watching him. He had not heard the soft *whoosh* of the linking chamber door slide open. But then, when he was deep in meditation, little distracted him.

Anna Leah stepped out from deeper shadows. "Forgive me. This time it's I who have startled you."

"You didn't startle me. It's all right." He stood up and noticed that his clothes were soaking wet. "I was about to leave. Good night . . . Miss Moineau."

"Why are you so frightened of me, Mr. Sinclair?"

Graham paused. "I beg your pardon?"

"You've seen my body. I have no unusual appendages. Your prejudice is only one of ignorance, you know."

"I have no prejudice against you."

"Yes. You do. It's a wall. Very high, very . . . thick. And it was not there, when we first met. It came only after you found out who I was. Seras frighten you terribly. Why?"

Graham met her gaze. "You don't frighten me. I simply disagree with your philosophy—with your adamant rejection of scientific and medical advances made available to you. It's you I find ignorant, Miss Moineau. You and all Contaminants who think as you do. Good night."

He was halfway to the door when she turned and said, "Happy birthday, Mr. Sinclair."

He stopped and looked back at her.

"No, you weren't thinking of it," she said, smiling. "Your lady told me."

"My lady?"

"Yes. She asked me to . . . she wanted a gift for you . . . a glass goblet . . . I'm afraid I've spoiled her surprise. I thought perhaps she had already presented it to you."

Graham watched her turn away, drop the white robe, and dive into the water. Some vague desire deep inside him drew him back toward the pool. In moments he had shed his own clothes, carefully hiding the small leather pouch inside an inner pocket of his jumpsuit. He dived in and surfaced, splashing water over the moss- and vine-covered rocks.

Anna Leah laughed, then clamped her hand over her mouth. "What changed your mind, Mr. Sinclair?"

Graham treaded water. The pool was both deeper and colder than he had expected. "I would have thought you would know better than I, Miss Moineau."

"You overrate my abilities. Please call me Anna Leah."

She swam to the edge of the pool, ducked under, then surfaced, throwing her head back to keep her hair out of her eyes. "So why did you decide to join me?"

"I dislike . . . being misjudged."

Her expression became serious. "Yes. You have been sorely misjudged. And so have I. Many times, Mr. Sinclair."

"Graham is acceptable, if I'm to address you informally as well."

Anna Leah pulled herself up onto the overgrown bank and dangled her legs in the water. "Come to the Sera commune and learn something about us, Graham Sinclair. Then decide if we are so terribly wrong in the choices we've made. At least do that. Will you?" She looked up at the blackness above her. "After this all subsides, of course. We won't 'contaminate' you by breathing on you, I promise."

"I don't know if I would be permitted. I'm to be transferred to the Keyote colony once the storm lets up."

"Of course you would be permitted to visit the Sera colony. Jonathan Baker has been trying to coax you into a visit for ages, hasn't he? To begin to understand a prejudice is the first step toward erasing it. How can you understand what we are all about if you don't see us for yourself?"

She had a very small waist, Graham thought, and although her long hair clung wetly to her body, he could see the delicate curve of her breasts. She slipped back into the water and swam away from him to the far end of the pool, near the waterfall.

"You really should, you know . . . come to visit us. I know you were the one who arranged the meeting. No matter what Vogel pretends. You organized it. And you were in control of it even in your silence."

Graham swam toward her. "Do you know everything someone thinks?"

Anna Leah seemed embarrassed. "Not always."

"Do you know what I'm thinking now?"

"Yes. You . . . want to touch me. But you're afraid."

"You have me at a disadvantage. I don't know what you're thinking."

Slowly she moved toward him in the water. He reached out and drew her close, fascination and fear so intermingled that he could not tell one from the other. Something within him awoke with the movement of her body as it slipped through his fingers. For an instant she was every desire and every loss he had ever suffered, and the sensation of passing warmth overwhelmed him. He wanted to reach out and hold her in an iron-tight grasp, to keep the cold from enveloping them both. But she had already moved beyond his reach, gliding on her back through the water, her eyes betraying a fear greater than his own.

She rose from the shallow end of the pool and quickly wrapped herself in the white robe.

"Please. Don't go," he said. The words surprised him. Impulsiveness was as alien to him as uncontrolled rage and yet he had done at least two impulsive things in the space of ten minutes. Something about this woman seemed to topple every rigid tradition ingrained in him. It seemed as if she radiated an energy that scrambled logic and shattered his reserve. He was embarrassed by his own sudden emotional imbalance. But he did not want her to go. He swam to the edge of the pool and looked up at her.

"The pain within you is too great," she whispered. "I can't bear it."

Before he could rise from the water she was gone.

Paris was asleep when he returned to the guest quarters, but roused slightly as he slipped into bed. She had, since the death of Haas, retreated into a torpor, eating little and seldom speaking. Graham accepted her withdrawn state as a natural reaction to grief, although he found that he missed her flippancy and irreverent high energy.

"I was dreaming," she said. "I was running in a field and the wind was blowing against my face and the sky was blue . . . so blue. I miss it. I want to go home."

"It's the dust storm, Paris. You'll feel better when it passes."

"No! Damn you! I don't miss *pink* skies!" She shoved away from him in the darkness and sat up, rocking back and forth. "I *hate* this place. The whole godforsaken planet. I hate it! I hate you!" She lurched from the bed and fled from the room wearing only the oversized T-shirt that had belonged to Haas.

Graham sighed and got up. It crossed his mind that an ascetic life on a womanless planet would have some appeal he had never considered.

In the corridor he met Waverly coming out of a room

belonging to one of the actors from the Sera colony. "Wrong door." She smiled, flushing slightly. "They look so much alike . . . the doors . . ."

"Did you see Paris come this way?" he asked, moving past her.

"No. What happened? A lover's tiff?"

Graham turned and looked at her. "I believe I saw Vogel looking for you, down corridor B. Shall I tell him where to find you?"

"God, no!" Waverly gathered up the hem of her robe and sprinted off in the opposite direction from corridor B.

It was in the fourth agricultural CELSS that he found her. She was standing at the far end of a wheat field like a shadow, looking up at the overhead dome.

"Leave me alone," she said, moving away from him.

"Paris, I don't know how to help you."

"I know you don't."

"In time, it will pass, what you feel now."

Paris turned on him. "What do you know about it, Mr. Sinclair? *Cloud Man!* You don't feel anything! Do you! You don't know anything about it. Tell me one thing you miss from home. From *Earth.* Tell me!"

Graham looked at her in the soft, artificial starlight and then turned away. He could not begin to list the things of Earth he ached to see again. To dwell, however briefly, on vivid memories of rainfall and the smell of autumn, of birds on the wing, the heat of a lathered horse after a morning workout, the icy crunch of snow under boots, and, yes, blue, endless blue skies was to court a pain he could not endure. Was that what she had meant, Graham wondered. Had Anna Leah felt the agony he had so carefully sealed off for the sake of survival? Could it seep from his pores like a subtle poison? Could touch be that powerful?

Without a word he left Paris in the field and made his way back toward the entrance to the CELSS.

"Graham! Wait! Oh, jeez, I'm sorry!" She ran after him, crying.

She reached him and stopped, seemingly unsure as to whether she should come any closer. "I . . . hurt so bad, I needed to hurt . . . somebody else. I didn't mean it to be you. I didn't mean . . . what I said. You just don't know how it feels to love someone so much and . . ." She shut her eyes, shaking her head.

Graham put his arms around her. "Haas was a good man. I'm sure he loved you deeply. It will take time, but the pain will lessen. I promise."

He could feel the tension in her ease. At first he thought she was crying again, but it seemed to be more a combination of laughter and tears.

"You dumb shit," she murmured. "All of you! All men are dumb shits. But I gotta hand it to you, Sinclair. You win the prize as the biggest dumb shit of all! No, I take that back. *I* win the prize as the biggest dumbest shit of all. You know why? Because I keep forgiving you for being such a dumb shit. I just love abuse. That must be it." She threw up her hands and stalked off toward the linking chamber.

Graham felt a headache coming on.

CHAPTER 25

He woke to a very off-key rendition of "Happy Birthday" sung by Paris as she sat cross-legged at the foot of the bed.

"You don't look a day over thirty-four, Sinclair. Bet you didn't know I knew it was your birthday. Today is"—she glanced at her watch—"one dash eight dash two zero five five point three five seven . . . A.D. Give or take a few microseconds."

The Paris he had come to care deeply for had returned. She started to slither over the edge of the bed but he caught her wrist.

"What?" she said, tossing unruly hair out of her eyes.

"Nothing. I just . . . it's as if you've been away . . . and now you're back. I missed you, Tucker."

"Yeah . . . I guess I was gone, kind of. I won't go away again. And I'm not leaving Mars. I'm a Grit, not a Lark. Stay right there."

She hung halfway off of the bed, rummaging for something on the floor. "Uh-oh."

"What's wrong?"

She sat back up, a cloth-wrapped object in her hands. "The bugs," she whispered. "They're gone."

"Baker had them removed at my request. He tells me there aren't any others. I've checked and haven't found any so far."

"Good." She handed him the wrapped object, smiling. "Remember where you were on your last birthday?"

"I was on the *Olympus Mons*."

"Right. Did you have a party?"

"Not that I recall."

"Oh, poor baby."

"I believe I was in a coma at the time."

"Oh, yeah, the inoculations. Well, open it already."

He untied the string around the cloth and unwrapped the goblet.

"That girl, your vestal virgin, she made it. Do you like it?"

Graham sat up in bed and held the blown glass up to the light. "It's beautiful, Paris. Thank you."

"Now you'll have something to remember me by, *us* by, and they can't take it away from you since it's Mars-made, right?"

"It's excellent workmanship."

"You should see it in the sunlight. It makes colors like you wouldn't believe. It looks clear now, but in the sun it's like . . . nothing I ever saw before. Kind of like all the light in a prism and then some."

Graham carefully wrapped the cloth back around the glass. "I don't know your birthday."

Paris rolled out of bed. "Don't be rude. Women don't have birthdays after twenty-four. We have . . . a yearly crisis. Get dressed. You don't want to miss Jacob's breakfast sermon. I just love hellfire and brimstone on toast. If it weren't for the condition of my soul, I'd be tempted to stay here, you know? There'll be room once the Jovis group leaves."

Graham watched her dress. "What's wrong with your soul?"

"I'd have to spend too many years on my knees to pray it out of purgatory."

At breakfast Graham checked the communication board to see what work detail he was assigned to for the following ten-day cycle. He had found the somewhat primitive approach to farming as practiced by the Jeremians oddly pleasing. Almost all work was done by hand. Robotics performed most CELSS functions at the SURF base and in the other communes, he had learned, but here, agriculture had taken on a spiritual symbolism that appealed to him. He was able to follow the harvest of a crop through the stages of preparation and observe the culmination of effort placed on the table at the evening meal. The breaking of bread took on new meaning for him, and he had regained a keen awareness of flavors, which had eluded him for longer than he cared to re- member. At home food had become a ritual over which business was conducted. In private, even though the most succulent foods had been available to him at a moment's notice, he often forgot to eat unless Ti reminded him. Sustenance had become an irritating necessity, time-con- suming and boring. The erosion of his awareness of con- sumption had been so gradual that he wasn't sure when it had slipped away. Now, a potato on his plate could have been the one he had dug from the soil himself only that morning. The only thing lacking in his exposure to basic farming techniques was that he toiled in fields during a perpetual midnight, overhead lights substituting for sun- light.

"We're assigned to the same CELSS," Paris said, point- ing to the schedule. "I'm glad they took me out of the hatchery. I couldn't look at those sweet, fuzzy yellow chicks knowing that I could be devouring one of them someday. I'm going vegetarian . . . any day now. It's frightening. I'm beginning to like guinea pig too much. Were you always a veggie?"

"More or less," said Graham, scanning the lists for Anna Leah's name. She was assigned to the food prep section, he discovered.

"Paris, this is possibly a tactless question, but . . ."

"Hey, only you A-Class types worry about tactless, Sin- clair. The rest of us wouldn't know it if it bit us."

"I was wondering what Anna Leah asked for, in ex- change for the goblet . . . the one you gave me. What kind of barter?"

"She wanted more sand."

"Sand?"

"The kind she used for the goblet. The Seras are always experimenting with soil samples we bring them. This was some from down in the Valles Marineris. She gave me a sample of it. Said she could use as much as I could bring her. You gonna court her with a ton of sand?" Paris wrinkled her nose. "Not the height of romantic gestures."

"Do you have the sample with you?"

Paris looked exasperated. "No, I don't carry sand around on me, Sinclair. It's back in the room. I know where the stuff came from. There's a place, down below Pod 8 in the Ophir Chasma. It's really white, or maybe it's crystal clear. I don't run into it very often. It makes nice glass, though."

Graham nodded. "Yes. It does, indeed."

Baker was down in the docking hangar overseeing the reassembly of a rover engine when Graham found him. Mechanical components laid out reminded him of a dismembered creature. Robotics, especially, made him think of severed arms or of a genetics experiment gone bad. It was a weakness held over from childhood, he knew, to perceive life and personality within inanimate objects, but the habit had clung to him, however much he tried to suppress it.

"What's up?" Baker asked, wiping his hands on a cloth.

"How soon am I to report to the Keyote colony?"

"I don't know. When the storm lets up and it's safe enough to travel, I suppose."

"Would it be permissible to visit the Sera commune first?"

Baker smiled. "Any particular reason?"

"Because I haven't seen it yet."

"That the only reason?"

Graham frowned slightly. "Isn't that sufficient? You've encouraged me to go there. Now I want to go."

Baker hopped up on the platform where Graham stood. "I just find it curious that once you were so adamant about *not* exploring the Seras and now . . ." He grinned. "Couldn't have anything to do with the influence of one particular member of the Seras, could it?"

The intimations, for some reason, irritated Graham. "No. I simply feel that we may be overlooking some export possibilities. The Seras are developing exceptional skill in craft areas, especially glassmaking. With proper marketing and promotion, Martian glass could possibly become a highly coveted product on Earth. Equivalent to Venetian glass during its peak in the Middle Ages."

The look in Baker's eyes shifted from subtle ribbing to genuine excitement. "You know something, you may be right. We could be sitting on our most valuable commodity. I mean, it's right under our noses and"—he paused— "right now, in the air. Mars itself. A touch of space exotica for those too timid to travel to the planet. By damn, Gray, I think you're on to something!"

"You might test-market some limited pieces by placing them in art exhibits —a touring exhibit in various centers of culture. Make them unattainable at any price. Then there could be a few, only a few, pieces offered at Sotheby's or some other auction house. Their very rarity will make them quite sought after. I'm sure of it."

Baker nodded. "Create the demand, then control the supply. It's so simple. And so brilliant. Somebody should have thought of it before. Is it legal?"

"The demand would be somewhat orchestrated at first, as with any new product. The supply, by its very nature —by the fact that it would be handcrafted—would be limited. It's not an artificial control. It's legal."

Baker slapped him on both shoulders. "I knew you could do it! If anybody could, you—" His face froze for a moment. "Uh . . . I mean, this kind of thinking is in your blood, right?"

Graham saw the sudden shift in the man's demeanor, as if he was suddenly embarrassed, caught in some vague deception.

Baker wiped his hands again on the cloth, not meeting Graham's eyes. "It's . . . a great idea. Talk to the Seras about it. See how they feel . . . Let them know how important it could be, to all of us, Graham. To our survival as a planet."

Graham watched him wipe roughly at his hands. "It's very important to you that Mars thrives, isn't it?"

"Yes. It is."

"You would do anything necessary to insure its successful colonization?"

Baker continued to examine his hands. "Yes. Almost anything."

. . .

The change was imperceptible at first, like an attempt to compare various depths of blackness. Slowly the global darkness lessened. The sky beyond the domed enclosures began to have a murky red tinge to it during what corresponded to daylight on the planet. Wind velocity died down to mere hurricane status.

"I give it a couple more cycles." Vogel sighed, tossing guinea pig bones onto his plate.

Paris turned to Graham sitting beside her at dinner. "I still have to translate cycles into weeks and months to comprehend time. He's talking like about three more weeks, right?"

Vogel belched. "Right, Sugar Cakes. Then the fun jobs start. Like digging out. 'Dozing the road if you can find it. Relocating the pods to see if they survived."

Baker, carrying a plate, came over to the table. "May I join you?"

Paris looked up. "Bake! You can talk!"

"And eat." Baker nodded, sitting down. "Got the wires out today."

Waverly peered at his food. "Poached eggs. Wonderful."

"It beats blended anything," Baker said.

"I was just telling the Larks here," said Vogel, "that—"

"We're not Larks," Paris corrected.

"You ain't a Grit, Sweet Puss, till the next cycler has come and gone and you ain't on it, all right? As I was saying . . . what was I saying?"

"Digging out," Waverly prompted.

"Yeah. Right. I was just thinking, it will be great once we get the monorail . . . no more shoveling sand."

"What monorail?" Paris asked, popping grapes into her mouth.

Vogel turned to scowl at her. "Eat and keep quiet. Maybe you'll learn something, okay?"

"Not if you're the one doing the talking," Paris snapped, picking up her plate and cup.

Vogel shook his head. "Cloud Man—Sinclair, you got to teach your woman some manners. One of these days, if she don't wise up, pow, right in the chops."

Graham rose and leaned across the table. Very softly he said, "Never lay a hand on her, Vogel. Never."

Baker cut into an egg. "Very good advice, Vogel. I'd listen if I were you."

"Hey, I'm kidding, okay?" Vogel slurped some wine. "I don't hit women. Ask Florie. I am not a violent man. Except in bed." He laughed and nudged Waverly in the ribs. "Right?"

Waverly looked bored. "Right," she said. "In bed you're a tiger, Dumpling."

Graham escorted Paris from the room. There was to be a musical concert presented that evening in the Congregational Garden, a combined effort by the Jeremian choir and musicians from the Sera colony. For the past several weeks entertainment had been offered by the Seras, despite volatile protests from the more conservative religious faction within the Jeremians' group. Graham had attended with Paris, surprised at how much he needed to hear music to offset the incessant sound of wind and sand buffeting the modules. On the first occasion there had been some disagreement as to whether or not he would be allowed to attend the gatherings since the program contained selections by Mozart and Chopin. Siegler was opposed to Graham's presence, arguing that by strict interpretation of the law it was music of Earth and Graham was no longer allowed such pleasures. The Seras threatened to boycott the concert. In the end Graham not only listened to Mozart and Chopin but heard three selections from a new musical that had opened on Broadway after his departure from the planet.

Paris linked her arm through Graham's as they strolled along the corridor toward the Congregational Garden. "You're getting territorial. Feels nice. Being your territory. Sort of."

"I claim no territory, Paris."

"I know that."

"You're free to do as you please. We are not bonded."

"I know that. It pleases me to pretend, okay? You started it, remember."

Graham elected not to pursue the subject, recognizing that the path would no doubt end with Paris in a sulk or a rolling fit of temper.

"So what's this monorail thing Vogel was talking about?"

"Just some long-term planetary goals."

Paris nodded. "From that big hush-hush meeting you won't talk about?"

"It wasn't hush-hush. It isn't my place to discuss it, that's all."

"Says who? Siegler? Really, Graham, what can anybody do to you? Think about it. You're the only—okay, I'll say it—*convict* on the whole blessed planet. You step out of line and what are they going to do to punish you? Send you home? Stand outside without a MEMU? There's no death penalty. They can't do that. So they're going to build a monorail. Big deal. It's about time."

"Underground."

Paris stopped walking. *"That* would be major. But the sensible thing to do. They're going to really do it? Won't it be awfully expensive?"

"Yes."

"The Mars Commission will go for it?"

"If continued investment in Martian colonization is deemed equitable."

"Oh."

Graham watched her sifting through possibilities.

"Then we can kiss it good-bye, huh?" she said. "Mars will never pay off. Not in our lifetime. If ever."

Paris looked like a child who had just been told there would be no circus that year. Or any year thereafter, Graham thought. "That's where you come in. And all the Ventures," he said, relinking arms. Briefly, he explained the tentative direction of the conference and the exporting plan as they strolled. By the time they reached the Congregational Garden the room was crowded.

"So, have you told *her?"* Paris nodded, looking toward Anna Leah who was sitting with Dr. Krolov and two actors from the Seras.

"Not yet."

Paris shook her head. "Only you would come up with a plan to restructure an entire planet in order to impress a woman. God, you do think big, Sinclair."

"That was not my intention."

"Of course not. Wouldn't it be simpler just to jump her bones? I'm sorry. That was crude."

"Yes, it was."

"Jealousy makes me say things I don't mean to say . . . out loud."

"I've noticed."

"I apologize."

Graham cleared his throat. "Apology accepted."

Paris gazed down on the stage below where robe-clad musicians were assembled. "But it *would* be simpler just to *ask* her to . . ."

"Paris . . ."

"Okay."

CHAPTER 26

There was a noticeable shift in the general mood of the entire colony as each day grew a bit lighter and the stinging winds howled less savagely. The more stringent faction within the Jeremian commune, whom Graham had learned to distinguish by their burlap-colored robes and consistently pursed lips, even seemed less critical of their joy-loving brethren.

"I'm glad this storm won't interfere with the arrival of the next cycler," Baker said, handing Graham a sack of apples from the stepladder. The orchard was filled with workers who could do what the robotics could not do— distinguish what was ripe from what was not ready. Although the human labor was slower, in the long run the bounty was greater, Graham discovered.

"What happens if a storm is in progress when a cycler arrives?"

"Things get very crowded aboard the 'Notchka. The cycler can't hang around, so it dumps new arrivals and leaves, minus Martian passengers who are stuck on the planet. They have to wait until the next cycler. It's the miners who crack fastest when that happens. Things get real testy." Baker put two fingers to his lips and gave a sharp whistle. "Filled basket here," he yelled to two other workers.

"Did Vogel show you his plans for the tunnel fuser?" Baker asked, climbing higher on the ladder.

"No."

"The guy may be a shrimp in the grace and etiquette department, but the little bastard is a mechanical engineering genius. Come by my room after dinner tonight. I'll show you what he's done so far."

"Could we meet elsewhere?"

"She won't be there. What have you got against Siegler?"

Graham simply looked up at the man and then dumped his sack of apples into a basket.

"Well, you're not her favorite person, either," Baker continued. "And I don't understand that, particularly. Other than that you never react quite like she expects you to."

A sudden shout went up throughout the orchard as sunlight broke through the dusty overcast.

Baker glanced up and squinted. "Even pink sky looks good after a while. I've spoken with the Seras and with the Committee at SURF. You will be allowed to visit the colony as long as you like."

"Good."

Paris sat on the bed watching Graham pack his few belongings into a duffel bag. "I should feel happy you're going to the Sera colony. You'll be a little closer than if you were at Keyote . . . I mean, we could like visit, maybe. Only, if you were at Keyote, I would feel . . . I mean, unless you like hairy chests, there's not a lot of temptation, if you know what I mean."

Graham carefully wrapped the glass goblet within T-shirts. "I'm due back at SURF on sol 530 for the arrival of the next cycler. Will you be there?"

Paris nodded. "I'll be there."

"As a passenger?" Graham did not look up from his work. He hoped the question sounded as casual as he tried to make it.

"Yes."

The answer washed over him like a spray of ice needles. For weeks he had tried to avoid thinking about what she might be deciding. Above all, he did not want to sway her toward a decision she might regret and for which she might later blame him. He did not want her to leave. But he did not want to be the cause that would make her stay on a world she hated. He forced his hands to continue folding clothes, folding and refolding with unnecessary precision.

Paris moved to the end of the bed and placed her hand on top of a T-shirt. "Did you hear what I said?"

"Yes."

"Graham. Look at me, dammit. I was kidding. I'm not going, okay? I'm a Grit! I just wanted to see if . . . you cared if I left. You would miss me, wouldn't you?"

"Yes. I would miss you."

"That's all I wanted to know."

"Paris . . ."

"Hey, Sinclair, the way I look at it, I'm out ahead. Back there, nobody's missing me at all. I tell you, the loneliest feeling in the world is to come home, when you've been gone on a trip, and you arrive and nobody's there— there's nobody to say, 'Hey, welcome back. I missed you.' It's an awful feeling. I'm staying, like it or not."

He didn't consciously put his arms around her. He didn't even remember reaching out, but she was there, in his arms, for a long, very silent minute.

Rovers moved out of the air lock in twos and threes, like ants on a reconnaissance mission after a rainstorm. Graham, riding in the lead rover from the Sera colony, was surprised at how completely the road had disappeared.

Anna Leah moved carefully back toward his seat, her long braid falling over her left shoulder. "I'm sorry traveling conditions are so cramped. We should arrive by early afternoon with a quick stop by Pod 4 to see if it's still functioning."

Wade Ross, one of the Sera musicians, who was now acting as copilot, glanced back at them with undisguised hostility. He was lean-boned and lanky with straight dark brown hair that hung below his collar. His eyes were a hard blue. A furrowed frown that stressed the hardness marred what would have been a striking handsomeness.

"It wouldn't *be* crowded without the excess baggage. He should have been put to a vote. We don't have to take on somebody just because SURF says it's fine."

"He's our guest," Anna Leah said, tightening ropes on a box of medical supplies.

"He's not one of us!"

"Wade, I repeat, he is our *guest*. Please treat him as such."

The man returned to his copilot duties. "The Cloud Man . . . they won't be pleased. I can tell you that."

She smiled at Graham. "Sometimes I forget that prejudice works both ways. Not all Seras are as close-minded as Wade. He has a great deal of bitterness toward Perfects."

Graham raised an eyebrow. "Perfects?"

Anna Leah shrugged, sitting in the seat across from him. "People . . . like you. The genetically blessed, you might say."

Graham suspected that Wade Ross was, in some vague way, exhibiting what Paris would call territorial breast beating. He had seen the man gravitate toward Anna Leah on every public occasion during their stay with the Jeremians. He had finally asked Baker if the two were betrothed. The answer, which somehow relieved him, was no.

"This is the first time you've been separated from him for an extended length of time, isn't it?" said Anna Leah, watching him intently.

"I beg your pardon?"

"From Jon Baker. Since . . . you first met him."

Graham thought for a moment. Had it been only a year and a half? Earth seemed decades behind him.

"I thought at first that you felt ill at ease because you were alone with us," she said, "but I believe it's perhaps mild separation anxiety, after all. Don't worry. We won't let anything happen to you."

Pod 4, though almost buried in red dust, proved to be in good working order. The two rovers following them were waved on and did not stop. Graham stayed aboard the vehicle with Anna Leah while Wade and Sam Edwards, the driver, quickly replenished emergency supplies within the pod.

"You'll have your work cut out for you," she said to

Graham as they watched the two men move across the sand to the pod entry hatch. "The Seras don't always recognize their gifts. Wade is a very talented musician. He can pick up any instrument and make it his own. He doesn't understand that it doesn't come easily to everyone since it comes so easily to him. Sam Edwards crawls inside characters the way you and I put on clothing. Because he acts so beautifully he doesn't know his own gifts. It won't be easy to convince these people that they may have talents that Earth would pay good money for. Glassmaking and pottery fell to us because there was a need for it and no one else seemed interested. If you can convince them that exporting our crafts would be beneficial to the planet, I'm sure they would do it. It's the convincing part that will be hardest."

"I haven't convinced you, either, have I?"

"No. Not yet."

The Sera colony lay nestled between Ascraeus Mons and Pavonis Mons like a cluster of crystal bubbles. It was a smaller community than that of the Jeremians, but larger than the Ventures commune. The air lock permitted only one rover in at a time, and there was a wait of approximately fifteen minutes between the entry of each vehicle. While they waited their turn, Graham noticed that the architecture that extended beyond the original prefabricated hub and spokes was modeled after the Ventures to some extent. Geodesic domes of variegated colored glass glittered like a fantasy palace or more like giant sleeping turtles, Graham thought. Alien turtles lying dormant on an alien red beach. For a moment he almost craved the stark, utilitarian architecture of the SURF base, certain that he was about to receive a sensory overload from a surfeit of strangeness.

"We aren't carnival freaks," Anna Leah said softly. "You needn't resort to your childhood monsters to prepare for us."

Wade turned to look at Graham. "Boo," he said, and laughed suddenly.

Without warning, Sam Edwards, a beefy, thin-haired man, contorted into a drop-shouldered hunchback, slack-jawed and twisted. In a suffering cockney rasp, he groaned, "Wah-tah! Me beloved Ezmer-rahldah! Gimme wah-tah!"

"Oh, hush, both of you," Anna Leah warned.

"He can't hear you." Wade pointed to his own ears, seeming to delight in Graham's momentary puzzlement. "The bells. Made him deaf, poor old Quasi. You know, I've always thought *The Hunchback of Notre Dame* would make a hell of a fine opera. What do you say, Cloud Man? Want to be my Broadway Angel and back a musical? An A-Class Perfect like you could afford it from loose change."

"Write your opera and I'll see what I can do," Graham said, meeting the man's gaze.

"You'll see what you can do?" Wade nudged Edwards, who had regained a normal appearance. "He'll see what he can do. Hey, Sinclair, am I wrong or didn't they strip you of your last credit before they booted you off the planet?"

Edwards started up the rover as the outer air lock slowly opened. "A creditless philanthropist doesn't carry much punch, don't you know?"

"I have friends."

"You *had* friends," Wade snorted.

"Wade . . ." Anna Leah began.

"Perfects, A-Class in particular, don't touch tarnish. Of any kind." Wade jerked a thumb toward Graham. "The man is tarnish, Anna Leah. That's facts. Head-to-toe tarnish."

Graham continued to watch the man, his own face impassive. "You've already written it, haven't you, your opera?"

Wade retreated almost physically, turning around in his seat.

Graham nodded. "Failure is part of the gamble, Wade, one of the possibilities. But only one of the possibilities."

The rover dipped down into the air chamber and the doors clanged shut behind it. No one spoke as the carbon dioxide was exchanged for oxygen.

The difference between the Jeremians and the Seras was apparent from the moment the second air lock opened. The color was what struck Graham first. Where the Jeremians garbed themselves in muted browns and cream and beige, the Seras arrayed themselves in splashes of purple and orange, magenta and turquoise. The men were as colorfully draped as the women, and Graham was reminded somehow of a cross between a Renaissance fair and a peculiar period during the twentieth century when the culture of the youth broke with tradition, shattering all rules, all customs. It had been a time of great social upheaval that touched every segment of society, according to historical reflections on the period.

Anna Leah embraced a number of people, introducing Graham as she went. There were strange names, reminiscent of American Indian names, Graham thought as he followed his hosts toward the central hub. He didn't feel unwelcome among them, nor did he feel accepted. There seemed to be polite wariness at best. He thought he heard quick murmurs as he passed, but was not certain. Whatever they thought of him would determine how well they would accept any proposal he might offer. The feeling was not unlike business dealings he had experienced in new territories where computers were barely known. One had to understand the people and how they thought before business could commence.

"Conditions are somewhat crowded," Anna Leah explained, "since the arrival of the last cycler. We were working on an additional module when the dust storm stopped everything. It would have been completed by now, otherwise. You'll have to bunk with the singles. I hope you won't feel too uncomfortable. Wade, would you show Mr. Sinclair around? I have a backlog of things that can't wait."

The man, clearly irritated, grabbed up a duffel bag and a guitar case. Graham followed him down narrow steps and through somewhat snaky passages. Wade was making little effort to point out anything, so he had to assume things from glimpses as they passed various rooms. There seemed to be a well-equipped media center with walls of books and video discs, a grotto with a waterfall where nude bathers splashed and swam, a number of workshops where potters were at work, and an open area with furnaces where glassblowing was done.

"I thought you were bonded to the leggy one," Wade

said, leading Graham into a large rounded room with a low dome. "How come she didn't come with you?"

"Actually, we're just friends." Graham looked around, mildly intrigued. The room reminded him of an Arab encampment on the desert. Soft, intricately woven rugs covered the matted floor. Dyed gauze curtains separated various cubicles where cushionlike bed pallets lay, piled with bright-colored pillows. Sunlight filtered down through the turtle dome, creating muted patterns across the central open area. There were no chairs or tables or stools. Cushions, instead, served as makeshift furniture. Large ceramic tiles placed upon several cushions served as a tabletop or writing surface or game board.

"You can stow your stuff over there." Wade pointed, placing his own belongings inside a curtained area across the room. The thin veils were drawn back during the day to create the illusion of more space. Graham counted ten pallets.

"Am I taking someone else's bed?"

"Not that he would notice." Wade shrugged, plopping down on his own pallet. "If you don't mind ghosts, that is." He pulled off heavy boots. "So you're not bonded to her and you slept together under Jacob's nose and weren't roasted alive for your sins. Not bad. Maybe you A-Class Perfects rate privileges the rest of us never considered. God knows you got everything else on a silver platter. Is it true you broke the jaw of the old man's son?"

Graham began to unpack fresh clothing, anxious to peel out of the LCG. "Could you direct me to the hygiene compartment?"

"Through that archway. Well, yes or no?"

"Yes."

"Why?"

"It was a personal matter."

"Those others . . . the ones you killed on the *Mons,* and on the *'Notchka,* were they just personal matters, too?"

Graham stripped and wrapped a towel around his waist. "Do you believe every rumor you hear?"

"Only the interesting ones. I also hear that you pulled some ninja moves on a T.E. Knocked him across the room without touching him. How true is that?"

Graham gathered up shower articles. "As true as you want it to be, Wade."

"Could you teach me how to do it?"

"No. Excuse me."

The colony's infirmary seemed the logical place for him to begin, Graham suggested to Anna Leah that evening after dinner, which was served in a main hall around low tables and piled cushions.

"They might resent your presence," she said, peeling an orange. "Seras are very sensitive about medical people. You must remember, most of us have been poked and prodded from the time we were in utero. Jema Marie is medically trained, but she's also one of us."

Graham had met the fiftyish woman earlier in the day. She reminded him of a midwife and she looked none too well herself.

"I have no other training to offer you," he said. "I don't want to stay here as a noncontributing guest."

"What about your skills as a T'ai Chi instructor? There are those here who would benefit from such training."

"Would it be a fair exchange?"

"We would consider it of value. Especially to those whose health is somewhat delicate and find strenuous exercise too demanding. You could also teach us your method of meditation if it's allowed."

A trio of singers entertained the colonists after food had been cleared away, and then Wade and three other musicians played several original songs he had recently composed.

"What is your impression of us so far?" Anna Leah asked as they walked back to the singles' quarters.

"I doubt that I need to tell you. I like your world, Anna Leah. I may not agree with your philosophy, but I like the world you have created for yourselves."

"We don't frighten you, then?"

"No. You were never . . . no."

It was the laughter and the music that charmed him most. It flourished everywhere. The Seras, it seemed to

Graham, made the celebration of life a full-time occupa-
tion. The Jeremians would have called it hedonistic, he
supposed, but the Seras sought out beauty in everything
they touched. The highly focused creativity among them
startled him. So too did the death rate. There were two
cremations in a period of less than four cycles. It was as if
they desperately needed to leave behind a token of permanence to balance out shortened life spans. And so they
left stories and poems, paintings and sculpture, music,
dance, and drama. And everywhere there was laughter.
Would the intensity of their creative drive have been
blunted had they chosen medical and scientific alternatives, he wondered. "Brief flames, burning brightly,"
Maggie McKay had said of them. And still Graham ab-
horred their choices, looking upon them as a form of
barbaric self-sacrifice.

He began the T'ai Chi instruction with some reluctance, only to discover that his novices seemed to come to
class fully prepared to address the spiritual aspects of the
discipline as well as the physical. He had considered himself a poor teacher, not only unworthy to pass on to others
what he had not yet mastered himself, but also incapable
of communicating a philosophy that was infinitely complex in its simplicity. Unlike the SURF base students, who
seemed to care only for the movements in physical terms,
the Seras bombarded him with endless questions. Some
were already students of Taoism and challenged Graham
much as he had challenged his own masters when he was
a youth. Their eagerness embarrassed him, for he could
now see his own foolish hunger reflected like a mocking
memory. And the student who mirrored him most was
Wade Ross. Had this man come to his attention within his
former world, Graham thought, he would have been sin-
gled out, groomed for an executive position. At twenty-
four, he had the qualities much in demand for corporate
leadership. Only the anger had to be reined in, somehow.
And Graham did not know how to teach him that.

Most of the men of the colony shunned barbering as a
precious waste of time and so cultivated beards and hair
that was often almost shoulder-length. Graham, adapting
to his surroundings, followed suit. When he was not
teaching, he was learning. The Seras, proud of their skills,

taught him the basics of pottery throwing and glassblowing. Wade tutored him in guitar. It was only in those brief
periods that the animosity that radiated from the man
abated.

"So you really think all your A-Class Perfects will covet
whatever our little cottage industry produces," Wade said,
watching Graham practice chording. They sat on the rugs
in the singles' quarters, which was empty except for two
men engrossed in a chess game over in a corner.

"I believe so. The pieces I've seen so far would be valued even if they had been produced on Earth."

"We're that good?"

Graham handed the guitar back to the man. "Yes. Let
me hear something from your musical. Or is it an opera?"

"It's not ready and it's an opera. You're not finished.
Keep practicing. You're awful."

"My fingers hurt."

Wade snorted and began playing an intricate melody.
"You never worked up a sweat in your life, much less any
calluses, am I right? You probably hired somebody to
work up calluses for you. Maybe you got one little callus
—from pushing all those buttons."

Graham watched him play. There had been calluses,
he thought. The hardness had crept upon him silently
until his soul was safe from pain. There had been such
distance between his mind and dangerous emotions that
the barriers had sealed him off from life. Only now was
he learning that to have nothing was to treasure everything equally.

"What you're playing, is that from your opera?"

"Yeah. There's a theory that Hugo's Quasimodo may
have suffered from neurofibromatosis. Most people still
call it the Elephant Man's disease, but Merrick had another disorder called Proteus Syndrome."

"I know."

"I carry that in me. A blueprint for making monsters.
Back home I had to declare that for all to see. I wore a
metal wristband that warned everyone that my seed was
poison. Because I refused sterilization and I refused genetic tampering, I was an Untouchable. It's still an imperfect science, genetic engineering, no matter what you've
been led to believe. Coming here, to the Seras, was the

first freedom I ever knew. Here, you're the freak, Sinclair. You're the only Perfect among us."

"Anna Leah . . ."

"Her imperfections are her own business. Nobody has to declare anything here. Leave her alone. I watch you watching her. Just stay away from her." Abruptly Wade got up and left. The two chess players turned to look at Graham. He picked up the guitar and returned to his chording.

CHAPTER 27

Siegler's fingers searched for the loose wisp of copper hair at her neck and tucked it back under control. Baker followed her reluctantly into the observation studio, a section of the SURF base that was ordinarily forbidden to him.

The walls of the large room seemed to be made of rectangular screens, and every screen that was on showed a different focus of activity from various communes. Members of the SURF scientific team, wearing high-level security clearance ID tags, monitored the activities at stations around the room.

"I thought you might like to see how your protégé is doing," said Siegler, pointing out a row of seven TV screens along one wall. Four of the screens were on but not in working order. Three other screens monitored various sections of the Sera colony.

Baker examined his shoes. "I don't want to observe him this way, Risa. I told you that."

"Well, you'd better get a look at him while you can still see him. He's managed to screw up four of our cameras so far. It's just a matter of time before he finds the rest. He's also scrambled eight of the ten listening discs." She gestured to another row of screens. All seven were on the blink. "He was a busy boy while he was with the Jerrys, too. I don't understand how he knows where to look."

Baker, unable to suppress his curiosity, glanced at the three remaining screens that were still functioning in the Sera colony. "It's part of his corporate training, I would imagine. Some of those business dealings are more elaborately guarded than military secrets. Where is he? I don't see him."

Siegler folded her arms. "Oh, he's there, blending in like a chameleon. Look at the screen on the right."

Baker moved closer, peering over the shoulder of Robert Conroy, one of the SURF staff workers. "That's Graham? What happened?" The dark-bearded man sitting on the floor, bent over a guitar, looked nothing like Graham Sinclair, he thought.

"He's . . . adapting to the environment." Siegler leaned toward the monitor. "Can't you pick up any sound?"

"He flushed the singles' quarters disc yesterday." Conroy shrugged. "That's nine. One to go."

"Great." The woman slammed a file down on a desk.

"I'll lay odds," said a second worker, "that he finds number ten before the next cycle."

"He's tampering with government property," Siegler snapped, glaring at Baker, "and it's all your fault. Monitors are beginning to blank out over in the Ventures now, too. I suspect it's that Tucker girl. He must have told her to do it. Or one of the others. He's systematically blinding the project."

"How long has he been playing guitar?" Baker asked Conroy.

"About two cycles."

"Is he any good?"

The man nodded. "He learns fast. He's practically got Wade Ross in his pocket. That's no small feat. Ross is the most militantly hostile member of the Sera commune. I have to hand it to the man—Sinclair knows what he's doing. If he can influence Ross, then he can just about direct the power of the whole commune. Anna Leah is another matter."

"What do you mean?"

Siegler examined notes left by an earlier shift. "You

know her better than anyone, Jon. You know she sees through games. If Sinclair tries manipulation with her, she'll spot it. So far he's been the quintessential gentleman and guest. I thought you said there was an attraction between them."

Baker turned away from the screen. "I never said that."

"I thought you said—"

"I was mistaken." He brushed past her. "Excuse me."

Siegler watched him leave. "Jon, remember your priorities. You've already tampered with the project in irreparable ways. Don't do further damage or you'll be eliminated from the program altogether. I have people I must answer to also, you know. I can't keep making excuses for you."

Baker paused at the door. "Maybe I'm doing exactly what I was meant to do. In some cosmic plan bigger than your little laboratory experiments, Dr. Siegler. Maybe I'm meant to be the proverbial monkey wrench."

"Jon . . ."

He was halfway down the corridor before she caught up with him.

"They could order you off the planet," she warned. "Don't do something stupid." She grabbed at his sleeve and he pulled away.

"Risa, I quit. I don't want any more to do with this damned . . . project. I can't wash clean of it. The sleaze won't come off. I respect the man. He doesn't deserve what all of you are doing to him."

"But it's working! Can't you see that? Graham Sinclair is the catalyst that may well determine the future of life on Mars. You believe in that. You want that as much as we do."

"How can you justify your own prime directive of non-intervention and do what you're doing?"

Siegler shoved her hands into the pockets of her lab coat. "We're not . . . interfering. It's like dropping a new bacterium into a culture dish—whatever happens or doesn't happen is entirely up to the participants. No one is forcing the man to save the planet. But he just may do it. Yes, I'm sure the colonies would have established a cohesive unity someday on their own. But it might have taken

generations. The Mars Commission doesn't *have* generations to wait. They're under pressure themselves. No government will continue to underwrite a losing proposition
indefinitely. They need to see some evidence of prosperity
and growth, some effort toward independence. Graham
Sinclair is the only hope we have right now."

She reached out and gently stroked Baker's cheek.
"Don't walk out on the project, Jon. We need you. Please."

Baker leaned against the wall and sighed. "Promise me
one thing."

"What?"

"If he should ever find out why he was brought here,
tell him I was never . . . I didn't want to be a part of
this. I wanted no part of the plan. Tell him the truth."

"He'll never find out."

"Just . . . promise me."

"You'll stay?"

Baker slowly nodded.

"You'll stop meddling?"

"I'll do whatever I have to do in order to live with
myself."

"That's not overly reassuring."

"It's the best I can do."

CHAPTER 28

Graham's nose itched, but he couldn't take his hands from the spinning pot. He was spattered with clay and yet the smoothness beneath his fingers soothed him. He could feel the shape evening into uniformity and balance under the slightest pressure. There was an aesthetic pleasure in the act that almost mesmerized him. He liked throwing pots, he decided, better than blowing glass.

"Not bad for a beginner." Paul Cole, the master potter, wiped his hands on his apron. "A few more cycles and you'll be a right decent craftsman." The barrel-chested man had vociferously resisted Graham's intrusion into the commune until he had found himself in what he perceived as a dominant role, teaching the Perfect something of his art. That Graham recognized the beauty within unshaped clay pleased him. He was unaware that it was he, not the clay, that was being so skillfully turned.

"We must convince him to stay longer, then," said Anna Leah, approaching them from behind. "He leaves with the arrival of the next cycler."

Cole looked up. "He's going home? I thought . . ."

Graham lost the steady pressure on the clay and the shape wobbled. The soft walls buckled and the pot collapsed into ruin.

"See what happens when you don't concentrate?" Cole scolded.

"He's moving on to the Keyote colony," Anna Leah explained.

"Those paeans to the theory of de-evolution? They'll eat him for breakfast. Sinclair, are you a masochist? Do you enjoy monosyllabic conversations?"

Graham scraped the clay off the potter's wheel and scratched his nose. "I haven't been there yet. It's the only colony I haven't seen."

"Taking the grand tour, are you? Going up into the hinterlands, now. Why? The miners aren't colonists. They're here for what they can get, then they're gone. They won't be interested in any unifying ideas you might propose." Cole slammed a lump of clay onto Graham's wheel. "They don't care about any of us, or the future of Mars. Why bother?"

"It's something to do. It interests me."

Anna Leah removed a pale blue-and-wine-colored scarf from around her neck. "Here, this will keep your hair out of your eyes." She folded the scarf into a sweatband and tied it around Graham's head. Briefly her fingers brushed his forehead. They felt cool and he resisted an impulse to touch her, to grasp her fingers and hold the coolness until they warmed.

"Graham, I came to talk to you about the Grace Banquet tomorrow. I thought you should be aware of a special . . . custom we have . . . why this ceremony is special." She glanced up at Cole. "Have you explained it to him?"

"I was going to get around to it." The man frowned. "But Perfects will never understand."

"If you're referring to your custom of ritual suicide, I know about it. Wade Ross told me."

Anna Leah pulled a bamboo stool over and sat beside him while he worked the clay. Cole excused himself to attend to other matters. "I don't expect your approval of our custom, Graham. I just didn't want you to be shocked, once you found out. We value, above all, our right to decide things for ourselves, about our selves. Sula Watson has begun to show symptoms of her . . . genetic inheritance. She's in a great deal of pain. And she chooses not to extend her existence until she's incapable of purposeful contribution. She has the option to withdraw with grace and dignity. Without condemnation from anyone."

Graham kept his eyes on the clay in front of him. "She has other options that might extend her purposeful contributions."

"She's well aware of the medical avenues available to her. It would simply prolong her decline. It would not cure her."

"The *cure* was in the hands of her parents. Before she was ever conceived." Graham's fingers pressed harder into the lump of clay.

"Her son is Akim Watson."

He looked up, the clay momentarily forgotten. "The concert pianist?"

"The same. If Sula had accepted sterilization . . . or if her parents had opted for genetic engineering . . . Every choice we make alters the world in some small way. No one is more acutely aware of that than we are."

Graham had felt, in the time he had spent among the Sera colonists, a subtle shift in his attitude toward the group. Although he did not wholly agree with their philosophy, he had come to respect their courage and pride and their fiercely guarded independence. He was daily taken aback by their splendid reach for perfection in their arts. He watched dancers push themselves to sweaty exhaustion, demanding that final nuance in an arch of the body, a leap a fraction above the one before, a turn more exquisitely executed than the last. There were the singers and musicians who seemed to work tirelessly to shape sound into a harmonious whole more keenly tuned than anything he had heard on Earth. Perfection produced by imperfect, flawed beings. Slowly he was beginning to wonder if perhaps there were not gifts to be offered to the gene pool by these misfits after all.

"You needn't come to the banquet if it makes you feel uncomfortable." Anna Leah rose to leave. "But you would be most welcome to join us. No Perfect has ever been a part of it before. Sula asked me to extend the invitation to you."

"All right. I'll come."

"Good. It will please her to have you there."

He had expected the evening to be somewhat macabre in nature, a forced gaiety and ebullience in the face of imminent loss. He had never attended an Irish wake but supposed that a Grace Banquet might be somewhat similar, except that the guest of honor was alive and alert. To Graham's surprise, however, the evening was filled with loving gestures and not a few tears. Sula Watson moved among the guests like the consummate hostess, sharing favorite memories and bequeathing her material possessions. Within the commune she had been a muralist. Her favorite themes were fantasy-filled jungles and tropical dreamscapes. Graham admired her work and knew that on Earth her paintings would be highly prized. Only recently had she turned to Martian landscapes, and it was through her eyes that Graham first began to see the beauty of the planet to which he had been banished.

There were circle dances after the feast and he found himself pulled into the music, hoping to touch Anna Leah, however briefly, as they spun and swirled about the room. It seemed as if everyone had selected their brightest, most vivid colors to wear that night. Earlier, in the singles' quarters, Wade had offered him a loose shirt heavily embroidered with a radiating design across the chest. "Gifts are not given lightly here," he had explained. "To refuse is an insult. You reject the person."

"Then I accept." Graham inadvertently gave a slight bow, which had been the custom in his dealings with the East. Wade seemed not to notice. "I regret I have nothing to offer you in return."

"That's not the point. It's not an exchange. Not like you're thinking. It's more like the left hand offering an orange to the right hand. With us, it's an acknowledgment of interconnectedness. Anna Leah didn't give you her scarf on a whim. She made a proclamation for all to see. She accepts you as one of us. I never thought I'd let a Perfect into my world, or that there would be something I could learn from you."

Graham studied the design on the shirt. The needlepoint had been done by Chera Pursell, who had died the previous winter. Although he had never met her, he had learned to recognize her legacy wherever he looked. "You're a quick student."

"I don't mean the T'ai Chi."

"Then what have I taught you?"

Wade seemed embarrassed. "Maybe . . . you don't want to hear it."

"I'm not easily offended."

The man paused, waiting for another member of the Seras to pass through to the shower room. "We're outcasts by choice. I mean from Earth. You . . . never chose to come here. You're an outcast in the extreme. No one asked you to come. No one on Mars wanted you here. You have no *place* anywhere. You don't belong. You've taught me how to . . ." He looked down, examining his callused fingers. ". . . how to cherish . . . what I have."

Graham wasn't sure what he had been prepared to hear, but whatever it was, he was not prepared for the bluntness of the man's summation of his life. He had managed to block out the gravity of his situation during most of his waking hours. The less he examined it, the less impact it had. Only Paris, first in her innocence, then in her own anguish, had reopened wounds he had kept hidden.

"I'm sorry. I shouldn't have told you that. I just want you to know you're welcome to stay here, as long as you like. I mean, after you've checked out the Keyote colony, you've got a place here with us, if you want."

Graham swallowed. "Thank you."

The emotional turbulence had not left him throughout the evening. The purpose of the celebration only added to the ambivalence he felt toward these people.

"You're sweating," Anna Leah said, sitting down beside him on the oversize pillows after a particularly dizzying dance. "I never would have taken you for a dancer, but you move quite well."

"How long does this continue?"

"Through the night. But it grows quieter. Sula has already made her departure."

"What?"

"She has already retired to her bedchamber. We take turns throughout the night sitting with her. We tell her things we always meant to say . . . Did you want to speak with her?"

"She gave me one of her paintings . . . I wanted to tell her . . ."

Anna Leah rose and held out her hand. "Come. I'll take you to her."

He followed her along matted corridors to a section of the commune he had never seen before. Here were private cubicles, on the order of small apartments. Many of the doors were open, and each living space seemed to offer the unique tastes and interests of the inhabitant. All looked curiously inviting. Graham wondered if one of these was where Anna Leah slept.

"Yes, my quarters are there, at the end of the corridor," she said, then blushed. "Oh. You didn't ask me that, did you?"

"Not aloud. But I thought it."

"Forgive me. I try not to do that. It makes people feel uncomfortable sometimes."

They stopped before an open door. The room was dimly lit and two women sat near a bed draped in pastel netting and garlands of flowers. Graham was vaguely reminded of a book illustration he'd once seen of the burial of a Viking princess, the boat festooned with blossoms and veils, drifting out into a hazy mist.

"Remember," Anna Leah whispered, "she can hear you, even if she appears to be asleep."

Graham entered the room slowly and the two women withdrew. Sula Watson lay as if dreaming the sweetest of dreams, her chocolate skin smooth, her face free of pain.

He had never touched her during their brief friendship and was now sorry that he had not. He sat down beside the bed and placed his hand over her long graceful fingers. They were still warm, still holding life. Part of him felt a flash of rage. The talent that would be stilled by dawn was a loss that was appalling to him. He felt an urge to shake her back into life, to force her to breathe and open her eyes. This was a custom he would forever reject.

"Sula," he began. "It's Graham Sinclair. I . . . wish . . . I want you to know of the gift you've given me. You've shown me beauty in a land where I saw no beauty. I thank you for that . . . I just wish . . . you could have stayed with us . . . longer . . ."

The woman's eyes fluttered open and Graham drew back, startled. "Oh, I'll be around, one way or another." She smiled sleepily. "A mote in God's eye, maybe." She took a deep breath and patted his hand. "Good-bye, Graham Sinclair." She closed her eyes, drifting back into what would become a final sleep.

Graham, not knowing what else to do, gently slipped from the room.

"Do you want to talk about it?" Anna Leah asked as they made their way back to the festivities.

"No. Suicide goes against everything I value. But I can't be inside Sula, to know her pain, either. I'm trying to understand your ways. It's difficult."

"I know. But you've come a long way in the time you've been here. And you've given many of us something, too. You've taught Wade compassion . . ."

"Pity."

"No. Compassion. It was a great lacking in him. He's beginning to understand that perhaps perfection is defined by something other than genetic purity. The bitterness within him would not allow him to see that there really is no total perfection in life. Nor is there meant to be. There wouldn't *be* any life. Our need to create, to move and rearrange, to *make better,* is due to our need to reach toward that wholeness we all lack. It's the very pain of our imperfections that causes us to reach inside and find whatever gifts we may have. Those with the greatest pain, the greatest need, speak most eloquently for those who have no voice. Nijinsky is said to have defied gravity in his ballets. It was his madness that drove him to reach for the impossible. And what of Van Gogh? Suppose mood stabilizer implants had been available to him? We would have nothing of his genius and passion. And Mozart and Beethoven and Schumann and Poe, and all the others. A few minor genetic adjustments in the womb and . . . what a bland heritage mankind would have reaped."

"And what of the potential Mozarts and Nijinskys and Van Goghs who lie in cribs until they waste away, vegetables from birth because of . . ." Graham stopped, his momentary anger in retreat.

"Because of people like me?"

The silence between them was filled with mute bludgeonings.

"It's all right," she said finally, moving ahead of him. "There is no one right answer. I know that."

"Anna Leah, is there no common ground for us? Is there nothing on which we can agree?"

She turned and looked at him. "The future of Mars. We agree on that. Life here should thrive." She shrugged slightly. "It's a beginning."

CHAPTER 29

The last of the packed glassware and pottery was placed aboard the rover. Graham was mildly surprised by his own accumulation of possessions in the time he had lived among the Seras. He had, in fact, left some things in storage since he wasn't sure of the accommodations awaiting him at the Keyote colony. The way Haas had once described living conditions at the mining facility, he doubted that Sula's painting would have space there to hang.

Wade Ross, Anna Leah, and three members of the Seras who were escorting the colony's merchandise to Earth accompanied him on the journey back to the SURF base.

They stopped at Pod 3 to eat and stretch, and saw signs that the Jeremians had been there earlier in the day. There were fresh blankets and food preserves in the storage compartment. Anna Leah set out several pottery cups on a shelf.

Wade moved around the pod, his eyes searching for something. "What do you think?" he said to Graham. "Are there bugs here?"

"Most likely."

"Where?"

"I've shown you how to look for them. See what you can find."

Everyone watched the man as he prowled about the room searching out the monitoring devices.

"This should be brought up at the next council meeting," said Anna Leah. "It's an outrage."

Wade groped under the stone slab table in the center of the room. "Found one."

"There should be another within five meters of that one," Graham cautioned. "The camera is probably under the vines."

"Maybe we shouldn't tamper with it," said Gabby Reed, one of the women who was returning to Earth. "It might be helpful if someone's in need. At least we'd know they could see and hear us."

"But nobody would come, Gabby. That's the trouble," said Wade. "They just watch and listen, record bits of data, and file it away. Right, guys?" he addressed the stone walls, and kept searching.

Anna Leah sipped hot tea. "Well, shall we stay here for the night or drive straight through in shifts?"

"Straight through," said Ron Harper, the one male returnee. "It gets crowded as hell at the SURF base before the cycler comes. I don't want to bunk in the corridors. It's going to be bad enough aboard the 'Notchka."

"I rather like it," Paula, the third returnee, said. "It feels so . . . primitive. You never know when a fight's going to break out."

"You especially like it if the fight's over you." Wade nodded. "Ah, got it." He removed a small disc from a ledge where it had been hidden under a tumble of vines. Both listening devices were unceremoniously tossed into the fountain. "Now for the camera."

Graham had coached the three novices in the ways and manner of the high-level art world they would be entering when they returned to Earth. They would be sent directly to Jasmine Wyncote for further instruction and final polishing. She would know what to do, he knew, and with any luck there would be a message from her upon their return.

Gabby, a petite blonde, tugged at the collar of her gravity suit. "God, it's miserable in this thing. How much longer till we peel?"

Wade checked his watch. "Another hour to go. Two in, four out. No cheating."

"I can't believe I grew up lugging all this tonnage around. It hurts!"

"You volunteered, Chunky Cheeks."

The girl slapped at him. "I do not have chunky cheeks, Wade Ross. *You* walk around in a gravity suit for hours and see how you like it."

The weighted suits were a cumbersome necessity for anyone contemplating return to Earth gravity. Graham, out of curiosity, had donned one once during his stay with the Seras. After half an hour of routine movement he was totally exhausted. "You have to build up your endurance time," Wade had cautioned, watching him strip out of the leaded material, which resembled elasticized chain mail. "You planning a trip, Sinclair?"

"No. I just wanted to . . . remember what it felt like."

"Feels like hell. Earth does."

"Wade, don't mention to anyone that you saw me wearing a gravity suit. It will just make things uncomfortable for both of us if the Committee hears about it."

"How come?"

Graham rolled the material into a cocoon shape and placed it in a steri-cleaner compartment. "It's on a list of things forbidden to me."

"Gravity suits? That's crazy."

"Crazy or not, I'm not allowed access to them. I have no need of them, you see."

There had been a look in Wade's eyes that seemed to register for the first time the enormity of Graham's difference. "I keep forgetting," he said softly.

"Most people do, after a while. I don't wear a number, or prison clothes, or chains, but I am still a prisoner here. For the rest of my life."

It was soon after that that Wade had shown him the completed libretto for his opera.

Phobos was high in the night sky when Ron Harper tapped Graham on the shoulder for the next driving shift.

"There's coffee up front strong enough to sprout hair on your tongue. Paula made it. Blame her."

Graham, coming out of a dream, was momentarily disoriented. He had been on the Trans-Atlantic Sky Rail and thought Ti was shaking him awake, complaining about the insolence of one of the conductors.

Anna Leah was already in the driver's seat when he moved up to take Paula's copilot position.

"Would you rather drive?"

"I don't know how to pilot a rover," he said, adjusting the seat for more legroom.

"And you such a daring race car driver," Anna Leah chided. "It's time you learned. Trade seats with me."

Graham hesitated. "I'd rather learn to drive during daylight."

"There's plenty of moonlight. You've done it before. Move over here."

She pointed out various gears and mechanisms, and Graham lurched off the road.

"Less pressure on the foot," she said, laughing. "Watch that rock. Now you're getting it. There's nothing to it. Coffee?"

He sipped the steaming drink and drove in silence for several kilometers. "I didn't tell you that," he said finally.

"I did it again?"

"I never told you I raced cars. When was I thinking it?"

"I don't know. It was just . . . there. It just came."

"How? In words? Pictures?"

"I don't know. Sometimes it's like running a video on fast forward. By the time the image registers, it's gone. But you can recall it like a memory. As if the memory is your own. It used to be a little confusing. Sometimes it still is."

"You've always had this . . . ability?"

"Yes. So did my mother and my sister."

Graham handed her the emptied cup. "Your sister?"

"Yes. When we were small, everyone was worried that we were mute. We talked all the time. Only not out loud. Matina was four years older and . . ."

"Matina?"

"Yes. She . . ."

"Where do I know that name? She's not with the Seras . . ."

Anna Leah watched him in the darkness, the tracking screen lighting her face. "She died. When she was twenty-one."

"Baker."

"Yes. They were bonded. He must have told you about her."

"I didn't know that she was . . . He never elaborated and I never asked."

After a silence, Anna Leah said, "It was childbirth. She died in childbirth, and no, I'm not going to fall over dead anytime soon. I happen to be quite healthy. And I know you didn't ask. But I'm telling you anyway."

"Why are you angry?"

"Your fear makes me angry."

"I'm not afraid of you. I told you that."

"Well, you lied. You can't lie. Not to me, Graham Sinclair. You're afraid to . . . love someone who could die on you. We're all going to die. I could outlive you, you know. Life is not a contract. Nobody gets a guaranteed number of years, no matter . . ."

Graham stopped the rover in the middle of the road, leaned over and kissed her. It was the most unplanned thing he had ever done in his life. From the back of the rover came enthusiastic applause.

Anna Leah drew back, seemingly more flustered by Graham's move than by the audience of four, all sitting up in the bunks, watching them.

"At this rate we'll never get to the SURF base," Wade grumbled.

"It was nice," Paula said. "Leave them alone."

"I'd give it an eight." Ron nodded.

"Does this make you betrothed, Anna Leah?" asked Gabby.

Embarrassment was not an emotion Graham experienced often but he felt it now. "I'm . . . I apologize."

Anna Leah slid the partition to the cabin shut. There were muffled boos from the other side. "Apology not accepted. We'll discuss this later. Drive."

The discomfort of the ensuing silence grew intolerable as Graham examined the rashness of the moment. Why had he done such an unprovoked thing, he wondered. To act without constraint was an abhorrence to him. It conveyed weakness. Impulsive behavior was allowable, even appealing in women, so his grandfather had taught, but it was never to be condoned in his own conduct. "An impulsive decision will lay you open to the vultures, boy. Never forget that. Once you've shown them your Achilles' heel, they'll bring you down. Spontaneity equals self-destruction. Never let them know what you think. Never." Even when he had broken Baker's jaw and gone on the smashing rampage, the wrath had been directed with controlled deliberation. It was only when he was around this woman that he lost control. She was intoxicating in a way that left him bewildered and hungering even as he feasted on her closeness.

Anna Leah cleared her throat. "I won't accept your apology because . . . I don't want you to be sorry. That you did what you did."

"It was an unforgivable breach of etiquette on my part, Anna Leah. For that, I am sorry."

"You've never impulsively kissed a woman before?"

"Not . . . impulsively."

"Were you ever bonded to someone?"

"No."

"Betrothed?"

"No."

"But there were women . . ."

"Yes."

A faint pinkish glow in the east grew brighter as they drove on in silence. "I don't know how long I'll be attached to the Keyote colony . . ." Graham began, "but if . . . after a time . . ."

"You would be welcome to stay with us."

"And we might pursue this . . . further?"

"If you like. Yes."

"I would . . . like that."

"Good."

CHAPTER 30

One section of the SURF base was traditionally set aside for barter between the colonies during the arrival of the cyclers. The Jeremians brought cloth, preserved foods, cheeses, honey, and bamboo furniture to trade. The Ventures bartered contracts for CELSS additions, labor skills, and wine. A great quantity of wine. The Seras brought glass, pottery, loomed rugs, and handcrafted jewelry made of polished native stones. The departing Keyote miners were the biggest customers in the jewelry area, Graham had noticed, handing over credits for the souvenirs to take home to wives and families.

The SURF researchers observed everything through their hidden cameras and, in return, gave out medical supplies and equipment that had been ordered from Earth through the Mars Commission.

Graham was sitting with Baker in the commissary when Paris arrived. She stared at him, clearly confused for several moments.

"Gray? Is that you?"

He got up, and she grinned. "My God! It *is* you under all that hair. You look like—like a Sera. No offense." Laughing, she hugged him. He put his arms around her, marveling at the ease with which they touched. He hadn't realized how much he had missed her.

"I hardly recognized him myself," Baker said as Paris joined them. "If it hadn't been for . . . ah . . ."

Graham looked at him. "The cameras," he prompted.

"Well, I didn't really . . . only once. You'll be pleased to know you've put them all out of commission now. Siegler is pissed. That should please you even more."

Paris reached over and stroked Graham's hair. "Jeez, you can almost braid it. Don't cut it. Let it grow. And the beard. I like it. It hides that A-Class gloss. That pedigreed, manicured look."

"Good thing she's a friend." Baker smiled, sipping a drink. "Heaven knows what she'd say if she hated you."

"So where are you staying?" she asked.

"In the medical section," Graham said.

"Oh. I'm over in Section D. I was hoping maybe . . ."

"I'm sharing quarters with three other medics."

"Oh. I'm not. I mean, I have a room to myself. Some of us are just lucky that way. Let me know if they snore. I mean, if you can't . . . Baker, don't you have things to do?"

"No."

"Then *find* something to do, why don't you? I think I hear Siegler screeching for you already."

Baker chuckled and got up. "Graham, don't forget the meeting at eighteen hundred hours with Tillman. And maybe you'd better think about a barber. He's not crazy about you coming, to begin with. Looking like a Sera won't go down well. The miners aren't fond of them as a rule."

After Baker had departed, Paris moved closer to the table. "So. You're still going up there."

"Yes. When the cycler leaves."

"For how long?"

"I don't know."

"Is this unification of the colonies business still in the works?"

"Yes."

Paris fiddled with a paper napkin. "And her? Is she still in the works? Your vestal virgin?"

Graham watched her fold the napkin into a child's fan, then smooth it back out. "Why didn't you ever return my calls, Paris? I thought we were friends."

"We are. I was busy. We've been surveying down in the Marineris. We're building two new pods over in the Sinai Planum. I wanted . . . to stay out of your way, okay? So, tell me, did you boff her yet?"

"Paris, stop it."

"Sorry. I'm just a naturally crude type. Ventures are C-Class all the way. Didn't you know that? But we're a cut above Keyote cretins, at least." She wadded the paper into a ball and tossed it across the table. "I'm sorry. I don't know why I do that every time I'm around you. It's like a compulsion. Do you know how many times I've gone over our opening conversation once we met back here? I've worked it threadbare, let me tell you. My favorite one was that I'd be down in the CELSS and you'd come up behind me and just kind of slip your arms around my waist and I'd spin around and be surprised and say . . . I don't know . . . that part always got fuzzy. But it would be the *right* thing. And you sure didn't have all that hair."

"I missed you. There were times I really wanted to talk to you."

She finally looked up at him. "You mean that?"

"Of course."

Paris brightened visibly. "We found some more of that special sand. Brought it to barter."

"Good. Anna Leah will be happy to get it."

"I'm thrilled she'll be thrilled. So have you seduced her yet, or what? Is that a better word? Seduce?"

"The topic is not open to discussion, Paris."

"You haven't. What have you been doing over there all this time then, besides growing hair?"

"Learning."

"About what? Certainly not about sex. What will it take to get you moving, Sinclair? You need a pimp lawyer to set up the deal? Is that how you A-Class types negotiate courtship? You want me to talk to her for you? I could tell her how . . ."

Graham rose, grabbed Paris by her right wrist, and yanked her to her feet.

"Ow. What are you doing?"

Without a word, he dragged her from the crowded room and out the door.

"Graham, stop it. Let go. Where are we going?"

He marched her down corridors, ignoring the stares of those who turned to watch.

"My fingers are turning purple, here, O Brute One. God, what a beard does for the gonads. Let go!"

Graham did not let go, nor did he loosen his grip on her wrist. They reached the Exercise Module and he pulled her through doorways until they reached the pool. Without pausing he flung Paris into the water, fully clothed.

Several men already in the pool began to laugh, applauding the gesture.

Paris surfaced sputtering and swam to the edge, ignoring Graham's hand as she pulled herself out of the water.

"Damn you, Sinclair! Why did you do that?" She wrung her hair, then shook it like a wet hunting dog. It began to curl resolutely, even while dripping.

"Because I couldn't hit you."

"Do me a favor. Next time hit me."

"If you'd rather."

Paris bent over and lunged at Graham, butting him in the middle like an incensed mountain goat. He fell backward into the water to the accompaniment of whistles and cheers from the women in the pool.

"I'd rather," Paris said, and squished off to change clothes.

Aaron Tillman eyed the notorious Cloud Man from the far end of the table, allowing his disapproval to register on his face. Graham Sinclair looked nothing like the image Tillman had conjured based on the numerous rumors and stories he'd heard about the man. He looked like someone who would be more comfortable moving chess pieces around a board than tossing men in a brawl on the *Ninotchka*. Although he was clean-shaven, he wore his hair long, pulled back and tied at the neck in the manner of many of the Seras.

"If he comes to Keyote, the hair goes," Tillman declared, more to Baker than to Graham. "I don't want any trouble. I can't guarantee his safety as it is."

"Graham can take care of himself," Baker offered, pacing the floor between the two.

"So I hear. If he goes out of control with us, I'll have him tranqued and shipped back to you in a box. I need a medic, not a candidate for an M.S.I. If he's scheduled for one, maybe he should have the implant done before he comes to us."

"Graham Sinclair is probably more stable than either of us, Aaron."

"Yeah? What about the woman he tried to drown just today? You call that stable?"

"A love tiff." Baker shrugged, looking to Graham for help. "Right?"

Graham didn't respond.

"Right?"

"Something like that," Graham said, finally.

Tillman's frown deepened. "We don't need any of that crap, either."

Graham eyed the broad-shouldered man, deciding that he was perhaps in his late forties. Touches of gray had begun to spread from his temples into his black, bristle-cut hair. "Mr. Tillman, wouldn't it be more advantageous to bring the families of the miners to Mars than to lace their food with Dar-Quel 25? Do they know they're being drugged?"

"Who told you that?" Tillman's scowl twisted a notch toward apoplexy. "Who told him that? I don't want him! He's trouble! He'll cause trouble at the mines!"

Baker stared at Graham. "Who told you that? Nobody knows that."

Graham clasped his fingers together and sat back. "It would seem to me that the Keyote Mining Corporation would be able to enhance production output and entice the labor force to stay longer if they weren't cut off from their families for such long periods. As things are run now, the workers function far below their normal capabilities. Your accident rate record is abysmal, simply because their reaction time is impaired. Thanks to their drugged state."

Tillman got up, furious. "Who told him all this? Do you know what this could do to morale if it gets out? If we have another riot like the one in '49, it could grind everything to a halt. The bastard has never set foot in the colony. How does he know all this if one of you didn't tell him?"

Baker sighed. "I don't know. Graham, all of this is privileged information. How did you know about the Dar-Quel 25?"

"I watch it come in on the cyclers and I watch it go out. Keyote is the only colony that loads up on boxes of it. Count the number of beds occupied by miners. Ninety percent of the accidents and injuries sent to the SURF base hospital come from Keyote. The level of DQ 25 in their systems measures far above the recommended dosage. That's why they cause so much trouble when they hit SURF during the arrival of the cyclers. The dosage is stopped cold and it sends them into an emotionally labile state. They're out of control."

"Just what I need—a medic who thinks. Jon, the man is walking anarchy. I don't want him."

"You don't have any choice. The Committee is sending him. It's been approved."

"The hell with the Committee! I'll go straight to the Commission. I won't have this man set foot in the colony. He'll be a disruptive influence. I know it!"

Baker kept his eyes on Graham. "The Commission approved it. Graham Sinclair is to be transferred to the Keyote mining colony without further delay. The decision is no longer yours to make, Aaron. If you challenge the Mars Commission, they'll be after your butt. I guarantee it."

Tillman slammed a portfolio of papers down on the table and stalked out of the meeting.

"Why in God's good time did you antagonize him like that, Gray?"

"It needed to be said."

"Not *now*. He's going to make things miserable for you. You know that, don't you?"

"Then maybe he has to go."

Baker rubbed his face in exasperation. "The Keyote Mining Corporation is not one of your companies, Graham. You're not back on Earth. This is Mars! You can't fire Tillman because you don't like the way he runs things."

Graham got up. "But somebody can. And somebody will." At the door he turned and looked at Baker. "And you don't need to remind me of where I am, Jon. I know exactly where I am."

Paris lay in bed munching cookies, so engrossed in the video on her headset that she did not hear the door to her quarters hum open. Nor did she see the figure approach her bed. By the time she became aware of him, he was standing directly over her.

"Damn! Scare me to death, Sinclair." She removed the headset. "What happened to the beard?"

"Gone."

"But you kept the ponytail. Good. I like it."

"Paris, why is your door unlocked? Haven't you learned anything?"

She sat up in bed, on her knees. "I can take care of myself now. Look at the muscle on this babe." She flexed an arm muscle of unimpressive size.

"Astounding," Graham said, clearly unastounded.

"Cookie?"

"No, thank you."

"Then why are you here?"

Graham glanced at the mirror across the room. It had been covered by the bed sheet from the second bed. Two listening discs, like an awkward pair of earrings, lay on the dresser, balanced one on top of the other to cancel out sound. "They . . . snore," he said, smiling slightly.

Paris grinned. "Oh, poor baby."

"About today . . ."

"I deserved the dunking."

"I know that."

"Take your clothes off and come to bed. We have things to discuss." Paris pulled back the covers and patted the bed.

Graham undressed as she shoved a clutter of books, cookies, and headset movie discs onto the floor.

In the darkness, beside her, Graham felt a contentment he hadn't realized he had missed. "Why is it," he said softly, "that this is our only neutral ground?"

"I don't know. Maybe . . . it's because this is the only place where we've defined the rules?"

"You may be right."

"And it helps if you don't bring up your other women in my presence."

"I've noticed that."

"Unless you want to criticize them, that is."

"I'll keep that in mind."

Paris curled close to him, sounding sleepy now. "And I'll try not to bring up your other women in my presence, too."

"Good."

"How many other women *are* there, Sinclair?"

"I'd rather not itemize tonight."

"Graham, don't go to Keyote."

"Why?"

"It's very . . . ugly there. Haas told me some awful things about it. It's dangerous."

"I won't be in the mines. I'll be in the medical facility."

Paris sat up on an elbow. "It's not the mines, it's the people who are dangerous. They don't think like . . . we do."

"I don't believe that, Paris. Haas was a miner before he joined the Ventures. He was a good man."

"Well, he wasn't like the rest of them. He never belonged at Keyote. Even he knew that. Did you know he left me a wealthy woman, Mr. Sinclair? I forget how many credits. If I went back to Earth I could rub noses with all your old A-Class friends. He never even told me he did it—named me as his sole beneficiary. And we never even . . . I don't feel rich. Do the rich *feel* rich? When you were a little kid did you know you were rich? Or did you think everybody lived like that?"

"I was . . . made aware of it. By other children."

"By the so-so rich, huh?"

"And by my mother. She made me aware of its excesses. And my grandfather, who made me aware of its power."

"If you had all your money back, all the credits . . ."

Graham sighed. "Paris, I don't want to talk about this."

". . . what would you do with it? I've got all this wealth and I don't know what to do with it. Money is practically worthless here. What would you do if you had your umpteen billion-some-odd credits back?"

There was a long silence before he spoke. "I would try to buy my freedom."

"To go home?"

"Yes. To go home."

CHAPTER 31

The six rovers moved over the dusty terrain like a caravan of mechanical insects. Graham sat in the rear section of the lead vehicle keeping an eye on two of the new miners, who were showing early signs of a flare-up of Martian Fever. The Transition Escort assigned to the fresh arrivals had done little to alleviate their anxiety, seeming bored by the few questions the miners asked. Tillman, also in the lead rover, had not said a word to Graham since the meeting almost a cycle ago.

A stocky blond woman with close-cropped hair sat across from the bunks where the two men lay, watching impassively as Graham urged them to drink from the canteens he had packed. "It's bitter, but it works," he said.

"Martian cocktails?" she asked as he replaced the canteens in a duffel bag.

"They've been called that"—Graham nodded—"among other things. Dee-Dee Brew, 'Notchka Novocaine, Gut Grinders."

"They're that, all right. But they stop the chills." She eyed him up and down. "You one of them? One of the freaks? The Contaminants?"

Graham was mildly surprised to find that the labels angered him.

His reaction must have registered on his face briefly,

he thought, for she quickly amended her question. "I mean the Seras. No offense. I mean you look like one of them, sort of . . ."

"Does that bother you?"

"No. I just wondered, that's all. I'd heard about you people back home. Coming here, to live, I mean. You don't seem so . . . different. On the outside anyway."

"He's not a Sera," Tillman said, moving back to check on the two sick miners. "Go ahead, tell her who you are. Maybe she'd like your autograph. Tell her your name."

Graham did not look up from his work. He opened a plastic bottle and shook out several yellow capsules.

"Tell her!"

"My name is Graham Sinclair." He propped up the miner in the lower bunk while the man washed down the pills with another swig from the canteen.

"The Cloud Man?" The woman sat back, staring at Graham as if she were watching a myth materialize before her.

"In the flesh," Tillman said. "So, are they going to live or die?"

"When do we reach Pod 5 at Sharonov?" Graham asked.

"Why?"

"It would be good to stop awhile and let them rest."

"Oh. I thought you were going to tell me we'd have to bury them."

"Thanks a lot," the youth in the upper bunk mumbled, not opening his eyes.

"Hey, Potter, you look pretty near dead to me."

"I live only to knock your teeth down your throat."

Tillman laughed. "About all you can do is sweat on me, kid. The pod's out of commission. We can't stop there. We have to drive straight through. Sorry."

"They need to rest," Graham said.

"They're resting. We're not stopping." Tillman glared at him and moved back to the front of the rover.

The blond woman watched Graham gently wipe Potter's face with a damp cloth. "So you're really him. This will be something to write home about." She held out her hand. "L. A. Atkins."

Graham hesitated, then reached out to touch her fingertips.

"And A-Class, at that," said the woman.

"What does L.A. stand for?"

Atkins did not appear to be a blushing kind of woman but a rosy splotchiness crept into her face. "Just L.A. I answer to that. Or Atkins."

"Lace Arabella," the man in the lower bunk mumbled.

Atkins kicked the side of the bunk. "Stow it, Malone. If you were a well man I'd deck you."

Malone opened his eyes to gaze up at the woman. "Your mother must have wanted a girl. She should have called you Burlap."

Atkins leaned forward. "Well, your mother got a girl, Sweet Pea."

The man swung his right arm out and backhanded Atkins in the face, bloodying her nose. Graham had to step between them to stop the antagonistic banter.

"And you're opposed to the use of Dar-Quel 25," Tillman muttered to Graham later, after the miners had drifted off to sleep. "Do you have any idea what we'd be up against without it? These people have nothing left to lose, coming here. They're corner fighters. They've been backed into no-escape corners, and they're fighting to survive. No one else would be willing to come to Mars. Nobody in his right mind would drag his family here."

"They're afraid," Graham countered. "They weren't adequately prepared for the environment."

"They knew enough to know what they were getting into. And the payoff seems worth it to most of them."

"Is it worth it to you?"

Tillman didn't answer, but gazed out at the darkening plain. A thin crust of snow covered the ground in shadowed patches. The land in the Acidalia region was less cratered, Graham noted, and there were several sloping hills on the horizon. The soil itself seemed to be a darker hue and somewhat less powdery. He spotted the solar wand of Pod 5, but the rovers kept moving, heading into the twilight.

"Why is the Sharonov pod out of commission?" he asked Tillman.

"It was damaged during the last dust storm and lost

pressure. Everything was killed off. Nobody's gotten around to repairing it."

"It's one of only two sanctuaries between Keyote and the SURF base. I'd think its repair would be of paramount importance. Who's responsible for looking after it?"

"Nobody."

"There should be—"

"Well, there's not. You want the job, Cloud Man? You want to be a pod keeper? We can just drop you off if you like." With that, the man headed for the front of the rover.

The repair and maintenance of the pods near the lower colonies seemed to have been a shared concern, as far as Graham could tell. The Ventures were always out checking on their status and viability. The attitude of Keyote puzzled him. The colony was by far the most isolated outpost on the planet. It seemed logical that they would be the most concerned about the safety links that connected them to the SURF headquarters.

Guy Wallace, the Keyote Transition Escort, moved back to check on his charges. "How are they doing?"

"Potter's lapsing into a delirium. It would help if we could stop for a while."

"Tillman won't allow it. Maybe we can get him to stop at Pod 6 tomorrow. We're passing through the Chryse Planitia right now. Viking I landed a few degrees southeast of here. I forget the year."

"July twentieth, 1976," Graham said.

"Right. I knew it was seventy something."

The man seemed uncomfortable but unable to find a way to withdraw. "Can I ask you something?" he said, scratching his chest absently.

"What?"

"Well, there are stories . . . about you. Things people say they saw, or thought they saw . . ."

"I didn't kill a Transition Escort."

"But you levitated him. You never touched him, but . . ." Wallace shrugged. "They saw you do it."

Graham opened an infusion cartridge. "If that's what they thought they saw, then I suppose it's what they saw."

"And the rover?"

"What rover?"

"The one you lifted off of Haas . . . How . . . ?"

Graham taped the cartridge to Potter's arm and set the infusion rate. "Wallace, get out of my sight. I'm busy."

L. A. Atkins watched the man move awkwardly to the front of the rover. "You just about walk on water." She chuckled.

"Any day now," Graham mumbled, checking Potter's vital signs.

"I've heard stories about you, too."

"It seems to be a popular form of entertainment here, for some reason."

"Cloud Man stories?"

"Yes. I don't know why."

"Mars needs legends. And there's a grain of truth, they say, behind all myths. There are even stories about you back on Earth."

"I don't care to hear them."

Atkins lay back down in her bunk. "They say you seldom sleep. That doesn't seem to be an exaggeration. If you want, I'll keep an eye on them while you sack out."

Toward dawn Graham was becoming concerned about Potter. His fever continued to climb despite the LCG he was wearing. Malone seemed to be sleeping comfortably, his fever broken.

Tillman watched as Graham tried to get the youth to swallow some medication. The rover bounced and the liquid spilled, wetting Potter's clothes.

"You've got to stop," Graham told the man.

"He'll be all right as soon as his fever breaks."

"Stop the rover, Tillman. Now."

The man started to argue, then nodded. "Twenty minutes. That's it. I'm sending the rest of the caravan on. There's no sense in holding everybody up because of one weepy Lark."

The other rovers rumbled around them, kicking up dust as they snaked toward the distant hills. The ensuing silence was broken only by Potter's congested breathing.

"Some really get hit hard," Wallace said, watching Graham work. "Others hardly notice the fever. Is he going to be all right? He sounds terrible."

"I think we should turn back," Graham told Tillman.

"It looks like an anaphylactic reaction to something he was given at SURF."

"We're not going back."

"He needs help. There is little I can do, at this point. He needs to be taken to the SURF hospital."

"We're closer to Keyote. Why can't we take him there?"

"How much farther is it?"

Tillman shrugged. "Nine hours, tops. If we move it. Sitting here is not going to get us there sooner."

Graham moved toward the front of the rover, away from the bunks. Tillman followed. "Potter doesn't have nine hours. Radio SURF and tell them to send a hover-lander."

"You sure you aren't overreacting to a little Martian Fever?"

"Do it, Tillman."

"I can't."

"Why?"

"We're out of range."

"What do you mean?"

Tillman's frown deepened. "The radio is out. We could communicate with the rest of the rovers in the caravan, so I didn't think it would matter. I didn't think we would need . . ."

Little made Graham angrier than blatant incompetence. His intolerance for slipshod performance within the Corporation was legend and those guilty of bungling were swiftly excised. His temptation to berate the man for his lack of forethought was tempered only by the immediacy of the emergency and the closeness of the quarters.

"How far is Pod 6?"

"An hour, maybe a little more."

"Take him there."

"Why? What good will that do? It'll slow us up even more, dammit!"

"Just do it." Graham didn't wait to continue the argument, moving back to the bunks.

Atkins was bathing Potter's face. "He coughed up blood."

Wallace frowned. "What does that mean?"

"That we're going to lose him if we don't get help."

The rover bounced and dipped, rolling at an unprecedented speed.

Getting an unconscious man into a MEMU was almost impossible, Graham discovered. By the time the solar wand of Pod 6 appeared on the horizon, Potter's labored breaths were beginning to sound like a death rattle and his pulse was thready. His skin color was dusky, indicating cyanosis. Graham adjusted pressure and oxygen levels in the youth's hard suit to assist his struggle for air.

Malone had recovered enough to make his own way into the pod without assistance. Wallace and Tillman placed Potter on a blanket that they then dragged through the narrow tunnel entrance. Atkins followed, helping Graham bring in the few medical supplies aboard the rover. Lindsey, the driver, opted to stay in the vehicle, to try to repair the radio transmitter.

As Wallace and Tillman eased the sick miner onto the stone-slab table in the middle of the pod, Graham quickly slipped out of his MEMU.

In a voice meant to fill an auditorium Graham turned and spoke to the room at large. "Siegler! I know you can hear me. Send help. We need a hover-lander. Cal Potter is approaching Code Blue. If you don't come, he'll die. You're a part of this. I have addressed you and the decision you make involves you, either way. You can't . . . your research be damned! Siegler, he's just a boy!"

Atkins, climbing out of her hard suit, leaned over to Tillman. "Who's he talking to?"

"I don't know. God, maybe."

Wallace looked at Graham. "So now what?"

"We wait."

"For what?"

"For him to die," Tillman mumbled.

Malone struggled to extricate himself from his MEMU. "The kid was going to get rich here. Send it home to his family. He's got a younger sister and two brothers, he told me. His old man is dead. This was going to turn it around for him. He never wanted to come to begin with. Tillman, if that kid dies I'm personally taking it out of your hide. That's a promise."

Collectively, they eased Potter out of his hard suit. Graham noted the fine rust-tinted foam at the corners of his mouth.

Lindsey entered the pod, carrying food supplies. "I thought if I went on to Keyote, we could radio SURF from there and they could send somebody. The rover transmitter is shot. There's nothing I can do to fix it."

Tillman nodded. "There's no sense in all of us waiting here. The pod can only sustain this many of us for a couple of sols."

"I'm staying," Atkins said.

"And I should stay," Wallace added. "But Malone should go on ahead with you. You can send a rover back for us when . . . I mean . . . once help comes."

After the rover had left, Graham opened up the medical chest in a corner and rummaged for implements he wasn't sure were there.

"What can I do to help?" Atkins asked, squatting beside him.

"Boil some water."

"Isn't that for having babies?" Wallace said.

"For sterilization."

"Oh. Right."

Graham had never performed a tracheotomy, and did not relish the idea of adding the experience to his résumé at the expense of the life in his hands. The boy's raspy breathing, however, told him that there was little choice left.

He felt for the thyroid gland. The trach opening would be placed just below. He made the incision.

Wallace, clearly unable to cope with the sight of blood, positioned himself across the room. "You sure you know what you're doing, Sinclair?"

"No."

"Great."

Graham worked quickly. "Hand me that plasma cartridge," he instructed Atkins.

The woman opened up a package. "I can apply it. Your hands are full. What rate shall I set it?"

"Six, one."

"I used to be a nurse," she said, dabbing at the throat incision with gauze.

"Why did you leave?"

"The pay sucked. Water mining sounded like the answer to my dreams."

Graham inserted the airway and noticed a dramatic improvement in Potter's skin color.

"Nice work, Cloud Man. Medics aren't supposed to know how to do that."

"A little extracurricular reading."

"Is he going to make it?"

Graham shook his head. "Not unless . . ."

Two MEMU-suited figures appeared in the archway of the inner chamber of the CELSS pod. One of the two men was Baker. The second man Graham didn't recognize.

"We were in the neighborhood," Baker said. "How is he?"

Graham was already easing Potter into his hard suit for the transfer to the hover-lander. "I didn't think she would respond."

"She didn't. There was a slight mutiny in the observation studio. I'm in deep shit and I don't even care. Let's get him out of here."

Atkins and Wallace simply stared at Graham after the men had gone.

"How did you do that?" the woman said finally. "Tillman is still hours away from Keyote. How did they know . . . ?"

Wallace cleared his throat. "Hey, I don't know what your religion is, man, but I'm converting."

Graham excused himself and withdrew to an adjoining chamber to meditate. An awareness of the exhaustion now washing over him made him realize the extent of his anger. It was an emotion with a voracious appetite, sucking energy into a fireball that needed only a target to be unleashed. Unless the tension could be channeled, the energy redistributed and balanced, it would wreak havoc within.

Graham closed his eyes and concentrated on breathing, but Siegler's face blocked his concentration. The rage swirled into a white-hot sun. For a flickering instant he saw a room filled with rectangles of light. The rectangles were stacked uniformly, like walls, and there were silhouetted figures observing the patches of light. Graham's curiosity made him try to cling to the image, but it faded and Siegler's poisonous beauty overrode his thoughts again. She would have to go, he realized. The policy of the SURF researchers would have to change, its clinical non-intervention challenged and brought to an end. Life on Mars could no longer be treated as a controlled laboratory experiment, with people holding no more value than rats pushing buttons for food. Graham felt the explosive energy disperse and balance within him. A decision had been made and a direction upon which to act formulated. Now he could disengage and escape.

CHAPTER 32

"Hey, Cloud Man. Sinclair." Graham opened his eyes. Tillman was squatting before him. They had waited for the return of a rover from Keyote for almost eighteen hours. Graham had shown Atkins and Wallace how to make vegetarian stew and left the decision as to what to donate to the pod up to them while he retreated to meditate. He wasn't sure when he would again have the opportunity.

"The kid's going to make it. He was already at SURF by the time we got to Keyote. I don't know what you did exactly, but Potter owes his life to it." Tillman stood up and offered his hand to Graham. "On behalf of the Keyote Mining Corporation, I want to welcome you aboard."

It was dark by the time they reached the colony. From a distance it gave the impression of a city of modest-sized skyscrapers. But the twinkling white lights were not windows. They merely defined the complex piping and venting systems that rose above the habitat itself.

The air lock was as large as that of the SURF base, Graham noticed, easily capable of accommodating landers as well as several rovers at a time. Keyote was the only colony aside from SURF that had its own fleet of landers, Tillman informed them. "They're not as comfortable as the landers you came in on, though. They're more like workhorses, I guess you could say. The pilots call them mules. All they do is haul filled water cylinders into orbit. Once the cylinders are hooked up they look like silver sausage links trailing behind a cycler."

Much of the Keyote colony lay far below ground. Graham was reminded of an ant farm he had once been given by his father when he was five. The gift was meant to educate. What it had taught Graham was that he never wanted to live his life only horizontally and vertically. He had released the ants into the garden and broken the glass walls that had imprisoned the tiny creatures. He had fully expected his father's wrath and punishment of some kind but nothing happened. It was never mentioned again. Now, he realized, he was the ant in a far larger colony, and eyes still watched his every move.

Much of Keyote appeared to be constructed of metal from its own refinery. There was little of the erratic rough-hewn charm of the Ventures' burrows, or the serene simplicity and organization of the Jeremian colony, or the free-form gypsylike comfort of the Sera commune. Keyote was utilitarian in the extreme. Even the aboveground CELSS modules were scientifically stripped of whimsy and aesthetic pleasure. Robotics tended the plants with laser precision. No vine wandered beyond its designated area, no leaf curled inappropriately.

Graham's cubicle was cell-sized, with riveted metal walls and floor, aluminum-colored and bare. The bunk bed, which filled the left third of the room, had plastic storage drawers beneath it. The hygiene compartment was approximately the size of the one in a rover, he noted, vaguely pleased by the small token of privacy. There was a fold-down desktop, which also served as a table, and one stool. A small entertainment unit in the wall at the foot of the bed contained a TV and an outlet for a holo-disc headset.

"You're lucky," Atkins said, standing in the doorway. "You're in the newer module. Down my way, there are no private hygiene compartments. There are designated times for usage. Women, even hours; men, odd. Which somehow seems appropriate. I'm heading up to the mess hall. Want to join me?"

Graham thought of the food liberally dosed with Dar-Quel 25. It wouldn't be in the water, since the slightly salty taste would reveal its presence. Nor would it be in fruit or raw vegetables. Unless he could find a way to prepare his own meals privately his diet would become severely limited, he thought.

"You unpacked already?" the woman asked.

"I didn't have much to bring. Most of my things are in storage at the Sera colony."

"What's it like, there?"

"Very . . . pleasant."

Atkins made a slight face. "Weren't you afraid you'd pick up something? They are Contaminants, after all."

"You were a nurse. You should know better."

"It's another reason I left the profession. Germs make me squeamish."

Graham smiled slightly. "I have to report to the infirmary first. Want to come along?"

"All right. I don't even like antiseptic smells anymore, though."

There was a constantly moving ladder lift that carried passengers, one or two at a time, elevator style, up and down clear tubes. The tubes descended far below Graham's section. The irony of being forced literally to live his life horizontally and vertically was not lost on him. The more he saw of his new surroundings, the more he yearned to return to the Seras.

Atkins lingered near the infirmary entrance while Graham checked in. Dr. Jonas Abrams, the head physician, greeted him with an enthusiasm he had not expected. "So you're the miracle worker I've been hearing about, Mr. Sinclair. You talk to walls and God answers. You come with glowing credentials from Dr. Krolov, I must say." Abrams was a small, wiry man, fortyish, with thinning pale hair cut in a burr. At first glance it gave the impression that he was bald.

"You'll be on the A shift to start, and then rotate every two cycles, through B, C, and D shifts. Glad to have you with us, Sinclair."

Graham felt almost as if his former identity had gotten lost in transition somewhere. He was somewhat bemused to discover that he almost had an impulse to identify himself as the Cloud Man, in case Abrams had him confused with someone else.

The mess hall was noisy and large, serving almost two hundred people at a time. It was a meat and potatoes affair, the beef shipped in by cycler at great expense to the company. Graham went through the line choosing nothing until he reached the salads and fruits.

"You a veggie, Sinclair?" Atkins asked.

"More or less."

"You can't live on that. There's rice back down the line, and soup."

"I'm fine, thank you."

Atkins looked down at her generously heaped platter. "There's something in it, isn't there?"

Graham simply looked at her.

"What? What do they put in it?"

"What do you think they put in it, L.A.?"

"Oh, damn."

They sat down at a long metal table. Atkins poked at the food with a fork. "It *looks* so good. Will I be able to taste the . . ."

"No."

"What will it do, exactly? Just . . . curb my sexual appetite?"

"Curbs everything."

"Will I feel it?"

Graham peeled an apple. "Probably."

"How?"

"A loss of energy. Sluggish reaction time, fuzzy thought processes, dulled memory, loss of enthusiasm and interest in . . . everything."

Atkins pushed her tray away. "Excuse me, I'm going after salad. Care for another apple, Sinclair?"

Graham shook his head.

He was in his bunk reading a medical text when the men came to him. There were four, each representing one of the shifts. There was hardly room for them once the metal door slid shut. The spokesman for the group introduced himself as Hollings.

"There's a rumor going around," he said. "It's been around before, but nobody much listened. It's about the food. Rumor is that it's doped. Is it true?"

Graham nodded.

"How do you know?" said a second man.

"I know."

"He's a medic. He could tell, right?" said Hollings. "What can we do about it?"

Graham carefully placed a bookmark in the text. "I don't know. What do you think you could do about it?"

"We can't stop eating," snorted the fourth man.

"But we sure as hell could stop work. Shut the damn place down till they stop doping the food," Hollings said.

"But they could just *say* okay, we stopped doping your food. How would we know for sure?"

"Random urine samples," Graham said.

"Yeah. That would do it." The third man nodded. "If it shows up, we boycott until it stops."

Two hours later Tillman barged into Graham's room. "I knew you'd cause trouble! They've shut down. Everything! You're responsible for this, Sinclair! Damn you! Everything's ground to a halt!"

Graham didn't look up from his book. "Maybe you'd better give in to their demands, then. Withdraw the Dar-Quel 25."

Tillman slapped his hand down across the book. "Then I hold you personally responsible for the consequences, mister. I want that on record. When they start killing each other, the blood is on your hands."

The mutiny was brief and triumphant, its success quickly attributed to the Cloud Man, and workers came to Graham to thank him. His sudden popularity made him feel uncomfortable. It had been much easier to deal with complete rejection, he thought.

They watched him go through T'ai Chi movements in the gym and asked him to teach them, and some became curious about Taoism and asked to know more. Graham found himself a reluctant teacher after his work shifts were over, his T'ai Chi classes growing larger by each turn of a cycle.

The expected eruption of violence among the miners did not come, although there were a number of couplings and a rearrangement of living quarters for those who elected to bond. Tillman grudgingly admitted to Graham a marked increase in production and a dramatic drop in work-related accidents.

"You've practically put us out of business here, Sinclair," Jonas Abrams said one evening at the end of Graham's shift. "The infirmary was always full, most often with steam burns or laser burns. And falls. A lot of broken bones from falls. Come on, let me buy you a drink. SURF sent up the latest news from home. If we hurry we can get seats before the throng arrives."

The video center held approximately a hundred and fifty people and seemed to be a major form of entertainment during the workers' off hours. Recent holo-films from Earth were cause for excitement.

Graham bent over some slides under a microscope. "Thank you for the invitation, Dr. Abrams, but I think I'll finish this work first."

"It can wait. Come on."

Graham looked up at him. "I'm afraid I can't."

"What do you mean?"

"I'm . . . not allowed to view material from Earth."

"Says who?"

"It's all right. I'm used to it."

Abrams put his hands in the pockets of his lab coat. "So, what if you walked in, anyway? Who's to stop you?"

"I would be stopped. Jonas, you know the rules about me. I know you were told what could and could not be mentioned around me. It's all right."

The man sighed. "Yes, we were told. But nobody from the Committee or the SURF Council is around now. Believe me, none of the miners would say anything. You've become a near saint in their eyes. Even Tillman would look the other way."

Graham returned to the slides. "They would know."

"How? They have spies? Watchers?"

"Something like that. They wouldn't punish me directly. They would . . . make things difficult for you."

Abrams laughed. "Ever hear of paranoia, Sinclair?"

Graham said nothing.

A medic came out of the nurses' station and whistled to Graham. "Hey, Sinclair, you got a call coming in from the Ventures. Want it patched through here?"

"No. Send it through to my quarters and tell them to hold. I'm on my way down."

He knew the call was from Paris. And he also knew that anything they said was monitored by SURF.

In his room he pushed the receiver and Paris came through, somewhat grainy, on the TV screen.

"God, what happened to your hair?" she said. "You got a Keyote crop. I liked it long."

"It's about time you answered one of my calls." He smiled. "You're not coming in clear."

"I'm just naturally out of focus. Sinclair, what the hell's going on?"

"What do you mean?"

"I've been out at Pod 11 near the Eos Chasma so I've been out of touch, then I come back to the colony and the place is crawling with SURF Security people looking for Baker. He's disappeared."

Graham took a deep breath. Some small restlessness within him had whispered niggling suspicions for the last several cycles. Baker usually contacted him on a fairly regular basis, but there had been no word from him since the rescue of Potter almost six cycles ago. He was certain that there had been repercussions from the incident but supposed they would have been of a mild nature.

"How long has he been missing?" he asked.

"I'm not sure. There are a lot of rumors. I heard he snapped out, stole a lander, and took off. When they caught him he went completely wild. This is what I hear, mind you. It doesn't sound like Baker. They had him in seclusion and somehow he escaped, shot somebody with a stun gun, and then he just . . . disappeared. They found an abandoned rover near Pod 3, so they think someone from one of the three lower colonies came and got him and he's in hiding. Security has been out combing the pods, in case he's holed up somewhere. They say he's dangerous. This is crazy. What happened?"

"I'm not sure."

"Another thing. What's this about you praying to sea gulls?"

That stopped Graham. "Where did you hear that?"

"The story's going around. You prayed to a sea gull and

saved somebody's life. Since when do Taoists talk to sea gulls?"

"It was *Siegler*. It's a long story. Paris . . . keep me posted on Baker. I'll find out what I can."

"Okay. Will I see you around sol 40? When the next cycler comes?"

"Yes."

Paris played with a curl. "I might have a surprise for you."

"What?"

"If I tell, it won't be a surprise, Sugar Face." She paused. "They . . . wouldn't hurt him, would they? When they find him. It's got to be a stupid misunderstanding, right?"

"I hope so."

CHAPTER 33

Graham had never ventured down into the older section of Keyote where the mining operation had first begun to build. Quarters were close, with each compartment holding six to eight miners in tiered bunks. Personal items were restricted to the space of a locker. There was a waiting list for private rooms like the ones assigned to the medical personnel. Graham found the conditions abominable and knew that the seeds of rebellion were waiting to burst through fertile soil. The miners had briefly witnessed the power they wielded during the work shutdown over the use of Dar-Quel 25. They would eventually demand better living conditions. It was just a matter of time.

"Hey, Miracle Worker, how's it going?" Malone said, greeting him with a slap on the arm.

"I'm looking for Potter. Have you seen him?"

"He's in the Game Room. Down the corridor, take a left at the junction. Then four, no, five doors down on the right."

The youth was engrossed in a holo-vid game in the recreation room. He had come by to thank Graham, awkwardly, upon his arrival at Keyote, the hole in his throat neatly closed, with only a slight indentation as a souvenir of the experience.

"Cal?"

Graham had to tap him on the shoulder to get his attention. "Could we talk?" he asked as the boy removed his headset.

"Sure. What about?"

Graham looked around. "Not here. Come with me."

He had gone over his quarters carefully and removed four listening devices. He could only hope he had found all of them.

"Hey, this is nice," Potter said. "You got your own private hygiene compartment, too. You gotta re-up before they even put you on the list for quarters like this."

Graham left the door open to avert any new rumors. "Cal, what do you remember about the trip back to SURF? In the lander?"

"Nothing. I just remember waking up in the infirmary with a million wires and tubes stuck all over me. Why?"

"Do you remember a man named Baker? Dark blond hair, about so tall. Gray eyes."

"No."

"He never came by to see you? To see how you were doing?"

"No. Who is he?"

"He's the one who came for you. In the hover-lander."

Potter's face brightened. "Oh, *that's* the guy? You gotta be kidding. He used to be a T.E.?"

"Yes."

"Oh, man. He's the guy they . . . I don't get it. Why would they lock him up for . . . ?"

"He was in seclusion?"

Potter nodded. "I didn't understand much about it. I was like in and out of it for a while there. But there was this guy, some T.E. they said, went nuts and shot a security guard with his own stun gun. They had him scheduled for an M.S.I. and he escaped. I don't know what happened to him. It sure created a lot of commotion at SURF. So he was the guy, huh? What made him snap out?"

"I doubt that he did."

•   •   •

Tillman's office was not large for a man in his position, and it showed evidence that he occasionally slept there. Graham had often made unannounced inspections at his various and diverse companies and could sum up a plant's situation in a matter of minutes by the appearance of the offices of those in charge. Too sleek and clean did not indicate that everything was necessarily under control. It simply meant that the office was for show and was not a functioning working space. Too much clutter told him that management needed help. A man who slept in his office either loved his work to excess or was drowning. In Tillman's case he suspected the former.

"I would like permission to go back to the Sera colony to collect some belongings I left in storage," he said when the man finally looked up from his work to acknowledge him.

Tillman put his hands behind his head and leaned back in his chair. "You're going to look for Baker."

Graham glanced around the room, wondering where the camera was hidden.

"Don't worry, they're not listening." Tillman opened a decorative wooden box on his desk to show him the listening devices, then closed it. "I let them hear what I want them to hear." He pointed to a large wall map showing a vertical cross-section of the Keyote mining operation. "There used to be a mirror there. I'm not a vain man, Sinclair, whatever you might think. I needed the wall space, so when the mirror came down the camera behind it 'broke.' Pity. So, do you think he's there? With the Seras?"

"I don't know."

"They've already been here, looking for him. You know they'll find him. There aren't many places to hide. It's not the Old West. A man can't simply head for the hills."

"All he did was—"

"Buck the system."

"—save a man's life. You owe him something for that."

Tillman leaned forward in his chair. "Sit down. We need to talk. I owe Jon Baker more than you'll ever know. But they will find him, and when they do, he'll be thrown off the planet forever."

"After a quick mood stabilizer implant."

Tillman frowned. "They were going to do that? Forcibly? They can't do that. That's illegal."

"On Earth. SURF can do it to anyone they please. Siegler doesn't like anything to interfere with her noninterference mandate. She's threatened me with one. Maybe you'll be next. Anybody who challenges the project."

Tillman rubbed his face. "Damn. I thought he was . . . that he had her under control . . . they were practically bonded. But I suppose sleeping with a snake doesn't mean it won't still bite you. This covert observation crap has got to stop. I just don't know how to do it. I'm in no position to challenge the Commission. They'll just yank me out of here and put in somebody who grovels quietly. So, you want a rover? They'll follow you there, you know."

"If I went by hover-lander I'd be back before they knew."

Tillman scribbled his signature on a clearance slip and handed it to him. "Go."

CHAPTER 34

He had to transfer into a MEMU in order to enter the colony, since the air lock wasn't big enough to accommodate the mule lander. The pilot, to Graham's surprise, was Jessup, the man who had harassed him upon his arrival.

"How long is this gonna take, Cloud Man? You're putting me behind schedule as it is."

"Not long."

The man grudgingly climbed into his own MEMU to follow Graham into the air lock. "I'm wondering what you had to kiss to get Tillman's nod on this little excursion. I don't like freaks. I better not catch something in there. I'm not getting out of the MEMU, no matter what. Contaminants give me the creeps."

"Have you ever been here before?"

"No. And I don't wanna be here now."

Graham smiled slightly. "Don't you know, Jessup, that here and now is the only place you can be?"

"Yeah, and you worship sea gulls."

The air lock slowly yawned open, and the two men entered.

Anna Leah was waiting on the other side of the inner air lock with Wade Ross and several other members of the commune. There was a look of relief on her face when she saw who had arrived unannounced.

"We were afraid . . ." she began.

Graham climbed out of his MEMU. "I know. I couldn't tell you I was coming." He glanced at Jessup. "I came to pick up some of my things."

Wade tapped Jessup's face plate. "You can come out. We're relatively safe."

Jessup didn't move.

Anna Leah quickly led Graham off into a chamber. "I knew *some*one was coming, but I didn't know who. Is he from SURF? The man with you?"

"No. He's a pilot from Keyote. He doesn't know why I've come. Is he here? Baker?"

"Yes, I'm here," Baker said, parting a beaded curtain. "We thought you were more storm troopers from SURF. Graham, you shouldn't have come. They know you're going to look for me. They probably have a cavalry of rovers headed this way now."

"Jon, what happened?"

"He interfered with the prime directive," Anna Leah said, motioning for them to sit on cushions around a small tiled table. "Now they want to eject him permanently from Mars."

"I won't go. They can't force me to go."

"They were going to force him to undergo a mood stabilizer implant," Anna Leah said, pouring hot tea.

"I couldn't take any more *non*intervention," said Baker. "We could see you and hear you, Graham. It was clear that the kid was dying. She just . . . sat there. Watching. So help me, I wanted to kill her. Do you know that 'Risa' means laughter? Now there's a joke for you. Four people, including me, walked out of there. It was a pathetic little revolt, but God, it felt good. I hadn't felt that good since I told my father what he could do with the whole Jeremian colony. He'll never forgive me, and I can live with that, and it only makes him angrier.

"Graham, do you know why you're here on Mars?"

"Yes."

"I don't think you do. I don't think you have any idea why they sent you here. It wasn't for punishment. They *needed* you. They needed your mind. To pull the whole planet together. You've got a gift, and somebody on the Mars Commission recognized it. You were never meant to come here. You were going to be sent to Antarctica. When it was suggested that you would possibly be more useful on Mars, that's . . . what they decided to do. Drop you in like a philosopher's stone. The Great Catalyst." Baker looked down at his hands. "I swear, Graham, I wasn't aware of their plans for you, at first. All I knew was that I was to escort a prisoner to Mars and help him become acclimated to the environment. For the first time, the planet I loved was being used as someone's lifelong torment. I hated that. I . . . wanted you to like Mars, to come to love it as I have. I want Mars to work. Matina's spirit is here. And my son's. I can't . . . just give them up, like none of it mattered.

"When I quit the T.E. service that's when they told me why you were brought here. I was given an ultimatum. Either keep working with you, steering you toward charted goals, or leave Mars for good."

Graham studied the dark mahogany-colored tea and the cup itself, bone china-thin and delicate. He wondered if Anna Leah had made it. "Then it was never a friendship?"

"Yes. It was. And it still is. Even if you want to break my jaw again. Graham, you'll never know how many times I wanted to tell you the truth. I had these nightmares where I was dying and you would never know what it was all about. Your part in their grand design."

Graham looked over at Anna Leah. "Did you know about this?"

"Not until Jon came to us seeking sanctuary. I knew something was troubling him clear back to the Summer Solstice, but he wouldn't talk to me about it. I don't know how long we can hide him. They'll keep coming back until . . ."

"They came here right away," Baker said, smiling slightly. "Risa's no fool. They lined the whole commune up and searched every chamber. Next time they come, they'll have figured out that there *is* no hunchback among the Seras. Sam Edwards is a makeup wizard."

"But by then, you'll be Jake Anders." Anna Leah poured more tea. "He died two cycles ago and we elected not to report it."

Baker shook his head. "She thinks it will work. It

might stall them a little, but they're going to check us against genetic files, Anna Leah. It won't work for long."

"What will you do?" Graham asked.

"Well, I sure can't go to my father. He'd turn me over, gift-wrapped. The Ventures are working on a new pod down in the Thaumasia Fossae, on the other side of the Solis Planum. I thought I might go there. Vogel hates Siegler enough to enjoy aggravating her for any reason."

Graham stood up. "You're not suited to live a hermit's life. This has to be resolved. What recourse is there if the authority in power is the source of the problem? Who has decision-making power above the SURF Council?"

"The Mars Commission."

"And who above them?"

Baker frowned. "I guess it would have to be the Interplanetary Council. But that's like asking to talk to God. God would be easier to talk to, come to think of it."

"The goal is to lift the nonintervention restriction from the Martian anthropological study. Only Siegler, as head of the project, wields the power to countermand that rule. The total invasion of privacy is also an issue that must be addressed. Their prime directive was compromised the moment my sentence was uttered in World Court. They're arbitrarily playing with people's lives, withholding or employing intervention in a capricious manner. It has to stop."

Baker shrugged. "I told you a long time ago that you can't break a system."

"But sometimes all you need to do is change one mind and you've changed the system."

"You'll never convince Risa Siegler that she's wrong. I know her, Graham. She believes in what she's doing."

By the time Graham returned to the air-lock hangar Jessup had been coaxed out of his MEMU and was being entertained by Wade and several other commune members with bawdy beer hall songs. He was also quite drunk.

"The man can't stand up," Wade pointed out, "much less fly. Looks like you'll be grounded until tomorrow."

Anna Leah smiled. "We're a bit crowded at the moment, Mr. Sinclair. Would you be opposed to sharing quarters with someone . . . for the night?"

"It would be my pleasure, Miss Moineau."

"Wade, would you see to Mr. . . ."

"Jessup," said Jessup, attempting to rise and failing, ". . . and thank you very kindly for your . . ." He searched foggily for a word. ". . . hospitality."

Graham turned to Anna Leah and said quietly, "You realize I'll be missed at Keyote. I haven't blocked all of the monitoring devices yet. By tomorrow SURF Security will be on its way here. Baker has to leave now, before they're alert to my absence. It won't give us much time."

"I've sent someone to tell him."

Jessup, sagging between Wade and Edwards, tried to organize his feet. "Man, I haven't had beer that good since the 'Notchka. Could I take a few cases . . . barrels . . . whatever back with me, do you think? I have credits. How many credits you want? Name your price."

As they helped him from the room he smiled at Anna Leah. "Damn good-looking woman, Sinclair. She got a sister? Hey, Ross . . . Wade . . . how about if you guys come up to Keyote sometime . . . like to put on a show, know what I mean? We could use some music up our way . . . Damn funny songs! We could pay . . . no kidding . . . it'd be great." Jessup belched. "And bring some more beer."

"How do you celebrate the Winter Solstice?" Wade asked.

"We . . . wave at it when it goes by. Nobody celebrates diddly up there. 'Cept leaving here, leaving Mars, I mean. Now *that's* worth celebrating."

Anna Leah walked with Graham toward her quarters. "A year ago the Seras would never have allowed someone like Jessup into the commune. But things need to change. And we're trying. We came here to remove ourselves from Perfects, to shut out those who had shut us out. But we can't live that way any longer. We've been considering ways to initiate some form of communication with Keyote. Maybe Jessup has provided us the means. Would they welcome our theater company, do you think?"

"Just don't start off with Shakespeare." Graham smiled. "You may have to work up to that. And I don't know whether Tillman and the others would allow alcohol. They're afraid of losing control of the miners."

Anna Leah's quarters consisted of a sitting room, a bedchamber, and a hygiene compartment, unprecedented luxury as far as Graham knew. Nowhere on Mars had he seen such extended privacy. The low ceiling and walls were draped with paisley cloth, giving the impression of a gypsy tent. Cushions, pillows, and low, tiled tabletops added to the Middle Eastern flavor. Soft, thick-woven rugs covered the matted floor. He had an impulse to remove his cloth boots, as if entering a home back on Earth. It also suddenly occurred to him that he had nothing but the LCG he was wearing.

Anna Leah emerged from the bedchamber with a cobalt-blue dashiki. "It was my father's. He wasn't as tall as you, but it should be comfortable enough." She would not look up at him, and he didn't need her gift of inner sight to know that his presence was making her very nervous.

"Anna Leah . . ."

"He would have liked you, I think. He would have approved of you. The shower is in there . . ."

"Look at me."

She stopped and finally met his eyes. "No one has ever . . . been here before . . ."

"Do you want me here?"

"Yes."

"Then I want to be here. Anna Leah . . . no one has ever been here before." He touched his chest. "No one."

She nodded. "I know."

He woke early and lay silent, watching her sleep. For several moments he was afraid that he would lose the image if it was indeed a dream, as it had been, so many times. Slowly he reached out to caress her cheek, and she moved sleepily toward the touch, as if seeking his warmth and nearness. At some point during the night he had unbraided her hair to feel its dark silkiness against his skin, and now it tumbled across her pillow and partially obscured her right breast like a Spanish mantilla.

He did not want to leave her as she slept, nor did he want to wake her. He wanted the moment to stretch like a carefully measured breath, one that would fill him completely and last forever.

She opened her eyes. Without a word she moved into his arms. He held her, slowly stroking her body, marveling at the smooth texture of her skin beneath his fingers, the way curves flowed one into another as in a classic marble sculpture. Sun-warmed marble breathed into life. He did not want to leave her. Ever.

"Don't go," she whispered. "Don't go back."

"I have to, Anna Leah."

"Stay here."

"They'll be looking for me. I have to give Baker time to prepare."

"What if it doesn't work?"

Gently he disengaged from her arms and got up. "Then know that I loved you." He reached around his neck and removed the small leather pouch. "Keep this for me. Until I come back."

"Graham . . ."

He bent and kissed her, silencing things he did not want to hear.

CHAPTER 35

Jessup was struggling to put on his LCG socks in the airlock hangar when Graham joined him. "We're in trouble," the man mumbled. "The place is surrounded by SURF Security, and these guys won't let 'em in. You don't do that. Cardinal rule number uno. Never deny entry. Unless you got plague or something." He stopped and looked up at Graham. "Oh, sweet Jesus. Don't tell me they got plague or something."

"They're looking for someone," Graham said. "You're not in trouble."

"Good. Will they let me out of here?"

"Probably not."

Wade ambled over and slapped Jessup on the back, making the man jump. "How's the head this morning?"

"It's been better. You guys are nuts. You can't keep them out."

Wade shrugged. "Looks like we're doing it."

"Is she with them?" Graham asked.

"Yeah. And spitting fire."

"You may as well let them in."

"He hasn't had enough time to get to . . ."

Graham glanced down at Jessup. "It will have to do. Let them in."

Wade sighed and whistled to the air-lock operators,

making a circular gesture. "Okay, curtain going up. All the world's a stage and I don't know my lines."

Graham watched the first rover move down into the air lock. "Improvise."

Risa Siegler was the first one out once the rover moved into the hangar.

"Where is he?" she demanded, glaring at Graham as a SURF Security team spilled out into the receiving area, stun guns poised.

"He's not here," said Graham.

"Of course he's here, or you wouldn't be here. Jonathan Baker's problems are none of your concern, Mr. Sinclair. Stay out of this."

"Baker?" said Jessup. "It's Baker they're after?"

Anna Leah moved down into the hangar and stood close to Graham. "He's telling you the truth, Risa. Jon Baker is no longer here."

"But he *was* here. Then you must know that he's very ill. He's in a very confused state. He's violent. We're only trying to help him. Tell me where he is, Anna Leah."

"No."

"Then you do know?"

Anna Leah hesitated. "Not . . . exactly."

"I know where he is," said Graham.

Siegler eyed him with undisguised loathing. "You brought this down on him, you know. He confused his priorities because of you. He needs help."

"I can take you to him."

"Graham, no!" Anna Leah drew away from him. "He's your friend! Don't do this."

"I'll take you to him under my conditions."

Wade made a move toward Graham but was blocked by one of the SURF Security guards. "Shut up, Sinclair!"

"What conditions?" asked Siegler.

"How badly do you want him?"

"We . . . want him."

"Enough to offer me clemency?"

Siegler laughed. "Not in your wildest dreams, Mr. Sinclair. Nor do we have the power to make such an offer."

"Then what's in it for me? If I lead you to him?"

"Bastard!" Wade shouted, lunging at Graham. A stun

dart dropped him into a fetal position and left him spasming on the concrete floor.

Anna Leah bent over the man and withdrew the dart from his thigh. Wade continued to jerk involuntarily, gasping for breath.

"Graham, don't do this. Please. Jon trusted you."

"Then that was his mistake."

"Hey," said Jessup. "Can I go now? I didn't have anything to do with any of this. I have to get back to Keyote before—"

"Not yet," Graham said. "So, what can you offer me, for Baker's whereabouts?"

Siegler folded her arms. "Why, how mercenary of you, Mr. Sinclair. I would never have thought it of you. What do you want? Aside from leaving the planet, that is."

"Drop the charges against Baker."

The woman smiled. "Now, that's the Graham Sinclair I know so well. He attacked a security guard. The man is unstable—"

"Drop all charges. No expulsion from Mars, no mood stabilizer implant, no . . . retribution whatsoever. His position as courier will be reinstated . . . and you will resign your post."

"Ask for both moons while you're at it. You've obviously talked to him. You could see that he was in an agitated state. I would . . . consider all but your last request, which is ludicrous. There would still have to be a hearing before the SURF Council . . . to determine his emotional stability . . . a small formality, if you will. To set the record straight. It can be written off as a temporary mental aberration. Something . . . unique, that will *never* happen again?"

Graham nodded. "Agreed. Before witnesses."

"Yes."

"I hold you to your honor."

"Of course you will." Siegler nodded. "You are, if nothing else, a gentleman."

"But a written agreement is in order," Graham added. "To circumvent any misunderstanding."

Siegler's eyes flashed darts of their own. "If you insist."

"I insist."

Wade was able to sit up, but could not stand without

help. Sam Edwards and two other commune members
helped him to his feet and half carried him off to another
chamber as Anna Leah ushered Graham and Siegler to a
room to draw up the document.

"Now," said Graham, once the signatures were witnessed, "I'll take you to him but it will have to be my
way. Send all the rovers back to the SURF base."

"Then he is here after all."

"No. We'll take the lander . . . the Keyote mule. Just
the two of us. And Jessup as pilot, of course."

"You promise that he'll return to SURF without any
argument?"

"You have my word."

"He *will* spend time in seclusion, you understand. It's
policy."

"I understand."

The lander moved above the red plain in a northeasterly
direction, its triangular shadow racing over the ground
far below. As they approached Tharsis Tholus Siegler
frowned. "He's with the Jeremians? His father would
never tolerate it."

"No. He's not with the Jeremians."

"Then where are we going?"

"You'll see."

Minutes passed. The somewhat crescent-shaped hills
along Kasei Vallis appeared on the horizon. "We're heading toward the SURF base," she said.

"Not quite."

Jessup began to descend. "These are the coordinates
you gave me. Now what?"

"Land," said Graham.

"There's nothing down there."

"Yes, there is. Pod 2 is down there."

Siegler turned and looked at Graham. "He can't be
there. We checked all the pods."

"Well, he's there now. Get into your MEMU."

The lander kicked up a thick cloud of rust-colored dust
as it settled carefully between chunks of rock. Graham
emerged from the mule first, then Siegler. The solar wand
above the pod mound was only a short distance away.

They were almost to the entrance when Graham turned and waved to Jessup.

The lander rose into the air.

"What's he doing?" Siegler shouted. "He's leaving! He can't leave! Stop him!"

"I told him to go."

"Are you insane? He's the only one who knows where we are!"

Graham gestured toward the pod entrance. "After you, Dr. Siegler."

"This is a trick. He's coming back. What do you think you're doing, Sinclair?"

"Illustrating a point. You have to crawl a bit, I'm afraid."

"You'd like that, wouldn't you!"

"To get inside. You have to crawl."

The woman reluctantly dropped to her knees and crawled into the narrow tunnel. Graham waited, then followed.

The pod was an early one, very small, and selected for that reason.

"You can remove your helmet," Graham suggested, climbing out of his MEMU.

"There's something wrong here." Siegler frowned. "The floor is wet. Why is the floor wet?"

"A plumbing problem perhaps."

She climbed out of her MEMU. "He was never here, was he? You lied. How unlike you, Mr. Sinclair."

"Oh, Jon Baker was here. We just missed him. Sorry."

"Where is this water coming from?"

Graham pointed to an overflowing pond in a far corner. "Something seems to be clogging the outflow. I suppose that's why he left."

"So what do we do now? Sit and wait for your man to return and rescue us?" Siegler waded through the water, which was now almost ankle deep.

"No one is coming back for us, Risa."

"He's the only one who knows we're here."

Graham shook his head. "No, *they* know." He pointed to a camera clearly visible among the vines covering the walls. "Smile for the camera, Risa. Wave to your friends. Talk to them if you like. Tell them to come and get us."

"I can't do that."

"Why not? They'll listen to you. Won't they?"

An aluminum canister floated across the floor. The water was now well above their ankles.

"You did this on purpose, didn't you? Well, I'm not impressed." Siegler sloshed over to the pond and plunged her arms down into the water, groping for the drain that kept the water circulating. "Damn! It's been pounded shut." She reached up to the rocks above the pond where the water cascaded from several cracks to form an enthusiastic waterfall. "Don't just stand there! Help me plug the holes to stop the water!"

"I'd rather not."

"What do you mean, *you'd rather not?*"

Graham moved over to the stone slab in the center of the small room. "Just that. I'd rather not." He hoisted himself up onto the table and crossed his legs. "Do you know literature, Dr. Siegler? Are you familiar with Melville's 'Bartleby the Scrivener'? I'm paraphrasing him, actually. I believe it was 'I prefer not to.' No matter what was asked of him, he simply said, 'I prefer not to.' Astounding power in that simple statement. Do you know what became of him, in the end? He isolated himself from his duties, and from society, and in the end, he withdrew from life itself. He was a casualty of a society that was indifferent to his silent, passive protest."

Siegler stared at him, her hair dripping. "You would do better to quote *Moby Dick*. What is your point, Mr. Sinclair?"

"What do you think the point is, Dr. Siegler?"

"That if we don't stop this water we'll drown!"

Graham watched a battered pot float by. "Yes. I suppose we will. It's filling somewhat faster than I anticipated."

"Than you *anticipated*? You set this whole thing up, didn't you? What was all that business back at the Sera colony? Playacting?"

"And very fine playacting." Graham nodded. "Wade wasn't expecting the stun dart, but it was a nice touch."

The water was up to Siegler's knees. "And all this is more playacting."

"No. This is quite real, Dr. Siegler. Unless you do something soon, you'll be the first person to drown on the planet Mars. That should be worth a small footnote in the history books, I believe." He pointed to the camera. "They're getting it all down. There will be no dispute. It will all be captured for posterity."

"What do you want?" she shouted.

"You know what I want, Risa."

"I can't commute your sentence. I don't have the power!"

"That's not what I want."

"Then for God's sake, what?"

"Lift the restrictions. On your *project*."

"I can't do that."

"You've *done* that. I'm here because of your omnipotent meddling—you and your *Committee. And* the Mars Commission. I was *brought* here for the express purpose of altering the face of Mars. I know that. You compromised your own prime directive by thrusting me into your world, into your little *experiment,* Risa." He pointed up at the camera. "*Tell* them! Remove your Code One directive."

"No!"

"Then drown."

"You'll drown, too!"

"Yes. I will. But you'll have the distinction of being first. I am, after all, a good bit taller than you. You'd best put your MEMU back on," he suggested, climbing into his own.

She moved clumsily in the hip-deep water and struggled back into her MEMU. "This is crazy. You're bluffing."

"Of all that you think you know about me, Risa, do you actually believe I would ever try to bluff someone?"

"Your own *Tao Te Ching* doesn't believe in interference," she sputtered. "What does it say? 'The world is ruled by letting things happen as they will. It can't be ruled by interfering.' That's all we're doing. Letting things happen as they will. Why should you resent that? You above all others should understand that."

"But you don't understand it. You don't understand its meaning at all. Your refusal to help someone—*that* is interfering. When you stand aside and willingly allow someone to suffer, you go against every instinct that makes you human. 'The Tao of Nature is to benefit, not to harm. The Tao of the sage is to serve without effort.' It takes tremendous effort to shut out cries for help, Risa. To deny any living thing its right to be makes you less alive, less than human."

The water was almost to her shoulders now. Graham reached down and pulled her up onto the table.

"You would let us both drown to make your point," she hissed, her teeth chattering.

"No. You are the one with the power. You're the only one who can do something. There's still time. If you lift the restriction they can send a lander. You know about the jade. About the pouch. You know its value in my life. I'm not wearing it. It's all I had to bequeath to someone. I gave it to Anna Leah."

The hot anger in the woman's eyes retreated, replaced by real fear. It seemed as if she really saw him, for the first time. And knew that he was not playing any game. He was fully prepared to allow himself to drown.

"All right! The restriction is hereby rescinded!" She looked up at the camera. "Conroy, did you hear me? Code One is dropped. As of now! Move! Get me out of here!"

Graham dropped his face plate down, clamped it, and sank beneath the swirling water.

"Don't leave me!" Siegler shrieked, twisting around, looking for him.

The pod was now an underwater grotto with only a pocket of air near the dome. Risa clung to a rock wall, her face plate fogging on the inside. "Oh, dear God, it's too late! It's too late!"

Suddenly she felt a tugging sensation, as if a strong undertow were pulling her from the stone slab. Water surged and swirled around her and she lost her balance, splashing and floundering in the MEMU like a plastic cork. By the time she righted herself, Graham was beside her, holding her up, and the water level was dropping rapidly.

"You knew?" she shouted, ripping off her helmet. "You knew how to stop it all along!" She swung at him and toppled over. Graham grabbed at her MEMU to pull her back to her feet before it filled with water. "We were never going to drown, were we? You wouldn't have let it happen."

Graham removed his helmet. "Yes, I would have let it happen. I was prepared for that possibility. I never bluff, Risa. Don't ever forget that."

By the time the flooded pod had drained down to knee-deep murky water, three MEMU-suited figures emerged from the outer chamber. One was Baker, the other two, Vogel and Waverly.

"I understand we got some plumbing problems here." Vogel sniggered. "We charge time-an'-a-half after hours, you know. Cripes, what a mess!"

Baker turned to Siegler. "A lander's outside. We've been sitting in the rover, waiting for the oxygen balloon over the pod vent to deflate before we could enter. I'm turning myself over to the SURF authorities. I'll go back with you."

Siegler wiped at her copper hair, a matted wet tangle, and clamped her helmet on, ignoring the man.

Baker looked at Graham. "You were right. About water. How does the Tao put it? 'Nothing under heaven is as yielding and receptive as water. Yet in attacking the firm and inflexible, nothing serves so well. Because of what it is not, it has no equal.' For the first time I understand what you meant."

Waverly shook her head. "This is going to take a while to restore. But damn, it was worth it. You should have drowned the bitch."

CHAPTER 36

Paris carried the toaster-sized wooden box down the corridor, blinking back angry tears. She had arrived at the SURF base early to await the first batch of mail and packages from Earth. She hadn't been sure what to expect from the woman, but she was certain that Jasmine Wyncote would respond to her request for a "special piece of interactive art." She had phrased the words carefully in the fax letter, which had been expensive, sent before she had knowledge of what Haas had left her.

Baker, wearing an LCG, met her as he was heading toward his own quarters.

"Paris, what's the matter?"

"Nothing. Bastard."

"And a good, good morning to you, too." He laughed. "If you're heading down to see Graham he's probably asleep. He was on night duty in the infirmary."

"He never sleeps. According to legend, the Cloud Man never sleeps. Didn't you know that?"

Baker touched her arm. "What's wrong?"

"I'm pissed."

"I can see that. At Graham?"

"No. At you. All of you. The ones who control his life. Yeah, the cameras are gone and Siegler's leaving and the only anthropological poking comes from researchers sent

to the communes—the good old-fashioned way, but . . ."
She sighed. "Some things aren't ever going to change, are
they?"

"Like what?"

Paris looked down at the box in her hands. "Keeping
Earth from him. Forever. I . . . tried to find out some
things—he didn't ask me —he never asks about Earth—
but I wanted . . . They knew, when the box came, that
it was for him. It was addressed to me, but they opened it
because it was from Jasmine Wyncote. It's just an old
wooden box with empty drawers, like to keep jewelry or
cuff links in. There was a letter in one of the drawers and
they took it. All of you are bastards."

Baker frowned. "May I see the box?"

"It's *been* searched already. I know he can't keep it, but
I just wanted to show him that I tried, okay?"

Baker took the dark lacquered box and examined the
inlaid mother-of-pearl designs on its sides and the carving
on top. It showed an old bearded man riding an ox. "It
looks Chinese, and very old," he said, running a finger
over the carving.

"I asked if I could buy a small piece of interactive art
from her . . . for a gift. I figured she'd know who the gift
was for. So did your jerk-face friends. Your *Committee*. I
thought they were going to body-search me before they
gave it back."

Baker placed the box in her hands. "Show it to him
anyway. He may . . . see things in it we don't."

He was asleep. She stood in the doorway where light
fell across his bed, and watched him. He was on his side
and the sheet covering his nakedness had slipped to an
enticing low just over his somewhat angular flank. Paris
had an impulse to tug the sheet a bit more toward the foot
of the bed.

He turned in his sleep and stretched, and she saw that
he was not wearing the jade pouch. Its absence solidified
further a creeping fear somewhere inside her that had
begun soon after what she referred to as the "water business." She had heard the story from Waverly and considered it another exaggeration in the growing myth of the
Cloud Man, until Baker confirmed its accuracy. During a
visit to introduce the anthropologist who would be stay-

ing with them, he told her what had happened and how
Graham had stood before the SURF Council and accused
them of complicity in the incident involving the young
miner. Risa Siegler was relieved of her duties and ordered
to return to Earth to face abuse-of-power charges at a
hearing by the Mars Commission. Baker, who was well
into his third cycle in seclusion, was released and all
charges against him dropped.

"Paris? Is that you?" Graham held his hand up against
the glare from the corridor.

She entered the room and touched a wall unit to bring
up the light. "Of course it's me. Who else would stand
around staring at your ugly bod? You're naked. How come
you never slept naked around me? Boy Scout."

He sat up and pulled the sheet around his waist.
"When did you get in?"

"About an hour ago. Remember I said I might have a
surprise for you this cycler? Well, it fizzled." She placed
the box on the bed.

His reaction was not what she expected. Indifference
was what she had expected or, at most, polite puzzlement.

He reached out to touch the carving on top of the box
as if he could not believe its tangibility. He began to
stroke the sides of the box, running his hands over its
lacquered surface, a slow smile replacing his sleep-fuzzed
exhaustion. "Where did you get this?" he said, finally.

"You recognize it?"

"Yes. It . . . belonged to my grandmother. How did
you . . . ?"

"Jasmine Wyncote sent it to me. There was a letter in
one of the drawers, but they took it. I'm sorry, Graham. I
really hoped to surprise you. They wouldn't even let *me*
read the letter. I hope they all die." She sat on the bed,
tucking her feet up, and faced him. "I asked her for a
piece of interactive art but she just sent this old box. So it
belonged to your grandmother? That's nice. It must be
real old, then."

"It is. About a thousand years old."

"Your grandmother lived . . ."

"No. It's been in my family that long. I thought it . . .
I was told that everything was sold at auction after . . .

Jasmine must have known and gotten it, or Ti must have told her . . ."

"So you're pleased after all?"

Graham nodded. "If they had allowed me one personal possession to take with me . . . I would have chosen this. You see, it *is* a piece of interactive art. Probably the first ever made. It's a Chinese puzzle box." He began to stroke and touch the box gently. A small drawer hidden in the side slid out. In it, wrapped in silk, was a gold ring. "My grandmother's. Here's a picture of her as a young girl. She was fourteen when my grandfather met her. It was not a union of love but . . . she loved, anyway."

Paris held the small photograph. "She was beautiful. She looks like . . . someone you could love."

He touched another side and a drawer within a drawer slid open.

"This is my mother and my father. It was taken two weeks before they died."

Paris held up the small hologram. "Handsome couple. You look like both of them. How . . . ?"

"They were murdered. During a corporate war. When I was fourteen."

Paris stared at him as he continued to open secret compartments in the box. "You never told me that. No wonder you never talk about them."

He glanced up at her. "I don't talk about them because I didn't know them very well. We spent very little time together."

Slowly he moved a number of designs on the box and swung open a somewhat larger compartment. "Here. She put the holo-discs in here. This is the real information. The letter was a decoy to satisfy searchers."

He held up the gold, wafer-sized discs. "There must be hours of information here."

"Do you have a headset?"

"No. I'm allowed to use one to study medical information or anything concerning Mars. That's it."

"Bastards," she muttered. "I have one. It's in my gear. I'll go get it."

He caught her arm. "Paris . . ."

"I know. You're going to bond with her. I'm glad. Really I am, Graham. I can give the box to her, like for a wedding present. That way, you'll still have it. There's nothing they can do about it."

"I wanted to tell you . . ."

"I guess we can't keep meeting like this, anymore, huh? No more roomies . . . I'll miss it."

Graham nodded. "So will I. Paris, don't let this affect our friendship. You mean . . . so much to me. More than you'll ever know."

"Yeah . . . same here."

Jasmine Wyncote materialized before him as if she were in the room and he could reach out and touch her. "I hope this finds you, Graham. I've tried to communicate with you so many times, but they know we're friends, so I suppose they screen things carefully. There's so much to tell you. There is a growing movement here concerning you. Writing campaigns by Universal Amnesty . . . groups concerned that banishing you to Mars could set a precedent and the planet might become a future Devil's Island for criminals . . . all kinds of political pressure groups are clamoring to have your case reopened. You aren't forgotten.

"Sometimes at night, I look for that slightly red-tinted star up there, and I wonder about you—if you're well, what you're experiencing. We're trying to get you home, Graham. Don't give up hope."

She pulled Ti in front of the camera. Graham was shocked. He was no longer a seventeen-year-old boy, but a young man. "He won't tell you this, but he's becoming an outstanding watercolorist. He's preparing for his first one-man show at the Galleria next month. And he's been commissioned by the Sierra Foundation to do a series on . . . well, you tell him, Ti. Talk to the man."

Ti bowed slightly. "Master Graham . . ." He turned to Jasmine, who had stepped out of camera range. "I cannot do this. He will never see . . ."

"Talk to him."

"Madam Wyncote has been very kind to me. You were right in sending me to her. She has shown me what was within me to give. I try to make you very proud of me,

Master Graham. I wish only to bring honor to you . . ." Abruptly he walked out of camera range.

Jasmine returned. "He's still very angry, Graham. With the authorities, the ones who did this to you. He's brilliantly talented. And we may never have discovered his gift if . . . how strange, the winds of Fate, no?"

She took him on a tour of the youth's paintings that hung about her immense studio. He worked large areas, creating such subtle beauty that Graham stopped the holo-disc to rerun the views. They were mostly landscapes, and the style was reminiscent of classic oriental brushwork, but there was an inner vision that the boy had brought to each painting that captivated the eye.

Jasmine went on to explain that the other holo-discs were filled with news and events of Earth. "As I understand it, you are completely cut off from home. We don't want you to return to us like Rip Van Winkle, waking in a world that has passed you by. Graham . . . we love you. Think of us."

He could not find her in the gym or the commissary or any of the CELSS modules and was on his way down to the changing room to see where she had been assigned quarters when he met Baker walking with another courier.

"Have you seen Paris?" he asked. "I can't seem to find her anywhere."

Baker looked puzzled at first. "She left, Graham."

"Left for the commune? She just got here. Why would—"

"She went out on a lander this afternoon. I thought you knew. I thought she told you she was leaving."

Graham felt a rippling numbness dropping down over him. "Leaving? Leaving Mars?"

"She didn't tell you?"

Graham shook his head.

Baker glanced at the other courier watching them. "Ned, can I catch you later?"

"Sure. Is he okay? He looks like he's about to keel over."

Baker touched Graham's arm. "He's . . . all right. He'll be okay. Gray, let's go get a drink."

"No . . . Jon, I want to talk to her."

"She's already aboard the *'Notchka*, Graham. You can't."

"Please. She never said . . . I just want to tell her . . . good-bye. That's all."

"I'll tell her for you."

"She could have said good-bye."

Baker looked out at the darkness beyond the covered walkway. "No, I don't think she could. I really thought she was going to make it. I thought she was a Grit."

"She was. You know she was."

CHAPTER 37

The bonding ceremony took place in the Congregational Garden of the Jeremian colony on the eve of the Spring Equinox, one Martian year and two cycles to the day of Graham's arrival on the planet. Two Earth years had elapsed since his departure, but he seldom measured time by Earth standards now, he realized. Time was measured by events. The Jovis group had begun its own colony and sent a representative to the celebration, and for the first time a number of Keyote miners participated in the festivities.

Graham had returned to the Sera colony after his work commitment was completed at Keyote and contented himself working in pottery. Word had reached them of the overwhelming demand for Martian glass, and orders for the product had swamped SURF headquarters.

Wade Ross, whose opera was being mounted back on Earth, was scheduled to leave on the next cycler to oversee the project. He escorted Anna Leah down the steps on the day of the wedding while Baker stood as Graham's best man. A tentative peace had been made between father and son, and Jacob, who presided over the ceremony, seemed more jovial than Graham ever remembered seeing him.

"He's got it in his head that I'm eventually going to

take his place, after all," Baker said as he had watched Graham dress in white robes that morning.

"Are you?"

"Absolutely not. But if it makes an uneasy peace between us, my mother is still happy. It will suffice until something stronger comes along, she says. Graham, I had hoped to have some good news for you, on your wedding day. But all I can tell you is that your case file is up before the Board of Review."

Graham turned and looked at him. "Why?"

"I guess the pressure groups are growing, back home. Everything you do here is news back there. You've become a major celebrity of sorts. The attention Mars is receiving, because of you, has caused a logjam of emigration requests. There's a two-year waiting list. If . . . your conviction should be overturned—now don't get any hopes up, but *if* it should happen, what would you do?"

"Go home."

"What about Anna Leah? She doesn't want to leave here."

"We discussed it. She's willing to return to Earth, if my sentence should be commuted."

"Graham . . . there can be no children from this union."

"We've also discussed that, Jon. But it's really none of your concern."

"It is."

Graham shook his head. "Anna Leah is not Matina."

Baker looked down at his hands. "I know. But there would be risks in a pregnancy. You both would be under unprecedented scrutiny. Are you prepared for that?"

"Were you?"

"No."

"Jon, be happy for us. Please. This is a very special day. There is a wholeness in my life that I never knew could be. You must have known it once. If you had listened to all the 'what ifs' and all the 'must nots,' you wouldn't have that memory. Nobody can take that away from you."

Baker nodded. "All right. No more advice. Go for it all.

You know, you look like some kind of bedouin sheik in those robes. You look . . . ready for a wedding."

Graham's one small sorrow was that Paris was not there. He had told Anna Leah of the bond of friendship between them and she had understood. He had not known, until Paris, that there could be a love that surmounted sexual barriers, that defined itself in terms of soul and spirit, or that such a love could encompass more than one being within his heart.

As he watched Anna Leah move down the garland-draped steps on Wade's arm, he felt an urge to weep. How far he had traveled, he thought, to reach this joy. Anna Leah, in a white sarilike gown and veil, seemed to float toward him, her dark eyes lowered.

Jacob graciously wove a touch of Taoist philosophy within the text of the ceremony, and Graham placed his grandmother's gold ring on Anna Leah's finger. There had been a brief controversy at SURF over the ownership of the Chinese puzzle box, but a written explanation left by Paris clearly stated that the gift was intended for Anna Leah Moineau. The SURF Council grudgingly relinquished its hold on the property.

The festivities continued for three sols, but Graham and Anna Leah escaped to Pod 8 overlooking Ophir Chasma for a brief honeymoon. Vogel, well into the wine that had been provided by the Ventures, dug an elbow into Graham's side during the wedding banquet. "I put the word out, okay? Pod 8 is outta commission for like the next couple of cycles. Or whenever you two get exhausted. Or"—he cackled—"more likely in Annie Leah's case, *bored* to death . . ." It took great restraint on Graham's part not to flatten the man's nose.

On sol 220 Wade left for Earth, escorting a large shipment of Martian glass and pottery. Graham's signature on pieces he had done was the Chinese character for "ox," his birth sign in the Chinese zodiac. Again, the SURF Council protested that it was a form of communication with Earth, which was expressly forbidden, but powers above the Council elected to let the small infraction slip by.

Although his skills and knowledge as a medic were still in demand and he dutifully reported to SURF for the arrival of each cycler, Graham was more interested in expanding his skills at the potter's wheel. The craft gave him immense pleasure and often substituted for meditation.

Members of the Sera theater company began to tour the colonies, presenting a repertoire of entertainments from musicals to classics and avant-garde works. "I never thought Keyote would sit still for *Antigone*," Sam Edwards said with a laugh during dinner one evening, after their return. "But they liked it. Graham, that place is some kind of hellhole. How did you stand it? They're packed in like Japanese mass transit at rush hour. The place is ready to blow. You can feel it."

"Tillman is aware of it to some degree"—Graham nodded—"but the company heads refuse to address their needs."

Anna Leah slipped a strawberry into Graham's mouth. "And they've become more sharply disgruntled now that many of them have been to the other communes and have seen how we live. How did the Jovis group react to the company?"

"No music. But we were allowed to do dramatic readings from the Scriptures. They seemed to approve of that. They took all the best weavers when they split from the Jerrys, so now the Jerrys send most of their cotton over to the Jovis colony. We brought some cloth back with us. Keyote gave us credits, SURF sent along some new crop samples, and the Ventures gave us more of the Marineris sand."

"Good. We can use it," Anna Leah said.

"The Jerrys gave us honey. I think we should try making some mead."

Graham stroked Anna Leah's long braid. "You may as well. It will simply add another color to our hedonistic image."

Anna Leah looked at Graham, then smiled. "You said 'our.' Did you know that? For the first time it's 'our' instead of 'your.' I do love you, Graham Kuan Sinclair. Did you know that?"

"I suspected it."

Edwards chuckled. "The honeymoon's not over, I see. Have you heard about the new soft suits they're working on at SURF? They combine everything you need in an LCG and in a hard suit, but they're more like a second skin. Amazing."

"Are they ready for use?" Graham asked.

"Not yet. But they're close."

Anna Leah adjusted a pillow behind her back. "It's about time they came up with something less cumbersome than a MEMU. I don't think they even make hard suits with expandable middles."

Both Graham and Edwards turned to stare at her.

"Just thinking ahead." She shrugged.

"How . . . far ahead?" asked Graham.

"About seven and a half months, or twenty-two cycles."

Edwards clapped Graham on the back. "Congratulations! Honeymoon's over, after all. Hey, everybody!" The man stood. "A toast! The first native Martian is among us!"

As carefully as he tried to mask his concerns, Graham was unable to hide the swirl of conflicting emotions from Anna Leah later that night. She addressed his fears as well as several of her own. "I don't want them to know yet, at SURF," she whispered in the darkness.

Graham gently rested his hand over the flatness that would soon change, as if to shield the delicate life from things they both knew awaited its first breath.

"They never left Matina alone, from the first moment they knew. All the eyes, watching . . . waiting . . . all the poking and probing . . . I don't want that."

Graham moved down to kiss the warmth of her stomach. "No one will touch you, unless you want it, Anna Leah. I promise you that. It will be your way."

She absently combed at his hair with her fingers. "Think of girls' names."

He paused in his kisses. "You know? For certain?"

"No . . . I *feel* that it is. Graham, would you mind if she were . . . like me?"

"I hope she looks just like you."

"I don't mean that. She might be . . . like me."

Graham worked his way back toward her lips. "Nothing would please me more."

"And nothing's going to happen, but *if* it did . . ." He tried to stop her words with his kisses but she turned aside. ". . . help her to understand . . . to not be afraid of what she knows . . ."

"Anna Leah, you will be her teacher . . ."

"Yes. Graham, don't let them make her a freak . . . don't . . ."

He pulled her into his arms and silenced her fears and his own.

CHAPTER 38

"Graham, there's a comp-call for you from SURF," Jema Marie said, picking her way down through the herb garden. Several members of the Ventures and the Seras, including Graham, were working on an extensive CELSS addition that would include a number of multichambered private dwellings.

Waverly, overseeing the plumbing involved in the project, had admired the designs Graham brought to her, and chided that she thought it was the mother-to-be who got nest-building urges, not the prospective father.

"What do they want?" Graham asked the old woman, not looking up from the careful transplanting of greenery to make room for piping systems.

"It's Jon Baker. He just said it was urgent."

Edwards looked at him, his spade poised. "It might be . . . you think the Review Board . . . ?"

Graham climbed out of the trench and started to jog toward the communications chamber.

"You're tracking dirt," the woman scolded.

Graham kicked off his shoes and ran.

Baker's face on the screen did not look like good news. "It's Keyote," he said. "They're in total revolt."

Graham worked to slow his breathing. The momentary surge of hope cracked into brittle shards of slow anger. "That's no surprise. We all knew it was coming sooner or later. Why tell me?"

"Because they're asking that you speak for them. The miners are holding the company officials and they want you to negotiate their demands before the Corporation."

"No."

"They're going to kill them, Gray. If we don't do something. They demanded you, specifically."

"I can't leave here. Not right now. Anna Leah is almost . . ."

"A lander is already on its way to you. We need your help. Keyote is desperate."

"Go to them," said Anna Leah, moving slowly into the room. "I'll be all right."

Graham turned to her. "Why are you up? You're not even supposed to be out of bed."

"I thought the call might be news from the Review Board. Graham, the sooner you go, the sooner you'll be back. We won't start the production without you." She leaned close and kissed him. "Hello, Jon."

"I haven't heard anything from the Board, Anna Leah. Not since the last rejection."

The disappointment earlier when the Board had turned down his appeal to return to Earth had not affected Graham as deeply as it had Anna Leah. "I want this for you," she had wept, "because you want it so badly. You ask for so little. And it's the one thing I'm powerless to give you." Graham had, thereafter, not allowed the topic to surface.

"I wouldn't be so insistent," Baker apologized, "but it is an emergency, Anna Leah. Several people have already been killed in the rioting."

"Jon, I want you to go with him, to Keyote," she said. "And I want the Board to know about it."

Smoke was curling into the sky above the mining facility by the time their hover-lander reached the colony.

"That's the E Section." Baker nodded. "It's been sealed off from the rest of the habitat."

"Is there a leader?" asked Graham. "A spokesman for the miners?"

"Yeah. You."

"I mean now. Who's been making the threats and demands thus far?"

"There seem to be several. Hollings does the talking, for the most part, but Jessup is involved, and Malone. Jessup is hotheaded, but I don't think he would kill anyone. Malone has a record back on Earth. He was leg-monitored for five years on a burglary conviction. Hollings has leadership potential but he doesn't know how to direct it yet. I don't know if he can stop the killing once it starts. The deaths so far have been accidental, as far as we can tell. They were trapped in the E Section when the seals blew. Once the oxygen is gone, so is the fire. I don't know how much damage was done. Some of the deepest sections are flooded, so we were told."

The lander moved slowly into the air lock.

"This could have been prevented," Graham said. "The Corporation overestimated the miners' tolerance for insufferable working conditions. I must admit that I *under*estimated it. I'm surprised that the revolt didn't happen much earlier."

Once the lander entered the docking hangar it was surrounded by miners carrying laser bores.

They were escorted through various chambers and corridors to the Communications Center, where Hollings greeted them solemnly.

"You're our only hope," he said, shaking Graham's hand. "If they don't listen to you, it's all over. The killing starts. We've got everybody rounded up in the theater—all the Keyote staff and security."

"Where is Tillman?"

"Malone's got him in his office."

"Bring him down here. And Abrams."

While they waited, Graham read the list of demands. "There isn't one thing on this list that isn't within reason," he said finally, handing the paper to Baker. "In fact, there are things I would add."

"Graham . . ." Baker began.

"You people are in no position to negotiate, with what you're asking," Graham continued, ignoring Baker's warning look.

Jessup frowned. "What do you mean? You just said it was within reason."

"Precisely. Everything on that list you *should* have. You leave no room for negotiation. If you want this," said Graham, spreading his hands apart, "then you ask for this." He extended his hands farther apart. "You also have to offer them something beyond the lives you're holding. You've got to give me something to offer them that they want."

"The lives of a hundred people won't be enough?" Hollings asked.

Graham shook his head. "Human life has never been good bargaining material. If you start killing them, it's all over. You know that. You've choked the goose."

"We've got nothing they want. We've got nothing, period." Hollings snatched the paper from Baker and wadded it into a ball.

Graham moved about the room, flicking dials and pushing buttons. TV screens flashed on. "Yes, you do have something they want."

"What?" said Jessup.

"A commitment to stay longer. To put in more time than two Earth years at a shot. Production is hampered by the revolving work force. You have to train almost a third of the entire colony every eighteen cycles. Just as you get a skilled, seasoned worker, he's ready to leave."

"Who the hell wants to stay longer than he has to?" snorted Jessup. "You'd be off this planet in a minute if you had the choice. You gotta be crazy to want to stay here."

"I'm not saying you have to make it a life commitment. Just . . . a reasonable time frame. If I can show them potential profits and losses incurred by a change in personnel turnover, then we have real negotiating leverage."

Hollings looked at Jessup. "I'd go for it if my family were here, but I won't bring them to Mars, to this."

"You've seen the Jeremian colony," Graham said. "And, Jessup, you've been down to the Seras at least four times now. What about a family colony along those lines? A place totally separate from Keyote? Once the monorail is completed you can travel to another colony in a matter of minutes. You would go *home* after a shift is over, not to a space the size of a bunk and a locker."

Hollings shrugged. "Let me talk to the others. We'll have to think about this."

Tillman was shoved through the door by Malone and a second miner carrying a stun gun. The man's face was bloodied and his nose looked broken. From the way he favored his right shoulder, Graham suspected a broken collarbone.

Baker glanced at Graham, clearly upset, then helped Tillman into a chair.

"You look better than I expected," Graham said to the man.

"Then you must have expected me to be dead," Tillman muttered. "Things are busted inside. Ribs, I think. Don't know what else."

"I've sent for Abrams. We're working on a proposal that might be agreeable to all parties. But it may take some time."

Jonas Abrams arrived, and Graham was relieved to see that he had not been beaten. But he looked terrified.

"I'm going with Hollings to talk to the miners," Graham said, "and Jessup is going to take Tillman over to the infirmary so Dr. Abrams can take care of him. Baker will line up the communications systems so that the SURF Council and the Keyote executives on Earth can hear what we have to say."

"What about me?" Malone said. "I don't like this. I don't like us scattered."

"Do you trust me?" Graham asked.

"You're the only one I do trust."

"Then stay here with Baker."

After the miners heard Graham's ideas they were enthusiastic but wary. "When's the monorail going to happen?" asked one man. "We keep hearing talk but we don't see any action yet."

"The tunnel bores should be arriving on the next cycler," Graham said, "but Mars is short on manpower."

"Hell, we could do it," said another miner. "If there's pay involved, of course."

"You think a four- to six-year contract would be the

thing to offer? To get them to listen to us?" asked another miner.

"Yes."

"I've seen the Jeremian colony," said a woman in the back of the room. "It's heaven compared to this place. I could handle going home to a place like that after my shift. I say go for it."

The time delay between Earth and Mars made communication tediously slow and awkward. It reminded Graham of a slow-motion tennis match in which there was enough time between each volley to play a quick game of chess or read several chapters of a book or complete a half-hour errand. The negotiations dragged on, far into the night. Tillman, bandaged and clearly in a great deal of pain, was permitted to lie down on a cot in the communications studio between transmissions.

By dawn, a tentative agreement had been reached and the hostages were released from the theater unharmed.

Graham arrived back at the Sera colony just in time to help Anna Leah deliver their daughter on the eve of his thirty-sixth birthday.

"You can tell them that she has the right number of fingers and toes," Anna Leah said, placing the infant in Baker's arms. "And you can inform them that she is healthy, beautiful, and has, I believe, blue eyes, though they may change. Graham's father and his grandfather had blue eyes. We have no idea where the blond hair came from. But they may not touch her. Nor will we allow any photos, videos, interviews, or speculation as to her genetic heritage."

Graham watched Baker hold his daughter and wondered if the man felt as awkward and frightened as he felt each time he cradled the tiny perfection. Anna Leah had finally coaxed him into picking her up on his own, and her cries were lusty and that frightened him still more. Fatherhood, he was discovering, did not instinctively come to him. But a fierce sense of protectiveness did.

"Her name is Lien. L-I-E-N," Graham said. "You'll have to include the phonetic spelling as well or they'll say *Lee-*

yen. It's *Lay*-ehn. It's Mandarin for lotus. Her middle name is Kendall."

Baker looked up at him, his eyes suddenly filling with tears.

Anna Leah sat beside him. "Your son was the first, Jon. Lien will carry his name. We wanted that for you, and for Matina. We would like you to be her godfather. We've chosen Paris to be her godmother but we don't know how to reach her, to tell her."

"I know where she is," he said softly. "I'll pass the news on to her."

Lien Kendall Sinclair, blissfully unaware of her instant fame and her future, yawned and curled a tiny hand around the man's finger.

CHAPTER 39

It was at the urging of Wade Ross that Graham and Anna Leah finally consented to allow a family portrait to be released to Earth. The man had returned to Mars filled with Broadway triumph, no longer the sullen outcast. "Graham, it can only help your cause," he argued when they had first refused. "You have no idea of the impact you have back there. You're like some outlaw legend. It's amazing. Every time I was interviewed about *Quasimodo*, they'd come around to you, somehow. They'd get real excited when they found out we're friends. Before I knew it, the whole interview centered on you. They've got this cult thing going, everybody wearing a bracelet or pin with a sea gull on it. It's supposed to symbolize freeing you."

Anna Leah began to laugh. "I wonder if Risa Siegler recognizes her part in the myth. Graham, let's do it. One family portrait."

"No."

"It would let them know that the first native Martian has no antennae. And Wade is right. You need to remind them that you're here, and that you want to come home."

"I won't do it. I will not use my daughter to try to get back to Earth."

"If we don't allay their fears and satisfy their curiosity,

it will just grow. Someday Lien may want to visit Earth. She won't be able to avoid what will happen. At least this would lift some of the mystique. I want to do this." With much reluctance, Graham consented.

The arrival of each cycler brought more and more baby gifts, until finally they had to request that such gifts be donated to various children's hospitals and charities on Earth. Graham watched Anna Leah make tiny gravity suits for their daughter, so that she might someday withstand a gravity much greater than that on the planet of her birth. Whether she would even be able to tolerate Earth was an unknown. The SURF researchers kept a polite distance, but watched her development carefully.

Anna Leah was reelected to a second term as commune leader and was called away periodically to colony Council meetings at the SURF base. On those occasions Graham was left in full charge of the baby. He plunked her into a backpack and worked at the potter's wheel while Lien slept or happily drooled down his back. Slowly he slipped into fatherhood and began to marvel at all the miraculous firsts in his daughter's life—sitting up alone, her first tooth, her first steps. The only first that had not made an appearance on schedule was Lien's first word. She did not speak at all.

"Graham, I want to try something with Lien," said Anna Leah one evening. "Take her into the playroom. I've put a blue ball under a box. There are red and yellow balls under two other boxes. I want to see if she . . . knows where the blue ball is."

Lien, her wispy pale hair in a tiny ponytail, looked up at her mother as Anna Leah smiled and said nothing. The child toddled over to the middle box on the floor and lifted it. The blue ball rolled out and Lien clapped her hands.

"But you didn't even tell her yet," Graham said.

"Yes, I did. Now I want you to try it. I want to see if she can hear you. I'll take her into the bedchamber. Tell us when you're ready."

Lien seemed delighted by the game and went to the blue ball without hesitation. Graham got down on the floor and she waddled over to him.

"Lien, can you say 'ball'?" he asked.

She tried to put the ball in his mouth. He laughed and
she chortled, snatching the ball back.

"Have we got a problem?" he asked Anna Leah.

"Not yet. But we may have to start insisting on some
verbalization eventually. She doesn't understand that not
everyone can do this. I remember why I finally began to
speak. Out of frustration. It was as if everyone else around
me was deaf, except for my mother and my sister. Speech
was so slow and silly, but I was forced to learn it, as if
studying an archaic language."

That night, in bed, Anna Leah moved close and whispered, "I think we should have at least seven."

"Seven?"

"It's a nice number."

"Well, I'll see what I can do." Graham chuckled.
"Whose idea was this? Yours or Lien's?"

"She wants playmates. She's a year and a half, Earth
time. I thought you should know that number two is already coming along."

Graham kissed her. "Is it a boy or a girl?"

"A surprise." She laughed.

He was at the potter's wheel when Baker came to tell
him. At first he thought that it was another rejection by
the Review Board, but the look on the man's face told
him the news was far worse than that.

"Graham . . ."

The vase he was working on buckled into ruin and a
detached coldness began at his fingers and moved inward
like an implosion, draining the heat from his body. He
saw Wade standing behind Baker, his face strangely gray
in color. Graham thought that it looked as if clay had
replaced his skin. The room grew hushed.

"Anna Leah . . ." he began. "Where is she?"

Baker shook his head. "She was coming back here
after the Council meeting and she wanted to get back
early, so . . . there was a lander . . . It . . . we don't
quite know why . . . it just . . . crashed. Graham . . .
she . . . there were no survivors."

Things seemed far away. He wanted everything to be
so far away that he could no longer see, or hear, or feel, or

think, or breathe. There had been no time to prepare. There had been no warning.

There were vague images he remembered, later, things that held him transfixed for hours, and he remembered people around him, touches and whispers that tried to offer small coals of warmth, but the cold that wrapped itself around him was impenetrable. He remembered hearing a baby crying somewhere and knew it was something he should attend to, but the cold twisted tighter, freezing him into immobility. And he allowed the numbness to envelop him until he no longer heard anything.

Paris walked along the arched corridors of the Jeremian commune with Baker. "We heard the news about four months out from Earth, aboard the *Westminster*. I'd wanted to surprise him, to show him I could finish something I started out to do. First woman T.E. I wanted him to be proud of me. Do you think he'll talk to me?"

"Paris, he may not even know you're here. He doesn't talk to anyone. He's very withdrawn. After Anna Leah's death he just stopped everything. He left the Seras and came here, alone. It's as if Lien no longer exists for him. I thought we were going to lose him when he had a bad flare-up of Martian Fever. He's still not back from it. It's hard to get him to eat, or move, or respond at all."

"Does he meditate?"

"No. He sleeps. SURF wants to pump him full of 'jollygoods' to see if he snaps out of this. I keep holding them off. Graham is in there someplace, and I think he will heal himself. But it's going to take some time."

Baker stopped at a door and knocked softly. A bluerobed woman answered.

"We never leave him alone. It just seemed that someone should be here with him, in case he . . . checked in," Baker said, gesturing for Paris to enter.

The room was in darkness except for a light above the bed. Paris was jarred by the gaunt figure who only faintly resembled Graham Sinclair. He was dark-bearded, with straight raven hair that reached his shoulders. His skin had no color at all, it seemed, almost matching the whiteness of the pillow and sheets. His hands, curled into fists, rested on his chest.

"He hangs on to the jade. He won't let go of it," Baker murmured. "Sometimes he rubs a thumb across it. That's about it."

"He hasn't eaten today," said the blue-robed woman. "If you can get him to swallow a little soup . . ."

Paris sat on the edge of the bed. *"Damn* you, Sinclair! I take a little leave of absence and you go and screw up your life! I can't leave you alone for a minute! Look at yourself!"

Graham opened his eyes.

"That's better," she said. "You look like crap, Sinclair. You really do."

Graham took a deep breath.

"That's good." Paris nodded. "Fill up the old Tan Tien. Do it again, deeper."

He blinked and reached out to touch her hair.

"Yeah, it's really me." She smiled.

He moved his lips and whispered.

She leaned close to make out the words.

"Why . . . didn't you say good-bye?" he murmured, his voice old and coming from far away, it seemed to Paris.

"Because I was coming back, silly."

Graham began to sob, deep guttural sounds that shook his whole body and would not stop. Paris wrapped her arms around him and rocked him. "Cry," she whispered. "Oh, please cry, Graham."

He did not heal quickly. There were days she couldn't call him back, and days he turned his head away when she held a spoon to his lips. And all the time, she talked to him, even when she wasn't sure he could hear her.

Jacob sat with him for an hour each evening, reading from both the Bible and the teachings of Lao Tzu, having a one-way theological argument in hopes of eliciting a response.

Wade came regularly and sat in a far corner of the room and played his guitar. "I'm working on a new op-era," he said one afternoon as Graham gazed out French windows that opened into a domed courtyard. "It's about an exile. But it doesn't have an ending yet. Tell me how it ends, Graham."

"He dies," Graham mumbled, not looking at him.

"No, I need a happy ending."

"Then don't . . . write about him."

"I was thinking maybe, at the end, he gets to go home."

"No. He can never . . . go home."

"He might. He just has to keep hoping. It could happen." Wade stopped playing his guitar and placed it on a chair beside the bed. "In case you feel like practicing a few chords." He stared out the window and said softly, "I loved her, too. You know that."

Graham looked down at the jade in his right hand and said nothing.

Tillman came down from Keyote to visit him. "I was here before," he said, standing at the foot of Graham's bed, "but you probably don't remember it. You were . . . you had the Fever, so I didn't think you'd know I came by. This is for you." He placed a scroll of paper on the bed when Graham made no move to accept it. "It's a copy of a petition we've sent back home—to Earth. Every blessed and cursed soul on the face of Mars signed it—asking that you be allowed to return to Earth. Even the Jovis bunch signed it."

Tillman paced the room, seemingly ill at ease. "I have this theory. I think they keep you here because of your meddling, Sinclair. Everywhere I turn, I see the results of your influence. The monorail is about completed, we've got a new colony going up near Sharonov for the families of the miners, I've got workers running around campaigning for various Council reps in the next election, and people keep coming in on the cyclers, asking if all these stories about the Cloud Man are true. 'Does he levitate?' they ask. 'Can he heal with a touch?' 'Does he bring back the dead?' 'Only the near dead,' I tell them. We've got to get you out of here before you become a damned saint. The more you do, the more they're going to keep you here. So, you've got to stop meddling."

Graham's eyes followed him as he moved around the room.

"I just wanted you to know that we're trying to get you the hell home. Don't . . . quit on us, man. That's all we need, people flocking to Mars on religious pilgrimages!"

There was a loud knock on the door and Vogel stuck his head in. "Yo, Sinclair, you talkin' yet? Tillman, how's tricks? Any more mutinies up your way?" The man sauntered in and went over to Graham. "If you're dead, Sinclair, you'd better let 'em know. Don't go 'round stinkin' up the place. If you're alive, I just come by to cheer you up. Actually we wanted to barter some supplies with the Jerrys, so I was in the neighborhood."

"Graham, this little turd signed the petition twice," said Tillman.

"Who's calling who a turd? Hell, I'd sign anything to get him off this planet. Florie's pestering me to death wanting a kid now. I blame him for that, if you want to know. I am not the fatherhood type. I don't *like* kids."

Tillman moved to the door. "That's because they're all taller than you, Vogel. Graham, you want me to throw him out before I leave?"

"Hey, Tillman, a broke nose improves your looks. See if you can do something about your ears now."

After Tillman had left, Vogel moved closer to Graham's bed and waved his hand in front of the man's face. "You in there, Sinclair? Blink or something. Listen, you know that special sand Annie Leah liked so much . . ."

"*Anna,*" Graham said, making the man jump.

"Yeah, that's what I said. Hey, it's good to know you ain't a total zombie . . . in a manner of speaking. Well, this sand is suddenly hot stuff back home, I just found out. Like, it's worth its weight in gold—its *Earth* weight, no less. Seems the molecular structure of the silica is a little different than anything they've come across and they want the stuff for some real special lenses and God knows what all else. It's gonna make yttrium superconductors obsolete. They want it bad and are willing to pay stellar credits for every gram we send back to Earth. Now we got all these Lark prospectors wandering around in those new soft suits like they think Mars is theirs for the taking and I don't like what I see happening. Two of 'em just killed each other over a little bag of the stuff—over *sand,* for chrissake. I figured you might know what to do.

If you're planning to stick around, that is. If you're going to kick off, sorry I bothered you. I just thought the Seras should have like first dibs on the stuff. They wanted it before anybody else did."

"I don't care what you do with it."

Vogel looked at him and shrugged slightly. "She was . . . a real special lady. I'm sorry it happened, Sinclair. I mean that. Nobody should have to go through what you been through. I mean, if something ever happened to Florie . . . I don't know what I'd do. But I wouldn't fold up and quit. She'd be mad as hell if I did that. Her ghost would nag me to death, telling me to get my can in gear and get on with life. Leah, she's too polite to nag, but I think she'd have to be pretty unhappy about how you're pissing your life away like this because of her. You got a little girl to think about. She's got nobody if you roll over. I know where that sand is. And I'm not telling nobody. If the Seras want it, it's theirs."

He was sitting in a bamboo rocker out in the small courtyard, his lunch left untouched on a nearby table, when Paris found him. "Good, you're finally out of bed."

"Where did you go?" he asked. There was a faintly accusatory edge to the question.

"I had to check on the new colonists I brought to Mars. I can't spend every minute spoon-feeding you, Sinclair. I can't neglect the new Larks to take care of you night and day." She uncovered a dish on the tray. "Eat."

"I'm not hungry."

"Eat anyway."

He looked up at her. "You're really a Transition Escort?"

"Yep. Licensed and everything." She held out a bowl of soup and he took it. After two spoonfuls, he set it aside and picked up the jade in his lap.

"That's not enough, Graham. Three more, then I'll stop pushing."

He wouldn't look at her, but kept stroking the jade, frowning.

Paris sat down at his feet and crossed her legs. "Gray, what's wrong?"

"You're going to leave again, aren't you?"

"Not for a while. There are four more cyclers in service now, so I can head back anytime. It doesn't have to be right away."

"But you will leave."

"Yes. And I'll be back. I understand now why Baker was a T.E. You get caught *between* worlds somehow. You can't quite leave Mars. She keeps a little part of your soul. I had no idea the sight of red dust would make me so happy. I was even glad to see Waverly and Vogel. They're coming over for the celebration, you know."

Graham looked puzzled. "The Summer Solstice?"

"No. That passed a while back."

"I . . . lost some time."

"Yes, you did. A pretty hefty chunk. A lot of people are piling in here for this Occasion. That's with a capital O, of course. That's what I came to tell you. There's going to be a lot of doubling up. You're going to have to share your quarters with another woman, Sinclair."

"You?"

"No, I'm sorry to say, but I guess I can contain my rampant jealousy in this particular case." She glanced toward the open door to his room. "Ah, here she comes now. Here's your roomie."

Baker came out into the courtyard carrying Lien.

"Everybody's coming from all over to celebrate Lien's first Martian birthday," Paris said, getting up to take the little girl into her arms. "God, she's beautiful, Graham. And smart! Quiet though. Like her father. In Earth years she's almost two. Aren't babies starting to talk by then?"

Lien saw her father and beamed, thrusting both hands out toward him, her tiny fingers clutching desperately at the air. Paris placed the child in the man's lap.

Graham closed his eyes. "Take her away, Paris. Please. I can't . . . Jon, take her." He placed a hand to his eyes, fighting tears. "Please! I don't want . . ."

Lien reached one hand up to touch his lips. "Daddy!" she said. "Daddy, Daddy, Daddy, Daddy!"

Graham wrapped his arms around his daughter and began to rock her as he wept.

CHAPTER 40

Graham watched from the doorway as Lien folded clothing into a wicker trunk. At fifteen she bore an uncanny resemblance to her mother, he thought, except that her hair had remained pale gold and her eyes were gray-blue. But there was a sameness in her bone structure and in gestures and in the nuance of movement that made certain memories almost more than he could bear. He had returned to the Seras soon after Lien's first Martian birthday and slowly regained his strength. His only consuming interest became the raising of his daughter. He repeatedly declined to be nominated as commune leader, but eventually found himself politically involved as the head of the Inter-Colony Council, which set policy for the planet at large. He had watched new colonies spring up and settlements spread throughout the northwestern quadrant of the planet. The years had slipped by so fast, he thought, watching Lien pack. Even the Martian years had spun by too quickly.

"Tell me again," she said, "about the birds in Singapore."

"You've heard it ten thousand times."

"Then I want to hear it ten thousand and one times. Go on, tell me. 'On Sundays . . .' Don't leave anything out."

Graham sighed. "On Sundays, when I was very little, I

went down into old Singapore with my grandmother . . ."

"Lihwa, whom you called *Nai Nai* . . ."

". . . yes, and we would go for tea in an open pavilion
where people brought their songbirds in bamboo cages.
The cages were hung on chains suspended from the ceiling and all the birds sang while the people sat at round
tables and listened and drank tea and ate small cakes.
And one Sunday I heard a bird that sang so beautifully
that I refused to leave until my grandmother offered the
owner what amounted to a small fortune for the bird. My
grandfather, when he heard what she had done, thought
the expense was outrageous, so my grandmother said we
would return the bird immediately. She took me out into
the garden and held the cage while I opened the door
and let the bird fly away. It was returned to where it belonged . . . which was all I had wanted to begin with."

Lien stopped folding her things. " 'And the songbird
came back to the garden and sang every day from the top
of a willow.' Do you think they still do that? Bring the
birds out on Sundays? It seems so odd, the repetitious
naming of sols, but I hope they still do that."

"It's an old custom. They may."

"When I visit Ti, do you think he would take me
there?"

"I'm sure he would."

"There are so many things I want to see and do. Blue
skies will seem strange. Nothing is domed? It's just . . .
open? I can't imagine that. And oceans. I want to see an
ocean that tastes of salt."

Graham moved into the room and sat in a bamboo and
rattan chair as she began filling a second trunk. He had
taught her all he could, and now it was time for schooling
beyond books and discs and computers. It had been difficult to give his consent, to allow her to leave Mars, but he
had always known that she would leave him one way or
another. He also understood her insistence on the story of
the songbirds of Singapore one more time. He had tried to
prepare her for the curiosity she would provoke wherever
she went on Earth, simply because she was who she was.

"But there are a lot of children on Mars," she had said.
"That's silly."

"But you were the *first*. And you'll be the first native-born Martian to visit Earth. And above all, you're *the Cloud Man's* daughter. You're going to attract attention no matter what you do. You must promise me you'll go nowhere without an escort . . ."

"Bodyguard." Lien grimaced. "Don't sugar it with euphemisms, Daddy. You want a bodyguard."

"Lien, there are people there who still harbor a great deal of anger because of what happened a long time ago . . ."

"But they can neutralize the Clouds now."

"Nevertheless, a great many people died, and some still look upon me as the one responsible. I worry for your safety. I can't allow you to go to Earth unless you are given full protection at all times."

Reluctantly, she agreed to his conditions.

The Mars Commission itself had finally reinstated Graham's freedom to receive news and information concerning Earth after he told the SURF Council he was unable to educate his daughter about a planet he no longer knew. Nor could he permit her to travel to a place about which he knew so little. He had managed to guess about the antimatter that had finally been harnessed as a propellant for space travel, shortening six-month trips to a matter of weeks, and Paris had smuggled news discs to him periodically during stopovers. But he knew he needed to offer Lien more than guesses and snippets of information about Earth. The Commission agreed, and the ban was lifted.

Ti, who had begun an immediate correspondence with Graham once communication restrictions were removed, had extended an invitation to Lien to visit when she came to Earth to go to school. The man had attained great prominence in the art world and had, to Graham's mild amusement, returned to Singapore to live in the highly coveted Old Chinatown district.

"I now understand, Master Graham, much that youth and ignorance blinded me to," he said in a letter disc.

Jasmine Wyncote, who had taken Wade to her bosom during his trips to New York, begged Graham to allow Lien to accompany the man for a visit. "They'll see that you're not a myth," she coaxed. "You have a flesh-and-blood child, and you are not to be forgotten."

Graham would have felt much more secure, he decided, in sending his daughter to an Earth that had forgotten him completely.

Wade knocked on the open door. "Lien, one trunk max, kiddo. If you forget something, your dad can send it to you. And as one of the heirs to the Marineris Silica Corporation, you have unlimited credit upon which to draw."

"No, she doesn't," Graham said. "She is on a limited budget. It's the one thing I can't seem to get across to her."

"I want a banking chip," said Lien.

"No. No banking chip. Jasmine is going to teach you the concept of frugality. It's one of the stipulations of this trip."

"What about this?" She held up a gravity suit. "Do I have to take it along?"

"You should be wearing it now," said Wade.

"I hate it. What if I can't stand the gravity once I get there?"

"Head for water. Whenever I feel like I can't lift the weight any longer, I get in a pool. It helps."

For an instant Graham remembered another pool in a tropical enclosure, and Anna Leah's body slipping through his fingers. He glanced up to catch his daughter watching him.

"Why was it dark?" she asked.

"That wasn't for you to see, Lien. That was private."

"But it was so . . . strong. I couldn't help it. I feel close to her when you do that. I know her so well through you. It was . . . a dust storm. Oh."

Wade looked at her. "You can't do that with outsiders, Lien. They won't understand it, and you'll scare them. There's still a lot of prejudice back there. Be careful of your gift."

"Will I have to wear a wristband like you do, when we arrive?"

Wade nodded. "But it will simply say 'Genetic Information Unavailable.' "

"I don't like that—being tagged like animal breeding stock."

"Well, that's why I live here." Wade smiled. "We far outnumber Perfects, don't forget. I've only met one I had any tolerance for, and that's only half the time. They're a vanishing breed."

On the morning of her departure Graham felt the symptoms of a flare-up already starting. He swallowed several yellow capsules and meditated in the solarium garden until it was time to go.

"Daddy?" She came into the garden wearing a white soft suit, and bent over him, her long golden braid falling over her left shoulder. She kissed him on the cheek. "You better get ready if you want to see me off. Promise me you won't miss me too much."

"I promise."

"Why do they insist we wear the soft suits if we aren't even going to be out on the surface of the planet?"

Graham stood up. "Just a travel precaution. Better to have it than to wish you had it."

Wade was already at the monorail station when they arrived. "I sent your luggage on ahead to SURF," he said. The platform was crowded with Sera colonists, all of whom had come to see Lien off. There was a great deal of hugging and shedding of tears. Sam Edwards picked her up to kiss her good-bye.

"I expect to hear from you regularly, young lady."

"Sam, keep my father busy, will you? Don't let him get all moody like he gets sometimes."

"Ah, don't let him think too much." The man nodded, beginning to quote. " 'People go mad if they think too much.' "

"Medea," said Lien. "Robinson Jeffers's *Medea.*"

"On the nose, sweetheart. We're so far behind in production right now, your old man won't have time to think. I guarantee it."

The ride to the SURF base was swift and almost silent. Graham had not experienced motion sickness for years, but suddenly felt nauseated and excused himself briefly once they arrived at the SURF terminal. The base had grown to the size of a small city in the last decade, still the hub of all arrivals and departures, and still overcrowded until the cyclers left. A second space station was in full operation and a third was being constructed.

Paris greeted them, slipping an arm around Graham's waist. "Baker's coming in from the Jeremian colony to see you off, Lien. He said not to let you off the planet till he gets here. Who would have thought that the man would go and get religious on us? Filled his father's shoes after all."

Wade snorted. "Well, the Jerrys of yore bear little resemblance to the Jerrys of today. I'd say they were more Taoist than Christian, with a little mystical sea gull thrown in. He was talking not long ago about sending missionaries to Earth. Now that's a kick."

Paris wiped sweat from Graham's face after Lien had gone with Wade to check in and get seat numbers on the lander. "Hang on," she whispered.

"I'll be all right."

"Of course you will." She patted his buttock. "Got a place to stay, sailor?"

"I wasn't planning to stay over."

"Plan on it. You're going to be too sick by evening to go back. You might as well head for the infirmary as soon as she leaves. You're a shade past green now."

"It's motion sickness. It will pass."

"Graham, I'm a T.E. I know a flare-up of Martian Fever when I see it. It's a lot less prevalent these days with the new inoculations, but all you old-timers still come down with it periodically."

"Old-timer?"

"Oh, excuse me. You're only fifty-one. You're in the youth of middle age. Forgive me."

"Paris, how can I let her go?"

The woman gently stroked his back. "Because you have to, and you always do what you have to do. She'll come back."

"What if she doesn't?"

"She will. Like that songbird. You remember? You let it loose and it came back and sang in your garden."

Graham shook his head. "It didn't. It didn't come back. I made that part up for Lien, when she was little. It never came back."

Paris wiped at his face again with a white handkerchief. "Maybe it did, and you just never heard it, mixed in with the songs of all the other birds. Graham, I think we should get you over to the infirmary."

"Not until she leaves. Go find me some Dee-Dee Brew."

"That stuff can kill you."

"Please. You know where to get it. It helps."

He was sitting on a bench against a wall when Baker found him. "Am I too late? Did she leave?"

"She's somewhere over there with Wade, getting checked in."

"You look . . ."

"I know. Paris went to find some Brew."

Baker sat beside him, silent for several minutes. "You can handle this," he said softly. "Remember, 'to give birth and nourish, bearing but not possessing,' this is part of the Prime Virtue."

Graham looked at him. "I doubt that Lao Tzu ever experienced parenthood."

Lien returned, flushed with excitement, and hugged Baker. She avoided looking at her father, but placed a hand on his shoulder as he sat, waiting.

Baker took Wade aside to talk to him and Lien whispered, "Daddy, I'm scared."

"All things new are a little scary. Lien, here, I want you to have this." Graham held out a delicate gold necklace. A small piece of jade hung from it. "The Seras fashioned the gold from your mother's ring. I contributed the jade."

"It's from your piece?"

"Yes. That way, if you ever feel that we're far apart, you'll remember that we're always joined." He fastened the necklace around her neck.

She kept her eyes downcast. "If I look at you, I'll cry. I'll come home. I promise you."

It had been hard to let her go. It almost felt as if he were losing Anna Leah all over again, he thought. He wasn't sure if it had been the inner tearing or the fever that fogged the first several sols after Lien's departure. He had spent the time in the infirmary sweating it out, with Krolov poking medications at him. The dread of returning to the Sera colony and the aching silence of his home was tempered somewhat by the fact that Paris accompanied him.

"You're sure you want me along?" she kept saying while they waited for the monorail train.

"I want you to stay with me during your R and R. I don't think I can go back there alone right now."

Paris watched the sun setting in a particularly pink sky. "Looks like we may be getting some dust pretty soon. That was really sweet of Vogel and Waverly to come see Lien off like that. I swear Vogel was almost misty-eyed. I guess we all mellow a little in our old age."

"How long are you going to keep this up?"

Paris looked puzzled. "Keep what up?"

"This back and forth business. The T.E. job."

"As long as I enjoy it. Why?"

Graham shrugged. "I just thought you might want to settle down someday. If you do, there's room . . . I have plenty of room . . ."

"Is this some kind of proposal?"

Graham looked out the windows of the empty terminal. "Some kind, yes."

Paris gazed out the windows, too. "I'll . . . take it under consideration. I don't cook."

"That's all right. I do."

"I still like roast guinea pig."

"Don't expect me to fix it. You'll come to love vegetarian."

"Just . . . roomies, like?"

"If that's how you want it."

"I *am* terrific in bed, Sinclair. I just thought you should know that."

"I always assumed you were."

"Oh."

The train rolled in with a breathy *whoosh* and they boarded. "I accept," said Paris.

Graham felt the presence in front of him but couldn't take his eyes from the pot turning so smoothly under his fingers. Lien had weathered her first Earth months and reported only one serious attack of homesickness for the salmon skies of Mars. She had spent a great deal of time in Jasmine's pool but was gradually becoming acclimated to Earth's gravity. There was a growing harmony in Graham's life, and he saw its influence in all the pottery he was shaping.

"Mr. Sinclair? Sir?"

"What?" Graham wet his fingers, not taking his eyes from the clay. The voice was youthful and male.

"Sir, I was wondering if we might talk?"

"I don't give interviews."

"No, sir. I didn't come to . . . my name is McKay, sir. Cadet Kuan McKay. My mother said I should come to see you while I'm here . . . on Mars."

Graham looked up, the pot totally forgotten. He was tall, boyishly handsome, with obsidian-colored hair, and there was a faint hint of almond to his dark eyes.

"Maggie McKay is your mother?"

"Dr. Margaret McKay. Yes, sir."

"How . . . old are you?"

"Seventeen." He held out a white box. "My mother sends her greetings. She told me to give this to you."

Graham wiped his hands on his apron and took the small box. Inside, tucked in tissue, was a plain white teacup and a saucer.

"She . . . said she hoped you would be pleased with her gift."

Graham began a slow smile. "Tell . . . your mother that I am very pleased with her gift. Kuan, do you know that your given name is the same as your father's middle name? It has been in his family for a thousand years."

"No, sir, I didn't know that."

"Do you know who your father is?"

The boy looked down, then directly at Graham. "I . . . believe you are. Sir."

"Did your mother tell you that?"

"No, sir. I just . . . no, sir."

"How long will you be here?"

"Two months . . . uh . . . six cycles, sir. On a work-study program. Then I have to return to the Academy."

"Have you seen anything of Mars yet?"

"Very little. I came straight here."

"Then I'll have to show you around. Six cycles doesn't give us much time."

Sam Edwards suddenly burst into the studio, out of breath. "Graham, did you hear?"

"Don't tell him!" Paris shrieked, running in behind him. "*I'll* tell him! Don't you dare tell him!"

"I already know."

Paris caught her breath. "How could you already know? Baker just got here with the news. Why aren't you excited? How could you know?"

"Paris, Sam, I would like you to meet my son, Kuan McKay . . . Sinclair."

"What?"

Sam Edwards began to laugh. "That's not the news we were bringing, but congratulations."

Baker entered the studio. "Why isn't he excited?"

"He doesn't know," Paris said, still breathing hard.

"Know what?" Graham said.

Baker looked at Paris. "I'll do the honors, if you don't mind. Graham, we just got word from the Review Board. You're going home. Back to Earth. Effective immediately. You can go *home!*"

Graham began to wash spattered clay from his arms. "I am home, Jon. I already am home." With that, he walked out of the room with his son.

"You'll have to see the Valles Marineris at dawn," he said. "There's nothing on Earth quite as spectacular . . ."

Off to Explore Mars
EUGENE MALLOVE

MARS AT LAST!

Mars is so near we can almost touch it. In fact, more than a few of us already *have* run pieces of the planet through our fingers: Mars rocks from Antarctica, gouged from old Mars thousands of years ago—by glancing meteoric impact some say—and lately fallen onto the ice fields of Earth's southern pole, coming then into the hands of intrepid explorers. These may be the first pieces of another planet to be handled by people of Earth.

A few months ago an old star-gazing friend phoned to offer me one of these pieces of Mars. No fooling!—a genuine Mars rock authenticated by respected scientists schooled in planets. Its composition and signature of elements is indisputably Martian, something that could not have been known before the Viking landing missions in the 1970s sifted, fathomed, and analyzed the substance of Mars.

I drooled with want, having dreamt of touching the sands of Mars since grammar-school days. I would have bought it in a flash at the ridiculously low price of $1,900 per gram (six grams minimum purchase, please), but the fee didn't tailor well with my budget. But what a bargain!

The Apollo Moon rocks came back to the tune of $60,000 per gram (and *they're* not for sale), and Mars is so much farther away. Alas, this Mars quester will simply have to wait for another Mars rock to be found, its blackness blighting the barren, frigid desert that is Antarctica.

Why would anyone want a pet Mars rock? Is it simply the call of the distant and heretofore unreachable? Are we *off* to explore Mars? Are we literally on our way, or have we merely gone off course, gone off the deep end, or gone entirely off our Mars rockers? Poets and writers of science fiction have chronicled the imaginary life of Mars past and Mars future. We have not stopped dreaming of civilizations on Mars. Not very long ago at the turn of the century, the French Academy of Sciences offered the huge sum of 100,000 francs, the Prix Pierre Guzman, to the first person to succeed in communicating with a world *other than Mars*! In that quaint age of planetary optimism, it was considered too easy to rouse the attention of the presumed Martians. Now we know better, but still we dream.

What is the mysterious allure of the Red Planet that has drawn Earthians to Mars throughout the ages, and promises to take us bodily there within the next twenty years to initiate a Martian civilization? Simply put, the answer is "because it's there," and we are who we are, creatures of adventuresome spirit. Like any other daunting challenge, humanity will take this one up and go to Mars in the next several decades, now that it has the means. Mars, after all, is another *place*, another world, and if we have learned anything from the record of life on this globe, it is that organisms tend to seek out and fill virtually every available ecological niche once they have the wherewithal to do so. Above all, Mars is the only planet or moon in the solar system with an atmosphere, water, and other surface resources that colonists could use to satisfy virtually all of their needs.

Indeed, we *do* have the means to go to Mars and have had it for some time now, but we have lacked the will. Willy Ley, the noted chronicler of the birth of spaceflight, could write with considerable justification in 1960, "The first expedition to Mars may take place in 1975, if not earlier." It galls would-be Mars explorers to think that human beings might be striding the valleys and basins of Mars right now were it not for the stubbornness of strife among the planet's nation-states. Nothing new under the sun after all—over two thousand years ago, one civilization named bloodred Mars after its god of war, a tradition that runs through recorded history of naming the red celestial apparition after the deadly and horrid. Warlike Mars is immortalized in the astronomer's symbol—the circle with projecting arrow, which does double duty as the biologist's notation for male. The arrow is a spear and the circle little doubt a shield.

The Moon having been won (or so we thought), as the U.S. Apollo program wound down in the early 1970s, high-level political plans circulated in the Nixon administration to select Mars as the next goal for the country's newly found space-faring talents. None other than Vice President Spiro Agnew, one might dimly recall, was the temporary champion of a manned Mars expedition—a landing by Americans on Mars before the year 2000. Alas, Mars was not in the cards as the nation's space program spun down like a dying record, even though groundwork was being laid for a major resumption in the 1990s. We had to build our space shuttles first and get the taste of "routine" spaceflight.

That routine, of course, was rudely and tragically shocked by the *Challenger* accident in January 1986. In 1989, the space shuttle has been reborn. We will soon be using our tiny fleet of shuttles—*Discovery, Columbia, Atlantis,* and *Endeavour,* the *Challenger* replacement—to loft a mammoth space station in the late 1990s, an ideal leaping-off point for Mars expeditions. The Soviet Union has brilliantly pioneered long-duration spaceflight—the sine qua non of multiyear Mars expeditions. We have learned that the medical and psychological sequelae of such human feats of endurance are not to be underestimated. The Russians have also already established a space station, *Mir,* much smaller than the projected U.S.-Canadian-European-Japanese model, but a space station nevertheless.

But why Mars? Why a world that comes closest to Earth but once approximately every two years (closer to twenty-five months)? Why not stay near Earth or simply return to the Moon for more extended stays? Some in the space community advocate establishing a lunar base first as both a training excercise and a staging point for the base on Mars—more than one hundred times farther removed. Dedicated Mars advocates consider the plan for a Moon base first to be an unnecessary diversion and perhaps an economic obstacle to Mars exploration.

In the final analysis, the search for extant or extinct extraterrestrial life, and matters of the human spirit, are the best reasons for going to Mars. On the other hand, there are many practical as well as scientific reasons to go. We have already traveled vicariously to the Martian surface two successful times—the U.S. Viking missions in 1976. We sampled the soil of Mars and found it apparently wanting in microbial life.

There are still some true-believing scientists who think that Mars microbes really were shown to exist by the Viking experiments. In their opinion, the data were contradictory at worst, and ringing with the signature of life at best. But recently other scientists have conceived quite convincing physico-chemical mechanisms to explain those initially startlingly Viking reports that seemed to tell of new life. Skeptics please note, however, only two landing sites have been examined for possible evidence of life on Mars—a far cry from what would be necessary to certify the whole planet barren. And what *were* those greenish patches on exposed Mars rocks that were discovered by Viking scientist Dr. Gilbert Levin in an image returned by one lander? Could these have been hardy Mars lichens, akin to one of the most adaptable plant species on Earth?

One of the most compelling reasons to go to Mars is to study how it came to be the frigid desert that it is—with an average equatorial temperature of $-60°C$—because of the great evidence that it once had a much more temperate clime and massive flows of surface water. Could the same tragedy eventually befall Earth? We are talking about comparative planetology, the effort to find out why Earth is Earthlike, neighboring Venus a hellhole, and Mars a planet that "almost made it"—or *did* make it and then lost out in the life game that apparently anoints rocky worlds with fragile but seemingly stable biospheres. Why does Gaia live on through the eons, while "Marsia"—if ever it was—came to a bitter end?

Studies to explore the science of planetary destiny have been conducted, and certainly could continue at much less expense with robotic vehicles. But there are even more compelling reasons why people should go to Mars and go there soon. Spaceship Earth is stewing in the juices of fratricidal conflict, and though the world may need a large dose of "love-sweet-love," it desperately wants an outlet for energies that have traditionally expressed themselves in warfare. Since 1988, the 120,000-member Planetary Society, based in Pasadena, California, has circulated a Mars Declaration, which says in part:

> Mars is the world next door, the nearest planet on which human explorers could safely land. Although it is sometimes as warm as a New England October, Mars is a chilly place, so cold that some of its thin carbon dioxide atmosphere freezes out at the winter pole. There are pink skies, fields of boulders, sand dunes, vast extinct volcanoes that dwarf anything on Earth, a great canyon that would cross most of the United States, sandstorms that sometimes reach half the speed of sound, strange bright and dark markings on the surface, hundreds of ancient river valleys, mountains shaped like pyramids and many other mysteries.

The other reason why humans should go to Mars may sound silly, and certainly no one in the 1950s—not even Wernher von Braun—could have said this: It's just getting to be *so easy* to go to Mars, why the hell *not* go! Technology is a very organic process that has evolved to make both space exploration and its expense much more doable and affordable. The annual fraction of the U.S. GNP (sustained over a period of years) that would once have been required to go to Mars was perhaps 1% at the end of the 1960s with its $2.5 trillion GNP (constant 1986 dollars). With an almost doubled GNP, the present cost of a stylish Mars voyage would likely be less than a tenth of that annual expenditure.

Wernher von Braun published the first thorough, state-of-the-art (for its time) engineering design for a Mars expedition in 1952, *Das Marsprojekt*. Von Braun had done the work in his spare time during 1948, and his "sole computational tool was a slide rule." In the preface to *The Mars Project*'s 1962 English translation (University of Illinois Press, 1962), the great rocket pioneer wrote, "My basic objective during the preparation of The Mars Project had been to demonstrate that on the basis of the technologies and the know-how then available (in 1948), the launching of a large expedition to Mars was a definite technical possibility. . . . Fourteen years ago we thought it was, but now we know it: the road to the planets is open."

More than a quarter century has gone by since Von Braun made that pronouncement. It is now the computer age and space technology has undergone revolutions that would have amazed even prescient space pioneers. Inertial and celestial navigation have been perfected to a high art, and space tracking systems routinely accomplish wondrous feats. Digital communications systems bridge billions of miles with ease, returning fantastic imagery from robot explorers. We have found ways to squeeze virtually every last calorie of available energy out of reliable liquid-hydrogen/liquid-oxygen propulsion systems. And we have learned that men and women can live in space successfully for long periods.

Since Von Braun's ten-vessel space flotilla—a seventy-person interplanetary expedition—there have been numerous studies that companies, universities, and every manner of Mars aficionado have made about reaching, exploring, and colonizing Mars. It gets simpler, cheaper, and more obviously doable by the decade. So sooner or later, we're going to begin that immense journey from which there will be no turning back.

COLONIES OF MARTIANS

The first Mars expedition by people, not robots, is almost certain to occur early in the twenty-first century, perhaps by the year 2010. The interplanetary transit to the fourth planet by contemporary chemically propelled rockets will be on the order of seven to nine months. Nuclear rocket propulsion systems developed in the 1960s would get us there more efficiently or quicker, but it will be decades—if ever—before the collective political will is mustered to take them out of mothballs. However we travel there in the beginning, the journey will not be brief. Traveling so far and long to meet a planet, it would be wasteful and shortsighted not to make that very first trip the beginning of a permanent human presence on the Red Planet. This is the most important way in which the first Mars expeditions will differ from the Apollo flights. In fact, before manned spacecraft ever touch the surface of Mars, we may well have dispatched to Martian soil an advance automated landing mission that would deliver provisions and portable oxygen and propellant-producing factories. The advance supply base would begin functioning and remain for the long haul, awaiting the arrival of Marsnauts and helping to ensure their safe return to Earth. The initial crew members will rotate back to Earth as new explorers arrive every two years. Some will not return to Earth for more than one cycle or may choose never to go back.

The most important concept to bear in mind about colonizing Mars is the art of defying apparent natural laws by pulling oneself into the air by the shoestrings—the "bootstrap" philosophy. When settlers crossed the Atlantic hundreds of years ago, they didn't bring with them all that was eventually to be on the North American continent. Rather, they brought simple tools and supplies that were to be the seeds of a continental culture based on indigenous resources. They were aided in no small way by trans-oceanic trade and sustenance, but everything that grew up in the New World didn't arrive fully formed. It was seeded and nurtured by the vast resources of the continent and the multiplying human population.

The same will be true for colonizing Mars. The difference will be that before beginning to populate Mars we will have a much more complete understanding of how extraterrestrial resources could be marshaled for the task. Before leaving England, the Pilgrims didn't study the greenhouse cultivation of corn or techniques to purify precious water. For many years, however, the "Mars Underground" has done precisely that and more, studying many times over every facet of hypothetical Mars missions.

What is the typical Mars environment like and what are the resources on which the first Martians may rely? Mars at 141 million miles from the Sun on average—its elliptical orbit is highly eccentric as planet orbits go—is about 50% farther than Earth from the source of solar illumination. The intensity of sunlight at Mars is thus less than one half that at Earth's orbit. The planet's orbital period is about 687 Earth days or 668.6 sols, a sol being the duration of one Mars day (24 hours, 39 minutes, and 35.238 seconds). One wonders what chronobiological effects will result from the slight but forced resetting of human biological clocks by this new regime of day and night.

Not only is the Martian day similar to Earth's, but at present the tilt of its rotation axis with respect to the plane of its orbit, 25 degrees—the cause of a planet's seasons—is similar to Earth's axial tilt, 23.5 degrees. While Earth's tilt is thought to have been relatively constant throughout geologic time, the tilt of Mars almost certainly has undergone wide excursions, accounting perhaps in part for its likely radical changes in climate over the eons. It is thought that a mere 700,000 years ago, the Martian spin axis was tilted only 16 degrees from perpendicular to the orbit plane. Yet only 100,000 years before that, the axis was tilted 33 degrees! The geological record in the layered Martian poles caused by this tilt cycling and other kinds of orbital changes is priceless, not only for insights about Mars but for what is has to say about Earth's climate changes. For the first Martian scientists, the poles will be among the hottest spots on the planet.

Mars is also a very small world, about one half the diameter of Earth and with only about one tenth the mass of our planet. The result: a gravitational acceleration at its surface that is a pleasant 38% of Earth's. That might be especially helpful to Marsnauts with shaky space legs from many months of interplanetary weightlessness. Very important for early Mars exploration is the planet's relatively low escape velocity of 5 km/sec (the velocity required to depart permanently from a world's gravitational clutch), in contrast to Earth's 11.2 km/sec. Rockets designed to escape from the Martian surface can be considerably smaller in the ratio of their initial to "burnout" mass than vessels with equivalent engine performance that struggle mightily to leave Earth.

A blessing for easy departure from the Martian surface (less air resistance), but woeful for Marsnauts attempting to survive is the thin Martian atmosphere that at the surface ranges in pressure from 6 to 15 thousandths that of Earth at sea level. The meager Martian air is 95.3% carbon dioxide, 2.7% nitrogen, 1.6% argon, a disappointing 0.13% oxygen, and a few hundredths of a percent water vapor. Apart from the atmosphere's stultifying effect on terrestrial life, the planet's surface is thus far more exposed than Earth's to solar ultraviolet radiation, protons from solar flares, and cosmic rays. Mars colonists will require not only pressure suits and life-support systems, but also shelter from celestial radiation. They will probably live in underground tunnels and hollows or in light, pressurized structures that will be covered with Martian soil.

Though the Martian atmosphere may be thin, it is substantial enough to allow an approaching spacecraft to take advantage of the technique of "aerocapture" or "aerobraking"—using gasdynamic drag to decelerate the vehicle, thus conserving retrorocket propellant. It would be possible for a ship arriving from Earth to dip into the Martian atmosphere momentarily to kill off some of its energy, skip out into space, and then go into an elongated elliptical orbit of the planet. It is a tricky maneuver, but well within the ability of present astronautical engineering.

The Martian surface is windswept and fraught with periodic intense dust storms that stir its thin soil and mix and distribute it planet-wide. The soil will be a great boon to colonists, however, in that Mars-dozers could mound it over structurally light habitats to provide radiation protection. Enriched with the right nutrients, especially nitrogen extracted from the atmosphere, the soil of Mars will support plant life within pressurized greenhouses. Not only will plants help to generate oxygen and provide the colonists with part of their food supply, but they will be a welcome psychological benefit.

The character of the Martian surface is set in the deathly cast of world with little if any plate tectonic activity—no continents float on a fluid mantle. To be sure there are stupendous Martian volcanoes—presumably extinct—and striking, deep canyons that dwarf comparable features on Earth. The Martian soil is reddish gray, presenting a boulder-strewn terrain resembling some terrestrial deserts. Erosional evidence suggests strongly to some scientists that Mars once may have had enough water to form a layer one kilometer thick. Since little of the water could have left the planet even after billions of years, many believe it must still remain as subsurface permafrost a few meters down or as deep liquid aquifers, one or more kilometers below the surface.

Some Martian water is clearly apparent even now. The dry atmosphere has in toto only about one cubic kilometer of water, but if necessary, the colonists could extract it. To remove a mere kilogram of water from the Martian air would require the efficient processing of millions of cubic meters of gas. Fortunately this can be done, and it is only a matter of generating the requisite amount of energy via solar, wind, or nuclear power systems.

To roving Martian colonists, as to the canal-building native Martians imagined by Percival Lowell at the turn of the century, the planet's polar caps may be the real mother lode of water. The northern and southern caps have "permanent" residual diameters of 1,000 kilometers and 350 kilometers respectively. They have a layered appearance as seen in space imagery. At the height of winter for one hemisphere, its cap reaches to about 55 degrees latitude from the equator. In summer, the caps retreat and become diminutive, their frosty dry ice layers having sublimed back into the atmosphere. Each cap consists of several kilometers depth of water-ice, extensively overlain and augmented by CO_2 ice during each hemisphere's winter season. In fact, the low atmospheric pressure on Mars is regulated by the cycle of polar region carbon dioxide freezing and subliming.

Silently drifting across pinkish Martian skies are two potato-shaped moonlets, Phobos and Deimos ("Fear" and "Terror"), that will be indispensable resources in the first wave of Martian colonization. The moons are so diminu-

tive that they were overlooked until American astronomer Asaph Hall noticed them in 1877. Phobos and
Deimos are respectively only on the order of
(16.7 × 13 × 12 miles) and (9 × 7.4 × 7 miles) in dimensions—very irregular in shape. These two chunks,
which in all likelihood are captured errant asteroids or
else residual primordial planetesimal building blocks of
the planets, are remarkably convenient way stations and
bases from which to conduct the first remote-controlled
exploration of Mars. The two moons may also possess
reserves of hydrocarbons (hydrogen-containing organic
compounds) that are absent on the Martian surface,
chemicals suitable for propellant and material processing.
Some suggest that the moons even possess frozen water a
kilometer or more beneath their surfaces.

Dr. Fred Singer of Virginia's George Mason University
was one of the earliest to suggest that a Phobos-Deimos
mission (a "Ph-D" mission) be the first step to Mars. He
made his proposal in 1969 and followed in 1977 (the cen-
tennial of the moons' discovery) with a more complete
study of Ph-D for then NASA administrator, James
Fletcher. He has argued that a manned mission to Phobos
and Deimos would be "quicker, cheaper, and safer and
would produce a much greater scientific return" than a
manned landing.

If a manned scientific base were established on the
outer moon, Deimos, it would be possible to sequentially
dispatch to the Martian surface numerous small roving
landers. From the vantage point of Deimos, round-trip
communication time to a lander would be virtually in-
stantaneous and would allow, for example, "real-time"
human interaction with the craft—not possible from the
distance of Earth. A human being at a Deimos base would
be able to interact with Mars rovers via teleoperators—
remote manipulation technology that provides tactile sensory feedback to the human controller. She would be able
to look out through the rover's television eyes, sense its
bumpy ride, anticipate dangerous obstacles, and pick up
intriguing Mars rocks with her surrogate hands.

Each of the Martian moons have negligible surface
gravitational acceleration, making escape from a moon
literally a hop, skip, or a jump, but causing some medical

difficulty for inhabitants due to prolonged near weight-lessness. Back and forth trips to the Deimos base from Mars could be frequent and would be greatly facilitated if it were possible to manufacture rocket fuel, such as liquid hydrogen, from the moon's resources.

Incidentally, like Earth's Moon, because of "tidal lock" the moon Phobos always maintains one face toward its planet, thus facilitating direct surface observation and communication. Even though it requires more energy to escape Mars from Phobos orbit than from Deimos orbit, some would argue that Phobos might be a better vantage point for some observations of the planet's surface. This early reconnaissance of the Martian surface from Deimos or Phobos would identify resources on Mars for sustaining the surface-dwelling colonists who would follow. The moons would likely become way stations for pioneers arriving from Earth.

The location of the first surface colony on Mars will likely be near the planet's equator, not only because climate in the equatorial region is most mild (the least seasonal temperature variation), but because a craft ascending from the surface could achieve the biggest velocity boost into orbit via the planet's rotational velocity. From a primary base on the equator, expeditions would set forth to other regions—at first to establish scientific stations and subsequently mining, agricultural, and manufacturing sites. Water-ice "mining" would undoubtedly be one of the first industries on Mars, and what better way to transport it than by pipeline. At last Mars would have its canals! Gas-filled blimps could also transport blocks of ice from point to point.

Apart from establishing a rudimentary economy based on the resources of the planet, the main objective of the first wave of colonists would be the scientific exploration of the new world. High on the list of scientific priorities is the search for either extant or extinct Martian life. Specialists would hunt voraciously for evidence of fossils, the remains of prebiotic chemistry locked within exposed canyon strata, or viable microbes existing on the surface. Some "far-out" scientific speculations could be addressed, such as the possibility that terrestrial microbes in the distant past managed to reach the Martian surface and began an independent biological evolution. The mechanisms that could have allowed them to escape from Earth and to survive an interplanetary voyage remain unclear and make interplanetary panspermia seem unlikely, but who knows?

There is also that highly symmetrical mysterious Martian "face" that stares vacantly into space from the Cydonia region, a visage or illusion that was captured several times in Viking orbiter imagery. Artifacts of an ancient Martian civilization, a sentinel monument placed there by an extraterrestrial culture that visited the solar system in ages past? It seems extraordinarily improbable, but who knows? Perhaps the well-known power of Mars to twist and distort wishful human imaginations will only grow stronger and more bizarre once humans explore the world in the flesh. One can barely begin to imagine the kind of space-faring tales and myths that will spring from the colonists' early adventures and misfortunes.

Will we hear of the "curse of Mars" to explain accidents or the dementias brought about by long-duration spaceflight and lengthy separation from Earth? Will "ghosts of Mars" haunt lonely explorers? Will there arise a Martian religion, and if so, who or what will be its prophet? What will be the music and songs of Mars? Indeed, the poetry of Mars may already have begun in the body of a 10,000-line saga, *Genesis: An Epic Poem*, published in 1988 (on Earth, of course) by one Federick Turner, who has rendered a Homer-like account of the future colonization of Mars.

POWER GENERATION ON MARS

Without abundant electrical and thermal power to sustain the basic needs of Martian settlers, the whole enterprise of colonization would wither like a plant without sunlight or water. Moreover, because of the critical life-sustaining function of power generation, it must be reliable and backed up in depth. Early Martian colonists, in particular, may need to have two or three independent means of generating at least their subsistence power. The first colonists will no doubt arrive with small nuclear power plants capable of generating tens to hundreds of kilowatts of electrical power and from which "waste" heat could supplement environmental heating needs. To power remote instruments and devices, the explorers may also employ small radioisotope thermoelectric generators, of the kind the Vikings and other outer planet explorers have used. Nuclear power may be anathema to many Earth-dwellers, but on cool Mars with its much diminished sunlight it will be the great sustainer of life. Estimates are that for each colonist a bare minimum of about a kilowatt of power will be required to operate life-support systems—about the power level of a contemporary microwave oven running on full power. More power than that will obviously be called for in a robust, flexible colony that intends to become a viable economic entity, so more capable energy sources will be essential.

Nuclear power will for some time be an expensive, imported technology, though it is possible to imagine a "domestic" nuclear power industry emerging on Mars. Gradually, however, other forms of power will emerge, notably solar power and, yes, wind power! Tenuous as is the Martian atmosphere, relatively high velocities occasionally prevail in certain areas and may make wind-generated electricity a realistic option. One possible use for this wind-produced electricity is in a process that dissociates the abundant Martian carbon dioxide into oxygen for breathing and carbon monoxide for rocket fuel—to be burned in liquid-carbon monoxide/liquid-oxygen engines. Thus, extracting the energy of motion of the Martian atmosphere will be the means to make further use of that same resource in propellant for rockets, aircraft, and even land rovers.

The average wind speed on Mars is estimated to be about thirty miles per hour (within a few dozen feet of the surface), which combined with the low density of the Martian atmosphere would make wind power not viable by terrestrial standards. But Mars is not Earth and the economics of power generation for a Mars colony—transport costs to Mars being the main driver—will make wind power attractive. It may be possible to locate some of the most promising wind-power sites on Mars by inferring their presence from orbital reconnaissance mapping that identifies windblown sand deposits. Certain Martian canyons as well as the slopes of the more prominent volcanoes may make particularly attractive wind sites. Some investigators have suggested that the leeward side of raised-rim Martian craters would offer particularly suitable conditions for wind power.

Martian wind machines will bear little resemblance to terrestrial windmills, which usually have their main power-generating axis horizontal to Earth's surface. In all likelihood, mechanical requirements will favor a vertical power axis turbine with high efficiency aerodynamic blades that are upright and rotate in merry-go-round fashion. Depending on the site and other variables, it is possible for such machines to generate amounts of power per unit of mass comparable to Martian nuclear reactors, i.e., tens of watts per kilogram.

Solar energy captured by advanced high-efficiency photovoltaic cells is another possible source of energy for Martian colonies, even though the sunlight reaching the surface of Mars is only about 50% that on Earth. Dust storms on the planet on occasion will significantly reduce and modify the light reaching solar cells at the surface, but the simplicity of solar power will still make it an attractive component of the Martian power mix. But both wind and sunlight are not nearly as reliable as the splitting of atoms, and it is hard to imagine early colonists staking their lives on chancy environmental power supplies.

There is a remote possibility that the Martian equivalent of geothermal power could be tapped. However, Mars does not appear to have the plate tectonic activity that normally would induce hot spots on a planet's surface. Any such hot spots, if found, would certainly become sites of great interest to the new civilization. "Areothermal power" (as in the Greek god Ares) would be relatively easy to extract using steam turbines or other straightforward technologies.

LIFE SUPPORT ON MARS

At a bare minimum, colonists will need safety from the
Martian elements, a breathable atmosphere, food and water, and adequate disposal of wastes. It is relatively simple
to provide protection from windstorms and radiation that
strikes the Martian surface: merely berming Martian soil
around cylindrical structures, or creating tunnels and
caves beneath the surface will do. In large measure
wastes could be recycled, certainly on the earliest missions on which the costs of not doing so are painful indeed.

Obtaining a sufficiently oxygenous atmosphere with
adequate pressure is more problematic. The congenial enclosed atmosphere will have to be chemically won from
the existing CO_2 atmosphere, stripped from Martian water, and extracted from the planet's soil or rock. This is
possible through various chemical processes that are dependent on significant energy input from the earlier mentioned power sources. Initially, operations on Mars will
require continuous local production of consumables for
the habitable atmosphere. Gradually, there will be a shift
to "closed cycle" environments in which plants, microbes,
and higher fauna provide the biological production of oxygen and the recycling of waste gases.

On Earth even today experiments are under way, such
as the Biosphere II closed life-support system project in
the U.S. or the Bios test in the Soviet Union, to evaluate
the possibility of completely closing the life-support
loop. The concept is the so-called Controlled Environment
Life-Support System, or CELSS, in which even wastes are
reprocessed biologically. In such a system, some portion
of the biota needs to be harvested to provide food for the
sheltered inhabitants.

Life-support loops undoubtedly can be completely
closed, given an adequate input of nonchemical energy
from the outside. Scientists and engineers worry more
about subtle, creeping contamination of a habitat's life
processes by unusual toxins, insects, or microbial imbal-
ances. These are matters that will require very long-term
study, not months or years but decades. And just as we do

not know everything about the intricacies of our terrestrial environmental loops, so Martian colonists will have to live with unknowns and uncertainties in their own miniature life enclosures.

TRANSPORTATION ON MARS

The surface area of Mars is by marvelous coincidence approximately equal to the combined area of all the continents on Earth. So even though Mars is a much smaller world, it has a large area that will be reasonably accessible to explorers. It will be no small feat, for example, to get from a site near the tallest Martian volcano, Olympus Mons, in the northern hemisphere, past or through the huge, several miles deep Valles Marineris canyon, to arrive at the Argyre Basin in the southern hemisphere a quarter of the way around the planet.

Surface traverses on foot by Marsnauts in advanced flexible space suits will be limited to several miles, so powered transport will be necessary. The first Marsmobiles are likely to be direct descendants of the Apollo lunar rovers, each of which sported four wire-mesh tires. Such compact "open-air" vehicles running on batteries or oxygen/hydrogen fuel cells providing electricity will suffice for exploratory jaunts up to tens of kilometers from base. For longer trips, the equivalent of a large van with an enclosed life-support atmosphere will be desirable—a mobile laboratory from which to carry out explorations. Colonists will eventually travel smooth, dusty roads that some of the first Mars-dozers will scrape from the rough boulder-strewn regolith.

Unlike the airless Moon, the possibility of transportation through the atmosphere arises in the case of Mars. Both balloons and airplanes are possible. Hydrogen-filled blimps could carry people and accompanying large freight payloads from point to point. The hydrogen, of course, would come from the electrochemical dissociation of Martian water. There would be no fear of hydrogen fires or explosions à la Hindenburg in the predominantly carbon dioxide Martian air. In the thin Martian atmosphere, a blimp would have to be a few hundred feet in diameter to support one person.

Gossamer-thin solar-powered balloons are also possible. Some designs envision a combined helium- or hydrogen-filled balloon linked in one of several ways with a black, solar-heated hot-air pouch (open on the bottom as in the classical hot-air balloon). Plans for automated scientific missions to Mars in the 1990s already include the use of such balloons to make photographic and radar reconnaissance traverses across the planet.

Marsplanes will have to be rocketlike in one respect: If their engines rely on combustion, since the Mars atmosphere has little oxygen the planes will have to carry not only fuel but oxidizer. Researchers at NASA's Jet Propulsion Laboratory have already designed a long-wingspan Marsplane weighing several hundred pounds and having a range of several thousand miles that it could cover at speeds of a few hundred miles per hour. Much larger craft could someday accommodate people. Each Mars base or city will no doubt have a special airport facility to receive such vehicles.

We must not forget rocket transport. Owing to the relatively thin Martian atmosphere, quasi-ballistic suborbital flights will be possible if sudden access to another part of the planet is called for—perhaps for a medical or environmental control emergency. Recall that the Martian atmosphere can be processed to produce rocket propellant. Nuclear reactors or solar collectors could heat the main component of the Martian air, carbon dioxide, and break it down to oxygen and carbon monoxide. The carbon monoxide itself could be used as a rocket fuel. Or the oxygen could be used to combust liquefied methane (brought to the surface from chemical plants on Phobos or Deimos). Martian water could of course be electrolysed to produce the energetic liquid-hydrogen/liquid-oxygen propellant combination.

THE MARTIAN SOCIAL ORDER

To guard against dissolution and chaos due to unforeseen psychological and social developments, the initial Martian settlements will organize themselves with a strong hierarchical command structure in the military mold common to naval vessels. There will be opportunity later for more democratic organization of the colony after the hazards inherent in small numbers have been passed. Moreover, this will be an explicitly determined political evolution based on preestablished milestones in the development of the colony and its companion settlements.

The landing party that establishes the first surface base will surely number less than one dozen individuals. In the initial small groups that may dot the planet, rigorously even male-female pairing will be essential for social and psychological health. The first colonists will have to play multiple roles as builders, engineers, horticulturists, physicians, and planetary scientists. As the populations of the first Martian bases grow through new arrivals with more specialized skills, the jack-of-all-trades demands on individuals will relax and people will be free to be specialists, the way they are on Earth. After the techniques of closed environment construction and life support have been mastered, there is no reason why the Martian population couldn't grow through reproduction and schooling of the young in survival and specialist skills.

An economic order will emerge on the planet as the dispersed colonies begin to specialize in activities such as mining, habitat construction, production of power-generating equipment, agriculture, medicine, and scientific exploration. The settlements will trade among themselves the necessities and baubles of civilization, instituting very soon no doubt a coinage of the realm. It may not require more than fifty years for the colonies to reach the ability to manufacture, independent of help from Earth, all but the most specialized products that they require.

Not more than a century may transpire before serious discussions of complete political independence from Earth civilization begin. Indeed, the Martian adventure should have that prospect firmly enshrined in whatever legal documents are cast to govern the colonies. It would be tragic to recapitulate the strife between colonies and founding nations that have been so common on Earth.

Having emerged with a more unified group objective and spirit, it is not too much to expect that the Martian colonies would be less prone to conflict than have been national groups on Earth. The dawn of the twenty-second century therefore may see the emergence of a United States of Mars that will be in the vanguard of exploration of the outer solar system and beyond. The interplanetary craft that will explore the nooks and crannies of the outer solar system's dozens of exotic moons and thousands of asteroids may be manufactured on Mars, Phobos, and Deimos. The 1.6% of the Martian atmosphere comprised of argon is an ideal propellant for high-efficiency electric rocket propulsion, the kind of drive that is ideal for interplanetary flights. Extraction of this valuable resource may be a key enterprise of the twenty-first century's burgeoning solar system culture.

Looking back at Earth, Martians will not view the white cloud-bedecked blue and brown marble espied by the Apollo astronauts in the 1960s and 1970s. Earth will be a bright point of light in pink Martian daytime skies, and an intense blue-white light when it graces the Martian night. The minimum time of a round-trip radio or television communication between Mars and Earth will be six minutes. More often it will be more like half an hour.

The travel time to Mars from Earth will never shrink to the extent that air travel has compressed the gulf between the East and West coasts of the United States. In the beginning, interplanetary transit will be many months. Eventually, fusion rockets and even antimatter rockets that are now only engineers' dreams will reduce the Earth–Mars voyage to a less tedious month or to a few weeks. Instead of plying a long arcing trajectory, such craft will set a virtually straight-line course between the two worlds. Unfortunately, there will never be any "Get-a-way Weekend Specials" to or from Mars.

The feelings of physical distance yet emotional closeness to the planet that gave birth to the new civilization is difficult for terrans—we of the mother world—to imagine. But beginning with the earliest days of Martian civilization, communication satellites in Mars-synchronous orbit will bind the new world together. Perhaps the colonists will take so much comfort in being linked intimately with sister colonies on the planet that removal from Earth will not bother them. How those emotions play out to strengthen or weaken the Martian culture is a saga yet to be written.

There may be solace in numbers, however. There is literally a world of difference between living on a planet with but a few dozen inhabitants and being on one with billions. Inexorably the human population of Mars will grow. Perhaps there will be several thousand Martians by the mid-twenty-first century, possibly millions by sometime in the twenty-second century. Such are demographics that toward the latter part of the twenty-first, the first native-born Martians may visit Earth on extended vacation cruises. They may be reluctant to go, except out of curiosity. It is to be hoped that life on Mars will continue to bear a closer resemblance to living in Vermont or Wyoming than to life in New York City or Los Angeles. Mars tourism can't be far down the road.

TERRAFORMING MARS: A New Earth

After several centuries, the United States of Mars will face a dilemma and a decision point much more wrenching than the quandary of global climate change faced by Earth civilization in the latter part of the twentieth century. Should the colonists remain indefinitely in their hermetically sealed chambers, or should they attempt to remake the hostile Martian environment in the image of ancestral Earth?

The word "terraforming" has long been in the lexicon of science fiction aficionados, since it was coined by writer Jack Williamson in the 1940s. Subsequently, planetary scientists and space engineers began to study the real possibility of terraforming, and what better place to start than with Mars? (In 1961, Carl Sagan did suggest the possibility of terraforming hellish Venus by infecting its atmosphere with CO_2-consuming bacteria.) But should world remaking be done at all? Will not Martian environmentalists rise in justified outrage to protest the changing of Martian deserts—pristine for eons—into the lakes, seas, and swamps of "transplaneted" human civilization? Whatever the outcome of the debate (We trust there will be no wars over terraforming, though who knows!), knowledge of how to go about the project will have been building for generations and will be ready to use.

Terraforming Mars will at a minimum require making the world's atmosphere more dense, i.e. raising its pressure. This will not happen overnight, needless to say. Even with the more advanced technology of the ensuing centuries, terraforming Mars may be a project that occupies centuries or millennia rather than decades.

Thickening the atmosphere of Mars will enhance the well-known "greenhouse effect," in which short wavelength solar radiation penetrates to the surface of a planet, heats it, and is reemitted as longer wavelength infrared radiation that is blocked by absorbing gases. Two indigenous greenhouse gases may help to remake Mars: water vapor and carbon dioxide. First, consider melting the water-ice or melting and subliming the CO_2-ice of the Martian polar caps. This could be done by blackening the now highly reflective surfaces of the caps. Perhaps a thin film of black chemical polymer could be applied—the equivalent of painting the poles. Alternately, aluminized mylar mirrors orbiting Mars could concentrate reflected sunlight onto the poles. As the pressure of the Martian atmosphere thereby increased, heat transport from the planet's equatorial regions would become more pronounced with the strengthening of the north–south air circulation.

Raising the atmospheric pressure on Mars would be advantageous in tempering the planet's harsh climate, but pressures comparable to terrestrial conditions would also allow settlers on the New Earth to roam the countryside without space suits. To breathe, they would certainly need to have tanks of oxygen and face masks, much as scuba divers in the ocean. With elevated pressures would come the possibility of freestanding ponds, lakes, and small seas.

Some researchers have even theorized that genetically engineered bacteria released into the Martian environment could begin a slow transformation of the mostly carbon dioxide atmosphere into an oxygenous one. So life itself, albeit this time under the direction of human beings, may eventually change Mars into a clement abode much as the dead Earth was transformed by the rise of microbial culture billions of years ago. As James Oberg so aptly expressed this vision in *Mission to Mars*, "The metamorphosis of old Mars into a living, terraformed planet would be more than a metaphor of the ultimate conquest of the god Mars' influence in all terrestrial civilizations, or of the victory of life over death which has been the spark behind so much human aspiration." It would be an event of galactic significance, a new planetary beginning.

WHITHER MARS EXPLORATION?

Coming back to Earth, so to speak, from these grandiose plans to transform Mars into a new world, wherein lies the hope for the exploration of Mars? Can we divine any sign that dreams of Mars colonies are nearer to being fulfilled than they have been in the past? In the last decades of the twentieth century we are beginning to come to terms with the threat of drastic global climatic change—forced by the greenhouse effect—and its accompanying worldwide physical and social disruption. Though in recent years the threat of nuclear warfare among the superpowers seems to have subsided, irrational acts of terrorism have become more common and Earth's teeming human population presses inexorably toward the ten to fifteen billion mark by the end of the next century. Environmental problems, energy problems, food problems, present and future pandemics—all exacerbated by exponentially climbing human numbers—often seem to squeeze out any prospect for romantic interplanetary quests. Yet perhaps precisely *because* of such problems, the yearning for Mars will have its day.

If the political community hasn't yet, the scientific community certainly does recognize the need to study the complex dynamics of Earth's biosphere in the widest possible context—comparing its workings to the different but simpler workings of a seemingly lifeless world. Mars is the essential control experiment for the good Earth. For that reason alone we must explore it. What the world also needs badly is a good transplanetary insurance policy. Once the human species is dispersed among self-sufficient distant worlds, the possible extinction of humankind in any imaginable cataclysm will become an increasingly remote prospect.

The last quarter century has seen the initial halting steps on the road to Mars. The first truly successful Mars voyage occurred when the U.S. *Mariner 4* spacecraft shot past the planet on July 14, 1965 and radioed back twenty-two exquisite close-up photo portraits of the partially cratered world. *Mariner 6* and *7* were also successful photographic flybys past Mars, albeit somewhat eclipsed by the millennial *Apollo 11* landing mission weeks earlier. In November 1971, *Mariner 9* was first to orbit Mars and send back extensive imagery that was later used to determine the landing sites for the highly successful U.S. Viking *1* and *2* landing and orbital missions. For many years, the Viking spacecraft sent back images of the surface of Mars and other scientific data, providing a tenuous but real, continuous connection between two worlds. The *Viking 1* lander sent back data from Chryse Planitia for more than six years. From a northerly region known to Mars cartographers as Utopia, *Viking 2* sent back data for almost four years.

Often forgotten is that the Soviet spacecraft *Mars 3* reached the Martian surface on December 2, 1971 and sent back radio signals for twenty seconds before becoming silent—victim no doubt of the then-prevailing dust storms. The previous month, *Mars 2* had reached the surface in silence due to equipment failure. These were the first human craft to touch the surface of Mars. Then after these and the Viking landings, a long hiatus. We have not returned to the soil of Mars.

Mars exploration suffered a temporary setback in late March 1989 with the failure of the second of two ambitious Soviet spacecraft that were intended to explore Phobos in situ. Both spacecraft were designed to rendezvous with and to explore the surface of Phobos, but failed to complete their exciting missions. The Soviet Union launched the twin six-ton spacecraft *Phobos 1* and *2* toward Mars in July 1988. Early on, in September 1988,

Phobos 1 tumbled out of control on the way to the planet due in part to a faulty command signal that was transmitted to it. *Phobos 2* entered Mars orbit and returned pictures of Phobos's surface from a distance of only 360 miles before failing excruciatingly close to its goal. *Phobos 1* and *2* each were to have deposited two scientific probes on Phobos's surface. Two of these were to have remained at fixed locations, while the other two were spring-loaded "hoppers" that would have jumped from point to point on the small moon. Both the *Phobos 1* and *2* mother craft were to have hovered for less than a half hour within 150 feet of the moonlet's surface, photographing it and testing the surface with various instrumentation—including one experiment that would have vaporized surface material with a laser beam and analyzed the resulting ions.

Many cooperative efforts between nations in the exploration of Mars by robot vehicles lie ahead. The Phobos missions themselves had a strong element of international scientific cooperation, including assistance by the United States in tracking. In an historic first, ten U.S. scientists formally participated in the missions. The Soviet Union has plans to send its probes to Mars four more times in the next decade, on each of the occasions in which the planets are properly aligned for the voyage. One of these missions, perhaps in 1998, may attempt to return samples of the Martian surface to Earth. In 1993, the U.S. plans to launch a Mars Observer spacecraft scheduled for 1994 injection into a polar orbit of the planet.

Engineers and scientists in the U.S. have been studying a Mars Rover Sample Return (MRSR) mission of their own that is designed to bring back to Earth or to the space station about ten pounds of carefully selected Martian soil and rock for chemical and biological analysis. If MRSR were carried out in the late 1990s or early 2000s, for several months a six-wheeled or tracked roving vehicle would roam the Martian terrain as far away from its landing craft as twelve to twenty-four miles. The rover would return to the lander, one stage of which would then ascend to the waiting Earth-return vehicle parked in Mars orbit making observations of its own. Because of the modular structure of the vehicles necessary for MRSR, there have been suggestions that the sample return mission would be an ideal opportunity for U.S.-Soviet collaboration in Mars exploration. However, in view of the recent Soviet failure with their two Phobos spacecraft, others may disagree.

The vicarious exploration of Mars by automated spacecraft only whets our appetite for a more intimate meeting with this still mysterious world. Whether the future human journeys to Mars will or should be carried out by nations separately—in the mold of Antarctic exploration —or by a consortium or consortia of nations is still a pending question. The answer is likely to be determined in the 1990s amid the chaotic winds of global political change. If decisions were made soon enough, however, planetfall could come before 2010. There is no question that if we can muster the resolve, there will be a way for people to alight on the sands of Mars to begin a world anew.

A BRIEF MARS
BIBLIOGRAPHY

1. VON BRAUN, WERNHER. *The Mars Project*. Urbana, Illinois: University of Illinois Press, 1962; published in German in 1948 as *Das Marsprojekt*.

2. LEY, WILLY, and WERNHER VON BRAUN. *The Exploration of Mars*. New York: Viking, 1960.

3. CARR, MICHAEL H. *The Surface of Mars*. New Haven and London: Yale University Press, 1981.

4. OBERG, JAMES E. *New Earths: Restructuring Earth and Other Planets*. New York: New American Library, 1981.

5. OBERG, JAMES E. *Mission to Mars: Plans and Concepts for the First Manned Landing*. Harrisburg, PA: Stackpole Books, 1982.

6. BOSTON, PENELOPE J., ed. *The Case for Mars*. American Astronautical Society "Science and Technology Series," vol. 57. San Diego, CA: Univelt, Inc., 1984.

7. McKAY, CHRISTOPHER P., ed. *The Case for Mars II*. American Astronautical Society "Science and Technology Series," vol. 62. San Diego, CA: Univelt, Inc., 1985.

8. LOVELOCK, JAMES, and MICHAEL ALLABY. *The Greening of Mars*. New York: St. Martin's/Marek, 1984.

9. MILES, FRANK, and NICHOLAS BOOTH. *Race to Mars: The Harper & Row Mars Flight Atlas.* New York: Harper & Row, 1988.

10. "Design of a Mars Colony." MIT Space Habitat Design Workshop (Fall 1988) Professor Ranko Bon, Instructor.

11. MEYER, THOMAS R., and CHRISTOPHER P. McKAY. "The Resources of Mars for Human Settlement." *Journal of the British Interplanetary Society* 42 (April 1989): 147–60.

12. CLARK, BENTON C. "Survival and Prosperity Using Regolith Resources on Mars." *Journal of the British Interplanetary Society* 42 (April 1989): 161–66.

13. FRENCH, J. R. "Rocket Propellants from Martian Resources." *Journal of the British Interplanetary Society* 42 (April 1989): 167–70.

14. HASLACH, HENRY W. "Wind Energy: A Resource for a Human Mission to Mars." *Journal of the British Interplanetary Society* 42 (April 1989): 171–78.

A dramatic new series of books at the cutting edge
where science meets science fiction.

THE NEXT WAVE
Introduced by Isaac Asimov

Computers, the space shuttle, biogenetics--what was once the domain
of science fiction is now business as usual. Developments in science
and technology are propelling us forward so fast that only a few dare to
speculate where we might go tomorrow.

Each volume of *The Next Wave* contains a fascinating scientific essay,
followed by a complete novel about the same subject. And every
volume carries an introduction by Isaac Asimov.

Volume One
Red Genesis
by S.C. Sykes
The spellbinding tale of a man who changed not one but two worlds,
with an essay by scientist Eugene F. Mallove on the technical
problems of launching and maintaining a colony on Mars.

Volume Two
Alien Tongue
by Stephen Leigh
The story of contact with a startling new world on the other side of a
newly discovered wormhole in space, with an essay by scientist and
author Rudy Rucker on the latest developments in the search for
extraterrestrial intelligence and the possibilities of first contact.

And coming in November, 1991
Volume Three
The Missing Matter
by Thomas R. McDonough
with an essay by Wallace H. Tucker

Look for the first two volumes of *The Next Wave*
on sale now wherever Bantam Spectra Books are sold

AN288 -- 7/91

First, there was a ship from beyond the edges
of our solar system.

Then, there was the mystery of the aliens themselves.

Now, there is the peril of a new Raman enigma...

THE GARDEN OF RAMA
by Arthur C. Clarke
and Gentry Lee

Years ago, an abandoned alien space ship entered the solar system.
On its journey past Earth, humanity reached out and explored the
mysteries it offered. They dubbed the ship "Rama," and it passed
into human history. But one thing was clear--the Ramans did
everything in threes.

With the coming of the second ship, humanity was prepared, and
sent a second exploratory mission to the next ship that came to
Earth. What no one expected was its sudden departure, with three
cosmonauts trapped on board.

The Garden of Rama follows those cosmonauts as they hurtle at
half the speed of light toward an uncertain destination. Threatened
daily by the mysteries of the Raman ship, the cosmonauts manage
to survive for twelve long years when it becomes increasingly clear
that they are headed for a Raman base -- and the heretofore unseen
architects of their galactic home....

Look for this dazzling new chapter
in the Raman saga
The Garden of Rama
on sale now wherever Bantam Spectra
hardcovers are sold.

AN295 -- 8/91

From two of science fiction's greatest storytellers
comes the stunning tale of a civilization
facing its greatest fears and its impending doom.

Isaac Asimov
& Robert Silverberg
NIGHTFALL

In 1941, Isaac Asimov published a short story about a
world whose six suns set simultaneously only once
every 2,049 years. When nightfall comes to the world of
Lagash, its people -- who have never seen the stars --
must deal with the madness that follows. The tale,
"Nightfall," named greatest science fiction story of all
time by the Science Fiction Writers of America, remains
a landmark of the genre.

Now, two of science fiction's greatest names join to tell
this story in all its immensity and splendor with a novel
that explores all the implications of a world facing
ultimate disaster. When academics at Saro University
determine that 12 hours of darkness are coming, a
group of religious fanatics called the Apostles of the
Flame begin to capitalize on the event, preying on the
fear of the general populace by "saving" converts and
damning non-believers. Both groups -- in conflict for
centuries -- know that the coming night will mean the
end of their civilization, for the people of Lagash have a
proven fear of the dark, and in the wake of unspeakable
horrors, must rally to save the fragile remnants of their
world.

Now available in Bantam Spectra paperback.

AN175 -- 8/91

Risking the world to reach the stars...

Fellow Traveler
by
William Barton and
Michael Capobianco

"A team to watch out for." -- *Locus*

As the new century dawns, the Soviets are reclaiming the high frontier. After a decade of social upheaval, they have embarked on a bold gamble to regain leadership in space exploration -- moving a massive asteroid into Earth's orbit to harvest its motherload of precious metals.

But the reactionary leadership of the United States sees the project as a potential weapon. They are willing to risk everything to stop it -- even the destruction of all life on Earth!

A vividly realistic thriller torn from tomorrow's headlines,
Fellow Traveler
is a powerful and prophetic tale of heroism and hope.

AN250 -- 6/91